THE GOLDEN FOUNTAIN CAFE

THE GOLDEN FOUNTAIN CAFE

[*La Fontana de Oro*: A historic novel of the XIXth Century]

BY

BENITO PEREZ GALDOS

TRANSLATED

BY

WALTER RUBIN

LATIN AMERICAN LITERARY REVIEW PRESS
SERIES: DISCOVERIES
PITTSBURGH, PENNSYLVANIA

YVETTE E. MILLER, EDITOR

1989

The Latin American Literary Review Press publishes Latin American creative writing under the series title *Discoveries*, and critical works under the series title *Explorations*.

Library of Congress Cataloging-in-Publication Data

Pérez Galdós, Benito, 1843-1920.
   [Fontana de Oro. English]
  The Golden Fountain Cafe: a historic novel of the XIXth century = La Fontana de Oro / by Benito Pérez Galdós; translated by Walter Rubin.
      p. cm. -- (Discoveries)
  Translation of: La Fontana de Oro.

   ISBN 0-935480-36-6
   1. Spain--History--Ferdinand VII, 1813-1833--Fiction.
   2. Spain--History--Revolution, 1820-1823--Fiction.
  I. Title II. Title: Fontana de Oro. III. Series
  PQ6555.F613   1989
  863'.5--dc20   89-8330
                                                  CIP

THE GOLDEN FOUNTAIN CAFE may be ordered directly from the publisher:

   Latin American Literary Review Press
   2300 Palmer Street
   Pittsburgh, Pennsylvania 15218
   Tel (412) 351-1477
   Fax (412) 351-6831

This edition has been translated with the financial assistance of the Spanish Dirección General del Libro y Bibliotecas of the Ministerio de Cultura.

The publication of this book has been made possible through the financial support of the Comité Conjunto Hispano-Norteamericano para la Cooperación Cultural y Educativa, in Madrid, Spain, and the office of Sponsored Programs, Limited Grants and Aid: University of Houston, University Park, Texas.

ACKNOWLEDGMENTS

I am indebted to the following people and organizations for having made this endeavor possible:

Javier Jiménez-Ugarte, Consul-General of Spain: Houston, Texas.

Dr. Yvette E. Miller, Editor: Latin American Literary Review Press, for her patience and valuable suggestions.

María Pérez Galdós de Verde, daughter of Benito Pérez Galdós.

Dr. Allen Matusow, Dean of Humanities and Fine Arts, and Professor of History: Rice University, Houston.

Among the Hispanic scholars whose work inspired my efforts: Professors M. J. Benardete, Rafael de Balbín Lucas, Joseph Schraibman, Pedro Ortiz Armengol and Juan López-Morillas, and my colleagues in the Real Academia de Bellas Artes y Ciencias Históricas (Toledo, Spain).

Dr. Thomas DeGregori, Book Reviewer: *The Houston Chronicle*, Ellen Wilkerson, Robert Boyd, David Weise, and Donald Hall for editing and proofing.

Lizette S. Moon, Van T. Moon III and Helen M. Connelly for typing and editing the manuscript.

Joseph Robinson for his support and encouragement.

María Teresa Pons and Ramón Bela of the Comité Conjunto Hispano-Norteamericano para la Cooperación Cultural y Educativa, in Madrid, Spain.

Last but not least, I give special recognition to LALRP Associate Editor Lisa Fedorka-Carhuaslla for her scholarly and careful editing.

Walter Rubin

This translation is dedicated to my wife,

Pilar,

for her endless patience with me.

THE GOLDEN FOUNTAIN CAFE

Preamble

The historical or novelistic events related in this book refer to one of the gravest and most interesting periods of political and social disorder; it began in 1812 and does not appear near terminating.

Long after this book was written it seemed opportune for me to point out that there is a relationship between the many events recorded here and something of what is occurring now, a relationship undoubtedly resulting from the similarity between the present crisis and the unforgettable period of 1820-23; this is the principal reason which induced me to publish it.

December 1870

B. P. G.

Table of Contents

Chapters

I	Saint Jerónimo Avenue, 1821	15
II	The Patriotic Club	31
III	A Patriotic Event And Its Consequences	41
IV	'Coletilla'	56
V	Coletilla's Companion	63
VI	Coletilla's Nephew	72
VII	The Inner Voice	78
VIII	Today He Arrives	83
IX	The First Steps	90
X	The First Battle	100
XI	The Tragedy Of Gracchus	108
XII	The Battle In Platerias	116
XIII	The Expected One Does Not Arrive The Arrival Of An Untimely Visitor	123
XIV	The Decision	129
XV	The Three Ruins	135
XVI	The Eighteenth Century	146
XVII	The Liberal's Dream	153
XVIII	Dialogue Between Yesterday And Today	156
XIX	The Abbot	163
XX	Bozmediano	172
XXI	Free!	180
XXII	Lázaro's Way Of The Cross	183
XXIII	The Inquisition	192
XXIV	Mystic Rose	197
XXV	Virgo Prudentisima	202
XXVI	Dissenters From The Golden Fountain	208
XXVII	She Stays Home Alone	215
XXVIII	The Handbag	221

XXIX	The Fateful Hours	226
XXX	Virgo Fidelis	239
XXXI	The Mysterious Meeting	249
XXXII	The Little Fountain	253
XXXIII	The Harpies Become Sad	261
XXXIV	The Conspiracy—Lazaro's Triumph	265
XXXV	The Nuncio's Biretta	274
XXXVI	Clarifications	285
XXXVII	Clara's Way Of The Cross	292
XXXVIII	Continuation Of The Way Of The Cross	300
XXXIX	A Moment Of Calm	309
XL	The Great Assault	314
XLI	Fernando VII	324
XLII	Virgo Potens	334
XLIII	Conclusion	345

Chapter I

SAINT JERONIMO AVENUE, 1821

The town of Madrid was the setting for many official festivities publicized by the daily *Gaceta* during the six unforgettable years between 1814 and 1820. Announcements in this influential newspaper informed the public of events worthy of celebration, prompting them to act accordingly. In response to all the publicity, the townspeople hung monumental banners and damascened tapestries along the thoroughfares. Huge posters on which Arriaza[1] wrote suitable verses for the occasion were placed on every street corner. Gay bannerettes were held high over the heads of the crowds by fraternities and other local groups. At these events the villagers were looked upon as invited guests added to the long list of mayors, public officials, gentlemen, priests, and generals. They were mere spectators whose passive functions were prescribed and directed in the articles of the program, and as such, they behaved as etiquette dictated.

During the period that we describe, (1820-1823), things occurred quite differently. The ceremony did not exist. People demonstrated daily without previous designation of authorized places published in the *Gaceta*, and with no necessity for arches, banners, or emblems. The whole town was set in motion. Its streets were turned into a great spectacle with tremendous rejoicing or noisy madness. The calm was upset by a single cry from that fellow called (by a hoax of history) *Deseado*, which is to say Fernando VII[2] whose favorite gathering places were next to the Palace entrance, City Hall, or the Church of *Doña* María of Aragón, located near the Spanish Parliament.

Those were critical years for the ramshackle, dirty, uncomfortable, unpleasant, and gloomy town! Madrid was no longer the opulent and grand locale of the age of the Tudors. However, the glorious days of the second of May and the third of December and the city's initiative in political affairs enhanced its prestige considerably. Moreover, it was the forum of the constituent legislation and the chair from which the brightest youth of Spain eloquently exercised the teachings of the new code of law.

In spite of all those honors, Madrid presented a very unpleasant appearance. Mari-Blanca, in Puerta del Sol Plaza, continued to be the most concrete artistic expression of Madrilenian culture. Immovable on its ugly pedestal, the statue, which in previous centuries had witnessed the uprisings of Oropesa and the mutiny of Esquilache[3], now presided over the revolutionary activity of this good town (which always converged on that site during its ovations and upheavals).

If it were possible to take the reader to the steps of San Felipe, capital of political and social gossip, or to seat him on the bench of the Mari-Blanca fountain, the meeting place of the common people, he would comprehend how different is that which we see today from what our grandfathers saw half a century ago. His attention would surely be called to the fact that many of the idlers who gathered there left at nightfall, to head toward the street called Saint Jeronimo Avenue or some other nearby thoroughfare. That crowd frequented the clubs, the patriotic meetings, The Golden Fountain Cafe, Grande Oriente, Lorencini, and The Maltese Cross. Among the groups some people stood out due to their solemn manner and protective gaze, and they appeared to be held in great esteem by the others. At times they seemed to try to impose silence on the multitude, and at other times by extending their crossed arms, they turned around as if calling for attention. All of this was done with an officious gravity which indicated either very great influence or no little conceit.

The majority headed for Saint Jeronimo Avenue. This was because The Golden Fountain, (*La Fontana de Oro*), the most attended, the most restless, the most popular of all clubs, was located there. We shall soon enter the revolutionary café. First let us cross, from Buen Suceso Street to the Los Italianos sections, the happy and lively Jeroniman Fathers' Avenue, which was then as it is today and will forever be, the most traveled street of the Capital.

Today, when you see that most of the street consists of private dwellings, you will not be able to understand that it was once a public thoroughfare occupied by the sad walls of three or four convents. It is impossible today to comprehend the darkness which they cast over the Carrera's entrance, the wide wall of the Victoria Monastery on one side and the dirty, corroded wall of Buen Suceso Street on the other. Further on, the Pinto nuns formed a battle line; over the wall which served as the extension of the convent could be seen the tops of cypresses planted next to the graves. On the other side of the street the Italian Hermitage camped in no less ridiculous manner than it does today. Further downhill was Espíritu Santo Street, which later became the House of Deputies.

The houses of the grandees stood between the convents. Down the street was the was façade of the Medinaceli Palace with its broad emblem and countless windows, its garden on one side and its house of worship on the other. The Valmedianos, the Pignatellis, and the Gonzagas were across the way. Further this way were the Pandos and Macedas, and finally, the Hijar's residence, which until recently displayed on its door the historical chain, the distinctive mark of hospitality offered to a monarch. Private dwellings, stores, and public places took up a third of the street. We shall describe this part in greater detail because it is important to be acquainted with the grand setting where some important events of this story will take place.

Entering by way of the Puerta de Sol Plaza, passing the Victoria convent, one found a great portico, the entrance to one of the oldest houses, which, in spite of the decorative shield engraved on the keystone of the balcony, was in those days a neighborhood house where up to a dozen reputable families resided. Its noble origin was unquestionable, but it was somehow acquired by the neighboring community, which rented it in order to meet expenses. The entranceway, which had been wide enough for the enormous coaches of its former owner, housed the office of a notary, a secretary of certifications and documents. In the same entranceway, a little further inside, were the hardware and costume jewelry stands, owned by one of the notary's brothers, who had come to Madrid from Ocaña in order to make headway in business. His store consisted of three shabby lockers in which some packages of combs, a few sealing wax wafers, children's toys, and a big handful of rosaries with time crosses and medals were stored.

On the left-hand side, and especially in the corner next to the door, was a place where the public exercised an indisputable right. It was a urinary center. The public discharge had converted that corner into a center of uncleanliness. In the evenings especially, the liquid flow increased in such a way that the notary and his brother firmly intended to abandon the locale. The public was threatened in vain with heavy police sanctions by the legal voice of the notary. In spite of these threats the public did not renounce its custom, and the brothers would surely have had a bad time if they had forcefully impeded this urinary freedom. According to the happy expression of a patron of that locale, this law of custom was rooted in the nature of man and the unavoidable hospitality of the neighborhood.

Across from this classical entranceway there was a small door. One knew that it was a barbershop by the two Mambrino helmets, wrought in very fine Alcaraz metal, which hung on either side. While the exterior of this establishment was noteworthy, with its green door, white curtains, leech flask, and red letter poster, adorned with two vignettes worthy of Maella[4], one of which represented an individual being shaved and the other a lady being bled on one foot, the interior was even more noteworthy. Three helpers, headed by Calleja, the master barber, each week shaved the beards of about one hundred of the most recalcitrant liberals. There were arguments and discussions about the King, the Parliament, the Congress of Verona[5], and the Holy Alliance.[6] One could hear there the forceful harangue of the first and oldest official, who was said to be a relative of Porlier[7], the martyr of liberty. To the rhythm of the razor, he recited pleasant verses with political witticisms. The words *Camarilla, Coletilla, Trágala, Elío, La Bisbal,* and *Vinuesa*[8] formed the background of the conversation. The most outstanding person in the barbershop was its owner, Gaspar Calleja (the title of *Don* had been removed after 1820)[9], a hero of the revolution and one of the greatest enemies Fernando had in 1814. So he said of himself.

Further down was the linen shop owned by some Irishmen and established since the prior century. Along with satin and organdy, they sold Flemish and Catalonian lace, fine wool for vests, suede pants, and ties called *guirindolas* and *carrikes* with four collars, which were then in fashion. The owner was a stout and succulent Irishman whose flushed, lustrous, and rounded face was shaped like a Flemish cheese. He had the reputation of being extremely 'servile' (that is, a partisan of absolute monarchy). But if this was in fact true, the Constitutional state of the country, specifically that along Saint Jeronimo Avenue, forced him to hide it astutely. Those who accused him of having this ugly trait based their opinion on his reaction whenever Fernando or Amalia happened to pass by. The good merchant would hastily drop his measuring stick and leave his desk, run to the door, peer out anxiously, and watch the royal retinue with an expression of tenderness and loyalty. However, after the procession passed the Irishman would return to his habitual task, making all the protests against the King that his friends demanded. Near his store was a bookstore in whose meager window were displayed such books as *The History of Spain* by Duchesnes, the novels of Voltaire translated by an anonymous author, *The Nights* by Young, *The Sensitive Traveler,* and a novel, *Arturo y Arabella,* which enjoyed great popularity back then. Some works by Montiano, Porcell, Arriaza, Olavide, Feijoo[10], a treatise on the language of flowers, and *Guide for the Male Midwife* completed the inventory.

Next door, and in harmony with this literary temple, stood a perfumery and a costume jewelry store with some hunting objects, toilet items, and woodwork, all of them part of the customary trade in those days. Among the pomade and cosmetic jars, boxes of pins, and toys, was seen the archaeological profile of an old lady, who was housekeeper, clerk, and even the manufacturer of some drugs. Down the line there was another dark store, narrow, almost underground, where paper, ink, and desk items, and lastly, a support, or some other special orthopedic apparatus, were sold. On the door, hanging from a kitchen rack, dangled a handful of goose feathers, and in the deepest and most dismal part of the store one could see, like two owl eyes in a cavern, the radiant spectacles of *Don* Anatolio Más, the grand boss of that grand establishment.

Across the way there was a grocery specializing in aristocratic tastes. It had a famous oven which at Christmas time was used to roast more than four hundred turkeys of different types. Their partridge and rabbit pies had no rival. The cakes were very well-known, and nothing could equal the broiled suckling pigs which came out of that great laboratory. On fiestas, birthdays, and weddings, not to order the main dishes from the establishment of Perico el Mahonés (so they named him) would have shown undeniable disrespect. Doughnuts, biscuits, English cookies, and Astorgan sweets were sold at retail.

Not far from the grocery, one found the silk, thread, cotton, wool, skeins and ribbons of *Doña* Ambrosia (before 1820 they had called her Aunt Ambrosia). She was a respectable matron who dealt in yarn. The exterior of the store resembled the stage of a small town. Over here, like a banner, hung a piece of red flannel; over there, a sporty sash; further on, a skein, with its innumerable white strands, resembling the pistils of a gigantic flower. From above hung some shirt fronts, children's costumes, poplin trimmings, lines of handkerchiefs, slips, and draperies. Above all this, a plank of wood in the form of a sock was painted black and nailed perpendicularly to the wall to serve as the principal sign. Inside, however, everything was in harmony and good taste. The stool in the center served as a foundation for the massive hips of *Doña* Ambrosia, above which whose gigantic chest and corpulent bust stood out. She was an old-fashioned Spaniard, Manchegan—a native of Quintanar de la Orden, and a lady of very noble and Christian sentiment. With regard to her political ideas, a very important thing in those days, it suffices to say that after great debates along the street, the conclusion had been reached that she was extremely 'servile'.

These stores, with their respective displays and respective proprietors, composed the decoration of the street. Apart from this there was the moving and picturesque panorama formed by the masses who passed, as they do today, through that area. The fashions of the time were bizarre. Who, today, would be able to describe those sharp-pointed coattails? And what about those felt hats with upturned brim and high top, like a loaf of sugar? Can anyone nowadays understand such watch pendulums, as heavy as bell clappers, whose impertinent jingling emphasized the wearer's footsteps? And what about the boots *a lo farolé* and the old-fashioned puffed sleeves which would probably have been the ultimate degree of the ridiculous had they not been surpassed by the hyperbolic hairdos which made the head of a Christian look like that of a macaw?

The coaching society also showed off its most characteristic individuals. At least twenty times a day the grandees' coaches passed through this street of the neighborhood where they resided. Their coaches, which have long since been submerged in the obscure abyss of forgotten fashion, consisted of a sort of boat placed on an iron chassis. This chassis moved with the deliberate and solemn revolution of four wheels, with not more speed than was required to pick up mud and toss it onto pedestrians. The vehicle was a large box. For important days they were decorated with tortoise shell plaques. Generally, the coach walls were polished walnut or mahogany with very fine inlays of ivory or white metal. Deep on the inside of that apparatus one could glimpse the very aristocratic profile of some illustrious dignitary or some conspicuously ugly old lady. Behind the box, as if nailed upright on a board and held down by heavy tassels, were two long, heavy frock coats, which together with two enormous hats served to signify the presence of two solemn lackeys— symbolic figures of etiquette, soulless, motionless, lifeless. Elevated in front was the driver, who in clumsiness and fatness had only the mules as rivals, although they were generally more rational than he.

At the same time, the public vehicle, tartana, chaise, covered wagon, or covered cart, drawn by a line of emaciated beasts rolled on the other side of the street. Among all of this there were also the workmen with their loads, the errand boy with his strings, the water carrier with his bucket, the second-hand dealer with his sack and a pile of six or seven hats on his head, the blind man with his guitar, and a local native with his frying pan.

While we linger in this description, the groups advance toward the middle of the street and disappear through a narrow door, the entrance to a place which can not be very small since it has the capacity for so many people. That is the famous café and inn, *The Golden Fountain*, according to the sign above the door. It is the meeting-place of passionate and noisy youths, restless with impatience and inspiration, anxious to stimulate the passions of the people and to hear their thoughtless applause. A political club was organized there, the most famous and influential club of that era. Its speakers, then exalted neophytes of a new persuasion, have since directed the policy of the country. Many of them live today and are certainly no longer such believers in the beautiful principles they preached back then.

In reality, we should not concern ourselves with what many of those youths were to become in later years, since our story does not go past 1821. Then, a democracy born of the upheavals of revolution and national uprising founded the modern political criterion, which for fifty years has been working itself out with much difficulty. Great delirium somewhat debased the noble efforts of that youth which took upon itself the great task of educating public opinion, which until then had not existed. The clubs, which began by being eloquent chairs and arenas of scientific discussion, left the domain of their own functions by aspiring to direct public affairs, threatening the governments and imposing themselves on the nation. In this atmosphere it was inevitable that personalities would replace principles, that ambitions would be awakened, and what is worst of all, that venality, the cancer of politics, would corrupt. The true patriots fought for a long time against this type of infiltration. Absolutism, disguised with the mask of the most abominable demagogy, undermined the clubs, controlled them and finally sold them out. The fact is that the youth of 1820, full of faith and valor, was either too credulous or too generous. It may be that they did not know the deceit of their supposed friends or, that knowing it, that they considered it possible to overcome it by noble means, with persuasion, and propaganda.

A decrepit society, still conserving that inconvincible tenacity which distinguishes some elderly people, sustained bloody war with an exuberant and vigorous society called to the possession of the future. In this book, we shall be present at some of their encounters.

Let us continue our story. The curious people stopped in front of The Golden Fountain. The proprietors went to their respective doors. The barber Calleja, who demanded to be called Citizen Calleja, was also at his door, sharpening his blade and gazing over at the club and its patrons with a conceited gaze which seemed to say "If I were there." Some people approached the barbershop, forming a circle around the master barber. One of them hurriedly approached and asked, "What's new? Is something going on?"

The recent arrival was one of those individuals of indefinable age who seem either young or old according to the light or the expression on his face. His build was small, and his head sat right on top of the trunk of his body, with no more neck than was necessary to keep him from being completely hunchbacked. His abdomen protruded considerably, and he habitually crossed his arms over himself with the motion of affectionate preservation. His eyes were small and half-closed, but very lively, forming harmonious symmetry with his thin, long, and flexible lips, which in their most fiery moments of conversation moved forward forming an acoustic tube that gave his voice extraordinary intensity. In spite of his secular attire, there was something friarish in this person. His head seemed to be just right for the roundness of a tonsure, and the wide overcoat which covered his body looked more like a religious habit than an overcoat. His voice was unpleasant and bitterly irritating. On the other hand, his movements were extremely expressive and vehement.

In summary, we shall state that this man was named Gil Carrascosa. The Augustan Fathers of Móstoles had educated him. When he was ready to take his vows he left the monastery, leaving the good Fathers open-mouthed. At the turn of the century, through influential friends at the palace, he succeeded in being named abbot. But in 1812, he lost this endowed office and set aside the vestment. After that, he had been an ardent liberal until Fernando's return, when his relations with the favorite, Alagón[11], provided him with an income of 10,000 *reales* as a miserable civil servant. He was then an aggressive absolutist; but the pledge of allegiance to the Constitution by Fernando in 1820 made him change his opinion, even to the point of enlisting in a secret political society called *Los Comuneros* and forming a faction with the ultra-radicals. When we have the occasion to look into the private life of Carrascosa, we shall learn some details about a certain adventure he had with a beautiful woman some fifty years old who lived on Gorguera Street. We shall also learn of the bad moments that a certain student, a classical poet and author of the never-well-praised Gracchus tragedy, made him suffer as a result of that affair.

"Well, didn't it have to happen that way?" said Calleja. "Today we'll have a great session at The Golden Fountain. It will deal with asking the King to name a new minister because the one in power isn't to our liking. Alcalá Galiano[12] will speak."

"That ugly Andalusian?"

"Yes, the very same. The one who last month said, 'There is no pardon or armistice for the enemies of liberty. What do those dismal spirits want, those...?' He kept on speaking so beautifully, so beautifully..."

"He'll give them lots to worry about," observed Carrascosa. "What eloquence! What talent that boy has!"

"Well...I...*Don* Gil," declared Calleja, "while respecting your opinion, which to me seems so competent, I should say..."

At this moment, he coughed twice, let out a couple of grunts by way of preface, and continued, "I should say that, although I admire young Alcalá Galiano's talents more than anyone else's, I prefer Romero Alpuente because he is more expressive, stronger, more...Well, he says things more forcefully..., for example, 'He who wants force, force!' and 'Tyrants are not going to look for support in the staff of justice; they look for it by means of the guillotine, in the dishonored shoulder of the hangman!' And if I tell you that he is..."

"Well, I," replied the ex-abbot, "although I also admire Romero Alpuente[13], still prefer Alcalá Galiano because he is more precise, uses more reasoning..."

"You deceive yourself, friend Carrascosa. Don't compare that man with mine. Let me tell you that no orator in Spain can shine Romero Alpuente's shoes. What about that passage dealing with the underdogs, when he said, 'Down with the privileged; down with the superfluous; down with that luxury they call the King!' Ah! Yes, he's eloquent."

Calleja repeated all these speech excerpts with a great deal of emphasis and affectation. He recalled half of what he heard; and when the occasion arose, he began to reveal his oratorical arsenal, mixing everything up and using different fragments to create an insubstantial and nonsensical homily. We forgot to mention that this citizen Calleja was a corpulent and obese man. Although he seemed expressly made by nature to reveal the similarity that exists between a human being and a bull, his voice was so clucky, insignificant, and calf-like that it caused laughter when he recited scraps of speeches that he learned at The Golden Fountain Café.

"Well, we don't agree," answered Carrascosa, gesticulating with much aplomb, "because what does his eloquence have to do with Alcalá's? Alcalá is the type of man who, when he says, 'let's go,' gets everyone to join in."

"It's true," said one of the onlookers, who must have been a bullfighter, judging from his attire and the braid on the back of his neck. "When Alcalá attacks, the tyrants become hot under the collar....Well, the other day that was a pretty good jab he threw at the Inquisition. But what I like most of all is when he begins in a low tone and then his voice goes up, up, up..., I tell you that he is the finest matador among the orators."

"Men," affirmed Calleja, "I repeat that all those guys are nothing next to Romero Alpuente. You should have heard how many things he said against the clergy two nights ago. I'll bet you don't know what he called them. I'll bet you don't even know...It couldn't have occurred even to the devil himself. Well he called them...whited sepulchres! What a brain that man has!..."

"Don't insist, Calleja," grumbled the ex-civil servant with some impertinence.

"Come on over here, *Don* Gil," said Calleja, doing everything possible to deepen his voice. "I know very well who Galiano is and how the rest of them act. Come now! I've had their number since I first saw them. I don't have to hear any more than a single word from them to know what they are made of."

"I believe, *Don* Gaspar, that you are greatly mistaken; what's more, I don't know what makes you believe you are so qualified to judge," asserted Carrascosa in a very serious tone.

"What do you mean, that I am not qualified? I, who spend evenings listening to all of them, don't know them! Come now, some who are said to be very good aren't anything more than masters of hit-and-run."

"It's also a fact that Romero Alpuente is no pushover," replied one of the others present.

"Pushover?" exclaimed Calleja, livening up. "Why, he has talent bursting out at the seams!...And you, Carrascosa, who told you that I am not qualified to judge? How would you know it?"

"You ask who am I to make such a judgment. What do you know about speeches?"

"Come on, *Don* Gil. Don't try my patience! Let me tell you that I consider you a conceited ignoramus."

"Let's have some respect, *Señor* Calleja," exclaimed *Don* Gil, rather upset. "Have respect for those who are educated....I...I am a graduate in canon law from the University of Alcalá de Henares."

"Canon law, yes! Yes! That has to do with Latin. But what does that have to do with politics?...Don't stick your nose into those matters; they aren't for the thickheaded."

"You are the one who shouldn't stick his nose into politics," exclaimed Carrascosa, unable to hold himself back. "You ought to use the time you are not shaving your clients' beards to put your own house in order."

"Now listen here, Mr. Pedant of the University of Alcalá, Canonist, or whatever you may be....Go peel potatoes in the Móstoles Convent, where you'll be more at home."

"Gentlemen," said Carrascosa, turning as red as a tomato and looking around for support. Although he knew the barber for what he was, a chicken-hearted fellow, he dared not engage that massive eight-foot figure in a fight.

"Now, that I recall," added the barber disdainfully, "you haven't paid me for the leeches you took to that lady who lives on Gorguera Street, the sister of the Royal Guard's drum major."

"Are you also calling me a swindler? It would be better for citizen Calleja to remember the nineteen *reales* which my cousin, who owns the chicken shop on Main Street, lent him. Money that he has never returned."

"Come on now, both you and your cousin are cut out of the same cloth."

"Sure, but don't forget the four-string guitar that you stole from Perico Sardina the day of the picnic at Migas Calientes."

"The guitar, eh? Are you trying to say that I stole a guitar from him? Come on, don't start with innuendoes...," answered the barber, pretending to remain calm.

Don't come here with nonsense. We've got your number already, Mr. Straight-and-Narrow."

"Come now, you kept the collection from Saint Anthony's Day, fourteen pesetas. But back then, you were a royalist. You were stuck to Ostalaza's[14] tail so that he would put you to work in some office. In those days, you shouted hurrahs to the King, and during student masquerades, you gave him a bouquet of flowers at the Prado Promenade. Let me teach you a few things. Now listen carefully; although I am a barber, I have always been a liberal. Yes sirs, a liberal, although a barber. I am not a turncoat but an honest and liberal citizen like anyone else. Just take a look at those big shot royalists who now have changed their tune. After their denunciations, they had the jails crowded with people, and now the turncoats clutch onto the Constitution like bulls in the bullring, shouting 'Long Live Liberty' ".

Señor Calleja, you are insolent."

"You servile absolutist!"

This word was the greatest of all insults at that time. When it was uttered, there was no other recourse but to fight.

The ingenious instrument which industry has created for the improvement and care of half of the human race's whiskers was raised in the hand of the angry barber. The sharp edge was already flashing above the defenseless skull of the man who was a lay brother, abbot, and civil servant, when a providential hand intercepted the tremendous blow which would have split any full graduate of canon law from Alcalá into two slices. This was the robust hand of Calleja's wife. Disconcerted and quivering at seeing the terrible aggressive intention of her husband from a corner of the store, she left her chores at once. She put down the baby who was being nourished by one of her monumental breasts and, covering her bosom as best she could, ran to the door and freed poor Carrascosa from certain death.

The three figures remained there some seconds forming a handsome group: Calleja, with his arm raised and face lit up; his wife, who was as gigantic as he, holding his arms; and poor Gil, mute and petrified with fright. *Doña* Teresa Burguillos had the same massive and crude form as her husband, but at that moment she possessed a certain majesty of intention and brought to mind Minerva when she held back Achille's hand. The Agamemnon of the civil servants presented a not-too-academic picture.

"Citizen Calleja," she said in a very solemn tone, "don't waste your weapons on that hairless character. Save your arms for the tyrants."

Calleja then followed her advice, closed the blade, and saved it for the tyrants.

Don Gil took off from there, helped by some friends who wanted to avoid a catastrophe. Shortly after, the group dispersed.

The Amazon closed the door and continued her harangue without interruption. We shall not repeat the many fine things that she said as the baby once more took possession of the breast that had been so suddenly taken away. It is enough, in order to evaluate *Doña* Teresa Burguillos' worth, to say that she knew how to read, although with great difficulty, finding herself disposed to understanding things in reverse. With much effort and mumbling, she acquainted herself with some written speeches, committing them to memory. Encouraged by the barberish eloquence and liberal persuasion of her husband, she became a great politician. She was very enthusiastic about Riego and Quiroga.[15] She liked men with gifted tongues more than men of the sword, reaching the point of saying that she didn't know any gentlemen more gallantly discreet than Paco Martínez de la Rosa.[16] It is almost certain that at some point she expressed the desire to have Elío the barbarian before her, in order to pierce his heart with her scissors. Now let us enter The Golden Fountain.

NOTES

[1] *Arriaza y Superviela, Juan Bautista (1770-1837)* A neoclassical poet thematically dedicated to historical subjects, many reflecting anti-French and anti-constitutional sentiments.

[2] *Deseado (The Desired One)* A flattering epithet used to refer to King Fernando VII.

Fernando and Amalia (1784-1833; 1804-1829) Fernando VII, son of Charles IV and María Luisa de Parma, and Fernando's wife, Amalia (María Josefa), daughter of Maximilian of Saxony, whom he married in 1819. Fernando went to Bayonne in France and placed his crown at the disposition of Napoleon, who sent him to prison in Valencay. After his return to Spain, Fernando abolished the institutions under whose support he had waged the War of Independence (1808-1814). He was an anti-liberal absolutist. In 1820 Fernando pledged to support the Constitution of 1812, but he secretly worked to destroy it. He used spies and other forms of intrigue to undermine the liberals' efforts and to monitor their activities, strength and places of operation. In 1823 a French expedition helped him regain absolute power. Amalia's apparent virtues contrasted strikingly with her husband's lack of the same. Spain lost its Latin American colonies during Fernando's reign.

[3] *Oropesa and Esquilache* Historic uprisings that establish an antecedent to the revolutionary spirit of the 1820's, the period of *The Golden Fountain Cafe.* Esquilache took place on March 22-26, 1766.

[4] *Maella, Mariano Salvador de (1739-1819)* A Valencian painter who received his art training at the San Luca academy in Rome. In 1774 he

was named palace artist. His works are found in the Royal Palace in Madrid, the Cathedral of Toledo and in important sites throughout Spain.

[5] *Congress of Verona (Oct.-Dec. 1822)* Held in Verona, Italy by members of the Holy Alliance, to discuss among other matters the situation in Spain. Louis XVIII, King of France, was granted permission to intervene in Spain's constitutional crisis.

[6] *The Holy Alliance (1815)* Organized in Paris by Alexander of Russia, Francis I of Austria and Frederick William III of Prussia. A loosely knit alliance formed during the negotiation of the Second Peace of Paris, after Napoleon's defeat, it promoted Christian values in government and conservative trends.

[7] *Porlier, Juan Díaz (1788-1815)* A Spanish general, born in Cartagena, Colombia, who fought against the French during the War of Independence (1808-1814). He rebelled against the constitutional authority, was arrested and subsequently hanged.

[8] *Camarilla* An advisory board of individuals joined by a common purpose and who influence decisions made by a ruler or leader; a palace clique. The *camarilla* was sometimes clandestine and surreptitious.

Coletilla ('Postscript') A name often used to describe an informer or gossip. In its historic context, the name refers to Francisco Ramón Eguia y Latorre (1750-1827), the Captain General of New Castile. An intransigent absolutist, Eguia y Latorre served in Fernando VII's cabinet.

Tragala A song containing liberal verses directed against the supporters of the despotic government of the early 19th century. Its refrain began "Trágala, tú, servilón..."

Elío Francisco Javier (1767-1822) Commander-in-chief of Valencia and Cataluña against Napoleon. A traditionalist ambitious to achieve fortune and fame, and a strong supporter of Fernando VII. Led the uprising of Valencia in 1822 and was later condemned to death and garroted.

La Bisbal A general named Enrique O'Donnell (1769-1834) who was given the title Count of La Bisbal after an 1810 victory. La Bisbal was in charge of an army contingent sent to La Mancha to put down the uprising there. After 1820 he declared his support for Riego, but was forced to emigrate to France.

Vinuesa, Tomás (1770-1821) An ex-priest and supporter of the crown, he served as honorary chaplain to Fernando VII. He fought against France in the War of Independence, and when Fernando returned, declared his active opposition to the liberal cause. In 1820 he was arrested for plotting an uprising against the constitutional government. The *Comuneros* and other liberals pressed the court to award him a stiff sentence and he was condemned to 10 years in prison in 1821. But the following day a mob stormed the prison and assassinated him. He was honored by the government after the restoration of absolute power, in 1823. His killers were tried and executed in 1824.

[9] *Don, Doña* Honorific titles derived from the Latin *dominus*, master or lord. Originally a title of dignity conferred on very few of the highest nobility, later an expression of respect when combined with one's first name (*Don* Miguel, *Doña* Teresa). The use of these titles was discouraged by supporters of egalitarianism as a reminder of past social privileges and distinctions. It was often replaced by the less formal *Tío/Tía* ('Uncle' or 'Aunt'). The title *Don* might also be used facetiously to mock a poor or humble person.

[10] *Montiano y Luyando, Augustín de (1697-1764)* Founder and director of the Spanish Royal Academy of History in 1738. An academician and neoclassic writer. His tragedies *Ataulfo* and *Virginia* reflect French influence. He translated Racine's *Andromache*. His work was also influenced by Dryden and Addison.

Porcell, José Antonio (1720-1789) Academician, historian and poet of the Spanish neoclassical period whose style and content reflect the influence of Góngora. He is sometimes cited as an author living in one century who expressed himself in the mode of the previous century.

Olavide y Jáuregui, Pablo Antonio José de (1725-1803) An important figure in the court of Carlos III. A politician and writer born in Lima, Peru. His home in Madrid was a meeting place of Encyclopedists. Olavide was a close ally of the Count of Aranda and known for his liberal values. He translated and created adaptations of works by Voltaire, Lenerre, Sedaine and others. He was persecuted by the Inquisition.

Feijoo, Fray Jerónimo Benito (1676-1764) A famous Benedictine theologian and literary figure of the Eighteenth Century, known as one of the most learned men of the age. Renowned for his long works "*Teatro crítico universal*" and "*Cartas eruditas curiosas.*"

[11] *Alagón, Duke of* A soldier of great presence and an advisor to Fernando VII. A servile Captain of the Royal Guard, personally responsible for the King's safety. Known for his mastery of the art of intrigue.

[12] *Alcalá Galiano, Antonio (1789-1865)* A well-known politician and orator, one of the agitators of the uprising of 1820 in "Cabezas de San Juan." A member of patriotic societies, he distinguished himself as a public speaker in The Golden Fountain café of Madrid. A strong proponent of liberalism and the freedoms it advocated. Deputy to the Spanish Parliament during the period 1920-23.

[13] *Romero Alpuente, Juan (1752-1836)* A Spanish political figure, noted for his liberal ideas.

[14] *Ostalaza, Blas de (1768?-1835)* Palace chaplain and personal confessor to Prince Carlos. Executed for conspiracy in Valencia.

[15] *Riego, Rafael del (1785-1823)* A general who in collaboration with General Quiroga and a conspiracy of secret societies lead the January, 1820 "Cabezas de San Juan" garrison mutiny that finally imposed the Constitution of 1812 on the King. Fernando VII was forced to alter his absolutist system and to call a special session of the Spanish Parliament (*Las Cortes*).

A famous hymn called "Himno de Riego" was written by General Evaristo San Miguel and José Gomis, and sung by the triumphant liberals. It became the Spanish Republic's national anthem in 1931.

Riego was captured by French supporters of absolutism, who turned him over to the royalist authority. He was condemned to death, dragged through the streets of Madrid and hanged.

Quiroga, Antonio (1784-1846) A naval and army leader of liberal ideals. He headed a contingent of the 1820 León island constitutional uprising. In 1821 Quiroga became Captain of New Castile. As an ally of Riego, he was a fellow symbol of the liberal cause, forced into exile in England until after Fernando's death.

[16] *Martinez de la Rosa, Francisco ("Paco") (1789-1852)* A statesman, poet and dramatist of note. A member of the Congreso in 1813. President of the government (Council of Ministers) 1821-22, and 1831.

Chapter II

THE PATRIOTIC CLUB

At The Golden Fountain it is necessary to delineate two areas, two hemispheres: one corresponding to the café and the other to politics. In the first area there were a few tables reserved for café business. Way in the back, forming an angle, was the area where the sessions were held. At first the speaker would stand on a table to speak; later the proprietor recognized the need to construct a rostrum. The masses who gathered there were so considerable that it became necessary to set up additional benches. Somewhat later, as a consequence of the arguments which this club had with the Grande Oriente café, its political affiliations were defined. The radicals pigeonholed themselves in The Golden Fountain, and those who were not radicals were driven out. Finally, it was decided that the sessions would be secret, so the club was moved upstairs. Those who were seated below were paying customers, drinking coffee or chocolate; they heard the frightening uproar from above in the most heated moments of discussion and some, fearing that the ceiling would cave in on them along with the whole political heap, took to the hills, abandoning their inveterate custom of frequenting the café.

One of the matters which most concerned the owner was harmonizing (in the best possible way) politics and business, the club sessions and the paying customers. He directed conciliatory warnings that they not make noise; but this, it seems, was interpreted as a first step toward servility. The noise increased, and so the paying customers fled.

During the period to which our story refers, the sessions were still held downstairs. Those were the good old days of The Golden Fountain. Coffee drinkers made up the clientele.

Among the numerous defects of the place was that it could not be said to be excessively spacious; on the contrary, it was narrow, irregular, low, almost underground. The thick beams that supported the ceiling had no symmetry. In order to make it into a café. it had been necessary to tear out some walls, leaving the supports standing. Once a sufficient amount of space was obtained, the idea was to redecorate it in an artistic fashion.

The artists selected for this task were the most skilled painters of our town of Madrid. They cast appraising eyes on the narrow walls, thick columns, and awkward ceiling and unanimously agreed that the most important thing was to add capitals to those columns. They improvised some scrolls which appeared to have been inspired by an Estremaduran sausage, nailed them on and painted them yellow. Later, they decided on a papier-mâché border all along the salon, but none of the artists knew how to engrave a bas-relief, nor were they acquainted with the wonders of corrugated paper. It was agreed that the best thing would be to purchase a roll of painted paper at the recently established shop on Majaderitos Street and owned by a native of Marseilles. So a day later it was accomplished; the border was pasted on and set in its place by the waiters. The motif represented the skulls of goats, from whose horns hung garlands of flowers symmetrically entwined around bacchanalian staffs adorned with vines and fruits, all forming a funereal Anacreontic ensemble with very bad effect. The columns were painted white, then streaked with pink and green, intended to make one believe that they were jasper. On the front walls next to the entrance hung two mirrors about three feet in length, but not of one piece. They were formed from two sections of glass neatly joined by a bar of tin plate. These were covered with a green netting to discourage the exercise of "squatter's rights" by all the flies from the street. On each side of the mirrors were oil lamps supported by bases with the same unhappy bacchanalian theme. Each day they received, from an oil flask kept behind the counter, just enough fuel to enable them to burn weakly, smoking and stinking, until just after midnight, when their flame, exhausted, flickered and went out, leaving the apostles of liberty to save the country in utter darkness.

The smoke from the lamps, cigarettes, and the steam from the coffee had caused considerable deterioration of the gilded mirrors, yellow capitals and classical cornices. If it were not for tradition one could not have recognized the figures and color of the paintings on the ceiling, accomplished by Maella's worst student.

The furniture was simple, limited to a few rustic tables of wood painted to simulate mahogany with marble tops, and some court benches covered with oilcloth cushions whose horsehair stuffing happily protruded from innumerable holes.

The wide counter was set on a step, and on its façade was a plaque with its owner's initials entwined in confused hieroglyphics. Behind this platform stood the imperturbable figure of the owner, and to either side of him were two shelves which held up to four dozen bottles. Through half of the glass were also seen rolls, chocolate bars, and some oranges, (we say half because the other half did not exist, replaced by pieces of written paper expertly pasted on with red stickers.) An enormous cat wandered among the bottles, leaping from the shelf to its master's shoulders.

This cat spent most of the day curled up in a corner enjoying a slumber of happiness and gratification. He was a cautious cat who never interrupted a discussion, nor permitted himself to meow or knock down bottles during critical moments. The cat's name was Robespierre.

In this locale the impassioned youth of 1820 assembled. From where had those young men come? Some were from the Constituent group of 1812[1], an effort by a few which ended up giving light to many. Others received their education during the six years of oppression following King Fernando's return. Some sprang from the upheaval of 1820, which was perhaps more productive than that of the year 1812. What became of them? Some roamed as political exiles during the ten years of Calomarde.[2] Others perished in the unhappy days which followed the victory of St. Louis' hundred thousand grandchildren.[3] Those who managed to survive wicked Fernando vigorously defended the same principle. Others, believing to defend it, stumbled against the demands of a new generation. They discovered that the next generation was proposing more than they had, and they refused to follow along.

When the club was founded, its only objective was to debate political affairs in principle; nevertheless, little by little that noble arena, opened to enlighten the understanding of the people, was corrupted. The Fountainists wanted to exercise direct influence on the government. They solemnly requested the dismissal of a minister and the appointment of a representative. Two parties were delineated, the moderates and the radicals, establishing a barrier between them. But it degenerated even further. Since the passions of the people were aroused at The Golden Fountain, the government permitted these excesses in order to intimidate the King, who was its enemy. Meanwhile, the King secretly fomented excitement at The Golden Fountain because he saw it as a danger to Liberty. History has shown us that Fernando corrupted some of the speakers and sent in certain bullies who promoted riots and disturbances with the aim of discrediting the constitutional system. But the ministers who discovered Fernando's trickery closed The Golden Fountain Café, and then The Golden Fountain became agitated against the government and tried to overthrow it. The King encouraged the scandal by means of disguised agents; the club sided with the ministers; the

King took revenge and all became part of a circle of intrigue. The credulous patriots who formulated opinion there did not realize the hidden importance of their intentions.

But let us listen to Calleja, who is shouting for the session to open. Two elements of disorder were undermining The Golden Fountain: ignorance and treachery. In the first category Calleja, the barber, occupied a place of preference. This patriot headed a group as unruly as himself. This very gang carried on in such a disorderly way that when a speaker who was not of their liking went up to the rostrum they seriously considered stopping him from doing so.

In the evening to which we referred, our man was clapping his heavy hands so that they sounded like explosions, and the others were making a rumpus by striking their sticks on the floor. Those on the inside asked in vain for silence; among them were delegates, high-ranking military, and famous speakers. The rowdies would not be quiet until Alcalá Galiano went to the rostrum.

He was a young man, a little taller than average, erect, thin with a huge head, his manner open and frank. His face was very coarse and his head was covered with unruly hair. His mouth was big and his lips crude; but in the totality of his physiognomy there was a clear impression of noble boldness, and in his profound expression, the insight and fire of the creative faculty of his ancient race.

He began to speak by relating an event of the previous session which gave motive for the exit of Garelli[4], Toreno[5], and Martínez de la Rosa from The Golden Fountain. He pointed out the basic differences which were later to separate the moderates from the radicals, and described with precision and delicacy the condition of the government. But as he was describing in an even more eloquent and robust voice the past misfortunes of the nation, an incident occurred which obliged him to interrupt his speech. From the street was heard a strong clamor of voices which increased, producing a great uproar. The audience began to diminish and finally dwindled to the point that the speaker had no other recourse but to be silent.

The Andalusian was cut short and angry when he stepped down from the rostrum. The uproar outside was increasing. Finally, only five or six persons remained in the café. Since they wanted to satisfy their curiosity, they also left, accompanied by Galiano himself.

Within ten minutes The Golden Fountain was empty, and the noise outside was fading away. Each moment it was heard farther away because the wave of masses causing it were moving at a good pace. All indications were that another of those uprisings (so frequent during those days) had begun.

It was now late; the lamps had reached the third period of their very difficult iridescence, that is to say, they were at the point of going out completely and their wicks were giving off more odor and more abundant smoke than usual. One of the waiters had gone home and another was sleeping next to the door, snoring. The third had gone out with the patrons. Off in the distance was heard an echo of sinister voices, the voices of the public disorder that rolled around Madrid, disturbing the town.

The coffee pot remained still on its stand. Two clear points of light shone from behind it. It was Robespierre who approached his master and jumped onto his shoulders, placing himself in front in order to receive a caress. The owner of the café petted him affectionately on his back and the grateful animal raised his tail, arched his back, licked his whiskers and then, stretching with pleasure, returned to his corner where he again curled up.

Opposite the counter, and in the darkest part of the café, a human figure, invisible until then, began to reveal itself. This person was coming out of the shadow, advancing slowly toward the counter in the beam of the scarce light which brightened the place, making it possible to distinguish the shape of that quiet and strange personage.

He was a man advanced in age, but instead of the decline appropriate for his years he displayed fortitude, vigor, and energy. His face was bony, deformed, and massive in the upper part. His forehead had an exaggerated convexity, while his mouth and cheeks were reduced to wretched proportions. The absolute lack of teeth (which made his mouth into a concave vacuum) caused profound depressions to be marked on his lips and cheeks, which revealed even more the angular frame of his jaws. The tendons, bones, and nerves of his neck formed a series of articulated pieces whose mechanical movement was very conspicuous, in spite of the skin which covered them. His eyes were big and revealed they had once been attractive. Due to a strange phenomenon, while his hair had turned completely white his eyebrows kept the color of youth and were strong, rigid, and bristling. His thin curved nose must also have been attractive once, although finally, with the years, it had become thinner and more curved, reaching the point of being entirely like that of a vulture. Around his mouth (which was nothing more than a slit) and on top of his jaws (which were only a framework) grew a tenacious fuzz. The strong white sprouts of his beard, shaved weekly for some forty years, stood out rigid and shiny like silver wire. Two enormous ears, widespread, pendant and transparent, made the appearance of this face even more unusual. The extension of these cartilaginous pavilions reflected the extreme tympanic delicacy of the individual and seemed to increase instead of getting smaller with the years. His glance was like the stare of night birds—intense, luminous, and more sinister, due to the dark contrast of his large eyebrows, the elasticity and subtlety of his dark lids, which had widened in the darkness, revealing two very clear pupils. These eyes, besides seeing a great deal, seemed to illuminate what they saw. This gaze announced the vitality of his spirit maintained in spite of the deterioration of his body (which was bent forward, thin, and small in stature). His hands were very scrawny, making it possible to count the veins and nerves. His fingers, pointed and angular, resembled the claws of a bird of prey.

The skin of his forehead was yellow and wrinkled like the leaves of an old manuscript, and as he spoke the skin moved rapidly and refolded itself around his eyebrows, forming a series of concentric circles around his eyes which ended up looking like those of an owl. He was dressed in black and wore a velvet cap on his head.

When this man reached the counter, the café owner arose in suspicion. He went to the street door and listened attentively for a while. He turned around and peered through a small window which opened onto the patio. He then repeated the same operation at a door which faced the stairway. Of the three café waiters, only one was present, snoring on a bench. The owner awakened him and bade him good night. With the door barred, he returned, settled back on his stool, and observed the man with the cap as if he were expecting some great thing from him.

"What a mess you've started!" he said in a loud voice, knowing he could not be heard by outsiders. "Another nighttime disturbance! And they say that the Royal Guard is planning a great tumult. You, *Don* Elías, must know about it."

"Let them keep on, friend. Let them keep it up. They'll catch up with them," said the thin fellow in a deep and sonorous voice.

Putting his hand in his pocket, he pulled out a bundle which, by the sound it made on the table, clearly contained money. The proprietor looked at the bundle with a singular expression of fond attention while the old man calmly unfolded it, pulled out some coins, and began to count.

At the sound of the coins Robespierre opened his eyes, and seeing that it was nothing which interested him, he closed them again and fell back asleep. The old man counted ten half-doubloons and gave them to the proprietor.

"Come on now, *Señor* Elías," said the unhappy proprietor, "What can I do with only five doubloons?"

"For five doubloons you can buy the goddess of Liberty herself," Elías replied, without glancing at the owner.

"Don't hand me any of that. There are patriots here who will not say 'Long live the King' for all the money in the world."

"Yes, they are very upright gentlemen," exclaimed Elías in a tone of irony which was typical of his manner of speech.

"Go and offer money to Alcalá Galiano and Moreno Guerra."[6]

"Those who stir up trouble over there in Parliament are not the ones we are concerned with. We are dealing with those who make trouble over here."

"Well I assure you, my dear *Señor* Elías, that with what you have given me, I don't even have enough to buy the shoelace of the worst speaker in his club."

"I tell you that it is enough. The boss is not in a position to take on any more expenses."

"My! What a penny pincher the Absolutist is turning out to be. May a malignant tumor take him if he believes that the overthrow of the Constitution can be achieved with these miserly amounts."

"Wait and see, everything will work out all right," answered the old man with a sigh. As he sighed, he closed his mouth in such a way that it seemed as if his lower jaw were set into the upper one.

"But my dear *Don* Elías, what do you think I can do with only five doubloons? What do you think about that massive sergeant who spoke last night? They say he's an ignoramus, but the fact is that he makes noise and serves our purpose well. Each paragraph which excited the masses and inflames the public takes a tremendous amount of doing....And there are some who are so reluctant...! The night before last a guy, who usually accompanies Calleja the barber...What a bullish voice he had! He started to speak about the convention, and he said that it was necessary to cut the heads off the poppy. They applauded him a great deal and I confess that it was a great spectacle, although to tell the truth, I couldn't understand him any more than if he had spoken in Yiddish. When the session ended, I tried to invite him to speak a second time, but I don't know if he understood my intentions. The truth is that he said he was going to cut my throat, and for me to watch my step. What a scare he gave me! And I am so poorly paid! That speech delivered last night at the last minute by that young Valencian student cost me two servings of beef stew and two bottles of wine. Oh, if Alcalá Galiano and Flórez Estrada[7] only knew about these intrigues...I can assure you that I am going to enjoy laughing."

"Those are the poppy heads that must be cut off," exclaimed the old man, winking an eye and make a cutting gesture with his right hand.

"My, but it would be a pity because they're good boys. I tell you sincerely, from the depths of my heart, that although I am a devoted supporter of my absolute King, when I hear those boys, and especially when I observe Alcalá Galiano go up the platform and begin to speak in flowery, and then barbaric language, it puts such chills into me that my heart dances and I feel like embracing him."

"Let them shout. That's exactly what we are looking for. Look at this evening's riot: they're responsible for it. With more people like this, things will soon fall apart. That's exactly what the King wants. You will see how quickly they'll tear each other to pieces."

"But what can I do with only five doubloons?" repeated the café proprietor.

"As I told you before, the King is not in a position to squander. Moreover, a great deal of money isn't really needed for the people to lose their heads."

"You don't think so? Go and ask that sheltered lay brother who writes in *El Azote*. I had to pay him three doubloons out of the money you brought me last week. And then there's the young officer who delivered that strong speech a few days ago in which he said: '*Calendas Cartago*'...?"

"What you mean to say is: *Delenda est Carthago*."

"That's right: *dilenda* or *calenda*. It's all the same," said the proprietor of the café. "Well, that young officer has a stomach that just won't quit. I had to give him two rabbit pies as heavy as mill wheels. And besides, to get Andresillo Corcho to go shouting through the streets, as you saw for yourself on Sunday, I had to pay all his debts, including eight months back rent to his landlord, and I don't know how many small debts to his friends...Apart from all this, one receives nothing but scares, *Don* Elías. I'll repeat once more, as I told you before, that if the important liberals discover these swindles,they won't leave a bone in place in my body."

"Be careful, very careful, not to leave any written evidence. Don't address any letters to me. Don 't put a single idea in writing on this matter," said *Don* Elías severely.

"Tell me," continued the café proprietor, lowering his voice as if he feared that Robespierre would hear. "Tell me, when will the Royal Guard mutiny?"

"I don't know," Elías said, shrugging his shoulders.

"They say that the Holy Alliance has written to the King."

Elías was surely a very cautious man because he again answered dryly, "I do not know," as he had to the first question.

At that moment, once more, although off in the distance, he heard the same rumpus of voices which had caused all the people to leave the club.

"I believe that they intend to break into Toreno's house."

"Good, I am glad," said the old man, with sinister satisfaction. "I see that they are beginning to devour each other. It couldn't have happened any other way. Oh! Now I know the ways of this low-life. And what can happen? Can Spain remain for such a long time in the hands of a handful of desperate thinkers? If this were to last, I would doubt the Providence of our Lord, who resolves the problems of countries and stimulates the spirit of individuals. Spain is without a King, which is the same as being without life and without honor. Did Spain by chance have a Constitution when it became the greatest nation in the world? This idea of letting the people make the law is the most monstrous thing conceivable. When has it ever been seen that he who needs to be governed should make the laws? Would it be right for our servants to govern us? Here there is neither King nor God, but this will all end. I assure you that it will."

Upon saying this, the old man opened his eyes and clenched his fist in fury. The café proprietor, unable to resist the charm of so much eloquence, arose from his stool and embraced him. On extending his hand with enthusiasm, a bottle fell and rolled, striking Robespierre who, awakening suddenly, gave a tremendous meow and went to seek quieter places on top of the cooky pantry.

Elías pulled from his pocket a small black scarf to cover his mouth. He wrapped it around his neck and was ready to leave. The owner, with the customary officiousness he showed in that personage's presence, went to open the door for him. Day-light was beginning. The old royalist left without taking leave of his friend and headed toward his house.

NOTES

[1] *Constitution of 1812 (*Also called the *Cádiz Constitution)* Provided for a limited monarchy, a centralized administration and a Parliament to which the government would be responsible. Individual liberties, including the free use of property, were guaranteed.

[2] *Calomarde, Francisco Tadeo (1773-1842)* Minister of Justice from 1824-1833. Reputed to be an extreme opportunist. His ideas on jurisprudence were considered extremely pedantic. His name is often associated with a lack of class and dignity.

[3] *St. Louis* Refers to the "Cien mil hijos de San Luis" (the 100,000 sons of St. Louis.) The Holy Alliance agreed to authorize the intervention by French soldiers in Spain for the purpose of helping the Bourbon king defeat the revolutionaries who were keeping him from attaining absolute power. Under the direction of the Duke of Angouleme, in the service of Louis XVII, the insurrection of 1823 was put down.

[4] *Garelli y Battifora, Nicolás María (b. 1777)* A politician and distinguished professor of Jurisprudence, very active in the political life of The Golden Fountain and Lorencini cafés. Minister of Justice in 1822, he always maintained the doctrines of order and justice.

[5] *Toreno, Count of (José María Queipo de Llano y Ruiz de Sarabia (1786-1843)* A writer, historian and statesman who distinguished himself in the Spanish uprising against Napoleon. Due to his liberal ideas, he was imprisoned during the reign of Fernando VII. After the publication of the "Royal Statute" he was named Minister of the Treasury. Through his efforts at mediation the Civil War came to an end and the financial condition of the treasury was stabilized.

[6] *Moreno Guerra* Liberal minister Under Fernando VII.

[7] *Flórez Estrada, Alvaro (1770-1852)* Celebrated political economist and statesman. A liberal delegate to the Assembly in Cadiz, senator and minister of state. One of his economic treatises was translated into several languages.

Chapter III

A PATRIOTIC EVENT AND ITS CONSEQUENCES

Don Elías was crossing Saint Jeronimo Avenue when he saw a group of men coming toward him, laughing and shouting 'hurrahs' about Riego and the Constitution. Trying to avoid the encounter, he crossed to the other sidewalk, but they also crossed, and one of them stopped him.

There were five in the group, and at least three of them were very drunk. Our friend Calleja was apparently the leader. The others included a trader from Gilimón, a smuggler from Salitre and a gentleman well-known in Madrid for his swindles, who enjoyed great prestige in the flea market of La Cebada Square. The fourth was a young fellow, tall, thin and very dark, who had a reputation as a guerrilla fighter, and about whom many astonishing tales were told: of his role in the campaigns of 1809, and later, in the events of 1820. The sign of his feats marked his face with a sinister scar which extended from his forehead to his cheek, blinding him in one eye, and flattening half his nose.

The five stopped the old man.

"Kill him, kill him!" proposed the smuggler in a slurred voice, poking Elías in the chest with his cane.

"No, leave him alone, Perico! What good will it do to crush this bug?"

"Yes, it's *'Coletilla'*," exclaimed the scarred one, recognizing him. "*Coletilla*, Vinuesa's friend, the one who frequents all the clubs in order to inform the King of what is going on."

"Let's force it down his throat!" shouted the peddler, who was covered from neck to coccyx in a red sash, through the folds of which stood out the handle of one of those famous daggers from Albacete which give the police so much to do.

"*Tres Pesetas*, seize the little old man by the arm."

Tres Pesetas placed his hand on Elías's cap and threw it to the ground, leaving the old man's bald head exposed. A strong outburst of laughter welcomed this move.

"Look what big owl ears he has," added the guerrilla fighter, pulling him by his right ear until Elías' head touched his shoulder.

"Well, he doesn't have a bad head for playing pocket pool," said the smuggler, referring to *Don* Elías's bald pate, and he gave him a wallop on the head.

The royalist was pale with anger. He clenched his fists in nervous convulsion, and his eyes shone with tears of despair. Calleja, who seemed to possess great authority among those people, grabbed Elías's arm and exclaimed smilingly, with the licentious hilarity of inebriation, "Come on, four-flusher, come with us. "Citizens," he continued, turning to the others, "this guy is the great *Coletilla*, *Coletilla* himself. We'll be friends. He is going to introduce us to the constitutional King so that he will appoint us..."

"Ministers!" shouted the smuggler, raising his cane.

"Citizens. Long live the absolute King! Long live *Coletilla*!"

"Let's make him shareholder of the great community," said the smuggler. "The first test. Let him jump."

"Jump!"

"Jump!"

And one of them took Elías by the hand as if to make him jump, while another, pushing him brutally, knocked him to the ground.

"The second test," screeched *Tres Pesetas*. "Take this sword and jab one of us."

Pulling out a saber, he struck him flat with such a blow that Elías fell in the opposite direction.

"Say 'Long live the Constitution!' "

"You bet he's going to say it, and if not, I have something that'll make him say it," shouted the smuggler, pulling out his knife.

"This bum is the one who informed on El Cojo from Málaga," commented the gentleman.

"And he is also Vinuesa's friend."

"Men, this guy is none other than *Coletilla*, the great *Coletilla*," affirmed Calleja gravely.

Ferocity was painted in the eyes of the smuggler and trader. The scarred fellow grabbed Elías by the neck, and with his strong hand, pressed him against the ground.

"Let him loose, *Chaleco*. Leave him on the ground."

It is necessary to point out that the smuggler was known among those of his kind by the extravagant name of *Chaleco*.

"Leave him to me," exclaimed the trader. "Grab him by the neck. I want to see what those royalists have inside their bellies."

Unhappy Elías found himself in a very bad situation. He was commending himself to God with all of his soul when the unexpected arrival of a new person achieved a letup in the anger of Elías's enemies, saving him from certain death.

The new person was a tall, young attractive officer. He was clearly a person of noble family. In spite of his youth, he wore the epaulets of a high rank. He wore a long blue military cape and one of those old and awkward sabers capable of cutting any enemy's head off in one stroke. Seeing him intercede in defense of the old man, the others moved away with respect, and none dared to persist.

"Calm down men, leave that poor old man in peace. He's not harming anyone," said the officer.

"He's *Coletilla*, *Coletilla* himself."

"But you are five against one, and he is a poor defenseless man."

"That's exactly what I was saying," exclaimed Calleja, laughing drunkenly.

"Well, he has to say, 'Long live the Constitutional King.' "

"He'll say it when he's free. I vouch that he is a good liberal and a good man."

"Yes, but he is a servile scoundrel!" shouted *Chaleco*.

"And what do you intend to do with him?" asked the officer.

"Not too much," alleged *Tres Pesetas*, who was the most daring of all. "Nothing more than open a skylight in his belly so that his insides may attend Mass."

"Go home," said the officer firmly. "I'll protect him."

"You, sir?"

"Yes, I myself. Go on home, I shall answer for him."

"Well, if he doesn't say 'Long live...!' "

"Say 'Long live the Constitution,' " clamored all in unison, with the exception of Calleja, who was laughing like an idiot.

"Come on now," proclaimed the officer looking at Elías, "say it. It's not difficult to say, and besides, every good Spaniard ought to say it nowadays...."

"Make him say it!"

"Make him say it, and soon!"

The young officer insisted that Elías say those words to obtain his freedom, but Elías remained silent.

"Right away, little old man," declared the smuggler.

"No!" Elías cried out in a deep and quivering voice of indignation.

Tres Pesetas then raised the stick over the old man, and the others got ready to attack him, and it took all the officer's strength and prestige in order to prevent a fatal outcome.

"Say, 'Long live the Constitution!' "

"No!" repeated Elías, as though he had received inspiration from heaven, in a rage of supreme valor. "Down with the Constitution," he cried out.

The four heartless men roared with anger, but the officer appeared determined to defend Elías until the end.

"Get away," he said. "This man is crazy. Can't you see that the man is crazy?"

"Make him take back those words," declared the ever-laughing Calleja, who in spite of his drunken state, bragged about using parliamentary formulae with propriety.

"What do you mean by taking back those words?"

"Yes, he's crazy," affirmed *Chaleco*, "and if he isn't crazy, he's drun...drun...drunk."

"That's right, that's it, he's drunk," shouted Calleja, who finally had to lean against the wall to keep from falling to the ground.

Some neighbors were looking out. Several passers-by struck up a conversation with the venerable *Tres Pesetas*. It may be that a drunkard is easily distracted, or that the firm attitude of the officer had frightened them. The fact is that Calleja's four friends left Elías alone. *Don* Elías, helped by his protector, got up with great difficulty and put on his cap, which had nearly lost its shape under the smuggler's feet. The soldier, vigorously holding back *Chaleco*'s aggressive movement against Elías, grazed his left hand on the sharp pointed edge of the blade handle which the young fellow carried in his belt. This abrasion raised his skin a bit and caused some blood to flow. He covered his left hand with a handkerchief, and with his right hand he took the old man by the arm. Elías, on the other hand, bruised and broken, was weak, to the point that he could not walk without taking short steps and stopping often.

The soldier held him up strongly, walking with him very slowly. He asked him where his house was in order to take him there. Elías, without uttering a word, set out, pointing in the direction of Alcalá Street, then turning up Barquillo in order to finally reach Válgame Dios Street, where he resided.

The young officer was doubtless not very fond of silence, being of a joyful and communicative nature. Along the way, however, he began to speak with unusual volubility. The obstinate silence of the old man stimulated his tedious loquacity even more.

We cannot transcribe the exact words he spoke. From now on, our friend will accompany us in the course of this drawn-out story. Knowing his character as we do, it is clear that it will not be hazardous to put these, or similar, words in his mouth:

"My friend, one must deplore that in this imperfect human life the best and most beautiful things always have a bad side; a fatal darkness casts a shadow briefly over the luminous and resplendent. The best and most just institutions devised by man for the common good, in their first moments of application give strange results, which causes men of little faith to doubt their goodness and justice. The very men who manufacture a complicated machine hesitate in its first trials, unsure how best to regulate its function. Political liberty, the most beautiful attribute of man, applied to the government is the ideal of nations, but how difficult are its first days of practice. How the first tests of this machinery confuse us and cause us despair! The greatest obstacle to liberty is impatience. One must have perseverance and faith and wait for liberty to bear fruit. We shouldn't condemn it on the first day. Wouldn't it be an act of madness to pull out a tree in despair because it didn't take root, grow, and give fruit on the first day?"

It is probable that the officer did not use these exact terms; but there is no doubt that the ideas were the same. On concluding, he hoped to see that his harangue had produced some result in the old man. But the truth is, the old man was extremely absorbed and gave no indication of paying attention to his words. He seemed to be making other considerations from within, no less important and profound than what was said to him.

"It is deplorable," continued the officer, using a small gesture to give greater strength to his eloquence. "It is lamentable that the first rights conceded by liberty are misused by some men. The habit of liberty is one of the most difficult to acquire. We have to suffer for the mistakes of people who, because of their coarse nature, take more time to acquire this custom. Friend, let us not lose confidence as a result. You, who are doubtless a good liberal, and I, also very much one, will know how to wait. Let us not curse the sun because it hurts our eyes in the morning, when they suddenly emerge from a dream and darkness."

The young man stopped for the second time to catch his breath and to see if the old man's face showed signs of approval; he did not see anything in that peculiar face but abstraction and melancholy.

"Those fellows who stopped you," continued the young officer, "are not liberals. They are either secret agents of absolutism or crude illiterates without reason or conscience,

libertines without education, or salaried agitators. Will it be
necessary to deprive them of liberty and not to return it to them
until they receive education or punishment? Will there be
liberty for some and not for others? It has to be for all, or it has
to be taken away from all. Is it right to renounce the benefits of
a system because of the improper use that a few men make of
it? No! It is much better that a hundred men have liberty,
although they do not understand it, than for one single man,
who knows it value, to lose it. The evils that the illiterates
might cause are less than the tremendous good a single
educated person could do with it. Let us not deprive one
reasonable person of liberty by taking it away from one hundred
imprudent ones."

The young man stopped for the third time for two reasons:
firstly, because he didn't have anything more to say, and
secondly, because the old man, on arriving at his street,
stopped at a doorway and said, "Here."

The officer was going to leave his new friend, but he noted
that he was weaker by the moment and would possibly not be
able to get upstairs if he left him. The loquacious and prudent
young man entered the house, supporting the royalist who was
barely able to take a step.

Elías's home stood out in the middle of Válgame Dios
Street, where it looked like a palace. Artfully set between two
houses, it seemed there to be gigantic, although it had only two
tall storeys. The upper floor enjoyed the unique pre-eminence
of being occupied by our hero.

The façade was wretched, ugly. Downstairs served as an
office for the rackety business of an iron-smith who provided
frying pans, pump-hooks, and horse-shoes to the Barquillo
area. The balconies were faithful imitations of the hanging
gardens of Babylonia, for on them were many flower pots, and
many shrubs that were almost trees, together with three quail
cages and two decoy-birds which brought harmony to the whole
block at night. Between this jungle and those warblers hung a
pawnbroker's sign.

The entrance hall was narrow and very long. To reach the
stairway, which was at the back, one ran a thousand dangers
due to the twistings of the walkway where holes filled with filth
alternated with sharp pointed pebbles sticking up from the
surface. The stairway was narrow, and its walls, which had
been whitewashed in the time of Philip V, were in this century
covered by a venerable coat of dirt, with the exception of the
shiny area where people rubbed their elbows as they went
upstairs. On one of the flights there was no oil lamp but a

place for one, indicated by a drip stain of oil on the wall and above it a smoke stain. At the spot where both stains met, a blackened hook remained.

When they reached the second floor, the officer knocked. Someone must have been waiting impatiently, because the door opened immediately. A young girl about eighteen years of age opened it, and, upon seeing the downcast appearance of the old man and above all that he was accompanied by an unknown person, something quite unusual for him, she let slip an exclamation of fear and surprise.

"What is it? What happened to you?" she asked, closing the door after the two had entered.

Quickly walking in front of them, she opened the door to a room, and the three entered. The old man did not utter a word, and threw himself into an armchair with signs of pain.

"But, are you hurt? Let's see. I don't see anything," said the young girl, examining Elías with great solicitude, and taking his hand.

"It was nothing," said the officer, who respectfully took off his cap. "It wasn't anything. It happened a moment ago in the street. Five crude characters who met up with him wanted him to sing I don't know what, but the gentleman wasn't in the mood for singing; he refused."

The young girl looked at the officer with an expression of astonishment. She seemed not to understand any part of what he had said.

"They were drunkards who wanted to harm him, but luckily I passed by...have no fear. There is nothing wrong with him."

Elías seemed somewhat improved. He moved away from the young girl coldly, and his face began to look more calm.

"Oh! How frightened I was this evening," said the young lady. "Waiting for him hour after hour without his showing up...then those disturbances in the streets. At midnight some men passed by shouting. Pascuala and I hid inside. We sat in a corner, shaking with fear. How they shouted! Afterward, we heard many blows. They said that they were going to kill someone....We began to cry. Pascuala fainted, but I tried to keep up my spirit; together we knelt in prayer in front of the Virgin. Later the noise became more distant. We heard some moaning in the street. Oh! I don't want to remember it. I still haven't gotten over the fright."

The soldier heard those words with interest. As he listened, he scanned the room and looked over the kind person who lived there.

The house was very modest, but its simplicity and cleanliness revealed a peaceful well-being.

The young girl caught his attention more than the house. Clara was her name. She appeared to be older than eighteen but younger than twenty-two. Nevertheless, we are sure that she was not more than sixteen years old. Her stature was tall rather than short. Her figure, bust, her whole body was elegant in form, beautifully proportioned—the patrimony of the daughters of both Castiles. The color of her face, characteristically Castilian, was very pale, not that intense and feverish paleness of the Andalusians but the fresh and marble-white skin of the daughters of Alcalá, Segovia, and Madrid. Much sadness was reflected in her big, black eyes. Her nose was thin and straight, although a little too small. Her small forehead was well-shaped. Her mouth was beautiful. It was embellished by the attractive form of her chin and her neck, whose voluptuousness and roundness contributed to making her appearance one of the most enchanting that the unknown officer's eyes had ever seen. The young officer, let us say in passing, was a man of considerable experience in feminine matters.

Clara's hairdo could be rigorously described as provincial because she arranged it in a high chignon with three braids on the crown. This hair style was out of style in society, but beauty generally triumphs over fashion. Clara looked very nice with her pyramidal braids. Her attire was not that used by the well-to-do class, nor by the poor. That is to say, her dress was of light-colored fabric with a floral motif; the sleeves were narrow to the cuffs. Her waist was a bit high, and the cut of the collar was square and adorned in many laces.

The soldier's scrutiny lasted much less time than we have taken to describe Clara's appearance. For a few seconds the three sat motionless, facing each other without uttering a word until the old man, as if to continue an interior monologue, exclaimed in a sudden bout of anger, accompanied by a ferocious glance: "Scoundrels, dogs! I wish I had had a terrible weapon in my hand that would have done away with those despicable characters in a second! Ah! But, they aren't really to blame. The others are at fault, the wise men, the public speakers, those who educate them, those evil charlatans who profane the gift of the word in those infamous meetings of the Parliament. The ones who are to blame are the revolutionaries, those who rebel against their King, blasphemous against their God, scornful of the human race. Oh God of Justice! Will I never see the Day of Vengeance?"

The soldier was astonished and somewhat embarrassed. It seemed to him that what the old man had said was an indirect reply to his expressive dissertation while en route with him to his home. Although the reply was directed to him, he contained himself when he saw the expression of contempt and ferocity on Elías's face. His attention was concentrated in part on the royalist's companion. Clara looked at the old man with her customary indifference and at the same time as if she were embarrassed by the surprise her protector's words had caused.

The officer, a bit careful after the imprecations of the royalist, began to feel interest toward that poor little girl who, without his even knowing why, had inspired so much pity from the first.

A moment arrived in which the young fellow sensed his embarrassing situation. Elías continued his soliloquy in a low voice, paying no attention to the officer. It was time to leave, but he did not want to go without satisfying his curiosity and speaking a bit more with the young girl. He looked at Elías insistently and stepped closer, but Elías showed no signs of noticing him. He did not show gratitude, affection, or courtesy. Apparently, he was not made from the same mold as other men. Finally, seeing him so distracted, he resolved to use the old man as a pretext to speak to the girl.

"You have nothing to fear," he said to her in a low voice, moving toward the window. "He wasn't even hit. He's become terrified due to surprise and anger. He'll calm down."

"Yes, he'll calm down...a bit."

"And he'll be happy once more."

"Happy, no."

"Living with you, he couldn't be sad." This could pass for gallantry, but it had no effect on Clara. He looked again at Elías who kept on in the same attitude, gesticulating to himself. Now and then he uttered his favorite invectives.

"Damned dogs!"

The officer risked a question, lowering his voice and moving toward the window. He said, "Perhaps the question I want to ask will be indiscreet. Forgive the great interest I have taken in that gentleman and the desire to serve him in any way I can. Is he in his right mind?"

Clara looked at the soldier with an expression of great surprise, and as if the question were a revelation, she replied, "Crazy...?" and after a pause, she added, letting her shoulders drop, "I don't know."

The soldier's curiosity grew.

"Please don't take offense, but his conduct, his words in that dispute, and the gloominess of his appearance make me believe that he suffers from a mental condition."

Clara looked at the young fellow with an expression that was rather affirmative.

"I don't know," she said at last. "The poor thing suffers so much. I also suffer, seeing him this way. He's never happy; at times I think he is going to die in a rage of fury. He spends the evenings reading books or writing letters, and at times he talks to himself as he's doing right now. He frightens Pascuala and me both. We hear him get up and pace quickly, walking around this room. He goes out early in the day and stays out all evening."

The young officer's compassion for Clara grew as he saw the unhappy girl in the role of a martyr, suffering the abuses of the eccentric old man with resignation.

"But you," he said with the greatest of interest. "Aren't you a victim of his rough manners? Doesn't he mistreat you? In that case it would be a matter of declaring him crazy."

"Who, me? No," said Clara. "He has never mistreated me."

It must seem strange that Clara, without knowing the soldier, would make statements of the most intimate confidence to him. This, of course, would be unusual under ordinary circumstances but in this case, it was not so. Clara had always lived in the company of the old man. She was an orphan, had neither relatives nor friends, never went out, and spoke to no one. She wasted away in the desert of that house, with nothing more than her memories and hopes. Her character was extremely simple. Unforeseen circumstances had set before her a courteous and generous young man who, in order to satisfy his curiosity, employed clever recourses for the purpose of conversation. She told him all that he wanted to know. She told it to him, obeying a powerful need for relief, which arose from her isolation and melancholy.

The curious stranger did not dare to continue his inquiry. He was about to leave, unwillingly, when Clara saw that his hand was bleeding, and exclaimed in surprise, "You are hurt!"

"Oh! It's nothing. It's only a scratch."

"But you are losing a great deal of blood. Oh Lord! Your hand is mangled."

"Oh, it isn't anything...with a little water..."

"I'll bring it right away."

Clara left quickly and entered the next room. She returned shortly. She brought a wash basin, which she put on the table, and called the officer, who did not delay a moment.

"Do you have a family?" he asked, touching the water to see if it was very cold.

"Family?" replied Clara with her usual naturalness. "No. He used to love me a great deal. I want so much for him to get rid of those obsessions....He used to be very good to me and very happy....I was a child then."

"He used to be very good to you. And now he isn't?"

"Yes, but now...he has so many things to think about..."

"How long ago did he change?"

"A long time ago when there were many disturbances, and they said that they were going to kill the...was it the King? I really don't know who. But even before this he was almost always upset. When I was just a child....No! In those days, we used to go walking every Sunday. He used to take me to Chamartín, to eat in the country, with Pascuala."

"And now you never leave here?"

"Never," said Clara, as if the loneliness in which she was living were the most natural thing in the world.

The officer became more and more interested in this girl he had met so unexpectedly. He suspected more and more that this unhappy girl was the victim of the fanatic's brutalities. From where he was seated he saw the old man in an armchair, possessed by his mute frenzy. Then, looking at Clara, whose simple grace and melancholy frankness created a contrast with the ill-tempered royalist, his confusion, curiosity, and fears grew even more.

"And you don't go out to amuse yourself, to look around and relax after being cooped up here for so long?" he said in a rather emotional voice.

"What for? I become sad when I go out. The only time I see the outside is early on Sunday when I attend Mass at Las Góngoras Church, but when I am out it seems to me that I'm even lonelier than at home."

"Doesn't it matter to him whether you enjoy yourself and lead a pleasant life?" he asked, half-frightened by his own curiosity and glancing obliquely at Elías to see if he was paying attention to their conversation.

"But I don't want to enjoy myself. What am I going to do outside? He says that I should always stay at home."

"But, don't you have dealings with anybody? Don't you see anyone?"

"Yes, Pascuala, who is very fond of me."

The officer was now anxious to know who Pascuala was.

"And this Pascuala, is she a friend of yours?"

"She's the maid."

"Oh! I see....And don't you have other friends? At your age it is natural and usual to have the friendship of young people and above all one can not live this way. You must..."

"I'm fine this way. He tells me I shouldn't get acquainted with anyone."

"And he forces you to lead this very sad existence?"

"No, he doesn't force me. If I wanted to I could go out. He's never here. But...I...God spare me...Where would I go?"

The soldier didn't know what to think. What relation existed between that monomaniac and that youngster? Could he be her father, her husband..."No," he said to himself. "It's disgusting to suspect that the bonds of marriage exist between the two."

"Don't be surprised at my questions," he said, continuing anxiously, "but I'm very interested in both of you. Does anyone visit him? Doesn't anyone come to see him?"

"He is very well acquainted with some ladies by the name of Porreño. They belong to the nobility and were very rich."

"And they come here?"

"A few times. He's very fond of them."

"And those ladies, I presume, are good people. Don't they show any affection to you? Aren't they fond of you?"

"Fond of me? On one occasion they told me that I seemed to be a good girl."

"And nothing else? Didn't they say anything else to you?"

"Oh! They are very good ladies. He says they are very good. They say that one of them is a saint."

These declarations were made by Clara with a frank spontaneity that would move anyone listening to them. The reader, who still is not acquainted with this girl's infinite goodness, should not be surprised by poor Clara's loyal frankness and sublime indiscretion. During many years this unfortunate girl had seen no one but *Don* Elías, Pascuala, and every once in a while, the three melancholic effigies who were the Porreño ladies. Her existence was a prolonged silence and slow boredom. The only thing that brought back her spirit and given her some happiness were the forty days which she had spent in Ateca, a town in Aragón where Elías sent her to enjoy the countryside. This had occurred six months before these present events. Later we shall see why Elías decided on Clara's trip, and what came of it.

"But is it possible?" continued the officer, forgetting that Elías was nearby. "Is it possible that you spend your life this way, without any other company than the old man? And you haven't ever left this place, not even to go to the country?"

"Yes, I went away for a few days, six months ago."

"And where did you go?"

"To Ateca. He send me there. I became ill and went there to recuperate. I was in his home town."

"Oh!" said the soldier, happy to have found a motive, however small, for believing that that man was not completely inhuman.

"And did you have a good time?"

"Oh yes! I was very happy there."

"And do you want to return?"

"Oh, yes!" exclaimed Clara being unable to contain her enthusiasm.

"You shouldn't be here. You have the kindest heart that ever existed. For what reason, other than for the good of society, would God create such an ensemble of gracefulness and similar worth? How many people you could make happy! Have you never thought of this? Think about it!"

Clara seemed not to pay attention to his gallant remarks. She kept silent and with her eyes downcast, perhaps thinking about what the young man had suggested. Who knows what her reflections were at that moment?

The inquisitive one was waiting for a reply when Elías, looking toward the room where they were talking, exclaimed, "Clara! Clara!"

The soldier went over to him quickly, hiding his confusion, and said to him, "Sir, I didn't want to leave until I was certain you were better. I was just relating the incident to the girl, and I gave her an account of the effrontery of those men. Now that I see that you are at ease, I shall leave, reminding you that you may call on me whenever I might be of service to you."

"Thank you," replied Elías dryly. "Clara, accompany this gentleman to the door."

He had to leave. There was no pretext for his staying. His hand was bandaged perfectly, and his elderly ward had shown him the door. The impressionable young fellow did not know what to do in order to stay longer. He looked at Clara to see if he could read in her eyes the desire for him to remain, but she showed great indifference, even stepping forward to open the door herself.

He had no alternative. The soldier stretched out his hand to the royalist who in turn extended two cold and bony fingers. On arriving at the door, the soldier intended to begin the conversation anew, but the curtsy she made frustrated him. He stepped outside and stopped once more.

"Don't forget what I said to you! You can't live this way," he said going down the first step. "You must..."

"Clara! Clara!" shouted the fanatic from inside in a demanding tone.

Clara shut the door, and the soldier remained on the stairway, embarrassed and confused. His first thought was to knock again until she came to the door, but then he reflected on the boldness of such conduct. He went down the stairs slowly. "What mystery is there in this house?" he said to himself. On finding himself in the street, he felt greater curiosity and compassion toward the young girl.

"Is she his daughter, wife, niece, or ward?" he wondered aloud. Gosh! It was impossible to stop wanting to know the secrets of this household. How could he not want to hear them directly from Clara, who confided in him with such frankness?

He walked a good distance, stopped, and looked back at the house.

"She herself will not receive me," he said. "This has been an accident. If I return? On what pretext? That poor creature, how much she must be suffering. Her face looks as if she has been suffering a great deal...in the company of that animal and without seeing or speaking to anyone..."

Instinctively he turned back toward the house again, continuing his soliloquy. "Perhaps he will reprimand her for having spoken to me; perhaps while pretending distraction he heard everything she said to me. Did he feel offended? Will he mistreat her as a result?"

He entered and went upstairs, trying not to be heard. He reached the door and stopped. His hand mechanically took hold of the bell cord. If he had heard the slightest indication of an argument—the sour voice of the old man—he would have rung the bell with all his strength. He put his ear to the door, but heard nothing. A tomb-like silence reigned in that house. Suddenly, he heard the voice of a woman singing and footsteps walking rapidly through the vestibule where the door was. He heard the noise of her dress scraping the walls and her voice, a voice which passing by so near resonated with delicate and expressive timbre. It was Clara who was singing and running so briskly. Was she happy, perhaps? This was a new mystery.

The curious soldier felt even more confused. He let go of the cord, and step by step, very quietly, he went down the stairs looking both ways cautiously, like a thief. He went into the street, determined to leave. He reached the corner, stopped, looked back at the house, and at last undertook the route to his home, where we shall leave him for the time being, worried and confused. We shall leave him for the moment in order to occupy ourselves with those friends on Válgame Dios Street whose life and characters require narration and explanation.

Chapter IV

'COLETILLA'

The strange man we know by the name of Elías was born sometime in 1762 in the town of Ateca, an Aragonese locale which is between Sigüenza and Calatayud. His happy parents were Esteban Orejón and Nicolasa Paredes. He was an honest farmer, and she the only daughter of the most affluent land owner of the neighboring town of Cariñena. Exactly nine months after the marriage, a child was born. Due to the circumstances which preceded the pregnancy and birth, it seemed that the child was destined for great things. It happened that sometime about the fifth month of pregnancy *Doña* Nicolasa had a dream in which she saw the fruit of her womb, already grown and well on in years, carried off to heaven in a flaming chariot. Later on, the good woman began to dream every evening that her son was a Magistrate, a Prelate, an Alderman, a Canon, Dean, even a Bishop, King, Ruler, or at least a Pope or Archbishop.

Finally, the moment of giving birth arrived. Entrusting herself to God and a certain male midwife in Ateca, a man of great talent, she gave birth to a son. The child did not come into the world with any indications of being the chosen among the chosen. On the contrary, he was so thin, sickly, and emaciated that it seemed as though his mother, distracted by her perpetual dreaming of crowns and tiaras, had deprived his body of nourishment.

Even though he was born like any other offspring of man, some prodigies did not fail to exist on the outside. In the sky of Ateca was observed for the first time the meeting of the Seven Stars of the Pleiades with Mercury. The moon appeared in the shape of a ring, and lastly, a comet traveled through the dome of the sky. The town apothecary, who devoted himself to observing the stars, understood something about astrology, and he fancied himself a necromancer. He saw all those celestial things showing in the Ateca sky and said with great gravity that they were indications that the child would be a wonder and glory of the whole world. The meeting signified that two nations would unite against him. The comet meant that he would conquer all others, and the ring around the moon, as anyone could understand, was a sign of immortality.

"Because," said *Don* Pablo (which was the apothecary's name), "nothing in celestial circles escapes me. Whatever I conjecture has to be a reality, just as sure as this is chocolate."

As a matter of fact, it was chocolate of the best quality, from Torroba, that they drank, during the solemn prophecy, thanks to the Orejóns' grateful generosity.

At the baptism there was a party beyond anyone's imagination. There was a great abundance of wines from Aragón, large coffee cakes, very large buns, loaves of bread a half yard long, a large mutton leg, peppers from Rioja, and some cakes as large as a fist made by the Discalced Nuns of Daroca. The greatest attention was lavished on *Don* Pablo because of his predictions, which he considered worthy of being engraved in bronze and painted on tablets. Encouraged by the generosity with which they repaid his astrological work, he composed a ten-line stanza of octosyllables in which he called the Orejón family 'patrons of science.'

The child grew. Needless to say, during his infancy his parents' hopes seemed to acquire foundation. What a precocious child! Everything that the child did was amazing, never before seen or heard. He opened his mouth to articulate a syllable and recited a proverb. Did he cry for his mother's breast? According to the astrologer, he had spoken an incomprehensible aphorism. Two, four, six years passed and with age little Orejón's fame grew.

"Do you know what I saw, *Señora* Nicolasa?" said the apothecary one day, in a certain mysterious tone which frightened the good woman.

"What, *Señor Don* Pablo Bragas?"

"Little Elías was playing yesterday with some hens and struck the chicks with a rod which in stronger hands would surely have killed them. 'Son,' I said to him, 'why are you punishing those little creatures?' "

"Because they're chickens," he answered, "and I want to kill them."

"And what have they done to you, little tormentor?"

"I am commanding them to say 'cheep,' and they refuse to."

"See for yourself, *Doña* Nicolasa, see for yourself. This was out of the ordinary for the wisdom and depth it contains: *Qui pulli sunt*. The Dialectician said the same thing when he got the best of the Jansenists: *Quia heroeti sunt!*"

Doña Nicolasa Paredes, in all truthfulness, did not completely understand the meaning of the depth of her son's words, but grateful for *Don* Pablo Bragas's prophecies, she laid out a tablecloth and set in front of her friend a bowl of thick broth which would have been the envy of any priest of the San Cayetano order.

Elías grew. Following the prudent advice of a lector of the Dominican monastery of Tarazona who came to Ateca to preach on the patron saint's day, they sent him to study Humanities with the priests of that monastery. He was then twelve years old. His reputation there grew; after a short time, he was such a great Latin scholar that not even Polibius, Eusebius nor Casidorus could equal him.

He was fifteen years old when the family held a meeting to determine whether they would send him to the Seminary of Tudela or the University of Alcalá. But there were so many important reasons presented by *Don* Pablo Bragas in favor of Alcalá that the decision was made. The prodigy of nature was placed on a horse along with saddlebags holding some cakes and two liters of wine. After tears shed by *Doña* Nicolasa and some couplets which the astrologist rattled off, Elías left, heading toward the land of the immortal Cervantes, where he arrived after four days of travel.

Soon thereafter *Doña* Nicolasa gave birth to a daughter. During this event nature produced no strange effects.

Elías studied canon law and theology in Alcalá. During his studies, in which he showed great diligence, the teachers did not cease to praise him to high heaven, he who greatly honored the illustrious Orejón lineage. Some expected him to be a Luis Vives, others an Escobar, a Sánchez, a Vázquez, or an Arias Montano.[1] And in fact, the youngster was studious. He spent the evenings without sleep, devouring Eusebius, Cavalario, and Grotius. He daily digested a huge portion of the book *De Locis Teologices*; and when he went to class, he excelled. During this period the fundamental characteristics of his personality began to appear, manifested by extreme pride, excessive dryness in his dealings, and very rigid behavior. For this reason, his classmates had no affection for him.

But his reputation as a learned person was widespread. He returned to his home town, and, on entering it, the first thing he saw was the venerable figure of *Don* Pablo Bragas, who greeted him with a pompous bow from the waist. Beside him stood the mayor, the parish priest, and the most noteworthy people of Ateca, including the blacksmith. Bragas pulled a paper out of his pocket and read a speech, half in Latin and half in Castilian, which everyone applauded, except the honoree. At home were waiting *Señora* Nicolasa, who was aging, and Orejón senior, who was very well preserved. The little sister was now a young lady, but the poor thing had a reputation as mischievous rather than wise. There was a small family party with plenty of cakes of which half, it may be said with impartiality, were eaten by *Don* Pablo Bragas.

In his town Elías continued to be dedicated to his studies. His unsociability increased and his pride was more accentuated. His parents, however, noticed nothing and were infatuated with the young man. If at any time the rigidity of his behavior offended them momentarily, they were soon satisfied by hearing from Bragas's mouth a speech of praise—a speech whose epilogue was always a bowl of chocolate or a large slice of pork.

Elías was thirty years of age when he set out for Madrid. We do not know whether he made this decision because he dreamed of acquiring the glory which the stars, through the mouth of the wise man, had announced. Undoubtedly, he had prepared some plan. On arriving in Madrid, he struck up very intimate relations with the Trinitarian Fathers, who were as wise as nature. Similarly, he established a close relationship with a gentleman of the nobility who belonged to the illustrious house of the Porreños and Venegas family, the Marquis of Jarandilla. He took such a liking to this family that he served them faithfully in prosperity and was their majordomo even after their ruin, which occurred at the end of the war. In 1808, when war broke out, Elías left his sedentary practices, index books, digests and decrees to serve in the ranks of Echevarri and El Empecinado.[2] He fought the whole campaign of Navarra with Echevarri and organized a body of vigilantes in Castile upon passing Napoleon as he was returning from Madrid.

After the war was over, he passed through his home town. His father had died. His sister, now a woman, had married a farmer who was a relative; and his mother was crippled and ill. Bragas had lost his good humor and his fondness for the stars, but not his love for little Elías or his deep conviction: *the two nations would unite against him and he would conquer both of them.*

In Ateca he became aware of the growth that the Constitutional party was experiencing and the enthusiasm with which the Iberian Peninsula looked upon the Assembly of Cádiz.[3] We must point out that Elías despised the Constitutionalists. Since he had reached the age of reason, he had lived only with his intelligence and had not experienced in his youth the natural feelings of friendship and affection. At forty he was inflamed by a strong and extremely violent passion. This passion was the love of despotism, the hatred of all tolerance and all liberty. He was an enraged royalist, inhuman, and his fanaticism reached the point of making him capable of the greatest sacrifice, the sacrifice of a martyr. His character was vehement by nature, although diligent studies had restrained and distorted it. But upon reaching that period in which it was impossible for any Spaniard to ignore the great problems to be resolved, the hidden vehemence of Elías's feelings manifested itself. It was demonstrated not in the form of love, or avarice, or ambition, but in the form of political passion, frantic adherence to a system and profound hatred for the opposition.

As a result of this evolution of character, there developed in him a strength of will and energy that might have carried him on to the greatest deeds had the occasion presented itself. His intelligence, perspicacious and cultivated, lent more strength to his exaggerated feelings. The strange blending of his intellectual faculties, his great passion, and his uncontrollable behavior made him one of the monstrous beings which a superficial observation quickly characterizes as "a madman."

The Constitutional system collapsed in 1814, and Elías was happy. But even so, he did not live quietly. He began to participate in an active political life, which at times can become unpleasant. He struck up a friendship with the Duke of Alagón and a most odious clique. He entered the councils of the palace and felt himself honored with the friendship of that Prince who disgraced his country. Then, he took part in the veiled scheming of that infamous court.

The year 1820 came and our protagonist entered into the period of chronic anger, moral disorder, and frantic tenacity in which we have known him. We already have an idea of how he lived. His activity had doubled, and he conspired with a constancy the like of which has never been seen. Secretly in touch with the Court, he tried to organize a reactionary movement and adopted any means which would lead to the desired result. He visited the clubs, stirred up excitement, attended the meetings of the royalists, and even those of the liberals. He found out everything and took advantage of everything. But some accusations were already being sounded against him. It was now being said that he had belonged to the King's inner circle, and he was now pointed out as a conspirator. On more than one occasion, he found himself threatened by people who claimed to recognize him or in fact did recognize him.

All those who knew him by sight in the patriotic circles called him 'Coletilla', a nickname devised in Calleja's barbershop some days after the famous addition which the King placed in a speech of the crown. That literary appendix, which produced such a bad effect, was referred to as the *'Coletilla'* or *"Postscript"* by the public. The idea that Elías was a friend of the King united in the mind of the people a picture of the fanatic and that word *"Coletilla."* The names that the public engrave on the forehead of an individual, with their hot seal, can never be erased. So it is a fact that Elías was called *Coletilla* by everyone.

His few friends were the only ones who were careful not to call him by that name.

We shall conclude this chapter by dedicating a moment to one of its principal heroes. Our friend *Don* Pablo Bragas died in Ateca at the age of ninety-one of gastric fever due to the double effect of a bellyful of hash and a cold which he caught while examining the crossing of Arcturus with Mars on a January evening.

Since then, astronomy in Ateca has suffered a pitiful decline.

NOTES

[1] *Vives, Juan Luis (1492-1540)* Spanish humanist and philosopher, highly esteemed by Erasmus. His bibliography is extensive, and his collected works fill eight volumes. His ideas on pedagogy are considered to be of high intellectual merit.

Escobar, Sánchez, Vásquez Although their full names are not given, Galdós appears to be referring to scholarly theologians (perhaps Juan Escobar del Corro or Antonio Escobar y Mendoza; Tomás Sánchez or Pedro Antonio Sánchez; Gabriel Vásquez (1551-1604).

Arias Montano, Benito (1527-1598) A Spanish theologian and humanist of extraordinary erudition. An advisor to Felipe II, who allegedly sent him to Antwerp to direct the preparation of the Biblia Poliglota.

Eusebio, Pánfilo Reputed to be from Cesarea, where he was Bishop. He often referred to as the Father of Ecclesiastical history.

Cavalario, Domingo An Italian theologian.

Grotius (Hugo van Groot) A Dutch law scholar and historian. Official historian of the Low Countries. His work entitled "De Jure

Belli at Paci" is considered by many to be the real beginning of international law.

2 *War of Independence (1808-1814)* Outside Spain this is referred to as the Peninsular War. It was in fact the Iberian phase of the Napoleonic wars. Many harsh images of the violence of this period are depicted in the works of Goya.

Echevarri, Pedro de Agustín A famous combatant against the French in La Mancha, 1808-1811. Minister of Public Safety under Fernando VII, in 1814.

El Empecinado (Juan Martín Díaz, 1775-1825) A liberal military leader. An able strategist in guerrilla warfare. "El Empecinado" means "the tenacious one."

3 *Assembly of Cádiz (1812)* Refers to the historic parliamentary assembly held in Cádiz to develop the constitution, which set forth a distribution of power, established freedoms and established the administration of justice, severely limiting the King's absolute power.

Chapter V

COLETILLA'S COMPANION

In December of 1808 Elías served, as we mentioned, in a group which El Empecinado had organized in Segovia. They had several encounters with the French until Soult[1], in pursuit of Moore, met the guerrillas and made them retreat toward Valladolid. From Valladolid they kept advancing toward the north and reached Astorga. Elías remained in Sahgún with a few men, prepared to organize a large group there which would harass Ney[2] in his exit from Galicia.

There was a Segovian Colonel who, having married in Sahgún, lived there in retirement from military service. He was a man of high character, good heart, and a very well-cultivated intelligence. He had been rich, but Heaven or perhaps Hell had furnished him a wife, who even made-to-order could not have turned out so unmanageable, unsociable, and capricious. The poor soldier did everything imaginable to control the character of that frenzied woman, in whom nature seemed to have united all the bad qualities it generally employs in the creation of women. She began by becoming excessively devout, and her sanctimoniousness was such that she abandoned her husband and household in order to spend the entire holy day among nuns, solemn priests, confraternity brothers, and penitents, without occupying herself with anything but rosaries, scapulas, litanies, hours in prayer, passages from the Sacred Scriptures, and clerical matters. She lived between confessionals, locutories, the convent cell, and the sacristy like a wooden saint with its neck twisted, looking downward with a sour expression and the voice of a brooding hen.

During the few moments she spent at home she was unbearable. In everything her poor husband said she found sinful thoughts. All of his actions were worldly. She burned his books; used his money for pious works; filled his house with missionary fathers, clerics from the order of San Cayetano, and Premonstratensians, and whenever she spoke of conscience and sin, she began to mention names from the neighborhood, bringing up at a priestly gathering the lives and deeds of everyone, portraying the lives of the neighbors as scandalous and corruptive of good behavior. While touching on this matter, she suffered fits of righteous anger, and then became impossible to deal with.

But suddenly the intolerable and over-pious churchgoer changed to the other extreme. At the depth of her character was an excessive volubility. Changing suddenly, she adopted a very worldly way of life. She left home and roamed around kicking up her heels under the pretext that she suffered a strong emotional disturbance and needed distraction. She was accompanied by either a young soldier or a rascally abbot. Her husband, seeing that it was impossible to keep her at home, had to consent to her flighty life. Even though it cost him a great deal of his fortune, at least it freed him for some time from the insolence of that demon.

The third change in *Doña* Clara was worse. She began to believe that she was ill. There was no indisposition, ailment, chronic disturbance, or acute attack that did not come to afflict her body. She activated all the apothecaries, healers, doctors, and professors of medicine and visited all the mineral baths of Spain from Ledesma to Paracuellos, from Lanjarón to Fitero. The only thing which seemed to relieve her was for her to recite a detailed account of her ills to all the Theatins, Franciscans, clergy of the order of San Francisco de Paula, and Premonstratensians with whom she had resumed mystical relations.

Chacón, her poor husband, pleaded to heaven and even resorted to the efficient remedy of a spanking, which produced no other effect than to cause the ferocious insolence of that enemy to flare up again.

At the same time, the couple's savings were almost gone; the unfortunate husband trembled to think what would be the future of his poor daughter, who was then five years of age. The sick devout woman had, before becoming ill and devout, borne a daughter whose name, like hers, was Clara, and who was the sole fruit of that ill-fated marriage.

Doña Clara was cured when she felt it convenient. Once again she devoted herself to church matters, taking them so much to heart that there was scarcely a day in which she did not mortify herself with severe discipline that could be heard in the street. She kneeled with her arms extended in the form of a cross for a full hour. When she began to relate the ecstasies which came to her and the visions she had, they turned out to be the story of Sancho's goats. Her husband prayed to God to be set free from that living hell. *Doña* Clara loved neither her daughter nor her husband, and he, who had once loved her a great deal, ended up despising her.

Finally, *La Chacona*, as she was called in the town, once more left her devout existence and from one morning to the next she set off for Portugal for a breather. Happily, God enlightened her, and from Portugal she went to Brazil with some missionaries. Nothing more was heard from her. Her scrupulous and loyal husband breathed once more. He was free but poor, completely poor, with nothing but a small income. He was not concerned about the present but always worried when he thought about that unfortunate child who was going to remain in poverty.

In mid-December of 1808, the whole town of Sahagún, full of curiosity, went out to the principal road. Emperor Napoleon I passed through en route to Astorga in pursuit of the English. He arrived in the town, rested two hours, and continued on his course, followed by much of the army which occupied Spain. When the French, led by Napoleon, were far off, Sahagún rioted. All the young men took up arms, and, commanded by Elías and the Priest of Carrión, they were determined to fight the French regiments which on the following day were to pass through in order to join the main body of the army.

That afternoon Chacón embraced and tenderly kissed his daughter, who upon seeing her father's tears, began to cry without knowing why. The Colonel had a plan, the only one that gave him some hope of providing for Clara's future well-being. He had resolved to enter the campaign, to advance in his profession, and to follow the nation in that crisis, certain that he would be repaid for his services. He wrote to El Empecinado asking him for orders, and El Empecinado answered him, telling him to lead five hundred men from Sahagún and that he should strive to beat down the French regiments that were going to Napoleon in Astorga. The brave soldier, acclaimed chief of the group organized by Elías and the Priest of Carrión, left that evening, leaving his daughter in the care of two elderly servants. They situated themselves about one and a half kilometers away. With the dawn of the next day, the French bayonets were seen shining in the distance. The guerrilla fighters harassed them with scattered shots. At first the French delayed as a result of the surprise. But, recuperating a bit, they returned the Spaniards' attack. The battle was a bloody one. Elías and Chacón looked at each other in anguish.

"They are three times our size!" said Chacón, "but, no matter. Onward!"

They retreated to the entrance of the town. The fight there was horrifying. From windows and corners the peasants fired against the enemy whose ranks were decimated. The Colonel directed his men with unprecedented daring. Finally, the rest of the people joined the group. With one more effort, the

French were defeated. This effort was made and took many lives; but the French, not wanting to lose more men, undertook their withdrawal toward Valencia *de Don Juan.*

The whole town followed them with Chacón at the head; but he had not taken more than twenty steps when he was wounded by a shell. He cried out and fell, bathed in his own blood. The women gathered around him wailing on seeing him wounded. He uttered some words; his men returned to his side, and four of them carried him to his home. Before they arrived, he was dead.

Consternation reigned in the town because so many sons and husbands had perished. Mothers and wives cried out in bitter and painful laments. In front of the entrance to Chacón's house, a group of silent women contemplated the Colonel's bloodstained body, his forehead split open and his chest shattered. Some children, whose curiosity was greater than their fear, had approached the body daring to touch his fingers, spurs, and belt. Poor little Clara, terrified to see that everyone was watching her cry, began to call out for her father, whose death she did not understand.

"Whose child is this?" Elías asked.

"It's his daughter," responded the person who was holding her in her arms.

"Doesn't she have a mother?"

"No, sir."

"And what are we going to do with her?" asked Elías, looking toward the Priest of Carrión and the rest of the other leaders of the commotion.

Everybody shrugged their shoulders and kissed Clara.

"We'll stay with her," said two women who had served the Colonel when he was rich.

"No," said Elías, "I shall take charge of her. I'll take her with me. I'll bring her up."

Those women were very poor. Little Clara had inspired in them great affection. But by keeping her at their side, they would condemn her to their own poverty for the rest of her life. They considered *Don* Elías a person of position and character. Consequently, they did not hesitate about leaving the girl with him.

Nevertheless, she remained in Sahagún until 1812, the year in which Elías the royalist abandoned his weapons and went to Madrid. Clara accompanied him. She could not separate herself from her poor friends without crying a great deal, nor was she able to get used to looking at her protector face to face, since he frightened her terribly.

Her sadness was great as she awoke one beautiful May morning to find herself between the dark walls of the house we know on Válgame Dios Street. This sadness increased when she was taken to the convent school run by certain sisters of a famous order who taught the girls of the area what little they themselves knew. The school had all the gloominess of the convent without its melancholy cloister and sweet peace. Some elderly nuns directed it. Among them a certain Mother Angustias stood out for her contemptuousness, ugliness, and decrepitude. She used a very large cane to punish the girls and wore green spectacles which were used, not to observe the students better, but rather so that the poor little creatures would not know when she was looking at them. The girls got up very early and prayed. For lunch they were served garlic soup in which an occasional leftover chickpea floated. Afterward, they went to study, which was a reading exercise in which Mother Angustias's cane fulfilled a principal role. Then, for a period of two hours, they scribbled some badly-executed exercises on lined paper. Later on they had to answer questions by heart from a catechism. They sewed for three long hours until play-time arrived. Recreation took place in a dark, malodorous patio whose only vegetation consisted of a poor, anemic, yellowed carnation growing in a cast-off stewpot used as a planter. The girls played for a while in that pigsty until Mother Angustias rang from her room a sinister bell which called the sad angels of that dung heap to assemble around her cane.

After eating, Mother Brigida directed the rosary since Mother Angustias was unable to, due to asthma which cut off her voice from time to time. That rosary was interminable because after her infinite "Our Fathers," came the litanies, wounds, mysteries, brief prayers, orations, mystical couplets in praise of the Virgin, and quatrains. During that devout exercise, the evening came upon them without their realizing it. Often one of the young girls, fatigued by the moral weight of such monotonous and tiresome prayer, would yawn three times, and finally fall blessedly asleep. Protected behind her spectacles Mother Angustias observed the yawns and caressed her dictatorial cane without uttering a word to the guilty, waiting until she fell asleep, and then; the wrath of God! the cane struck, followed by a string of irascible insinuations. The other girls, who waited for any motive for distraction and enjoyment, seeing the pathetic figure their companion presented awakening abruptly, would burst into laughter, interrupting the prayer. Mother Brigida groaned; Mother Angustias cackled, and blows of the cane fell left and right.

At nightfall the lessons and the catechism continued. Mother Angustias would say to them:

"Now the ca...ca...techism, Mother Bri...Bri...Brigida, and the girl who does not know it to the atti...atti...attic."

And she went off to bed because she was suffering from difficult breathing spells and had to put cloths on her stomach every evening.

Clarita and the other girls of the school firmly believed that Mother Angustias did not have eyes and that her optical faculties resided entirely in those two fearful green glasses mounted on an old and rusty frame. In order to imitate her they cut out two round pieces of green paper from the cover of the catechism, pasted them on their eyes with saliva and almost died laughing. As they couldn't see a single thing with those patches on, Mother Petronila, who was a sour woman, surprised them one day at play. After giving them many slaps on the head, she prohibited them from eating or playing the rest of the day. What terrible hours the poor girls spent!

Another time they were in the school yard. It occurred to an emaciated tiny bird to enter the yard, passing by the roof and crashing against the walls, to alight on the sad carnation. What an uproar broke out! That was the biggest event of the year. With handkerchiefs, blankets, anything at hand, they pursued it until they caught it. They tied a string on one of its feet, and Clara hid him very well in a small box where she kept her needlework. Secretly, they fed the bird every night, but the little run-down creature became sadder and sadder. One evening, at the time when the prayer was to begin, Clara had the box open, and pretending to arrange something inside of it, she occupied herself with opening the little bird's mouth and forcing down some bread crumbs which she kept in her pocket. All of a sudden the bird set off in flight. It fluttered about the room with the string attached to its foot and came down, will you believe it, on the very head of Mother Angustias, who, on seeing herself disgraced in such a way, was so angry that her asthma suffocated her voice, and for ten minutes she gesticulated in silence, red as a tomato. Clara remained rigid with fear.

"Cla...Cla...Cla...rita!" exclaimed Mother Angustias, blind with rage. "You spoiled little brat. What irr...irr ...irreverence is this? This evening in the at...at...attic."

Clara was condemned to sleep that night in the attic, the ultimate penalty applied every once in a while for the more wicked and unusual infractions. Mother Angustias continued her cackling until she saw her terrible order carried out. At the hour at which they were accustomed to go to bed, Clara was taken to the prison, which was a dark, foul, and frightful garret. The poor child was terrified on finding herself alone in the darkness among a thousand formless objects, huddled on a single coarse, miserable blanket and chilled by a draft which entered through a small window. She spent a sleepless night listening to the scurrying footsteps of mice which resounded in her ears as if they were the feet of an army of giants. She curled up, wrapped herself with the whole blanket, and hid her feet, hands, and head. But, they ran over her, jumped, and came and went with a frightful squeaking. Also contributing to the child's fear was a quarrel between two cats on a neighboring rooftop, which launched lugubrious and inharmonious meows. The poor girl could not sleep. Daybreak found her curled up, soaked in a cold sweat, and shaking with fear.

Clara spend four years divided between these extraordinary events and the daily tasks of study and sewing, always terrified by the terrible fascination of Mother Angustias's spectacles. When she reached eleven years of age, Elías came for her and took her to his house.

The royalist at first did not know what to do with the girl. It occurred to him to make her a nun, but impelled by a sudden egotism, he resolved to keep her at his side. He was alone; his house needed a woman. What person would be better than Clara for this purpose? Her intelligence was not well cultivated, she only knew how to read, write, and do some elementary arithmetic. On the other hand, she sewed very well and could do all kinds of needlework.

Chacona's daughter grew up in *Coletilla's* home and became a woman....She grew up without the games, affable companions, joys, and beneficial recreation which happily lead from childhood to youth. Elías did not mistreat her, but neither was he affectionate. On Sundays he used to take her to a park, either to *La Florida* or *La Virgen del Puerto*. Once he took her to the theatre, and Clara thought that what she saw dramatized was all real. The Sunday strolls stopped when Elías had business matters and preoccupations which kept him away from home. Then, she limited herself to hearing Mass very early in the morning with the Gongoran nuns. In this expedition to hear Mass, she was accompanied by a servant from Alcarria named Pascuala, whom *Coletilla* had taken into his service.

This eternal confinement would perhaps have soured or perverted another personality less sweet and virtuous than Clara's. Clara came to believe the her way of life was very natural and that she should not aspire to anything different. So in this way she lived at peace, sadly happy, and at times lighthearted. Nevertheless, entire weeks passed by without a single stranger entering the fanatic's house. It seemed that all of society wanted to avoid the cage which enclosed their greatest enemy.

There was only one exception to that customary isolation. We have already said that *Don* Elías was a friend and servant of an old and illustrious house. After the ruin of the Porreños y Venegas family only three individuals remained, three venerable matrons who maintained friendly relations with the royalist. Every once in a while they used to visit him in the afternoon. They were very unsociable, intolerant, rigid, and proud. They never spoke to Clara except with grave words which saddened and depressed her. They were incapable of dispensing with the forms of etiquette, even in front of a poor young girl, and they were so ceremonious and stiff that Clara began to take a disliking to them. Whenever they came to the house, they left a shadow of sadness which remained a long time in the soul of the orphan.

In the last few years *Coletilla* had been entering, as we have said, the most intense period of his political frenzy. Anger was his normal state, and in his fantastic obsession it was impossible for that irascible soul to provide the charity and kindness that the poor child needed so much. On the contrary, he was very hard on her. He went for weeks without speaking to her. On other occasions, he reprimanded her harshly and without cause. He called her frivolous and scatterbrained. One day, upon seeing that the unhappy youngster had set her hair with less simplicity than usual and had dressed up, changing her natural elegance a little in accordance with the powerful instinct of fashion, which even the most withdrawn woman possesses, he scolded her, repeating many times the phrase which made her cry:

"Clara, you're going to the devil."

On other occasions, the old man took to keeping an eye on her and prohibited her from looking out from the balcony and opening the door. That is to say, he either abandoned her or made her suffer, depending on the state of his perturbed and cruel spirit.

Clara became ill. Little by little she was fading away like the carnation which grew with such difficulty in the school yard. Her sadness grew; she became pale and emaciated. Grave danger for her health was feared. *Coletilla* could not remain indifferent to the illness of his charge and called for a doctor who expressed his judgment very briefly saying, "If you don't send this child to the country, she'll die within a month."

The royalist thought that the girl's death would be a setback. He remembered that his sister lived in Ateca with her family and worked out a plan.

He wrote two letters, and some days later Clara entered the town with her heart overflowing with joy.

A beneficial reaction took place in her health and spirit, so long humbled by boredom and confinement. She recovered her spirits with the full enjoyment of nature and contact with happy people who paid attention to her and loved her. Those days were like a second life for the unfortunate martyr because she was materially restored to her normal self, acquiring strength, freshness, and vigor. Her eyes, accustomed to the darkness of four walls, now traversed a wide horizon. Her steps took her long distances; her voice was heard by jovial and frank friends, simple youths, and affectionate oldsters. Her happiness was understood and shared by others. Her innocent desires were satisfied. She knew friendship, family life, and confidence, and enjoyed a beautiful sky, pure air, simple and tranquil well-being, days of happiness, variety, and quiet and peaceful evenings.

But during Clara's stay in Ateca, certain things occurred which strongly influenced the rest of her life. We are going to refer to them because most of this story derives from them; because they are so important and serious, we shall leave them for the following chapter where the reader will observe them if he is resolved not to leave us.

NOTES

[1] *Soult, Nicolas-Jen de Dieu (1769-1851)* A French general sent by Napoleon to Spain. After five years of fighting (1808-1812) he was eventually defeated by the Duke of Wellington's forces.

[2] *Ney, Michel (1769-1815)* A marshall in Napoleon's army. A lifelong soldier who distinguished himself in battle and fought in Spain. Once a supporter of the Bourbons he later opposed their return as rulers of France and was subsequently executed after their restoration.

Chapter VI

COLETILLA'S NEPHEW

Marta, Elías' sister, had been left a widow with a son named Lázaro, who after studying Humanities in Tudela transferred to the University of Zaragoza. He was between twenty-three and twenty-five years of age, of a pleasant appearance, precocious intelligence, lively imagination, and was eloquent, very impressionable, vehement, and had an honest and noble heart.

New ideas, which were then profoundly stirring the hearts of young people, had found in young Lázaro a passionate believer. He was one of those young men who sprang from the confusion of a philosophy classroom and fought with zealous passion in the ranks of the political propagators who were then so important.

It happened that some students from Zaragoza initiated a dispute with the members of a certain political club. The dispute grew; the University authorities intervened and Lázaro was forced to leave Zaragoza, losing credits. This took place when Riego was removed from his command as Commander-in-Chief of Aragón. During those days there were riots and public demonstrations which the Government wanted to contain. Lázaro, who was near finishing his studies, knew the seriousness of the situation and the displeasure which his mother and grandfather, whom he loved a great deal, would feel. He wanted to protest, but it was useless, and he had to return to his home town, sad, ashamed, and full of doubts and fears.

But, on entering his house, beset by anxiety and remorse, he saw with his mother a stranger, who, from the first moment, produced in him a secret feeling of happiness, giving him consolation and hope, without his knowing why. Lázaro confessed what had happened to him without minimizing the seriousness of the matter. *Don* Fermín, his paternal grandfather, was concerned, and even angry, at first. His mother cried a bit.

The unknown person, who seemed to be there to gladden the house, diminished *Don* Fermín's anger and dried his mother's tears. Lázaro, with bowed head and damp eyes, stood before his judges and his defender without uttering a word. In all truthfulness, it was not necessary to say a word because the young girl defended him well without displaying great eloquence, without employing any other means than her clear and natural common sense and her transparent and generous sentiment.

Poor Lázaro was so upset that the stranger seemed to him to be an apparition, a being sent from heaven to defend him in that delicate moment. He waited for her to disappear upon completing her mission and looked at her with that silent amazement one feels in the presence of the supernatural and unknown. He knew nothing about the young girl, nor had he suspected that she ever existed. But, the image did not vanish. On the contrary, he continued to imagine her as though adorned with all the physical and moral charms which only the angels of this world possess.

Nothing more was said about the matter. Lázaro was forgiven, but he still felt bewilderment. They explained to him who Clara was, and why she was there; but in spite of the explanation, the student could not overcome the respectful and profound surprise that she had produced in him.

He felt shy and inhibited all day long, and his voice quivered when he spoke to her. Finally, he had to keep quiet for fear of coming out with a thousand foolish remarks. The following day he awakened with an enthusiastic joy which was suddenly followed by an unparalleled sadness. His confusion took on very diverse phases. Suddenly, he would be attacked by an insatiable desire for conversation which he was unable to control. Then again just as suddenly he would try to speak a word, but could not. He was a fervent politician, and in Zaragoza he had distinguished himself in the clubs by his eloquent harangues, which had made him famous. In his private conversations he also expressed himself with a great deal of enthusiasm and correctness. Now, however, he spoke about anything but politics. It seemed that for him neither the French Revolution, Rousseau's *Emile*, Talleyrand's *Letters*, or Voltaire's *Dictionary* still existed. He had forgotten about all that, and only thought about the most expressive and exact way of telling Clara that he had seen her in his dreams that night. He resorted to a system of circumlocution. Later he thought of expressing it clearly and to the point, but he recalled that allegories had been invented for just such occasions. He tried every means without achieving his objective.

Two or three days passed without his finding a way of getting to the point. When he was alone, yes. Then, he spoke to himself and even seemed to begin mysterious dialogues with that beautiful spirit which he found everywhere, accompanying him in his solitude and sleeplessness; a spirit full of light with the contours of a woman, who came out from the very womb of the night, motionless, silent, and serene to look at him. Before this spirit, Lázaro was very eloquent. He always succeeded in expressing what he felt. The poor fellow felt so much emotion that at times he had moments in which his entire body was affected, broken and oppressed by the great expansion of his spirit. He left the house because he didn't feel comfortable inside, but he went back again because he didn't feel right outside, either. Finally, he had managed to initiate a conversation with Clara. The first time he was able to speak to her for a full fifteen minutes he felt very angry. Angry? Why? After that he began to thank her. Thanks? For what? Then he begged her pardon. Pardon? For what? And after that he told her that he was going mad. Mad? His gait was erratic. He headed in many directions, but never arrived. He always found himself where he did not mean to be. However, in spite of these blind movements, if Clara happened to head somewhere, what a coincidence! She always seemed to run into Lázaro there waiting for her!

Clara's spirit was not subject to these strange disturbances. Always sensitive and happy in her innocent serenity, she let herself be carried along by the current of a life devoid of apprehension or disappointment. In her own place, in order to give peace to her spirit and rest to her fantasy, we might say, she lived without thinking about her life. If any thought made her sad, it was the idea of returning to Válgame Dios Street. It was friendship, almost unknown to her, that gave her the subtle delicacy which characterizes feminine emotion and the abundance of creativeness which embellishes and adorns it so much.

There was another girl of the same age and character in the town named Ana, daughter of a rich farmer. Clara and Ana became good friends after only a few days. Every afternoon they used to go to an orchard owned by Ana's father. There, entertained by their labors, they spent long hours conversing. During this communication between the two youngsters, Clara matured emotionally with unparalleled rapidity. For she had spent her youth in the company of an unsociable and eccentric old man. The innocent frankness and simultaneous exchange of ideas, in all of its beautiful, natural simplicity, achieved in the orphan's soul a discovery of herself which settled and enhanced her beautiful character even more.

As the two friends were going to the orchard, coincidence had it that Lázaro would pass by the gate at exactly the same moment the girls arrived. The conversations would start at four in the afternoon and lasted until nightfall. Not a single day during all the time Clara spent in Ateca did the girls fail to go to the orchard, and not a single day did Lázaro fail to meet them by coincidence. In those conversations, which grew more and more intimate, one sometimes noticed that, following her part in the staged dialogue, Ana fell silent or muttered asides in a stage whisper, while the good student and mischievous Clara talked very quietly and very close to one another. His face, distressed at times, at times pale, sometimes lively, and at other times sad, revealed that the subject of the discussion was interesting. What were they saying? Some long intervals in which one and the other remained looking at the ground permitted Ana to make some clever observations, the humor of which she appreciated and laughed at by herself. Clara and Lázaro seemed not to be in a laughing mood. They remained silent until a single syllable here and a gesture there stimulated the conversation once more. On occasion he began to meditate as if pondering what he was going to say. Lázaro had a good memory, but found himself in a situation in which he had forgotten all the admirable fragments of eloquence that he had prepared. What a coincidence! Were they speaking about the past, the present, the future? Were they outlining a plan, or carrying out a project? It is probable that none of this was the object of those intimate exchanges. Their voices only expressed a thousand anxieties from within; depicted certain disturbances of the spirit; formulated intensely passionate questions whose replies increased their vehemence; confessed secrets whose profundity increased as they were spoken; made vows, manifested doubts whose resolutions gave rise to another thousand doubts; asked explanations of mysteries, which engender endless mysteries; explained the inexplicable, measured the infinite, exhausted the inexhaustible.

At times Ana interrupted these impenetrable conversations, saying, "But, woman, don't you notice how your embroidery is coming along? What are you thinking about?"

Actually, Clara, who was embroidering a little head of an angel surrounded by a wreath of flowers on a canvas with colored wool, had made the eyes of red yarn and the lips black. All the colors of the flowers were so mixed up that one could not decide what they were. On hearing her friend's observation, Clara turned the same color as the angel's eyes.

Twenty to thirty days pass by very quickly when there are daily meetings in an orchard, eager chats, unresolved doubts, questions poorly answered, and little angels embroidered with red eyes. So that a day arrived on which Lázaro swore by all the saints in heaven that he would not let Clara leave. He became a nuisance when it came to this point; he repeated the same thing over and over again; or, it occurred to him to relate a dream he had the night before from which he came to the conclusion of the absolute impossibility that he and Clara could ever be separated. She became very pensive and said nothing for half an hour. Now and then the poor youngsters looked at the sky, as if the solution to their problem were written there.

They separated. Clara confided her sorrows on the bosom of her friend Ana. Lázaro confided to the depths of the night the great vertigo that he felt from within. He could not sleep, because an interminable and fast-moving series of confused reasonings mingling with vaguely perceived images kept him in an unconquerable and painful vigil. The morning light returned to give them hope. The afternoon brought them together, and the evening returned to sadden them. So the fateful day approached.

When one so fears the arrival of a day which is to bring some misfortune, the imagination has an extraordinary strength of hatred with which it personifies the detested day. The imagination sees this day approaching and sees it in the form of some kind of menacing monster, which approaches with raised hand and baleful glance. There are days when the sun should never rise.

But on the day designated for Clara's return to Madrid, the sun came out. How cruel! Its first rays carried sadness to the spirit of the two young people menaced by separation.

It seems that when a separation of that kind takes place, when a mysterious and fundamental unit, a unit constituted by the complementary totality of two individuals, is dissolved and destroyed, a catastrophe of nature should occur. But what we commonly call the elements are blind and insensitive. A continent is sunk and two oceans collide for the most insignificant mechanical causes which originate in the center of the earth's matter. But nothing happens, nothing moves in the inert and blind machine of the world when the grand, the immense equilibrium of the heart is altered.

That morning Lázaro felt an unknown grief. The day moved on; the student went to Ana's house and found her crying. He became frightened on seeing her cry. He returned to his home and wanted to enter the room where Clara was making preparations for her trip, but he was afraid of himself. He saw her come out later, pale and with her eyes tired from crying. Seeing that she was taking leave of his mother and grandfather, Lázaro ran outside for fear that she would also say good-bye to him.

He went out and walked hurriedly for a long time. He left the town and traveled quite a distance, far, far from the town. Suddenly, he heard the coach approaching. The youth stopped and went back; the coach passed rapidly. There rode the desolate orphan with her face hidden between her hands. The other passengers were laughing at her. Lázaro called out her name loudly. Without realizing it, he ran after the coach for a long stretch until fatigue obliged him to stop. The coach disappeared.

Night approached as he returned to the town. On passing the orchard, he noted that the birds, which usually slept there, were making a diabolical uproar with their wild songs and restless flutter. He quickened his pace so as not to hear them, and entered his house. His mother and grandfather were very pensive and melancholy. He did not speak to them; neither did they speak to him. He kept to himself. He went to his room and tried to read a book. He tried to sleep and to tear from his mind what seemed to be a burning iron crown which tormented and weighed heavily on him, but it was impossible. It was a radiation which, had it been visible, would have resembled a halo. In his fever he remained lethargic and in that lethargy he felt that his head was giving off lively flames which he couldn't stand and that his brains were boiling like molten metal.

Chapter VII

THE INNER VOICE

That young fellow was extremely impressionable, nervous, and of an idealistic disposition, inclined to always live in an imaginary world. No one equaled him in fabricating future events, connecting and using them in order to convert them into a very dramatic and interesting life. His mind worked involuntarily in the elaboration of these future events. He always had before him that great prospective event in which the principal role was undertaken by one figure alone, himself, Lázaro. This perpetual vision, a phenomenon characteristic of youth, took on tremendous proportions in him. His imagination possessed a powerful, creative force, and one can be sure that this great faculty was for him an implacable enemy, a tormenting demon.

With this personality, it was easy for all the great expansive passions to come out in him and for them to grow, ultimately carrying him to extremes. In those days, politics, proselytism, and the spirit of affiliation engendered in him great passions: civic heroism, self-abnegation, and that Catonian tenacity which manifests itself in some protagonists of any revolution. Underhanded venality, treachery, sanguinary cruelty, and vengeful rancor, which are seen in others, arise from political passion. Lázaro possessed this passion: he felt within himself the zeal of patriotism. He believed himself called to be an apostle of the new ideas, and he embraced them with ardent faith and noble sentiment.

But, do these unbreakable resolutions exist without a mixture of selfishness? Sublime egoism, but egoism nonetheless. Lázaro was ambitious. But what kind of ambition? An ambition directed only toward the moral exaltation of an individual, who aspires to a very simple prize, which is mere gratitude. However, the gratitude of Humanity or of a people is the most valued thing on Earth. He who is worthy of it will have it because a single man may be ungrateful, but a people, in the course of History, can never be. In a lifetime there is room for error, but in a hundred generations of a people, with each person correcting the others, there is no room for error. He who has deserved gratitude inevitably receives it, even though it may be too late.

Lázaro aspired to glory. He wanted to satisfy a certain vanity; each man has his vanity. That of the young Aragonese consisted of fulfilling a great mission, in achieving some gigantic undertaking. What he did not know with certainty was the nature of this mission. Young men like Lázaro do not like to specify things because they fear reality. They believe too much in predestination. Deceived by the splendor of the dream, they think that events should come to look for them instead of their looking for events.

After he left Zaragoza and went to Ateca, one figure perpetually accompanied him in those future scenes. What a fool! What do you intend to make of her? A queen. A queen from where? She will simply be the wife of a great man. Less than that, perhaps: the wife of an unknown man....He concluded by reducing the object of all his illusions to a peaceful retirement, to a happy marriage.

It was necessary to meditate and draw up a plan, to determine the simplest way of reuniting himself with her.

Clara was an orphan, and he was poor. Two strikes against him which had existed from the beginning. Ah! But he would work; he would be active, ingenious and astute. He knew he had talent. But should he be just a farmer? No! That wasn't for him. He must go to Madrid, make himself heard and make a name, and a good position, for himself. This would be a very easy thing for one who had so many talents. Was it not a certainty that Lázaro, upon arriving in Madrid, then as now the center of intellectual activity of the country, would acquire name, position, and fortune? Undoubtedly. They must already know of him by reference because of the speeches he delivered in Zaragoza. In that era the young folk easily made their way among the decrepit multitude. They, the youth, with all their energy of faith and the strength of their early years, undertook the propagation of the new ideas. They inevitably commanded respect, acquiring a high and envied social position. He believed himself superior. Why deny it? From the bottom of his conscience he heard a continuous voice which said, "I have merits. One must look for the events before the events come to look for him. Cheer up, then!"

These thoughts occupied Lázaro's mind during the days which followed Clara's departure. When his decision became clear, he noticed with enthusiasm that his intelligence acquired more vigor and his heart more daring. He felt himself capable of articulating the most profound, the most heated, and the most truthful ideas in defense of the noble principles of the ear. It seemed to him that nothing equaled his facility of expression, imposing logic, and picturesque and expressive witticism. In the deepest quiet of the evening, when in solitary places he would devote himself to his meditations, he listened to himself.

An eloquent voice resounded from within him. Mute and absorbed in thought, he heeded the marvelous inner manifestations of his own genius. He was his own audience, and it seemed to him that the spoken phrase had never achieved more beauty, surer logic, and more vigorous intonation. He applauded himself. He had the feeling that around him an infinite multitude of agglomerated shadows were also applauding. An intense clapping echoed, whose clamor filled the entire earth.

When he returned home he slept, and during his slumber the same voice, which moved thousands of hearts, continued to resonate in his brain. It was the voice which carried enthusiasm or fear to entire citizen armies. He concluded that from within there was a mysterious, sonorous entity, a loquacious spirit which constantly sustained a brilliant and energetic peroration in the depths of his soul.

Lázaro possessed the genius of eloquence. He knew it. He was sure of it. As each day passed by without a large audience, it appeared to him that those admirable words which he felt from within were lost in the vacuum and quiet of a desert. There was no time to lose.

He told his grandfather that he was going to Madrid. The poor old man began to cry and said between sobs and slobber that such resolution was very serious and should be thought over carefully.

"And what are you going to do there?" he added, wanting to sound worried. "You have such poor penmanship...!"

A certain *Don* Gil Carrascosa was then in Ateca. This is the same character whom we saw arguing with a certain barber in the first chapter of this story, and who also sustained a friendship with *Coletilla*. Lázaro's grandfather consulted the ex-abbot about Lázaro's decision. The ex-abbot was of the opinion that a letter should be written to his uncle. The old man took his pen in hand and without hesitation drew up this letter, which the royalist received a few days later.

Dear and respected Sir:

Young Lázaro, my grandson and your nephew, wants to go to Madrid. He has it in his head that he will be able to make a fortune there. He says he cannot remain in this town. In effect, dear Sir, this is bad. This year's crop does not even give us seed, and the poor boy has greater fondness for books than for the plow. I want to tell you, your grace, respected Sir, that Lázaro is a very bright young man. He knows many books by heart and has read four times from cover to cover a volume entitled *The Great Men of Plutarch*. He has assured me it is not a work of heresy, and if it were, it would not have been read in my time. He understands law, and at times he writes and fills a few notebooks with very good things, although I do not understand them. He is a good Christian, very respectful, and courteous with everyone. I shall not conceal his defects, respectable Sir, and by the same token that I love him, I shall tell your grace what his major defect is, so that perhaps you can reform him with your talent and great wisdom. The truth is that it will be difficult for him to fulfill his obligations in the court in Madrid, because he has very bad penmanship, and he does not show what he knows. I am very sorry to have to reveal this weakness of his. But my conscience must come first, and I would not hide his shortcomings for all the gold in the world. I believe, nevertheless, that with good teachers as there are in Madrid, he will be able to correct this defect if he applies himself. In this way, as time goes on, he will become fit for undertaking a post paying 2,000 *reales* in some secretariat, as did my respected grandfather, may he rest in peace. I want him to earn a living because I love him with all my heart. So I wish that your grace, with your great tact and universal wisdom, would inform me if it will be possible to bring out something of merit from the young man, telling me at the same time if I can count on your patronage. Do it, your grace, for God's sake, as he is your sister's only son and we, who are poor, cannot make him happy.

Your respectful and reverent servant,

Fermín

Three months passed without an answer from *Don* Elías. Finally, he replied, advising that Lázaro wait a little longer and saying that he would let him know if he could join him or not. A month later he wrote again, calling Lázaro to his side, and adding that his success would depend on his comportment and attitudes.

Lázaro was beside himself with joy. He wanted to leave that very same day, but the pleadings of his mother and grandfather obliged him to stay two more days.

The young fellow knew through family tradition that his uncle was very wise, and he had imagined that he must be a great liberal. Lázaro could not understand that a very wise man could fail to be a lover of Liberty.

Coletilla's letter arrived during the first days of September, 1821, while the first events which we have referred to were occurring. A little after the lamentable scene in the barbershop and the entrance of the soldier into Clara's house, Lázaro's trip to Madrid took place. Clara did not know beforehand which day Lázaro was to arrive.

We can now logically continue the course of events of this precise story. We shall leave Lázaro getting ready to travel. His mother and grandfather say good-bye to him in tears, and the mayor embraces him, saying that he foresees him occupying nothing less than a very high-ranking government post. The priest gives him two sweet rolls for the road, along with a tedious sermon. The student enters the coach and with more illusions than money takes the road to Madrid.

Chapter VIII

TODAY HE ARRIVES

Three days after the adventure described in the second chapter, very early in the morning, Clara was closeted in the room which served as her bedroom. The fanatic had told her a few hours before that he was expecting his nephew and that he was going to put him up there until they all moved to a new house which he planned to occupy.

Clara was entranced on hearing this news and could not utter a word because the surprise left her speechless. When she was alone, she closed herself in her room.

This was a small and unsymmetrical room; it was in the most innermost part of the house and had narrow windows of doubtful transparency which faced the patio. Due to its depth and narrowness, the patio appeared to be a virtual well. Opposite, and to the sides, three lines of small windows were open-air vents for so many other cells where noisy families were lodged. Clara's room had the benefit of a ray of light from 11 to 11:30, the hour at which it moved on to illuminate the tropical regions of the third floor. That ray of light never brought with it colors, landscape, horizon, or happiness.

The patio was a crowded area, the center of a human anthill. At certain hours many heads peered through those holes. This occurred during such great events as when the blacksmith from downstairs and the ironer from the fourth floor were resolving some matter of honor in the open air, or, when a vulgar woman on the third floor and a mender in front struck up an argument about the right to hang clothes.

Apart from all this, an Octavian peace always reigned; and, it was remarkable to see the amiable frankness with which the mat repairer asked to borrow a frying pan from the neighbor on the left and the intimate confidence with which the soldier on the fifth floor and the shoemaker were conversing. Some windows were joined to others by cords, like telegraph circuits. There were several clothes lines from which some ragged shirts hung. Every now and then one saw a slice of beef hung in the silence of the evening, or a fishing rod with bait controlled by the capable hands of a student from the garret.

The glass window of Clara's room was never opened. Elías had nailed it shut from the inside ever since he occupied the house.

If the view of the patio was unpleasant, the interior of the room had without doubt a certain charm, not because there were beautiful things in it, but because of the simplicity and modesty that reigned there and the careful cleanliness and neatness, which are the only distinction of the poor. In the foreground was a massive chest of drawers composed of six enormous compartments. Above the chest there was an old decorative piece of furniture that represented a figure of Parca with one of her hands raised as if to support something. In place of the clock, which had once hung from it, it supported in Clara's time a box lined with colored paper which held utensils of feminine needlework. In place of the crystal flask, a piece of chiffon now covered all this, secured by blue strips to the legs of the goddess who showed off on her profane breast a scapulary of the *Virgen del Carmen*.

A dressing table, three heavy chairs of glossy walnut, a sewing pad bristling with needles and pins, a footstool, and a mahogany bed of very massive design, covered by a blanket from Palencia, completed the household furnishings.

Clara stood in front of her mirror and was busy pinning up her thick braids of black hair, recently intertwined and finished with a roll of hair and a red bow. Two small curls, subtle strands of long hair twisted without care, adorned her forehead, and from her white temples, whose skin showed lightly the bluish line of some vein, fell two graceful locks of hair.

There is no better way to duly appreciate the classic form of a woman than when she raises her hands and rolls up a braid around her head, allowing the bust to be seen. The figure and the neckline in all its roundness, the muscles of the breast encircling the back, the angle of the elbows, and the smooth curves of the shoulder with their gracious lines tend to give harmonious sculptural expression to the whole figure.

Having finished her hair-styling, Clara cast a glance of desire and distrust at the last drawer of the enormous bureau where she kept her clothes. The fact is that she kept there with singular care a dress which Elías had purchased for her some years before, when he was less grim and grumbly. This dress was the most luxurious and beautiful that the orphan possessed and was the style and color most in vogue in that period. It had a body of black velvet with prolific lace motifs and an underskirt of straw-colored silk. It was adorned with a large band of black lace. She debated whether or not to take it out of the drawer. She wanted to wear it, and at the same time was afraid to wear it. She wanted to show off her best dress that day, but at the same time she feared being too attractive to him. Why? She hesitated, pensive and sad, not daring to bring out for public view a treasure hidden for such a long time. Why?

Because Elías had become so grouchy. He was so obsessive and scolded her so much without reason....What peculiarity! The week before she had been sewing and mending the hem of a dress which had been torn when he entered brusquely and said to her, "What are you doing here...? Always thinking about adorning yourself. Why do you busy yourself with these trifles?"

To tell the truth, she had not dared to reply, although she had a reasonable answer to that question, and sadly folding her work, she buried it in the bureau. Elías did not soften in spite of such a display of submission. On seeing her open the drawer he remarked, in an even more bitter and severe tone, "When I say that you have gone bad..."

But this was not the worst comment that the poor little girl listened to. Full of shame, she returned the dress to its burial place. This wasn't the worst she heard, for the old man lowered his voice as if talking to himself and said, "At last I'll have to make a decision about you."

My good Lord and for heaven's sake! What decision will it be? Will the old man also want to lock her up in that very same drawer like a useless article of clothing?

That matter of the decision had her worried for many days. She tried in vain to gauge the old man's spirit. Oh! But she didn't know how to delve into anyone's feelings. The only means that would have worked to find out about this decision would have been to simply ask him, and that she did not dare to do.

This was not all that happened; there was still more. Along dismal Válgame Dios Street there usually passed a flower girl who carried in her basket some bunches of carnations, two dozen roses and many, many violets. Clara used to observe through the windowpanes the movement of those fresh colors which attracted her spirit, those gentle aromas she eagerly desired to inhale from the balcony. One day she decided to purchase some flowers, and sent Pascuala for them. Clara took hold of them, kissed them a thousand times, put them in water, caressed them, and place them against her bosom. She could not resist the temptation to look at herself in the mirror with such adornment. Putting them back in the water, she at last let them rest in a vase which she was reckless enough to place where *Coletilla* always put his cane and hat. When he would arrive from the street, my, he will surely be gladdened to see those flowers. The flowers would give him a great deal of pleasure. What a surprise he will have. This was what she was thinking. She was certainly foolish.

The fanatic arrived and went to the table. As he set his hat down, it struck the vase which fell to the ground, scattering flowers and dousing his trousers with water.

The man became enraged, and looking angrily at the trembling orphan, shouted, "What are these flowers? Who told you to buy these flowers? Clara, what foolishness is this? You flirt! There is no hope for you. You've gone bad! So you also want to fill my house with flowers?"

Clara attempted answer him, but although she did everything possible, she could not say anything. Elías stomped on the flowers in rage.

"I'm resolved to make a decision."

That decision once again. "What decision could it be?" Clara thought in the height of her confusion and fear. After retiring to her room she thought about it and asked herself, "Does he want to kill me?"

That evening she could not sleep. At about twelve she heard Elías walking around his room with more commotion than usual. She even seemed to hear some words which were more than likely not very flattering. Clara, moved by curiosity, got up very quietly and little by little she approached Elías's door with great caution and looked through the keyhole. Elías was making gestures and walking back and forth. Suddenly, he stopped and went to a drawer and pulled out a very large knife, very large and very sharp, shining and elegant. He looked at it in the light, he examined it well, and then put it away. At seeing this, Clara nearly fainted. Trembling she returned to her room and after bundling herself well, fell asleep. She had not been so afraid since the night she had spent in *Doña* Angustias's attic in the company of mice. At dawn she calmed down a bit, but in her sleep a multitude of knives like the one she had seen came before her. At times only one appeared, but it was so large that by itself it would have been enough to chop off fifty heads at a time. She bundled up more and more, believing in the fantasy of her dream that the knife, in spite of its sharp form and shining edge, could not penetrate the bed sheets.

The following day she calmed down, and even laughed at having feared that Elías would have been capable of killing her.

Nevertheless, she did not dare to put on the dress. That beautiful sinful article of clothing was destined to sleep the dream of eternity in the most remote depths of the bureau, where it would be nourishment for the worms.

Clara had not been able to determine in her mind what changes Lázaro's arrival might bring about. In her great joy she could not see it as other than a happy occasion. She did not consider the events which might result from his arrival. Only some vague ideas accompanied that expressive and unselfish happiness. He would become a young man of position. Of course! Without stopping to think of the means, Clara thought about a change of destiny. Without her knowing how, there appeared in her mind an unresolved confusion—the idea of Lázaro's arrival and the idea of freeing herself from the somewhat disturbing (she was unable to give it any other name) guardianship of *Don* Elías. The idea of marriage came to her mind. It came to her, yes, several times, but it was really not an idea but only a confused image, a faint-hearted and somewhat fearful hope. Finally, she began to think, really think about it. A confused vision, we may call it. This vision occupied her mind constantly. Lázaro was going to be her husband. Clara, who also imagined the future, saw her husband next to her in another place, in another house, in other places, and in another land. And even in another world. Why not? That would be even better.

That day she was very happy; she laughed at the slightest provocation, blushed for no reason, and felt restless, without serenity. She remained pensive for a long while, and later seemed to be talking to herself.

It was probably nine o'clock when Pascuala returned and entered Clara's room.

Pascuala was a woman who standing next to Clara formed the most violent contrast possible between two specimens of the human race. She was an energetic and mannish woman reared in the fields of Alcarria. She was high breasted and broad-hipped, with red cheeks, a large mouth, small nose, narrow forehead, her hair pulled back and pinned in a knot, rough hands, and large black eyes.

She approached the young girl and said to her mysteriously, "Do you know what happened?"

"What?" asked Clara in alarm.

"I saw the young officer from the other day, the one who was here when *Don* Elías returned in such bad shape."

"And what about it?"

"What? Just that he frightened me because he said he wanted to come in, and since we are here alone, I thought that something might happen to me....Since I'm so tall and good-looking...and my face isn't half bad...you can see that for yourself."

"Ah! That officer from the other day? And, you say that he wanted to come in?"

"Yes, but he asked about you."

"About me? And what did you tell him."

"That you were fine. Then, he asked if the old guy was here. Now, you see how little respect he shows. The old guy! What disrespect! I told him no. He told me that he wanted to come in to talk to me....But, come now...I am a suspicious person, and I got an inkling..."

"What?"

"They can't fool me with pretty words. It's because I am so darn pretty."

"Don't worry," said Clara, laughing. "It's just that he is in love with you and wants to marry you. If only the tavern owner knew..."

"My Pascual? He'll never know....If Pascual ever found out that there is a young gentleman who gives compliments to Pascuala..."

We should mention that the charwoman Pascuala had as her boyfriend a certain Pascual who had established a tavern on Humilladero Street. That honest and noble relationship seemed to be well headed along marriage. And, since she was so *darn pretty*, it was very possible that the two Pascuals would be joined together before the Church in order to give children to the world and turn water to wine.

"But, I'm a rascal....I have something on my mind....Do you know what's on my mind?"

"What?"

"That he doesn't want to visit on my account, but on the contrary, because of you."

"Because of me? Don't be a fool," answered Clara, smiling with the greatest naturalness.

"Should I let him in?"

"No, be careful. For God's sake don't do such a thing. Do not speak to him again. What reason does he have to come here?"

"Although I'm such a doll, I suspect...I suspect that he doesn't want me a darn bit...because after all, I'm a servant and he is a gentleman....Well, he seems to be an important person. So..."

"For heaven's sake, Pascuala, don't say that again!" exclaimed Clara seriously. "But why does that man want to come here?"

"Come on now, to see you."

"And why does he want to see me?"

"Come on now, to see you."

"What a strange idea," murmured Clara pensively.

At that moment she heard the bell ring. They opened the door and *Coletilla* entered.

The two girls were still chatting when they heard a clamor of excited voices in the street, some shouts and hurried footsteps. The three peered out and saw that several groups were roaming the street. The best-known riff-raff of the area left their activities and went out in search of adventure. *Coletilla* cast a glance of rancorous contempt on those transients. Closing the balcony doors with a crash, he said: "Another upheaval!"

The two girls trembled, remembering the fear they had felt a few nights before.

"Ah! When will these things come to an end." observed Clara.

"Soon!" said the old men drily, sitting down and reaching for a letter on the table.

He read it; then, picking up his cape and hat, he said to the girls, "I'm going out. I have something to attend to. I'll be out all afternoon. My nephew will arrive tonight at about eight. I shall not return until ten at the earliest. Have him wait for me here."

Wrapping himself in his cape, he looked at a dismal clock on the livingroom wall, which marked time with a very gloomy beat.

"Don't open up for anyone. Be careful, very careful with the door. Close all the latches. When my nephew comes, give him something to eat and have him wait for me."

"But, how are you going to leave with all these disturbances?" said Clara with fear. "Don't leave us alone; we are very scared!"

"Afraid for me? What can they do to me. They'll be sorry," he murmured with restrained anger. "I repeat, be careful with the door."

And then, as if speaking to himself, he added in a low tone, "Yes, I must make a decision..., a good decision."

Clara could hear it and thought of the bureau, the dress, the flowers, the knife, and the decision, that cursed decision she did not know about. But even all this, which set her to meditating and feeling melancholy for a good while, was not enough to banish the joy overflowing her heart that day.

Chapter IX

THE FIRST STEPS

The crowds grew larger. The entire town presented a strange and disorderly appearance which was not itself an uprising, but does precede one. It was September 18, 1821. Most of the inhabitants of Madrid were out in the street. An anxious "What's new?" came from every mouth. On such occasions it only takes two to stop together for others to immediately join in, thus forming a dense crowd. Then everyone we see seems to have an evil expression. The most momentous event on such days is the arrival of the person who is believed to be 'in the know' about what is going to happen. The informed one lets the crowd gather about him and plead with him for details. He begins to speak in symbolic language so as to increase their curiosity. He sets as a condition that without their profoundest discretion and their promise to keep the secret, he cannot tell what he knows. All swear to him by all that is sacred that they will keep the secret, and finally the man begins to relate the matter in an obscure manner. Urged on by the listeners, he decided to be frank and throws out three or four heaps of lies which the others hungrily swallow, immediately disbanding in order to vomit the news out again to other groups: that sort of secret is very indigestible.

On the afternoon we refer to, our friend Calleja, an 'informed' officer of The Golden Fountain, was telling the crowd formed on Saint Jerónimo something that was, in fact, true.

"But, don't you know?" he said, lowering his voice and making gestures worthy of the Spartan who alone escaped from the battle of Thermopylae and carried news to Athens of that memorable catastrophe. "Don't you know? No later than tomorrow there'll be a civic procession in honor of Riego. His portrait will be carried through all the streets of Madrid."

"Good, good," said one of the listeners. "Should we permit them to mistreat the hero of Las Cabezas, the author of Spain's freedom?"

"The serious problem is that the government has decided that there will be no procession. But, the procession will go on anyway. The Golden Fountain club has decided on it, and so it will be. The portrait is ready. It's indeed a beautiful work. He's in uniform and the book of the Constitution is in his hand. A great portrait! My cousin, the one who did the Vicentini Café sign, painted it."

"And the government prohibits the celebration?"

"Yes, they don't like these events. But there'll be a procession, or we're not Spaniards. The government forbids it."

As a matter of fact, at that moment the street corners received an official bulletin in which the proclamation appeared prohibiting the celebration planned by the clubs for the following day. The government troops were on alert.

"And this evening we have an important session at The Golden Fountain."

"Look, Perico, save me a good seat tonight," said a young fellow of the group. "Save me a place since I have to go to the Agujero hotel to receive some friends who are coming in from Zaragoza."

And then he added mysteriously, addressing himself to another two or three people who appeared to be his friends, "Gentlemen, those chaps from Zaragoza about whom I have spoken to you will arrive this evening. They belong to the republican club there. Good fellows."

The group broke up. At the same time, the sinister figure of *Tres Pesetas* crossed the street, together with the no less unpleasant figure of *Chaleco*.

Three young men left the group together. They were three youths about twenty-five years of age. We cannot call them true fashion plates, but neither can it be said that they entirely lacked distinction and elegance. They were close friends who shared hardships and joys, the hardships of their poor student days and the joys of their popularity achieved from newspaper articles and speeches in the club.

One was a young man from a distinguished family, a second son who had been sent to study canon law and sacred theology in Salamanca with the object of becoming a priest and enjoying some profitable chaplainship which had belonged to his uncle, choir-master of the Cathedral of Calahorra. He would have become a chaplain with certainty and a bishop with a little effort. In fact, Javier, as he was named, might easily have become a bishop because his family had great influence, but the lad was not fond of the priesthood and was impressed by the new ideas. So, he packed up, lacking money but not daring, and set out on the road. He showed up in Madrid the same blessed year, 1820. He roamed the streets alone, but soon he had many friends. He wrote to his dear grandmother, who granted him a half pardon and some money—very little, because the family, although the most noble of León, was in a very precarious financial situation. Afterwards, he took off for

Zaragoza where he lived for a few months, figuring prominently in the democratic clubs. Then, he returned to Madrid neither very well wined nor dined but extremely happy. He used to write frenzied articles in *El Universal*. Content with his limited glory, he went through life poor but well-respected. He captivated everyone because of the amiability of his character and the generosity of his sentiments. In politics he professed very extreme opinions and belonged to the party then called ultra-radical.

The second of these three friends whom we describe was active in the same group. He was an Andalusian, twenty-three years old, thin, small, and agile. In Ecija, his native land, he spent his time writing verses to Marica, Ramona, Paca, the fountain, the moon, and to everything. But all routines become tiresome, and plain poetry is not one of the most entertaining activities. One day he found himself so bored that he thought about leaving town. Riego's army passed through there at that time, and the troops excited his curiosity.

He inquired and they told him that they were soldiers of freedom. This resounded in his ears with a certain pleasant harmony.

"I am going with them," he told his parents.

They were very poor and replied, "Son, may God be with you and make you good and happy. Behave yourself and don't forget us."

The poet followed the army. His parents wept. It is still rumored that three of the prettiest girls in Ecija cried for him in secret. Upon arriving in Madrid, the young man returned to poetry and composed verses about the King when he opened sessions of Parliament, about Amalia, Riego, Alcalá Galiano, Quiroga, and Argüelles.[1] This poet who, as we shall see, belonged to the classical school in all its vigor, spent some straitened moments in his courtly life. Afterwards, writing in a lawyer's home and filling modest functions for the periodical *El Censor*, he lived ever happy, always a poet, always a classic, and esteemed by his friends with the reputation of being reckless, but at the same time considered intelligent and good-natured.

The physiognomy of the third young man was not as pleasant, nor was there as much in his favor as in the case of the other two. Still, he was known as a good lad. As for his political opinions, he could not be accused of being lukewarm because he was a fanatic republican. Some ill-intentioned people said that deep inside he was a royalist and that his intransigent radicalism was a calculated pose. But we have no reason to accept this affirmation, which is perhaps slander. They called him *El Doctrino*, or the Charity Child because he had learned his alphabet at the school of San Ildefonso. Certainly his character held a certain underhanded astuteness and some of his mannerisms were noticeably affected. He was the illegitimate son of a glazier who as he lay dying recognized him as his own, and left him a small fortune. But the executors of the estate, to whom the deceased had given powers, took an inventory, which revealed that the glazier had not left a single item of value. *El Doctrino* would ask them for money, and they would then say to him, "Take this for six months." And they would dole out a little money.

But his friends helped him live. They kept him going, and they bought him a heavy corduroy frock coat. It was well known—and this matter was seriously discussed—that a short time before the period in which this story begins *El Doctrino* was spending more money than usual. When his friends asked him about the source of that treasure, he would respond evasively and change the topic of conversation.

These three youths were inseparable. Neither the passing misfortunes of one nor the fortuitous earnings of the other disturbed the peace. *El Doctrino's* six-month dole would disappear in Lorencini or at The Golden Fountain in two days' worth of coffee, chocolate, and sherry. But then, Javier would write a huge article on national sovereignty in order to buy some boots for the classical poet, and *El Doctrino* himself would pull from a hidden pocket one doubloon of the five he had in order to take care of the amorous needs of Javier, who had a certain problem pending with the daughter of a cavalry colonel, a man as cruel and fierce as a Cossack.

These three roamed the streets together, approaching the various groups, questioning everyone, and relating news items devised by the fertile imagination of the poet. Finally, in the early evening they headed for the Agujero Hotel, located on Fúcar Street.

Neither ancient nor modern architecture contain a monument that better deserves its name than does the Agujero ["Hole"] Hotel on Fícar Street. That name, created by the popular imagination, had become official and could be seen written in enormous and twisted letters of black smoke on the whitish wall of the façade. A wide portal, not very high, led to the inn. This door, whose frame consisted of an immense horizontal beam somewhat bowed by the weight of the main floors, was the entrance to a long dark narrow alley which faced the unkempt patio. This patio was surrounded by awkward wooden corridors in which some numbered doors were located.

On the upper floor stood the establishment owned by La Riojana, as the landlady was known, according to an enduring title that had been maintained during three generations. There the travelers, disjoined and worn out by the gentle movement of the coach, were served a piece of tuna with onion, some capon if it was Christmas or on San Isidoro they would be served small, discreet portions of tripe, thin slices of Manchegan cheese, stale partridge, and wine from Valdepeñas and Pardilla. This frugal meal, served in cramped quarters and on a not-too-clean tablecloth, was the first stop that the traveler made before continuing later on to the *via crucis* of the inns and hotels of Madrid.

Twice a day a harsh and growing noise increased the usual clamor of that neighborhood. Bells, the crack of the whip, and the clamor of wheels jumping from hole to hole and cobblestone to cobblestone were heard. The vehicle arrived in front of the entrance way, and here the coach driver proved his skill at maneuvering. The apparatus turned around. The animals entered the entranceway and behind them the vehicle. The noise was so considerable that the house seemed to be coming apart. The ship cast anchor; the beasts were unsaddled; and the driver climbed down from his throne. The travelers still kept their heads inclined and crouched due to the low ceiling above the crowns of their heads and were surprised to be still alive. They too dismounted.

If there were relatives waiting, embraces, kisses, and greetings followed. The driver was tipped meagerly, and each traveler went on his way, it being customary to first have a snack right there in La Riojana's inn before going up to Atocha Street, which was somewhat more inaccessible in those days.

This time, as the vehicle made its definitive stop in the patio, there was general applause. *El Doctrino* embraced his friends.

"Javier!"

"Lázaro!"

They embraced each other warmly. After the monosyllables of joy and surprise, the second said to the first:

"You're in Madrid...? Finally! Are you coming from Ateca?"

"Yes."

"Well, you couldn't have arrived at a better time. And our friends from Zaragoza? But where are you coming from? And the club...and our club...?"

"By now you must know that they closed it down on us. I was in Ateca for six months."

"And will you be here for some time?"

"Forever."

"Good. Here there are young people, life. And if I must tell you the truth...we're badly needed."

"Yes...eh?"

"Gentlemen, this is my friend, my friend and companion, the great orator of the Zaragoza club."

The other young men, travelers and visitors alike, gathered around the Aragonese youth.

Let us explain. While Javier was in Zaragoza, he had struck up a very close friendship with Lázaro. At the club, both propagated democratic ideas—democracy in 1820—which at that time spread rapidly throughout that noble city. Privately these two lads, alike in character and temperament, considered each other as brothers. They shared each other's money, ate from the same plate, and fused their sorrows and joys into a common sentiment. They had not seen each other since Lázaro's return to his home town.

"How happy I am that you've come here!" said Javier, embracing him once more. "Young men like you are badly needed. The youth of yesterday have become corrupt. Some lose their nerve, others turn back, and some sell themselves out due to a lack of faith."

"Gentlemen, let's go to Vicentini," said *El Doctrino,* leading his friends away.

"What do you mean Vicentini? Let's go to The Maltese Cross cafe! There are many Aragonese there; they are all Aragonese."

"This fellow isn't going any place but The Golden Fountain," said Javier, pointing to his friend.

"Long live The Golden Fountain, the king of clubs!"

"And the club of kings," said one who slipped away as if he had said a bad thing.

"Who said that?" exclaimed *El Doctrino* furiously.

"Don't pay any attention to him. He's one of those who believe in those slanders," Javier pointed out. "Let's go, gentlemen. This evening there is an important session in The Golden Fountain."

"You can take me there tomorrow," promised Lázaro.

"Why tomorrow? This very evening, right now! Are you going to miss the most important session that has ever taken place?"

"But how can I go this evening, if I have only just arrived? I have to go to my uncle's house."

"Do you have an uncle living here? Is he a liberal?"

"I presume so; I don't know him."

"And are you going there now?"

"Of course."

"What nonsense! Forget about your uncle for a while. Come to The Golden Fountain. It is eight o'clock. It is going to start now. When it's all over you can go home."

"I don't know....That doesn't seem right to me," said Lázaro bewildered.

"But, how can you miss this session? Alcalá Galiano, Romero Alpuente, Flórez Estrada, Garelli, and Moreno Guerra will speak. There'll never be a session like this one. What's the difference whether you go home now or at two? Your uncle will just think that the coach hasn't arrived."

"No, no, I'm tired. They may be waiting for me at home."

"You just have to go. Where does your uncle live?"

"On Válgame Dios Street."

"Lord, that's so far! Don't go there now."

Lázaro had a strong desire to go quickly to his uncle's house. It is easy to understand why. But, it was not humanly possible to do so because his affectionate friend took him almost by force. Moreover, the reasons by which he excused himself from that determination also carried some weight in his mind. The warm reception, and the news of a great session of the celebrated Golden Fountain, stimulated the enthusiasm to which his character was always inclined. He let himself be taken there.

Who knows whether there was something providential in that unplanned visit to The Golden Fountain. Without having shaken off the dust from the road—he was thinking—they would receive him with applause in the most illustrious and famous club of the monarchy. Perhaps, they already knew of his reputation for brilliant oratory in Zaragoza. What do you mean, perhaps? No doubt they had already heard of him. In his mind these thoughts mixed with the pride he would feel when Clara heard his name praised by others the following day. In the confusion of his imagination he saw himself glorified by success. Why? It was clearly providential.

In this way the resistance he had first felt began to diminish as they approached The Golden Fountain. But do not take him for a crazy man yet.

They arrived. The door was blocked by an immense crowd. But, *El Doctrino* with his followers, and Javier with

Lázaro and the poet, had a way of entering through the inside patio. The meeting was very tense. An orator was accusing the government of the destitution of Riego. He related what had happened in Zaragoza and accused the inhabitants of that city of not having defended their general.

"To discredit a hero is the greatest desecration. What did Zaragoza do? Oh, the city in which such a thing occurred remained silent and permitted the Commander-in-Chief to be deposed. It allowed a vile constable to stain the sacred investiture of authority by stripping it from Riego. (Great applause.) The pretext has been given that Riego fomented disorder throughout Aragón. That isn't true. It is a lie concocted in those darkened councils of a certain Palace which I do not wish to name. (Murmurs and laughter.) He is sent from headquarters to Lérida for being under suspicion, and his command is handed over to a political boss. Who is that political boss? He was always an enemy of Liberty. You all know him. He is a deceitful enemy of Liberty. Down with disguises! (Applause.) You know very well what they plan to do. That is, they plan to separate the good liberals little by little from public office in order to fill them with hypocrites who call themselves our friends and detest us to the bottom of their corrupt hearts. (Yes! Yes! Yes!) What are they trying to do? Where are they leading us? What is going to come from all this? What will become of the freedom we have won? Citizens, pay close attention! Don't worry! Be alert, and if not, alas for Liberty! (Good, good.) But, I repeat gentlemen. My strongest complaint is against the town of Zaragoza, which I once believed to be the greatest town on Earth, and it is not....No, it isn't! Why did it allow Riego to be deposed? Why was he allowed to leave? Is this the same city as in 1808? No. I shall say to that city: 'I do not know you, Zaragoza. You are not Zaragoza. You no longer know how to rise up as one, like a single Aragonese. You have let Riego be trampled on. Once, in the past, you saved us, but today Zaragoza, you have ruined us!' " (Enthusiastic and continuous applause.)

A young man stood up (he was Aragonese).

"I protest," he said with great energy, "against the accusations launched at my country, at the noble capital of Aragón, by that gentleman, whose name I do not know...nor do I wish to know it. (A voice calls out, "Alcalá Galiano.") My country has not forgotten its honor. What would you have us do against a decree of the constitutional government?"

"Disobey it," shouted several voices.

"Gentlemen, let me continue."

"Let him go on, let him go on."

"I protest in the name of my countrymen, and I affirm that Zaragoza is the city in Spain which through the years has always done the most for Liberty. Doesn't he accuse it of being a center of republican extremism? Hasn't it been said that is where the most dissolvent ideas come from, that a conspiracy is being prepared there in order to maintain the Republic?"

"I want deeds and not words," said the first speaker.

"Well, you shall have deeds. Don't you know that in Zaragoza a club exists whose influence and prestige reached throughout all Aragón? That club, called democratic, has for two years been the most enthusiastic and efficient assembly in the nation. You well know what has been preached there. The eloquent voices that have resounded there are officially recognized. The doctrine that has been created there has reached here." (Murmurs.)

"We don't know what that club is all about. You the Aragonese always speak to us of the Zaragozan club, and yet today we still don't know what it is. What is it? Lots of talk of democracy, but no success in developing political doctrine and forming a party. But, in the final analysis, what are the theories of that exaggerated club? I have no confidence in it. Who speaks at that club? Let us know their names. I believe that most of us who are gathered here should consider that insignificant gathering with the contempt that it deserves. (Voices and tumult.)

Many Aragonese stood to insult the speaker. As Lázaro listened to everything, his expression changed by degrees. His friends told him in a low voice that he should defend the Zaragozan club. Suddenly, an Aragonese stood up in the middle of the room, pointed to the place where Lázaro was sitting with the others who had arrived that evening and said, "Some gentlemen are present who belonged to that club."

Everyone looked at that spot.

"Well," said the orator. "If those men are here let them speak. Let them tell us what that club is and has done. We want to hear them. Let them speak.

"Here is the most outstanding speaker of the democratic club of Zaragoza!" said Javier in a loud voice, pointing to his friend.

"Yes! Yes!" cried all the Aragonese who were there in the place, recognizing their compatriot. "Defend us, defend our reputation!"

All eyes were fixed on Lázaro. How strange! At that moment a sudden transformation took place in the spirit of the young man. He felt confused, he made an effort to bow and tried to say something, but he was unable to speak. But they pushed him toward the speaker's stand, and there was no way out. If he did not speak, what would they say about him? Lázaro had shone in Zaragoza for his eloquence. He had learned to control a crowd, to overcome its resistance and bend it by winning them over to his any whim. But on this occasion, he felt himself a beginner, he did not recognize himself; he was afraid.

"Let him speak, let him speak!"

"Make way," exclaimed one of the most notable deputies of Parliament.

Lázaro had an inspiration. The image of his kind young friend gave him strength. Like those knights of old who used to invoke the sovereign aid of their lady before entering in battle, he tried to evoke all the images of glory and happiness that had stimulated him. Expanding his chest, he went up to the podium. From above he looked at a roomful of heads, each one shaped like a pine-cone, and felt like a blow the curious glances of so many eyes.

It seemed to him like an abyss. His face which had reddened with confusion, suddenly turned very pale. He would have preferred to speak with his eyes closed. These deputies, writers and eminent politicians whom he saw all around him, frightened him. But, he was stouthearted and managed to control himself to some extent. But, how would he begin? What was he going to say? With a supreme effort of intelligence, he pulled together his ideas, mentally formulated a sentence, and looked at his audience....The audience looked at him and saw that he was as pale as a corpse. Lázaro coughed. The audience also coughed. The first word was delayed. Finally, the speaker caught his breath, and defying that abyss of curiosity which had opened up before him, he began to speak.

NOTE

[1] *Argüelles Alvarez, Agustín (1776-1844)* Eminent orator and statesman. A strong advocate of Freedom of the Press and abolition of the Inquisition. As a representative of liberal ideals, he was sentenced by Fernando VII to eight years of military service in Ceuta. When the Constitutionalists triumphed, he was named Secretary of State (1820), but later was forced to emigrate to London. Queen María Cristina de Bourbon assigned him the delicate task of being tutor to her daughters Isabell II and Luisa Fernanda.

Chapter X

THE FIRST BATTLE

Lázaro had been somewhat rhetorical as a speaker in the august chair of the democratic club of Zaragoza. It seems that there had been certain formulas or expressions of speech which our young man had learned from his teacher of Humanities in Tudela, a learned scholar of Luzán's classical school. The young man, nevertheless, possessed the instinct of tribunal eloquence, which was dry, sonorous, incisive, and clear. The Golden Fountain, unfortunately, was on this occasion the declared enemy of rhetoric and an even greater enemy of set phrases and common remarks, and of the officious, foolishly courteous, and extremely boring preambles which are common in academic oratory.

Lázaro suffered an evil temptation (because it was certainly a temptation of the devil) to begin his speech with clichéd remarks about *his smallness in the presence of so many great men* and the *select and illustrious public*. He followed this with *his confusion* and *the need of their indulgence, his scant strength*, etc. The exordium was long—another mistake in judgement. Some voices called out, "Get to the point, get to the point!"

For Lázaro, it was a little difficult to get to the point. This was not strange, for he had not been prepared, nor had he yet recovered from the surprise. In vain, he formed a very expressive synecdoche; in vain, he attempted to control the audience with four litotes and two or three metonyms, but this was not the way. He came up with some generalities which seemed to him very new, when in reality they were extremely old. He concluded a paragraph with two or three Plutarchian adages which he thought fit perfectly, yet they evoked no reaction from the crowd. He waited for an ovation, but no one applauded.

Lázaro was accustomed to hearing applause from the beginning; this gave him encouragement. The coldness which he noted in the audience on that occasion disheartened him. He wanted to think about it. He was almost at the point of not knowing what to say. Nevertheless, he had some magnificent thoughts fixed in his imagination. But how strange! He could not speak them. He felt as if these thoughts were written before him, but due to a natural mystery, at that moment he could not find the oratorical form with which to express them. What a setback! Little by little even his voice grew hoarse. Without doubt, there was a malign influence in our friend's spirit. He spoke coldly at times. Sensing it, he tried to put more feeling into his voice, and ended up shouting too much. He lacked ideas; the images he sought faded, and words jumbled together in his mouth.

Oh, where were those inner perorations, full of life and vehemence and as persuasive as a divine voice? Where was that awesome logic which in the depth of his oratorical swooning teemed in his brain, suddenly too small to hold so many ideas? Where were the sublime thoughts, the descriptive eloquence, the picturesque power, and the concise and profound words of wisdom? Yes, he felt all of this boiling from within, inside that solitary and passionate Lázaro, who spoke about nature in the quiet of the night, who addressed society from the depths of a dream. The ideas, forms, and language, he had them all, he felt them all within him. But he could not, just could not express them in any way.

In all speakers there are two entities: the orator and the man. While the first addresses the multitude, the second stands back, remaining that is, also speaking. Two simultaneous speeches are produced by the same brain. One is verbal and voiced; let us leave it to the audience. The other is deep and silent; let us examine it. Lázaro described, scolded, refuted, expounded, and declaimed. On the inside the other voice seemed to say, "How badly I'm doing! They're not applauding me! What should I say now?...Shall I discuss this point?...I shall not deal with it...and that idea that occurred to me earlier...I can't remember it!" At the same time, he did not interrupt his speech. He continued defending the Zaragozan club. He explained a democratic system, and in addition gave a brief history of the Republic. But the inner voice continued to speak in this way, "I don't know what to do....Why don't they applaud me? I can hardly recognize myself...I had so many ideas...Where are they? Oh! I'm going to express this great idea, but I have already said it....But it has had no effect on them...I'll try to be careful with the phrase...This sentence is going well....How shall I end it? What a fix this is! I can't find the adjective...Devil of an adjective! Oh, I'll end with an apostrophe...there it is....It hasn't made any effect...they aren't applauding me."

Lázaro's afflicted soul spoke in this manner. He addressed the audience with a confused, winding, and uneven discourse, lacking in logic.

The coughs began. Speakers say that hearing coughs during pauses in their speech makes their blood freeze. Lázaro heard repeated coughs throughout the audience, which resounded in his heart like a sinister echo. He also coughed. The cough allowed him four seconds of rest. He made a desperate effort and pulled some ideas from the depository he had in his mind; he took control of them firmly and continued speaking, "There goes that one," said the inner voice; "there they go. I'll develop the theme in this way...no...,better this other way...no...better the other...somehow...Oh, there is someone laughing...and another there whispering. What a terrible cough!...Don't they like what I am saying now...nor even this...Have courage...I'll conclude this paragraph with a quote...there it is....Oh, but it hasn't had any effect, either."

A perfect parallelism is maintained between the words from within and the speech the public hears.

Oh, what mysteries there are in human intelligence, such strange phenomena, with relation to the human word!

Why did the Aragonese's speech fail? Did it fail because of the diabolical meeting of a thousand circumstances not related to the nature of his outstanding talent and facility of speech? Whose fault was it? His or the audience's? The public and the speaker tend to a mutual fascination. The public looks and listens. We cannot say which is more frightening; its gaze or its ear. The thousands of eyes make one dizzy. The attention of so many people, directed at a single voice, confuses and overwhelms. The speaker also sees and listens. He hears coughing. Because of it, Lázaro could have wished at some moments of that evening that he were deaf and blind. But the speaker has an advantage over the public. He has a weapon apart from his words: the gesture. He also fascinates, and he too carries in his eyes that vertigo which confuses and overwhelms. He generally looks down to see the public. He can move his arms and head while the audience remains as if by its feet and hands, immobile and solely attentive.

On that ghastly evening Lázaro and the public did not mutually entrance each other. They did not command each other's respect. They did not establish rapport. Lázaro did not persuade the audience, nor did they applaud the speaker. An unconvinced audience and an unapplauded speaker reject each other; they repel each other with force. "You should stop talking" is what the audience seems to say to the speaker. "You should take a walk" is what the speaker seems to say to the audience.

The Aragonese youth had succumbed to the worst of temptations: the temptation of being long and drawn out. A second more than usual is enough to end the audience's patience and turn its interest into disgust. Lázaro saw this moment pass without noting it. Undoubtedly, they did not understand each other. Did they mutually dislike each other? Perhaps, they had begun by fearing each other, but certainly, they ended up despising each other.

The strange thing is that if any one individual had been asked his opinion of the speech, it would perhaps, not have been unfavorable. But, the audience's opinion is not the sum of the opinions of the individuals who comprise it. No, in collective opinion there is something fateful, something not included in the laws of human feeling. Lázaro was clearly failing.

It occurred to him twenty times that he should conclude. But how? He did not dare. He was going to end it badly. What a horror! And if he was going to end badly, it would be better to continue speaking, to keep on and on. He looked for an ending and could not find one. And the end is so important! He would be able to rehabilitate himself with one moment of inspiration. The thought of concluding without applause horrified him. Consequently, he feared the end and avoided it. But he had to finish up. The coughs were followed by yawns, and the whispers by mumbling. He searched without stopping for a punch line. He went round and round the matter, striving for a graceful exit, but found no escape. The word slipped from his mouth. Words flowed continuously without a solution near at hand.

"It's time to finish," said the inner voice. "Conclude! I can't find the ending, and the ending has to be good....Lord, please help me! I'll summarize, recapitulate...But, I don't remember what I have already said....Shall I ask the audience to forgive me?...No, that would discredit me...." At last a final sentence occurred to him, and he began it. But as he got to the end, another sentence linked on with it, and then another, another, and another. His speech was an endless oscillation. The audience became impatient. Not a minute more. He reached the final period and resolved that it would be the last. He finally pronounced the last noun. Then, raising his voice, he followed it very slowly with three adjectives that modified it, and then had the courage to remain silent.

The last word of that unfortunate speech vibrated in space, alone, dry, sad, and with funereal resonance. Not one listener's applause did he draw, nor an exclamation of satisfaction. His voice had fallen into the abyss without producing an echo. It seemed to him that he had not even spoken and that his speech has been one of those silent, although eloquent, inner manifestations of his oratory genius. He stood in a desert surrounded by darkness. What had he said? Nothing. And he had spoken a long time. It was as if he had struck at a vacuum, as if he had wounded a phantom believing it to be a human being; it was as though the sun had shone in a world of blind men. He stepped down from the rostrum with his soul in grief, his heart oppressed, his head inflamed and confused. His face was bathed in a cold sweat.

Javier attempted, in vain, to rehabilitate him by giving him a few delayed claps of applause. The public, an implacable animal, ordered him to hush up. Lázaro had sufficient presence of spirit to look face to face at those hundred mouths, yawning in boredom. Robespierre the cat stretched his legs on the counter with the supreme expression of annoyance.

"I did very badly," said the speaker sadly in his friend's ear.

"You will do better on another day. You are a great man, but you haven't touched the core. After one of my lessons you will be up-to-date. Another orator is going to speak. Now, pay attention."

"No, I am going to my uncle's house. I can't stay here any longer. I'm overcome."

"Wait and hear what he's going to say."

A second speaker went up to the rostrum to relieve the boredom Lázaro's harangue had caused. As the multitude celebrated with mechanical applause the words of its favorite speaker, Lázaro slowly sank into profound melancholy. Nothing is more frightening than those moments of disillusionment in which the soul lies tormented by the pains of defeat. The torment of this situation consists of a certain absurdity which surrounds all memories of past illusions. All the words of intimate praise, of deep pride which had earlier caressed his imagination now resounded with an echo of ridicule in his poor downcast soul, full of shame.

"But I must try to pull myself together," said Lázaro to himself. "Yet how? Everyone is whispering about me, and if the subject of my speech comes up tomorrow, they'll all say that it was detestable, extremely bad. It will pass from mouth to mouth; it will reach the ears of all the people who matter to me. She'll hear about it. Perhaps she'll laugh at me. Everyone will laugh now."

The strangest thing is that once he left the rostrum, thoughts began to occur to him, magnificent resources of eloquence, superbly effective remarks and very fitting quotes. And he was sure that if he were to speak to them, he would draw great applause. But it was too late now. There he sat, mute and perplexed, and his spirit was overshadowed by a cloud.

Meanwhile, the new speaker digressed as he pleased through the field of History and politics and finally expounded on the need for a planned demonstration on the following day. All stood up unanimously shouting, "Yes!" Everyone promised to attend, and three or four who were in charge of the ceremony reported on the organization of the procession. The hour was set, and the gathering point designated. Bravos followed the applause; applause followed the bravos; and finally, the session ended.

The members began to leave, but the ignorant and rowdy group which always sat in the corner of the café did not care to exit without comment. Calleja stood on a chair and shouted, addressing his men:

"Men, let us sing a serenade to Morillo!"

The idea was received with an uproar. Morillo was the commander-in-chief of New Castile. An enemy of tumultuous mobs, he had taken measure to impede the procession. A part of the population flocked near his house on the evening of the seventeenth, stunning the whole thoroughfare with frightening tumult.

"A serenade to Morillo!" said Calleja, leaving The Golden Fountain. Gathering together everyone willing to participate, he prepared for the event about to take place.

We don't know where he came from, but *Tres Pesetas* was there. Our three friends and Lázaro were among the last to leave. Out of curiosity they approached the group which Calleja had organized.

Meanwhile, the barber crossed the street in two long strides and approached the door to his house. His wife came out to meet him.

"Citizen, did you speak?" she asked him.

"No, my dear little citizen. I couldn't tonight. But, tomorrow, I'll either speak or cut out my tongue. I have studied the introduction, and I'll not forget a single letter. When I speak, I'll eat them up alive."

"I don't think I should let you in," his wife responded gravely. "If I were the one who wore trousers, they would have heard from me by now. Even so, if I wanted to do it, I would have driven them nuts....If I wore trousers, I would go through those clubs and shoot my mouth off. Because I have many truths to speak here in my gut...."

"You'll see tomorrow evening whether I speak or not. It's just that when I am going to begin to speak my tongue feels tickly....And I become tongue-tied. But don't worry, I'm going to leave them dumbfounded."

"A serenade to Morillo!" a hundred voices shouted.

"Gentlemen," exclaimed one of the most famous speakers of The Golden Fountain, "go home, each of you, these public disorders are going to discredit us. Go home, stop shouting!"

This advice was greeted with prolonged whispers of reproof.

"Who is that royalist?" said a slurred voice that belonged to none other than the incomparable *Chaleco*.

"To Morillo's house," repeated Calleja. "Woman, bring me the mortar!"

The crowd increased with new arrivals from La Cebada Square and from the Salitre district. The members of The Golden Fountain had left, and the club closed. Only the three friends were left in the street with Lázaro, who was saying good-bye and heading for his uncle's house.

"Wait a second and see who comes out," said Javier, detaining him.

At that moment a person was knocking energetically at Calleja's door.

"What's up?" said Calleja, as he answered, breaking up a patriotic barbershop discussion which had commenced.

"Go immediately to bleed *Don* Liborio, he's very ill."

"Damn sick one. I'll bleed him tomorrow."

"It can't wait. Go right away," exclaimed the servant.

"Men, what should I do?" asked the barber of his friends.

"Don't go, Calleja; let him bleed himself. This isn't a night for bloodletting. Let's go to Morillo's house!"

"Men..., I should fulfill...as you now see...my profession. Science comes first.

"Don't go, Calleja."

"I'll come right back. Let us see," he added, opening the door, "citizen bring me the lancets."

His wife the citizen came outside, very grieved, and said to him:

"Come on, we have to give Joaquinito an enema, he's very ill. If you had seen what a terrible vomiting spell he had! Should I give him mallow?"

"Give him boiled demons, sister," exclaimed *Tres Pesetas* furiously.

"Take it easy, gentlemen," replied Calleja. "Mallow or oil? Let me see how to handle that, because for me...Why should I deny it, science must come first.

Lázaro insisted on leaving his three friends. He was very depressed and sad.

"Wait, men," said Javier, detaining him. "Wait and see what these barbarians are doing."

"What do you mean barbarians!" angrily exclaimed some men standing nearest to them. One of them turned toward his friends with so much curiosity that even Calleja himself abandoned science to defend their association. "What's that about barbarians, little gentleman?"

"Who are those good-for-nothing cowards?" said one.

"This is the Aragonese who prayed the Rosary to us this evening. What a way to give a speech!"

"It sure sounded like a Good Friday sermon."

"May the devil take me if I don't smash the teeth of those intruders," said *Tres Pesetas*, ready to do what he said.

Javier, *El Doctrino*, and the classical poet saw a storm gathering over their heads. But the classical poet, who was their truest enemy, did not become frightened and had the whim of calling the great Calleja a name. Sparks flew and battle was imminent. But they were so unequally matched that the four young men decided not to fight. They turned their backs and sped away toward Victoria Street. Many of their adversaries followed them, shouting and throwing stones at them. But the fugitives got away quickly and took refuge on Gorguera Street, getting through the portal of the house where one of them lived. They carefully locked the door from within. An enormous stone, tossed by the robust hands of *Tres Pesetas*, struck the door so powerfully that if it had hit anyone it would have smashed him to bits. Fortunately the youths were safe. Those on the outside, seeing that their prey had escaped them, left chanting a harmonious jingle praising the commander-in-chief of Madrid.

Chapter XI

THE TRAGEDY OF GRACCHUS

As soon as they heard their pursuers leave, the friends went upstairs. The classical poet lived there.

"Do you have anything to eat?" *El Doctrino* asked him.

"A magnificent feast," answered the poet. "A quarter kilo of Manchegan cheese and a bottle of Cariñena. We'll send for some fritters from the corner tavern."

Lázaro was frightfully hungry. He had not eaten since nine in the morning, and the fatigue of the trip, along with the mental effort, and great emotional fatigue of that evening had exhausted him to the point that he could not go on. He went upstairs with the others, physically unable at that moment to undertake the trip to his uncle's house. The retinue led by the classical poet moved up the stairs.

No trip to the North Pole is more dangerous than a narrow staircase in a Madrilenian house when total darkness reigns in it. You begin to stumble here and there. Suddenly, you hit the wall; run into a door; and the noise alarms the tenants. You come across a hat hanging on a lamp, which, although extinguished because of lack of oil, has just enough left to relight. All of this is tolerable if one does not bump into a crook who flees or the suitor on the way up, if you do not hear the jingle of the picklock who intends to open a door, if you do not slip on the substances deposited by the cats on the stairwell, or if you do not stumble on the amorous union of two stars courting on the last flight of steps.

Finally, the retinue reached the northern regions of the house, the heights where the poet had made his nest. They rang and the door opened. Our friends found themselves face to face with a drowsy-eyed, sour-faced woman. Her raised hand held a lamp, as if in imitation of the stairway lights. This lamp lit up a room which communicated with the room which the four men had entered. The lady snapped the lock on the stairway door. Saying good night in the leaden tone of an ecclesiastical response, she left. She had not taken more than four steps when she turned back. Wrapping herself in her robe with upright and reserved gestures, she said:

"For God's sake, *Don* Ramón, don't make noise. The area is disturbed by the uproar which starts up here every evening. Because you now see...one reason is all the gossip from the neighbors. The embroiderer has been going about saying that this is a tavern and that no one can live in this house. As you can see...I have to protect my reputation...."

The woman who was so zealous about the reputation of her house was its owner, *Doña* Leoncia Iturrisbeytia, a Basque, as her name reveals, about forty years of age, more or less, respectable, of good appearance, robust form, tall in stature, with a round face, and very good disposition, and extremely plain-looking.

"Leave us in peace, madam," answered Javier. "If *Don* Gil had been along with us we would not have been such an inconvenience to you."

"Come now, here you go again with your jokes, *Don* Javier."

"And when are you getting married, *Doña* Leoncia?"

"Who, me? Married?" said *Doña* Leoncia with poorly disguised satisfaction.

"Well, I hope you know that you are getting a handsome fellow. *Don* Gil is a man who'll make a career for himself....He is at a good age."

An outburst of laughter from the other two and a forced smile from the landlady greeted those words. The Basque woman had a suitor, *Don* Gil Carrascosa, who was a lay brother, abbot, and clerk, and just about anything else. Alarming rumors were spreading through the neighborhood concerning the existence of a certain somewhat intimate agreement between the classical poet and *Doña* Leoncia. Let us not delve into the sacredness of these secrets.

Doña Leoncia noted the presence of an unfamiliar face and tried to put on airs. She became serious and reprimanded the students for their lack of formality. Then, she made a pompous gesture, added some courteous remarks, and left.

"Good-bye, Ariadne, Antigone, Sofonisba, Penelope," said the poet when he saw her step outside. He was very fond of assigning her those heroic names.

Shortly after this farewell, some very prolonged and raspy snores were heard. It was Ariadne, Antigone, Sofonisba, Penelope who was sleeping within. How happy are the goddesses!

Javier and *El Doctrino* competed for possession of the bed. Lázaro made himself comfortable as best he could on a chair with three and a half legs. The poet remained standing, doing the honors of the attic. From the bureau drawer, he pulled out a piece of cheese wrapped in paper which had become transparent. A knife, bottle, and plate on which there were one-and-a-half rolls were brought in from another corner. The feast was prepared on the table, making it necessary to set aside two tragedies in heroic verse, a portrait (gnawed by rats) of a woman, a copy of the Constitution, an inkstand made of horn, and a slipper inside which there were scissors, a box of tablets, and half a volume of Crebillon's theatre.

The room was strange. The bed stood out as horizontal as possible on two benches whose boards supported a straw mattress with such an uneven surface that the person sleeping on it had to roll from summit to summit before being able to get to sleep. An esparto grass mat, very elegant back in the time of Carlos III, covered two-thirds of the apartment. *Doña* Leoncia's best efforts to stretch it out so as to cover the rest of the floor had been to no avail. An immense trunk sat next to the bed. Judging by the corroded state of the leather and the filth accumulated between the trunk and the wall it seemed that mice had assumed the task of colonizing the area. The walls were adorned with paintings; the most noteworthy was a pen sketch done by the uncle of the brother-in-law of the grandfather of the Basque lady, a man who had been a renowned calligrapher. The whole sketch was full of personages, lines, strange letters, signatures and pen adornments—a work so excellent that it was illegible. On the other hand, a small piece of needlework in a once gilded frame hung on the wall; it presented the youthful skills of *Doña* Leoncia's grandmother, an embroiderer of the finest kind. To the side of these family relics were a pair of figurines of the French Directory and a picture of the Virgen de Pilar simply pasted on the wall with four stickers.

Ramón poured wine in a glass which was passed from hand to hand; the cheese was distributed and the bread disappeared quickly. Lázaro showed no moderation in eating, because the truth was that he was very hungry and continually felt faint.

"Let's go, little Ramón," said *El Doctrino*, "read us some of that tragedy and make us cry, the one you call Petra."

"What Petra? What do you mean Petra?" replied the poet. "Don't be a barbarian; you mean Phaedra."

"Phaedra or Pancrasia, it's all the same to me."

"I have given up on that theme. It isn't anything new. What is more suitable now is a political theme."

"I like that."

"I finally decided on the Gracchus....Friends, what men they were!"

"Let's see," said *El Doctrino*. "Read us something of those Grajos. It must be funny."

"But listen here, you nut," said Javier. "Why not do a tragedy of current events in which men are like these of our time."

"Don't be a fool," said the poet, laughing heartily. "Nowadays, there aren't any real heroes."

"Stupid, then what do you call Churruca, Alvarez, and Daoiz?"[1]

"Yes, but they're dress-coat heroes."

Ramón had talent and poetic ability; but he was born in an unlucky period for letters. Cold classicism impeded the budding talents of one who, trained in French rhetoric and following the principles of the prosaic Montiano, rigid Luzán, and the unbearable Hermosilla[2], could make no use of the poetic elements which our society then offered him.

The people, patrons of the theatres, did not understand the dithyramb of the Greeks and Romans; and at the same time no poets succeeded in putting Spanish heroes into their productions. Nasarre[3], in the meantime, called Calderón[4] a barbarian and his drama, *La vida es sueño*, nothing more than delirium. That classical restoration was productive for comedy because it produced Moratín, the younger.[5] But drama, the pathetic fable which portrays the great disturbances of the soul and depicts the most visible elements of society, did not then exist.

A few tragedies were written. They were weak and lifeless works, because they were not enlivened by national inspiration; neither our people nor our heroes came to life in them. Now we realize that the heroes are stiff, like cardboard copies of the classic tragedies, always the same. Love of liberty cannot be conceived without Brutus, nor contempt for the Empire without Cinna. How can there be passion without Phaedra and fatality without Oedipus and patricide without Orestes and rebellion without Prometheus and love of independence without *Persas*? In our friend Ramón's time the young writers believed this, and there were some serious persons who found Crebillon more inspiring than Lope, and Rotrou greater than Moreto.[6]

The poet of whom we speak wrote his version of Alcestis, and in one of its acts, Bellerophon and various scenes of biblical tragedies, all in vogue at that time, also appear. Then, he had an inspiration and attempted to abandon such a common practice.

He though up a Subieski, a Solimán, an Arnoldo de Brescia, and lastly, a Padilla. But he had just started to write some verses when he turned back through fear to antiquity and concentrated on Gracchus. He began the opus and completed it a little before the events we relate.

We see him now seated upon the table with the manuscript in his hand, illuminated by a small oil lamp. *El Doctrino* and Javier were arguing over the possession of the bed with renewed furor. Lázaro, who was seated on the chair, had yielded to fatigue; and, leaning against that same bed, he awaited the first scene of the Gracchus.

Javier coughed and read off the list of protagonists of the tragedy, followed by a string of tribunes, lectors, centurions, patricians, towns, and slaves. Afterward, he described the setting, which was a public square, a scene of confidences, of meetings, of speeches, of secrets, of scandals, of trials, and of everything. Then, he began the act: The *first tribune* came out and asked the *second tribune* if he had seen Caius; the *second tribune* answered no to the *first tribune*; but then, the *third tribune* came forth and told the other two that Caius was in the home of the priest Ennius Sofronius who would come to confide his plans to them in the public square. They depart and, on leaving, the *man from the first town* says to the *man from the second town* that bread is expensive and that the poor people are eating their own elbows in hunger. This exasperates the *man from the third town* who swears by Neptune and the son of Maya that this must not go on. Each one returns from whence he came. Cornelia asks why Caius is so disturbed and sad; he says that Caius rejects *good meals of a plentiful table* in order to roam silently and to be absorbed by the banks which bathe *the slow Tiber's undulating current*. But soon, Caius comes in person to remove their doubts. Caius, alarmed by some words which the *third tribune* said to him behind the scenes, runs into his mother and orders her to listen and be fearful. In the face of such a command, Cornelia is all ears and begins to tremble like quicksilver. Caius tells her that the gods will help her in her undertaking. With this, she calms down and her trembling stops. He also says that Averno will swallow up the Earth before he fails in his purpose; the deer will drink— *of excellent foliage*—the briny sea; and the carp will be raised to the summit of the high peak of Tinacria. After these unburdenings, the curtain comes down, and each one returns to the town whence he came.

When Caius had made these pledges, *El Doctrino* closed his eyes, not too worried that Averno would devour all Italy, and began to snore gently, like a lazy god. The poet did not notice this incident, and began to read the second act. However, upon reaching the delicate point in which Cornelia relates to her confidant the dream she has had, Javier began to do the same and also fell asleep. As the poet penetrated into the labyrinths of the third act; when Senator Rufus Pompilius stood toe to toe with Senator Sextus Lucius Flacus—who, let us note in passing, did not look askance at Cornelia, even though she was a rather mature lady—; when all this took place, Lázaro, who had held out through courtesy, could not resist any longer. Settling down on the chair and against the edge of the bed, he gave some nods and also fell olympically asleep, commencing to dream asleep, which was when he dreamed the least.

The poet concluded the third act, in which there was an uprising. Before reading the fourth act, he looked about him and observed a scene of desolation.

"Asleep, oh Gods!" he exclaimed, still absorbed in the classical spirit.

But it was to be expected. Who could stand a tragedy with a busy public square, a virtual storehouse of hendecasyllables? Who could endure such a large dose of classicism at that hour, after hearing twenty speeches, and after having eaten?

Something was still lacking. The oil lamp, which doubtless was not fond of the classics, had been sickened by so many hendecasyllables up to that point that it refused to light up the public square any longer, and went out. Ramón closed his manuscript in the dark; he understood that the best thing to do was to emulate his friends. He got down from the table, wrapped himself in his cape, and stretched out on the blessed floor. In a moment he was as deeply asleep as the others. So ended the Gracchus tragedy. It has been impossible for us to determine if at the end Senator Rufus Pompilius gave Senator Sextus Lucius Flacus the hard slap on the face which he had promised him.

NOTES

[1] *Churruca y Elorza, Cosme Damián (1761-1805)* General of the Spanish naval fleet. From 1793-1814 he guided the preparation of a maritime atlas for the northern Western Hemisphere. He died bravely of wounds during the Battle of Trafalgar.

Alvarez de Castro, Mariano (1749-1810) A general distinguished for his resistance during the French siege of Georna. Renowned for his heroic valor, unconquerable energy and fervent loyalty. He was taken prisoner by the French and imprisoned by them in Figueras castle. He refused to sign the surrender agreement presented to him by the French. He became ill and died in prison under suspicious circumstances.

Daoiz, Luis (1767-1808) One of the heroes of the Spanish independence. Along with Pedro Velarde and Lieutenant Ruiz, one of the first to use his artillery against the French. Died while defending Madrid on May 2, 1808.

[2] *Luzan, Ignacio (1702-1754)* Distinguished poet from Valladolid, whose "Poetica" deals with the antecedents, form style, and content of poetry.

Hermosilla, José Mamerto Gómez (1771-1837) A famous philosopher and professor of Greek and Rhetoric. An admirer of Moratín Hermosilla translated Homer's Iliad into Spanish (1831).

[3] *Nasarre, Blas Antonio (1689-1751)* Professor at the University of Zaragoza and Librarian to Fernando VI. A member of the Spanish Royal Academy of the language. He considered Lope and Calderón to be corruptors of good taste. He held the opinion that Cervantes' plays were bad, and that they had been written as parodies of Lope's comedies. His opinion of the *Quijote* also created a stir.

[4] *Calderón de la Barca, Pedro (1600-1681)* Great Spanish poet and dramatic writer of the Golden Age. His plays are exceptional for the strong development of the characters, clever plot lines and a poetic fluidity of expression. Among his best known plays are *El Alcalde de Zalamea* and the philosophical drama *La vida es sueño*.

[5] *Mortín, Leandro Fernández de (1760-1828)* Comic poet. His frustrated love for *Doña* Francisca Gertrudis Muñoz left an impact on his outstanding work, "El sí de las niñas." He translated Moliere and Shakespeare into Spanish. His original comedies "El viejo y la niña," "La Mojigata," and "La comedia nueva o el café," are typical of his elegant and ingenious literary productions. He is considered by many critics to be one of the few giants of the neoclassical eighteenth century Spanish literary scene.

[6] *Crebillón, Prospero Julyot de (1674-1762)* A tragic poet and dramatist, member of the French Academy and author of "Rhadamiste et zenobie."

Lope de Vega (Lope Félix de Vega Carpio) (1562-1635) Outstanding and prolific dramatist, poet and writer of the Golden Age of Spain. Wrote 1,800 comedies, all of which were presented on stage, and half of which were published.   Innovator and critic of his contemporaries.

Rotrou, Juan de (Jean) (1609-1650)   A French dramatic poet considered by many critics to be one of the creators of the French theater.   A disciple of Corneille.   Among his productions are "L'Hypocondriaque" and his works of Spanish inspiration: "Cleagenor et Doridthée," "Laura Persecutée," "Don Bernard de Cabrera," and "Saint Genest" are tragic comedies inspired by Lope de Vega.

Moreto, Augustín (1618-1669)   A priest and dramatist of the 1600's. A poet in the court of Philip IV, he was noted for his pure and simple style.   A follower of the Calderonian school, he is thought to have introduced to Spain the *comedia de costumbres* drama.   Some of his works were later imitated by Moliere and Scarrón.   He wrote "El Lindo Don Diego," and adapted "El licenciado Vidriera" to the stage.

Chapter XII

THE BATTLE IN PLATERIAS

The sun and *Doña* Leoncia both appeared with the same splendor of beauty in the early hours of the following day. The landlady, on leaving idle her wool blankets, first gave attention to dressing her hair, a complicated act because it consisted of a conscientious restoration of the damages done to her person by the slow passage of years.

After combing loose her rather thin hair, she began to weave a bun which, if it had not received reinforcement from a puffy pad, would have been no larger than an egg. She proceeded immediately to make up her face, an operation carried out so cleverly and discreetly that not even *Don* Gil, who was the person who came closest to her during the day, knew the truth of her deceit. At times she used a special eyebrush, but this was only on certain days, and we shall not dwell on it for now. While she was involved in these tasks, her skirt was badly adjusted. She was corsetless and two-thirds of her massive bosom was carelessly uncovered when someone entered the house and, approaching the room of the goddess, softly knocked twice on the door.

"Who is it?" said the Basque, alarmed.

"Me."

"For heaven's sake Carrascosa, don't come in. I am..."

But Carrascosa pushed the door and would have opened it had it not been held on the inside by the easily frightened and modest lady who left her make-up and quickly adjusted her skirt in order to defend her fort.

"Leoncia, Leoncia, look, it's me, your Gil."

"*Don* Gil, *Don* Gil, don't be a nuisance. You always come when I'm tidying up. Wait! Go to the kitchen. I have to speak to you."

"I also have to speak to you," said Carrascosa, applying his eye to the keyhole, in an effort to see something.

Doña Leoncia did not delay in dressing. She adjusted her corset, put the last hairpins in her hair, applied two or three pins to her bodice, threw a shawl over her shoulders, and went to the kitchen.

"You know that I come here quite disturbed," *Don* Gil said to her, while the lady, who had approached the stove, made an effort to ignite the coal with straw. "You know that I am very disturbed, Leoncia, with what people are saying, and I come here so that you may dispel any doubts, because, in short, I have this weighing on my mind, and I can't digest it."

"What? Let's see....Let's see what absurd things are on your mind today."

"Nothing, except that people are saying that you..." the ex-civil servant stopped here, as if, in fact, something were caught in his throat.

"That I? Let's see what," said the landlady, blowing on the coals.

"That you...I mean...that that young fellow who writes verses and lives in the studio is sweet on you and that he is wooing you....The fruit vendor told me that he saw you going out with him for a stroll, and..."

"Don't repeat such stupidities," declared *Doña* Leoncia raising in her right hand a copper fire shovel she was using at that moment. "The fact is that since I am a woman of good reputation everybody has to occupy himself by saying whatever they feel like saying. Come on now, *Don* Gil! And you are engaged in gossiping with the fruit vendor. A fine mess this is! Don't speak to me again about mischievous rumors. The fact is that one cannot move a foot without the whole neighborhood saying why or why not."

"That's enough," declared Carrascosa. "I don't doubt that you are a very decent woman, but you ought to avoid having people gossip...because..."

"Don't speak to me about that. Gil, Gil, don't speak to me about that," said *Doña* Leoncia, pretending annoyance. "All you men are deceitful, and I have become very disillusioned....No..., I mean...very...I have already been told what men are like....If you don't believe it, look at that loan shark downstairs who gives his wife fifty smacks for breakfast."

"Oh, my Leoncia! And you think that I am not going to treat you like the docile little lamb you are?...Lord, don't be a fool; since we have to clear this up, and it's important to maintain one's good reputation, it would be a good idea for you to toss that fellow out of your house and for him to go somewhere else with his verses."

"Well, I say no. If they talk, let them talk. If they want to offend, let them offend. I'm a respectable woman."

"Jesús, Leoncia. And you will not indulge me?"

Doña Leoncia began to laugh heartily; and Carrascosa, who was not ready to get too serious about it that day, calmed down and ended up laughing, too.

"This afternoon I am going to a picnic in Chamartín with *Doña* Petronila and Juliana. *Doña* Ramóna is coming along, and if you come, you can sing those *seguidilla* tunes you know."

"I'm not in the mood for *seguidillas*. What riles me is that guy Ramón, who has me fed up. Look, look, Leoncia! If you get rid of him, I'll sing you *seguidillas* for four days straight. Oh, it slipped my mind—do you know that we are planning a procession in Las Maravillas? I'll get a balcony for you to watch from. It's going to be very spectacular, and there will be more than twenty-four saints' statues and all the confraternities of Madrid."

"Look, Gil, don't get involved in processions. I dislike them. So then, you'll come to Chamartín?"

"Yes. It's a good idea for us to go today because there is a lot going on in Madrid, and I suspect that there will be shots fired in the streets."

"Jesús and Saint Librada! Another uproar!" declared the Basque with her face disturbed and changing color. "But why?"

"It's nothing. Those crackpots from The Golden Fountain are going to parade the portrait of Riego around with music and everything. The authorities have prohibited the procession but they say that it will take place anyway. We'll see who wins. The people over there are already aroused. Soon we'll see the tumult."

In fact, the noise arrived soon after. A large crowd assembled in the nearby Santa Ana plaza, and the rumble of voices reached the peaceful abode of *Doña* Leoncia. The galician maid, who was returning from shopping, entered yelling in terror, and saying she had heard some loud cannon shots. Her cries awakened the three friends and Lázaro.

"What's going on?" asked Javier. "What's that uproar about?"

"What else could it be but the procession?" said *El Doctrino*.

Lázaro got up aching because of the uncomfortable position in which he had slept. It felt as though his backbone had been broken. They opened the balcony and looked out. *Doña* Leoncia entered the poet's room, shouting and gesticulating.

"Jesús, Jesús! Don't open the balcony or a bomb will fall in here! Don't you hear the cannon shots? Heavens, what loud shots!"

"Madam, you must be dreaming about those cannon shots."

"Don't be alarmed, Artemis, Electra..."

"Close that balcony!"

The four youths were too curious to be content with just looking out from the balcony. They hurried down to the street to join the crowd. Lázaro, having picked up his meager luggage in advance from the Agujero Hotel, planned to leave and go to his uncle's house immediately.

"Who is that young man?" asked *Don* Gil of the landlady after the four had left.

"I don't know who he is. They brought him here last night.

Carrascosa thought that he recognized the fellow as the nephew of a friend with whom he had dealings in Ateca. Interested, and wanting to make sure, he decided to follow them down. The four young men mixed with the crowd. It was impossible to take a step. The procession was organized, and soon the march was about to enter Atocha Street. Great confusion reigned among the masses, and the efforts of two or three persons to place the people in orderly rows and direct them were in vain.

Lázaro tried to leave for his destination but a sudden temptation made him stop, thoughtful and worried. When he saw that crowd, his imagination, downcast and lifeless since the traumatic café scene, returned to life, assuming its customary vivacity. The people were gathered there, prepared for a great demonstration. Confused and almost fearful of their undertaking, the masses were hesitant. They had neither steadfastness nor determination. Something was certainly lacking. Lázaro tried to control himself and resist the temptation. He left the crowd and then returned to it. "Yes," he was thinking, "something is lacking here. A voice is lacking."

The important moment had arrived, so vital in popular demonstrations, when the mob pauses, undecided, a thousand hearts disturbed by a single profound fear, a thousand minds with a single doubt. One voice is lacking, one which will express what they all feel. At this crucial moment we see a figure rise above thousands of figures and an arm, trembling with tension, extended over their heads. A strong voice puts into words the emotions which struggle for expression in many minds. That voice says what no mob can say, because the mob, which functions as a single body with security and decision, has no voice other than the savage rumble composed of an infinite number of unequal sounds.

Once that man has spoken, the crowd has said what it has to say. The crowd knows itself. It is able to gather and unify its forces. It has acquired what it lacked: conscience and unity. It is no longer an inorganic meeting of blind strengths. It is an intelligent body whose activity is directed toward a defined object, whether good or bad; regardless it leads toward it with decision and knowledge.

Lázaro was thinking. Would he be that means of expression? Could he be the motivating word of that blind and unconscious body? Would he speak or not? The masses, meanwhile, were milling around and had spread out over Angel Plaza. Lázaro followed the crowd as if fascinated. He drew apart, fearful of them and of himself. Yet, he could not decide to withdraw. Would he speak out or not? Surely, they would listen to him. Why not, if he were to say such great things? He was sure that he would speak well. The words he must say appeared as if written in space with letters of fire.

The portrait was now advancing, carried by four members of The Golden Fountain club. The music sounded, and the crowd surrounded the canvas. Everyone was in motion, but no one made the move to advance. They milled about in confusion. The spark was missing. Lázaro joined the whirling mass. His inner conflict was mounting, his excitement at fever pitch. His eyes blazed. Moving and eloquent phrases coursed through his mind. His heart beat rapidly. His temples burned, and he felt in his throat a sonorous vibration that needed only a little breath to become a strong and eloquent voice.

He saw that they raised the portrait and that the masses were milling in never-ending circles. He saw a multitude of white handkerchiefs waving in the air, rising from that whirlwind-like foam.

The unruly procession continued through Atocha Street and entered the Main Plaza. There the crowd spread out a little. But then, it tried to pass through the arch of Amargura Street in order to enter Platerías. The great monster calculated at a glance the number of its members and the width of the arch through which it had to pass. "The camel was going to pass through the eye of the needle." There was a convulsive movement of elbows; stomachs were compressed; bodies rotated; and some hats fell at the impact and the collision of so many heads. A few voices tried to bring order and to overcome the difficulty which was undoubtedly an obstetric problem.

"On with the portrait! Let the picture pass," they declared.

It was impossible. The people flocked together in such a way that the portrait could not get through. Finally, after great effort, the painting was maneuvered through the arch. Behind it, the mass of people followed in the greatest confusion. The multitude which filled the square stopped and waited. The portrait with its followers reached Main Street; but on arriving there, an unexpected surprise stopped the procession. Two ranks of soldiers formed in the Platerías extending beyond Villa Square. The pikes of a squadron of lancers shone in the distance. At the head of this troop was the Commander-in-Chief of Madrid on horseback, waiting with great aplomb and firmness. This man moved forward, followed by two or three others. Signaling with his saber, he gave the order to withdraw to the people carrying the portrait. There was a rapid consultation of looks between them. A civil authority also approached. With the utmost politeness, he told them to return to their respective houses and to cancel their demonstration, because the government was resolved not to let them take another step forward. The appearance of the troops vividly impressed those carrying the portrait; moreover, they had counted on the assistance of the Sagunto Regiment, which was confined and very well-guarded in its barracks.

Nonetheless, the crowd tried to advance, declaring that the demonstration was purely moral; they said that they did not plan to create a disturbance, nor was their attitude aggressive, and that it had no other object than to pay tribute to the hero who had given liberty to the country.

"Go home! Take the portrait back," said Morillo resolutely.

Defense was impossible. They had no weapons. The Government's anticipated weakness had turned into unyielding firmness. Some began to desert, parading through Milanesas Street and San Miguel Plaza. The portrait rested on the ground and was moved back and forth insecurely in the hands of its bearers, they spoke up, but it was useless. The people began to retreat. Some were shouting, and there were those who wanted to put up resistance against the troops.

Meanwhile, the crowd which occupied the plaza remained still. Who was the man who stood up among them, gesturing for attention and speaking to the applause of the crowd? The speaker, undoubtedly, spoke well. His words were received with great acclamations, but the continuous shoving and the shouts of those who were stepped on and crushed, did not allow him to release his feelings. Someone pleaded for silence, but silence in the entire square was impossible. Perhaps those who were arguing with the authority near the arch retreated on observing that the troop did not yield. Confusion then reached its maximum. The speaker continued his philippic, but he continued to incite the people not to yield in their determination to carry out the demonstration. He was flushed and eager. Each of his words was a whiplash which stimulated the masses to move forward.

Meanwhile, the troops advanced, clearing the square. Some were so daring that they put up resistance in front of the horses and shouted insults at Morillo and his men.

"Find the ones who are shouting," ordered the leader of the pike detachment.

The throng milled around. Many ran to escape. Others turned around and were dragged by the surge or, in a state of confusion, were undecided as to what to do. Lázaro stopped speaking.

"Who was shouting?" asked the Captain. "The ones who are shouting. Seize those who are shouting."

Lázaro tried to flee, but the strong arm of a soldier firmly detained him.

"Seize those who were shouting. That is the speaker. That one!"

Lázaro was passed from one strong hand to another even stronger one. He barely realized that he had been arrested. He thought that they would soon release him, and tried to free himself, although in vain.

"Keep moving, get going. Out of the square," continued the Captain.

And he was well obeyed because the people fled at full speed. The procession broke up. The portrait was left in shreds in the center of the square; the troops took possession of all entrances to it.

What became of Lázaro? A quarter of an hour later, honorably guarded, he entered through the gates of the Villa prison and was honorably handed into an extremely sad, dark, and filthy cell.

Chapter XIII

THE EXPECTED ONE DOES NOT ARRIVE

THE ARRIVAL OF AN UNTIMELY VISITOR

Of all the ways that the spirit employs to torment someone, the most terrible is waiting. There is no remedy for it. It seems that it should be easy to resolve oneself not to wait, removing the expected thing from one's imagination and living only for the present moment, without that painful anxiety keeping one off-balance.

When one waits in expectation, hours seem like centuries. When one waits for that which should have already arrived, the hours fly like seconds. At ten o'clock Clara's spirit was in suspense, quivering and attentive, full of restlessness and anxiety. Ten o'clock passes and the traveler does not arrive. The clock flies from eleven to twelve and from twelve to one. Pascuala was very fearful because the clamor of people in the street was increasing by the hour. The two women, seated in the inner room, said nothing; the maid did not tell those tales about nymphs and dragons which she had learned in her town; nor did the orphan laugh with the frank expansiveness and natural simplicity of her character. The two were very quiet. They were looking at each other with anxiety when suddenly a noise was heard on the stairway. After making certain that it was not what they were waiting for, one fell into indifferent depression and the other into serene, melancholy, and hidden restlessness.

Clara, at daybreak, entered the period of conjectures in which the spirit produces every imaginable torment. What had happened to him? Did the coach overturn? Could he have run into some thieves carrying large blunderbusses. Had he given up the trip? Could it be possible that he had amorous relations with some girl from his town? Was he detained by some faction of royalists? She thought of everything except what had really occurred. In moments like this, it is easy to calm oneself with just a bit of serenity, but no one feels serenity at such a time. A profound blindness takes the place of the normal clarity of understanding. It suffices to reason calmly and say, "He hasn't arrived? Something must have come up. He'll arrive tomorrow." But instead of using this logical reasoning, what one generally thinks is this: "Hasn't he arrived? Well, he has died, they killed him."

Nighttime, moreover, contributes to this torment. The night gives horrible forms to everything, both to material things as well as inner visions. Clara, who had not and would not be able to sleep, kept imagining undefined forms, blood and darkness. Such a situation produces fever. Feverish impatience overpowers the blood, which is agitated and flows as if the velocity of its circulation would speed up the arrival of the expected one. This disappointment of our desire is all the more horrible because it is slow and limitless. Ahead one sees only eternity. The changes that the next day may bring do not come to mind. The night and its loneliness seem to be endless.

The first glimpse of daylight, nevertheless, only increased her sadness. Yesterday! She had been waiting for him since yesterday! She wanted to go outside and run about asking everyone about the unfortunate young man. She opened the balcony and looked out into the street thinking that she was going to see him walk by, and looked over every passer-by. A person standing on the corner attracted her attention. He was looking at her intently. Certain that it was not Lázaro, she turned her face away and paid no more attention to him.

She closed the balcony because she was fatigued and felt an irresistible need for sleep. She went to her room and sitting down on a chair, rested her head on the bed. But instead of sleeping, she began to meditate with as much delirium and restlessness as during the evening. Nor had Elías returned. What could have happened to him? Maybe he had found him, and they were together somewhere.

At this point, Pascuala entered. She was coming in from outside the house. She approached Clara with an impertinent smile adorning the round and vast façade of her face.

"Do you know what has happened?"

"What? What happened?" asked Clara with interest.

"That young gentleman of the other day...well, the soldier...he stopped me at the corner."

"And what does that matter to me?"

"He says that he's coming here."

"Heavens! Here! And why is he coming here? We're all alone."

"Well, he seems to be a very proper gentleman."

"Really? I hadn't noticed."

"Didn't you see him here the other day...when *Don* Elías came home in such bad shape?"

"Yes, he seemed to be a good person. But why does he want to return here?"

"You can very well guess. My, what a tease you are!"

At that moment the pesetas that the soldier had given Pascuala jingled in her pocket. Then they heard footsteps on the stairway, and the bell rang very weakly.

"It's he," said Pascuala.

And before Clara could prevent it, the maid ran and opened the door. The soldier, whom we already know, entered the hallway, took off his hat respectfully, and approached Clara.

"Whom were you looking for?" asked Clara. "He isn't here. He has gone out."

"Not if the person I'm looking for is at home," replied the officer tactfully.

"Who? But whom were you looking for?"

"It is easy to understand that I'm not looking for that old man whose character repels rather than attracts people."

"But what do you mean? What are you here for?" inquired Clara with a slight expression of alarm. "I am alone. Go away."

"That's why I'm not leaving."

"If you don't leave, I'll yell, I'll scream," said Clara, resolved to carry out what she was saying.

"Then, we'll quarrel," asserted the soldier with a smile of friendly frankness which in part disarmed Clara's anger.

"For heaven's sake, he's on his way here! But just who are you? Why do you come here? Who gave you permission to enter? You are the one who came here the other day with him. Now, I recognize you, but I don't understand why you come here today. Pascuala! Pascuala!"

"Don't look at me as if I were an enemy. My entrance was unusual, but I'm neither a thief nor an assassin. I come as a friend. I bring peace and friendship. Don't be afraid, Clara. I come as a friend. We already know each other from the day when I came here supporting that poor man."

"Oh, and now you have the right to come here," asserted Clara in alarm. "Get out of here, for heaven's sake! I don't know you, and nothing you've said interests me. If he arrives..."

"That old man doesn't interest me in the least," answered the officer. "Before, he interested me somewhat. I thought that he was your relative, your husband, perhaps. But afterwards, I found out that he is a little tyrant whose only purpose is to torment a poor orphan so that she may die of sadness locked up here. I can't be indifferent to the fact that such a beautiful person, so friendly, so worthy of happiness, is spending her life in the hands of that beast."

"Oh, well, I'm just fine this way. I am very grateful to you for your kindness," answered Clara, "but it isn't necessary. For God's sake, please go!"

"No, I won't leave!" said the soldier, rather heatedly. "I've been worried for some days about the torment that you must be suffering. I feel a very strong desire to free you from that maniac, and I think that I'll achieve this purpose. I have passed by here a hundred times a day, and the gloomy appearance of this house has horrified me. It is a living death for such a beautiful creature. You'll laugh at me, I understand that. This interest I have taken in a person that I saw only once must seem strange to you, but we don't need to talk about that mystery now. What does matter is that you agree to do what I advise you. I want you to know that I have sworn to not let you die here of boredom and loneliness. I am sure that you, who with so much simplicity communicated to me the first time we met your misfortunes, will today have the confidence I need, will know how to appreciate the nobility of my intentions and will not oppose their realization."

Clara didn't know how to reply. She was confused by such generous and brotherly interest from a person whom she had seen so little. This would have inflated the pride of any other woman, but Clara was modest. She reacted with gratitude and shame in the face of that show of affection. She never believed herself worthy.

"I am very grateful to you, sir," she said, "but..."

The fact is that she could not tell him that she was happy and desired to continue that type of existence. What the officer said was true. It was impossible to live in the company of that beast. But was she not awaiting her salvation by means of another person? This thought induced her to reject even more energetically the offers that he was making to her.

"You don't know the person with whom you are living," continued the soldier. "You don't know him. I do. I've learned about his character and his ideas. Not only is he an extravagant and unsociable man, but he is a heartless fanatic, a ferocious man with perverse instincts and terrible plans. No! You can't remain in the custody of that man who is neither your relative nor your friend—he calls himself your guardian to make you a victim of his brutal pride."

Clara understood, by the vehemence with which the young man spoke, that his interest was sincere. She also knew that the picture he painted of the old man was not exaggerated. The stranger acted with the greatest nobility, sincerity, and good faith. He was one of those persons inclined toward difficult adventures that implied the dangerous rescue of suffering people. His chivalrous spirit and kindly heart found in that situation a motive of occupation and he dedicated all his activity toward the fulfillment of that noble purpose. Moreover, a fairly strong sentiment of congeniality toward that poor orphan pushed him to proceed with such diligence. Further on, we shall learn the name and background of this noble gentleman.

"But don't stay here any longer," said Clara. "How can you convince me that you are interested in my welfare, if by staying here you are proving just the opposite? It he arrives and finds you in his home..."

"He'll say nothing. That man is so wretched that he doesn't care about either happiness or your honor. He'll see it all with indifference. You can't count on any protection but mine."

The orphan, hearing these words, felt a chill in her soul. At the moment in which they were spoken they seemed to be a great truth. Her only legitimate and true friend would not arrive. Now there remained no other protection than that of a stranger.

"Only I, but that's enough," continued the young man in an affected voice. Follow the plan that I'll outline for you. Pay that old man no mind. I'll be for you all that a man with a heart and honesty can be. Have faith in me as someone who is going to save you....And now, Clara, I'm leaving. But I will soon return to give instructions to the poor prisoner whose happiness depends on me. How proud this makes me! I shall always be vigilant. If a new misfortune occurs, you will not need to call me. I'll be here to help you and cheer you up. You have no other protection left than mine. Think about it! Good-bye."

The decision of the stranger, who had worked his way into the secrets of the house like a fictional character, was firm. He had decided to undertake a noble adventure, moved by both a feeling of sympathy and his inveterate desire to do good.

If there was a bit of selfishness in him, we'll see it later on.

He was about to leave when Pascuala came out of the kitchen and said in fright, "The master!"

"Don't open the door, said Clara fearfully. "Wait! Hide yourself."

But Elías, who had a key, did not need to have anyone to open the door for him.

"It doesn't matter," said the officer, who was trying to calm Clara.

Coletilla opened the door and entered. He walked with his head down, absorbed in thought. He took some steps through the corridor still unaware of the intruder, but noticed a figure as he reached the end of the hall. He raised his head and saw a young man who respectfully nodded to him.

Chapter XIV

THE DECISION

"What are you looking for? Who are you? What are you doing here?"

"Don't you recognize me? I am the one who some days ago brought you home when you were in bad shape. I came to see if you had recovered completely."

"Yes. I am all right," he replied brusquely. Entering the room where the young man followed him, he said, "Did you want anything else?"

"Nothing else, I'm leaving. I just stopped by," he said with affected naturalness. "I am leaving and repeat that I am very concerned about your health."

"Good. You already told me so the other day," answered *Coletilla*, casting distrustful glances at Clara and Pascuala.

"Can I do anything for you?"

"Nothing more than to leave me in peace. Aren't you going to the procession? It's quite spectacular."

"I am not in the mood for processions."

"So you want to know what's going on in the royalists' houses," added the old man with the bitter and distrustful tone so typical of his character. "There is no conspiracy going on here. And if I were conspiring, I would do it in such a way that the young dandies from the national militia wouldn't catch me."

Clara was trembling. It seemed to her that the officer, offended by that insult, would pull out the saber he was carrying at his waist, and use it on the royalist's head. But he smiled disdainfully and said, "Friend, I see that you misjudge me. You can be assured that I shall not bother to denounce you. What harm can you do?"

"Harm...Me?" replied the fanatic with a ferocious grimace, which for him was the equivalent of a smile.

"The damage you may do will be slight and last for only a short time. That I can assure you. So I am going to do you a favor by leaving. Good day."

He went to the door while trying to express to Clara in a single glance what he had said before with many words, that is to say, that she should confide in him and wait. He would have liked for the young lady to accompany him to the door, but she did not dare to do so. When the soldier was outside, *Coletilla* turned to Clara, and with irritated gestures asked her, "Has that man been here a while?"

"No, sir. A moment before your arrival," responded Clara trembling.

"And why did you open the door for him? Didn't I tell you not to open up for anyone?"

"He came asking for you."

"For me? Rubbish!" answered Elías with fury. "He must be a government spy. I can imagine what the real truth is. He's a fellow who is courting you."

"Who, me? No, sir. I don't even know him, nor have I ever seen him," said Clara, trembling.

"Well, I have seen him hanging around this street. Yes, indeed, I've seen him. Don't deny it! You have dealings with him. You have spoken to him. You invited him here...."

Clara had never seen Elías so angry with her. His accusations so offended her innocence that at that moment she felt what she had never felt before: a secret aversion toward him.

"I have been a father to you, Clara, but you just don't know how to appreciate my protection," continued *Coletilla* with rancor. "You're an ingrate, a senseless woman. You abuse the freedom I give you. You take advantage of my absence from the house. But I swear to you that you'll straighten out. This very day I must make the decision that I had planned. Yes, this very day. Right away."

"I'm telling you that I do not know who that man is, who entered here asking for you. I don't know who he is, nor have I had dealings with such a person."

"Hypocrite! Do you think that I am taken in by your dead fly act? Such a timid girl. But your escapades will come to an end, Clara. You will never again disturb my peace again as you have today. I'm often away, and I don't want this house to become into a den of iniquity during my absence."

Clara couldn't believe those words. As we already know, she was not very skillful in replying when the terrible old man scolded her. And on this occasion, with her honor offended, she could not find suitable words for the occasion. She only denied the accusations and cried, a behavior which the royalist took as the ultimate expression of hypocrisy and deceit.

"Get ready to leave here, Clara. You don't deserve the sacrifices that I have made for you. Now we'll see whether you will buy flowers and arrange ribbons to flirt at the window. From now on you are going to live in the company of some people whose protection you don't even deserve. But they are so charitable that they will accept you out of consideration for me. Get ready! This very afternoon I am going to take you to the home of those ladies and there you will live. They will show you how to be a well-behaved woman and then we'll see if you return to your imprudent ways. We will see whether you depart from the righteous path. You will live with them; you will help them and serve them in their needs and they will teach you what you cannot learn in this house, alone and without direction."

"The Porreño ladies!" thought Clara with horror. They were such proud and conceited women, who always frightened her when they spoke to her, leaving her with a feeling of sadness she could not erase from her mind for many days.

"Those modern ideas," continued Elías, as if speaking to himself, "pervert even the most sheltered girls. These modern ideas, this social leprosy! It spreads itself without our knowing how. It's everywhere! Who would have thought...! It's now seen....Alone in this house...Clara, you'll go to those ladies' home. Bear in mind that you don't deserve it, because they are very important and virtuous people, free from the ills of the day. Imagine that you are entering a haven."

There was no alternative. Without her knowledge the fatal decision that had so frightened the orphan, had been irremissibly made. Clara was going to live with those mysterious ladies in whose house, according to what *Coletilla* was saying, modern ideas had not penetrated. He had wanted to do this for a long time in order to be able to live more at ease. He never would have dared to propose it had not the three venerable matrons, whose generosity never seemed to tire, suggested it to him. It was all settled. So *Coletilla*, after the scene we have described, did not want to delay the decision for another moment. He left for his friends' house to inform them of the decision, leaving Clara behind, overwhelmed by the deepest grief.

Let us say something about Elías' friendship with those three very noble ladies.

At the turn of the century, Elías had been the head majordomo of the Porreño and Venegas household. The ruination of this historic house dates from that same period. *Don* Baltasar Porreño, Marquis of Porreño, who had been an intimate adviser to Carlos IV, initiated a lawsuit against a relative, a descendant of the Marquis of Vedia. This fight lasted ten years and during it Porreño lost almost all his wealth, contracting frightful debts. Later on, he had the misfortune of supporting Godoy in the conspiracy of Aranjuez. Once Carlos IV had fallen, the new prince and heir to the throne missed no chance to do him harm. His brother, *Don* Carlos Porreño, committed the absurdity of becoming a French sympathizer during the war. The protection of Junot and Víctor served only to have him later condemned to perpetual exile.

That illustrious and powerful house reached the ultimate in ruin with the Marquis's death. Its creditors confiscated the family wealth without respecting the coat of arms. After the liquidation of the furniture and real estate, the only thing left for the family was poverty. Upon Fernando's return from France, he forgot that the Marquis had been his enemy in the Aranjuez conspiracy and conceded a pension to his sister. The male offspring of the Marquis had died during a voyage, sailing toward America. Of the ancient and powerful family only three ladies were left; the sister, the Marquis's daughter, and the daughter of his brother, *Don* Carlos, who followed Napoleon and died, it was said, in Prague on the way home from the Russian campaign.

After the sad end of the family, Elías stayed loyal to his old masters. When he returned from the war, he presented himself to those three glorious vestiges and offered his services once more, but the three ladies no longer had any estate to administer. Of their formerly abundant fortune there remained only a few meager wheat fields in the area of Colmenarejo and some vineyards of very little value next to Hiendelaencina. Management was reduced to a quarterly accounting of two tenant farmers who cultivated those properties. But the Porreños, after their decline, considered Elías a good friend and treated him as an equal. Oh, what decline can do! Nevertheless, the old majordomo, even in their conversations, never went beyond the respectful limits which separate "a son of laborers"—as he put it—from three ladies belonging to the most illustrious nobility.

They were not youngsters. The Marquis's sister, named *Doña* María de la Paz Jesús, was a little over fifty, although she was very well-preserved. Her niece—the oldest daughter of *Don* Baltasar—whose name was Salomé, constantly made intricate calculations to see by what manner her years could add up to be only forty. The third, named *Doña* Paulita, could never get rid of the diminutive. Daughter of *Don* Carlos, the French sympathizer, she reached thirty-two years of age on the day of the Incarnation. *Doña* Paulita was a saint.

They lived humbly, almost poorly, but with order. Several times they had suggested to Elías that he bring Clara to live with them for the reason that all alone in his house the girl would necessarily be contaminated by the ideas of the century. *Coletilla* did not accept at first, out of respect, but finally, he accepted the idea, and we have already seen how he was prepared to execute it. Moreover, *Doña* María de la Paz Jesús, who was a woman of great initiative, had conceived of a domestic arrangement very convenient for Elías and also for them. The plan was that Elías would occupy the second floor of their house, which they used for the storage of furniture from the grandiose old house, which they had not wanted to give up.

"Ladies, at last I am bringing the girl here," said *Coletilla*, as he greeted the Porreños.

"Good, friend," exclaimed Salomé, "bring her right away, this very afternoon."

"But, ladies," he continued, "that girl is shameless. You'll need to exercise extreme severity with her. Otherwise, it will be impossible to get good results."

"But what has she done?" exclaimed *Doña* Paulita, the saint.

Elías related the appearance of the soldier in his house. He told of the dangerous antecedents of Clara, of her desire to look attractive, the purchase of flowers, and her mending her dress. The three ladies began to get upset. Salomé intoned a prayer, and *Doña* Paulita made four crosses from her forehead to her stomach and from one shoulder to another.

"Don't worry, friend. We'll mend her ways," said María de la Paz Jesús.

"One can well understand her lewdness. The girls of today..." said Salomé, taking off her glasses, "they are all alike. And...well...since Clarita isn't bad looking...yes...such a sweet little face...shameless and attractive...well, that isn't beauty."

"But, *Don* Elías, is it really true that she has spoken to men?" exclaimed Paz with an archiepiscopal gravity she frequently showed in her speech. "But what kind of demon is that...? But it doesn't matter. We'll mend her ways. We shall teach her how to behave like an honest woman. Ay! decency has gone to the devil. What a century we live in!"

"Oh!" exclaimed *Doña* Paulita, after reciting the Lord's Prayer in a low voice, "these ideas of today...Heavens, what a society! But everything will change; the worst sinners are those who change their ways the fastest. Bring her over, *Don* Elías. I have confidence that that unfortunate creature will follow the righteous path, and she will, perhaps, become a saint. Isn't that what happened to María Egipcíaca?"

Elías showed by a series of nods that he was in agreement with their assessment. He left the house and returned an hour later, with Clara.

To understand what Clara found so intolerable in the royalist's decision, it is appropriate to describe the house in detail and its unusual occupants.

Chapter XV

THE THREE RUINS

The three Porreños lived in a modest house on Belén Street. The house consisted of two high stories, and although old, was not bad-looking, thanks to a recent stucco job. There was no heraldic motto, no doorman with chevrons in the entrance, no team of horses, no livery stable with a mother of pearl carriage, no ostentatious berth. But if on the outside there was no single object which might reveal the very aristocratic origin of its occupants, on the inside, however, were a thousand objects that produced curiosity and respect at the same time.

What had occurred was that during the family's ruination, in that profane liquidation and the embarrassing confiscation which occurred after the Marquis's death, the family managed to save part of the furniture from the old house—which stood on Sacramento Street—and transport it to the new and gloomy dwelling where it was arranged as well as possible. This furniture took up two-thirds of the house and almost the entire second floor, which also belonged to the Porreños. It was impossible for them to render unto the dishonor of an auction those inherited monuments, the witnesses of so much grandeur and misfortune.

In the hallway or anteroom, which was quite spacious, they had placed a bulky closet of darkened oak with Solomonic columns and thick sheets of white metal on the locks and hinges, and at the top, an oval with the Porreño y Venegas coat of arms, which consisted of six red bands in the upper part and on the lower part three flashing badges on silver and green next to the Saracen head encircled by a chain and a motto which read: "On the Bridge of Lebrija I perished with Lope Díaz." (We shall not detain ourselves in a prolonged explanation of this very learned slogan, which undoubtedly alludes to the death of the first Porreño during one of Alfonso VIII's expeditions in Andalusia.)

The walls of that waiting room were covered with portraits of fifteen generations of Porreños forming a historic family gallery. On one side was seen an ancient hero, from the time of our good King Felipe III, with a squalid face, a long and well groomed mustache, a pointed beard, and a ruff with three rows of pleats, in a black costume with some touches of lace, the cross of Calatrava, a sword with a luxurious hilt, and with armor and a chain of the Teutonic order. At his side hung a portrait of an erect lady in a stiff tailored suit, a long underskirt embroidered in silver and gold, and an enormous ruffle whose white and symmetrical folds circled her face like a halo of embroidery. On the other side of the room some white wigs, embroidered dress coats, and knight's shirts stood out; over here, a woman with a little dog, which gracefully straightened out its tail; and over there, an elderly lady with a hairdo two or three stories high, a fortress of rolls, plumes, and pendants. The gallery was a museum of clothes and hairdos, from the simplest and the most elegant to the most complicated and extravagant.

Some of these venerable paintings were pierced in the face; others had faded, and all were dirty, corroded, and covered with that classical dust which antique collectors love so much. It was scarcely possible to walk through the rooms where the three ladies slept, ate, and worked, due to the secular furniture that filled them. In the bedroom there was a double bed that looked like nothing less than a cathedral. Four voluminous columns supported the canopy, from which hung damask curtains whose original colors had faded to light gray with abundant worn spots, and some shameful patches of mending. In other rooms were two carved secretaries with innumerable divisions adorned in tiny decorative figures and inlays of ivory and tortoiseshell. One had a very old and worn figure of St. Anthony in a bright costume and carrying a bunch of flowers of recent creation. Across from it, in what had once been luxurious lignum frames, hung certain Chinese-style sketches, a gift to the sixth Porreño—1548—from his cousin the prince of Antillano, who went with the Portuguese to India. Next to this stood some Mexican vases with odd paintings and intricate symbols which seemed to represent some heresy. According to tradition preserved by the family, these vases, brought from Peru by the seventh Porreño, Admiral and Advisor to the King—1603—, were at first regarded with great fear by the devout wife of that gentleman. She resolved to throw them in the fire, believing that they were diabolical objects, the handiwork of the devil, as revealed by those cabalistic and incomprehensible signs. The only thing that stopped her was the opposition of the eighth Porreño—1632— the one who later became Advisor to the Indies and Lord Chamberlain of our good King, *Don* Felipe IV. Next to the bed stood a studded calf leather armchair, a silent witness of the three past centuries. Upon that durable leather had rested the adorned breeches of a gentleman of the Emperor's house. Perhaps, the armchair had even received the gentle buttocks of some provincial Father, a friend of the family, or perhaps supported the skinny thighs of some member of the Santo Oficio in the good times of Carlos II; and was later the honorable distinction of those persons who wore a tail on the occiput, that always seemed outlined in the frock, together with the rapier.

Not far from this monument stood two or three large chests with locks similar to those on the doors of a fortress. They were true fortresses where silver coins, chinaware, the family silver, and expensive jewelry had been buried. But there was no longer any treasure inside, with the exception of two or three dozen pesetas which *Doña* Paz kept in a stocking for household expenses. On top of these pieces of furniture were placed some empty wardrobes, and empty birdcages, and shelved on the wall was a four-sided folding screen, a piece which stood apart from all the others with its happy and youthful appearance. Its drawings were of French style, which the dynasty had brought to Spain, and on the five canvasses which formed the screen were displayed groups of discreet shepherds and shepherdesses with Watteau-styled wigs, a style which today is drawn on ladies' fans.

There was also—and if we recall correctly, it was in the living room, a clock of the same period with its corresponding gilded fauna. But this clock, which in the good times of the Porreños had been a wonder of accuracy, had stopped at twelve in the evening on the 31st of December, 1800, the last year of the past century. It had stopped, never to run again. This fact was significant in such a household. As of that evening, the clock did not function, and there was no way to make it run a second more. The clock, like its owners, refused to enter this century.

A mystic canvas of the authentic Toledan school occupied the center of the living room, next to the fourteenth Porreño— the happy father of *Doña* Paz—painted by Vanloo. The great painting represented, if our memory does not deceive us, the triumph of the Rosary and was an aggregate of small compositions in the form of an ellipse. In each one was a portrait of a Dominican monk, beginning with Vicenzius and ending with Hyacinthus. In the center was the Virgin with Santo Domino, kneeling. Its only defect was that in the place where the painter had put the head, moisture had made a very profane and ugly hole. But in spite of this, the canvas was the Sanctum Sanctorum of the house and represented the shared sentiments and beliefs of all the Porreños, from the one who perished with Lope Díaz in Andalusia, to the three ruined ladies.

In the room of the devoted one—we describe it based on hearsay because no male mortal could ever enter it—there was a Saint Librada, an image of the especially devout and faithful godchild of the third Porreño—1465. Over the years, good care was taken of it; it was put back together with enormous chunks of wax. The Saint was left with a neck so twisted that it evoked pity. Next to the bed—a modest and chaste piece of furniture, which we mention with respect—was the prie-dieu which no one, not even her aunts, approached. On it was raised a beautiful ivory Christ, disfigured by a white satin shirt embroidered with sequins and a very wide ribbon and a large bow which hung from his feet. The prie-dieu was a beautiful carving from the Sixteenth Century, but a carpenter of the Nineteenth Century, in order to repair it, had added pine strips more suitable for an olive barrel. The cushion where the saint's knee fell for four hours a night was so old that its origin was lost in the obscurity of time. Its color was not definable, and the wool stuffing was quickly falling out through large tears.

All of these relics, a memory of past glories, institutions, persons, and days past, had a respectable and solemn appearance. On entering that house and viewing those objects deteriorated by time, beautiful even in their state of decadence, the visitor was overcome by surprise and veneration. But the relics, the ruins which produced the greatest impression were the three noble and deteriorated ladies who lived there and who, in the moment of our story corresponding to this chapter, were seated in a row in the living room. María de la Paz, the oldest, sat in the center, and the other two on either side. One of them held in her hand a prayer book; another was sewing; and the third was embroidering with silver thread a small silk baby's dress which undoubtedly was destined to cover the flesh of some wooden saint. The three, seated with symmetry, silent and tranquilly absorbed in their prayer or work, presented a somber, glacial, and dismal picture. We shall describe the principal characteristics of this illustrious trinity.

María de la Paz—let us forget about using the honorific *Doña*, because we heard by coincidence that it pleased her to divest herself of that title—, the younger sister of the Marquis de Porreño, was one of those women who appears to be forty, and in reality is older than fifty. She was tall, stout, and robust, with a round face and prominent bosom, which protruded more than usual due to her peculiar insistence on adjusting it to the height used in the time of María Luisa. Her face, perfectly spherical, rested directly on her bust. Her hair, still black in spite of the years, was divided in two parts above the forehead, covering both ears and gathered at the back. Her nose was small and purplish. Her mouth was even smaller and so round that it resembled a red button. Her eyes were not very large. Her chin was prominent, and she had sharp teeth, one of which always protruded when she closed her lips tightly. From the visible end of her ears hung two enormous filigree earrings which resembled two weights designed to maintain her head in balance. On the left side, she had a large and very black wart, which looked like an offering placed on the altar of her face through the piety of some Catholic. Her body formed great harmony with her face, and on her small, red, fat hands shone many rings whose settings had been skillfully changed for imitation stones. Let us cast a veil over these sorry sights.

Salomé was entirely different. Just as the figure of Paz had nothing of aristocracy, that of Salomé was what tradition or fashion qualifies as aristocratic when it is beautiful. She was tall and thin, thin as a ghost. Her yellow face had been, in the time of Carlos V, a very beautiful oval. Now, it was an oblong thing which measured a quarter of the distance from the roots of her hair to her chin. Her skin, which had been finest jasper, now resembled the parchment certificate of an old patent of nobility, and the years were traced on it with wrinkles so marked that they resembled a scribe's complicated rubric. Who could say how many years were recorded there! Her arched brows were very delicate. Once they had curved smoothly, but now they were scanty and moved above the large eyes like two snakes. Her eyelids, blackened and almost transparent, were lowered like two floodgates when Salomé wanted to express disdain, which happened frequently. Her nose was sharp, and so thin and bony that her glasses constantly slid down it for lack of anything to cling to. This moved her to tie them behind her head with a ribbon. Finally, so that this effigy might be even more singular, her upper lip was enhanced by black down, symmetrically balanced by two or three hairs below the chin, of a length and vigor which any Muscovite might envy.

Chronic spite had given her countenance a repulsive grimace and a sinister tic which harmonized very well with the contour of her figure and with her attire. Her hair disappeared under a headdress of most unfortunate aspect, and her neck, which had been compared to that of a swan by a plaintive poet during Comella's time, was now thin, sinuous, and unadorned. The bones, tendons, and veins stood out like a bundle of cords; and when she spoke with emotion, those badly covered anatomical parts moved and shook like the sticks of a loom. Below all this the bosom of the lady extended in a narrow space, whose form, in that period, could not have been appraised from without by even the most experienced geometrician. Further down, the anatomy of her waist and body was also inaccessible to induction. This apparatus, as a result of nervous seizures, had reached the most complete state of inactivity. She wore a long black dress. Between the folds of a very wide kerchief of the same color emerged two extremely elegant white hands, admirable in form and smoothness. But her hands were not the only beautiful thing that one noticed in that ruin, no. She possessed another feature a thousand times more beautiful than her hands. It was her teeth. Her teeth saved her from general disaster and were beautifully preserved, with perfect regularity, gleaming enamel, and impeccable form. Oh! the lady's teeth were divine. They alone reflected the old splendor. When that vestige of the past was smiling—a rare thing—, when she was showing the two rows of teeth of incomparable beauty, contrasting with her disagreeable countenance, it seemed that beauty, happiness, and youth shone from her mouth, or that a light illuminated her face.

Doña Paulita, who never was able to rid herself either of the *Doña* or the diminutive, in no way resembled either her aunt or cousin. She was a saint, a dear saint. Her gestures were in harmony with her character, so much so that to see her and to feel the desire to pray an "Our Father" were one and the same thing. She constantly stared at the floor. Her voice possessed a nasal and uninflected timbre, like that of an altar boy with a cold. When she spoke, which was often, she did it in a "mechanical" tone, like children reciting their lessons—in the tone with which litany and praises to the Virgin Mary are recited. Watching her attentively, one observed that the mystical aura which shone from her was due more to a habit of facial expressions and attitudes than to a natural and congenital behavior. But do not assume that because of this she was a hypocrite; no, she was a real saint, a saint by conviction and zeal.

She possessed a remorseful and unpleasant countenance, pale, with circles under her eyes, and a coarse and dark complexion, and the space around her eyes looked discolored, as if she had just stopped crying. Her eyebrows were very dark and thick. Her mouth was a little large and had a certain inherent grace, almost disfigured by the remorseful pursing of her lips, formed by the silent modulation of holy words.

Anyone worthy of the singular privilege of being looked upon by her would have noticed in her eyes the inalterable firmness and glacial expression which are the most distinctive characteristics of the eyes of a wooden saint. But there were moments to which only the author of this book can testify. There were moments, we state, in which the pupils of the saint radiated extraordinary light and heat. It is indisputably true that the soul burning in divine love always manifests itself in a mysterious way and with symptoms that the superficial observer cannot appreciate.

Her dress was modest and nunnish, making it impossible to certify that beneath her veil there was anything resembling a head of hair, although we dare to guarantee that she had one, and a beautiful one at that. Her height was only average, and in spite of the modesty, scant elegance, and lack of *conceit* with which she dressed, it was certain that a worldly topographer, called in to appraise the shape of that saint, would not have found himself with such a lack of data as in the case of her illustrious cousin, the cardboard-like María Salomé.

Having met this illustrious trinity, we should recall some historic antecedents. Back in the 1790's, the Porreños had been rich. They displayed great pomp and enjoyed importance in the Court. Paz was then nineteen years old, so fresh, robust, and ruddy that a poet of the period compared her with Juno. Her cousins used to say secretly that she was very haughty, and her father, the fourteenth Porreño, assured us that there was no Prince or Duke worthy of such a flower. Her marriage was arranged with a young man of the illustrious house of Gaytán de Ayala, but it so happened that this fellow did not care for Juno; thus, the wedding was a dream. It is impossible to describe the pain that the unhappy girl experienced when María Luisa, one evening in the house of the Duchess of Chinchón made, with her usual malice, a rather spicy appraisal of our goddess's corpulence and plumpness.

This, nevertheless, was not an obstacle, to Paz's marriage, to an Irish gentleman in the employ of the English Embassy being agreed upon four months later. But the devil, who does not sleep, caused some difficulties at the last moment. The fourteenth Porreño was a Christian, very old and fearful of God; and a certain friar of the Order of Mercy, who used to visit the house every night and drink a cup of chocolate there, was bent on proving with the authority of San Anselmo and Orígenes that the little Irish gentleman was a heretic and nearly a Jew. The susceptible conscience of the Marquis was aroused, and after he preached a consolatory sermon to Paz, she was left without a husband. In this sad state, she became fatter and fatter, and she could not conceal this misfortune, even by lowering the waistlines of her dresses. Finally, in December of 1795, Paz married an elderly and bothersome relative who committed the singular absurdity of dying seven days after the wedding, leaving his wife stouter, but not pregnant. On the feminine branch, the Porreños remained without succession, which made the elderly Marquis, during his spells of melancholy, cry like a baby, foreseeing the sad termination of his glorious lineage.

Then the old man died. His son, *Don* Baltasar, Salomé's father, inherited the estate; and for her, whose beauty was noteworthy, the father had made marital plans which were expected to remedy the ruination that already threatened him. The litigation began to appear formidable, sinister, and horrifying, like a monster with multiple limbs. It had taken possession of the house, narrowing, devouring, and consuming it. A lawsuit is like a conflagration, but more terrible because it is slower. The illustrious house began to crumble. It was useless for them to prop it up here and there. The house was collapsing because the horrible monster did not cease its destructive activity. The only thing *Don* Baltasar managed was to conceal his ruin. No one believed that the powerful house was being devoured by creditors. Only Elías Orejón, who enjoyed without salary the pre-eminence of intendant, knew about it. *Don* Baltasar placed his hope in Salomé, whose basket hairdo had certainly pleased the young Duke of X—who was looking for a wife in the society gatherings of the aforementioned Duchess of Chichón.

Salomé was then a sylph. Nobody was her equal in elegance and delicacy. She dressed with the utmost grace and simplicity and danced the minuet in such a subtle and agile way that it seemed less earthly than is normally possible in the human figure.

The Duke fell madly in love with her. He got one of the most irritating poets of that time to write some amorous stanzas, which the passionate young man smoothly slipped into Salomé's hands as she left a dance. We are sorry not to have these stanzas at hand, because they are a significant and worthwhile document. The young girl answered in pure prose, but her style was no less expressive. They became friends. From friendship, they passed to courtship, and from courtship to wedding plans. *Don* Baltasar now felt confident about the financial situation of his house, but he received a terrible setback. Suddenly, the Duke and Duchess of X—opposed the marriage of their son. Salomé stayed in bed seven days with a toothache. Her father humbly listened to the sermon which the friar spat at him by way of consolation, and Elías Orejón immediately read to him some horrifying accounts that affected him like poison.

The young girl then began to lose weight. Through a friend of the family we ascertained that before the basket hairdo, which had strongly impressed the young Duke, there were reasons to believe that a lieutenant of the Royal Guard who paced Sacramento Street at least one hundred times a day was not entirely indifferent to Salomé. It is also a certainty that Salomé spent many evenings crying, and that the friar and the Marquis had intervened in the matter. The lieutenant was sent to Peru, and nothing more was known of him.

It is impossible to express what the poor soul of the young Porreño suffered from the terrible blow of the wedding cancellation. She was expecting I don't know what from that marriage. The mysteries of women! She cried for the lieutenant and raved for the young Duke. From those days on, the changes became apparent that led her to the state in which we know her. Indifference, bitter disdain, and impassivity appeared. Finally, they took complete possession of her spirit. As years passed, she became the most disagreeable person with the most disturbing behavior that one might imagine—she, who once had such a flexible character, such amiable behavior, such soft and admirable ways of winning people over.

On the other hand, *Doña* Paulita had always found consolation in her religion. Since childhood she had the reputation of being an angel. She was always praying and singing in choral style, imitating what she heard at Las Carboneras. On Sundays, she said Mass at a small altar which she had made herself. She also preached on top of the table to the great delight of the servants who came to hear her from all four corners of the house. As she became older, she manifested horror at *sarao* dances and theatres. The only thing which pleased her a little was the bullfight to which her father, a great *aficionado*, used to take her. She only attended the theatre when some religious *auto* of the Crucifixion was presented during the feast of Corpus, and then always with her confessor's permission.

At eighteen years of age, she listened with horror to the proposal of the fifteenth Porreño, her uncle, that she marry him.

"I," she said, "will be a daughter of Jesus Christ, or I shall live at home apart from the world, seeking in it a bulwark against the devil."

"All right, my child, if that is your pleasure," said her
uncle, "so it will be."

With the years her devotion increased, not a hypocritical
but a true devotion; legitimate, religious fervor. She had great
visions. When Lent arrived she disciplined herself, and the
servants said that in the late hours of the evening they heard
blows which she inflicted on herself. During the period of
decline, when they lived on Belén Street, she used to visit the
neighboring Gongoran nuns and converse with them for hours
at a time. She consulted them about her visions and counter
visions, relating her ecstasies and rages of divine love. On
other days, she arrived hurriedly to tell them how she had felt
some terrible temptations, but by drinking vinegar, had gotten
rid of them.

In this manner she spent the days in delicious
communication with the unknown, the same way in times of
splendor as in the days of decline.

These three fallen angels led a monotonous and gloomy
existence. Their house was the house of boredom. It seemed
that the three bored each other mutually and separately.

We have forgotten about another important tenant. It was
a delicate example of the canine race, a little dog who
represented the irrational element in the house. However, this
creature never showed the restlessness and joy inherent in his
age and breed. On the contrary, he was as melancholy as his
owners. In times of prosperity, there had been many dogs in
the house: two lap-dogs, a pointer, and six or seven retrievers
that accompanied the fourteenth Porreño when he hunted on the
estate of Sanchidrián. The canines disappeared with the decline
of the house, some due to death, and others because of the
implacable destiny of the family which separated them from
their most loyal friends. But in their decline, the three ladies
could not manage without a dog. It is a known fact that one
day, *Doña* Paz, coming from a visit to her friends, Las
Carboneras, passed through the Puerta del Sol and saw a man
who was selling some lap-dogs just a few days old. She
approached him with emotion and a certain shame, purchased
one for eight *cuartos*, and carried it off under her cloak.

Once the dog was installed in the house, Salomé gave him
a name, recalling mythological and pastoral lucubrations which
poets of the time of Chinchón had presented her with their
verses. She gave him the classical name Batilo.

This unfortunate creature was, at the time of our
description, stretched out at the feet of María de la Paz,

resembling in its posture the dogs or pups that sleep the slumber
of inert marble at the feet of the reclining statue of a sepulcher.

The Porreños used to rise at seven in the morning, drink
chocolate of the cheapest kind, and go to the Góngoras church.
They heard three Masses and part of a fourth. It it was Sunday,
they made confession. Afterward, they returned home. *Doña*
Paulita generally remained in the locutory in order to speak to
the wounds of Saint Francis. At one, they ate—there was no
maid—a decent stew which contained less beef than lamb and
some dishes prepared by the culinary instinct, not education, of
María de la Paz, who considered that having to enter the
kitchen was the worst of humiliations. Then, they did their
chores. Once a year, they visited a certain elderly countess
who maintained some sort of friendly relationship with them in
spite of their misfortune. At nightfall, they prayed as a trio for
a period of two hours and then went to bed. On submerging
themselves in those architectonic beds, true monuments of days
past, the three vestiges of the renowned Porreño family,
strangely alive in our days, seemed to weary of the modern
world and to return to their own century.

Let us conclude: the most inalterable harmony apparently
reigned among them. They seemed to have only one thought
and will. Paulita's asceticism was transmitted to the other two,
and Salomé's bitter misanthropy was similarly repeated in the
others. Happiness, pain, altercations of passion, and sentiment
were unknown in that region of apathy. The unity of the trinity
was a mystery. During normal periods of life, the three were as
one; the old regime manifesting itself in an equilateral triangle;
boredom was depicted in three different ways, but was
essentially the same.

Chapter XVI

THE EIGHTEENTH CENTURY

These were the venerable matrons with whom our poor friend Clara was going to live, and they were in the situation we described as Elías brought his adopted child into their living room. He stopped before the three ladies, bowing deeply. At the same time, the three women directed their most inquisitive stares at the face of the unhappy girl, who, with eyes downcast and soul oppressed, was unable to say a word.

"Is this the child you have entrusted to us, *Don* Elías"? asked María de la Paz Jesús.

"Yes, ladies. Since you are so kind as to accept her here...I hope that she will be grateful for such an honor and will respond to it with good behavior."

"One must correct oneself, child," said Paz. "And if it is true what *Señor* Elías has told us about you...and it must be true, if he says it...be seated."

The two visitors sat down on two benches, magnificent relics of the seventeenth century.

"Yes, it is true," said Salomé, with disdain and a certain fatuity. "You must mend your ways. This house, child, imposes on him who inhabits it very sacred duties. We do not permit the slightest scandal, and when we protect," she stressed the word *protect*, "a person, we begin by teaching what is owed to the protectors."

"These modern ideas," added Paz, "are everywhere, child. I am not at all surprised that their contagious influence has reached you. There is no longer any religion; men run uncontrolled toward their ruin; and if God is not merciful, the whole world will come to an end. You have to realize, child, that you have left a world of slime to enter another world, a more perfect one. God has enlightened your good guardian by placing you among us so that we can free you from the infernal ideas of the day."

She continued rambling on about the ideas of the day with arguments so strong and with such vehemence of style that Clara felt her curiosity awakened. Clara raised her eyes and began to look with astonishment at the Porreño effigy from whose mouth came such frightening eloquence.

"You are so good...! You are the only persons who can offer some consolation among the dangers of the day," said *Coletilla* with a voice less harsh than usual, since he was affable only when dealing with the Porreños. "You will make her understand what you have been and what you still are, because, although this world is turned upside-down, there are people left from that period who are still as great and noble as they were then. Clara, I want you to realize that you are living with the most worthy and elevated ladies of Spanish greatness who, besides virtue, possess all those qualities of the soul which distinguish them from persons of the lower class to which we belong."

María de la Paz swelled with pride, with all the elegance she was capable of. She breathed deeply and looked to one side and then another with perfect majestic royalty. Salomé looked on with afflicted calm at the mended and threadbare tapestries, the rickety and broken-down furniture. *Doña* Paulita gave a mystic sign and continued in silence.

Coletilla, upon expressing such a great thought stood up. Bowing to the ladies, he left, uttering something to the oldest of the three. Clara watched him leave. That man, who had inspired so much fear and who had always been a tyrant to her, in that moment resembled a guardian angel who was abandoning her. She felt an impulse to run and embrace him in order to leave with him, but she looked on in silence. When he had gone, she observed the three old women with terror, and two tears of grief and anguish ran down her cheek.

"Don't cry, child," said Salomé, "the sentiment that you manifest for your benefactor is wholesome, but what good are those tardy tears after having abused his goodness and having put the dignity of his house in danger?"

"I, lady?" exclaimed Clara in astonishment.

"Yes, you," affirmed *Doña* Paz, "the young people have lost their morals. It doesn't surprise me. We hope, nevertheless, that you will mend your ways. It is quite clear...with the ideas of the day. What could you do?"

"One must forgive," said *Doña* Paulita with a bittersweet and high-pitched voice which seemed to come from the depths of a church collection box.

"Yes, forgive, but one must also mend one's ways," indicated Salomé with the aplomb of a legislator. "If not, where would we end up, because forgiveness without correction produces worse effects than not forgiving."

"That is a point," answered the devout one, "difficult to resolve and which can lead us to fall into heresy. Forgiving is good in itself and by itself, as Father Antonio proved to me the other day."

"But, sister, what good is it to forgive if the evil is not corrected and if the evil persists?" said Salomé, becoming

interested in the controversy which altered for a few minutes
the stifling harmony of the trinity.

"Forgiveness in itself is enough to produce the effectual
grace in the forgiven one," replied the devout one, "and if it is
so, that the forgiven amend only with grace, then the correction
of the forgiver is ineffectual for the forgiven."

We forgot to say that *Doña* Paulita knew a little Latin and
that during the period of decadence she had devoted herself to
reading the *Florilegio Sagrado* and the *Theasaurum Breve
Patrum ac Sententiarum*.

The controversy concluded and María de la Paz, who
inclined more to sermons than to theological doctrine,
continued to harangue Clara, who, seated like a delinquent on
the bench, was terrified in the presence of such severe judges.

"The reputation of a woman," said the matron, "is a very
fine glass which fogs with the slightest breath of air. That
reputation which does not protect itself is not protected. We
have seen very honest women who, by not caring for their
name, have seen it stained for no reason. Reputation comes
first: take care of your good name, and if not, you'll have
nothing left, and even your own innocence will not console
you."

These doctrines on reputation belonged to the friar of the
Order of Mercy, who *in illo tempore* frequented the house. His
argumentation remained present in Paz's memory, and from
then on, she missed no occasion to bring it up, believing that
she was uttering from her mouth the same wisdom. The devout
one manifested with a "nonetheless" that she was not in
agreement with that doctrine, but the sermon, upset by this
small incident, then continued for a long while.

"And if not, tell me, child," said Paz, "what purpose does
a woman have in paying attention to the words of men, to those
whom the devil elects to propagate these modern ideas? You,
what do you aspire to on this earth? Due to your origin, to your
upbringing, you can't aspire to occupy a place in the world
which would allow you to do good for the less fortunate. Let's
see. I shall try to find out what your thoughts are on certain
things, child. What do you hope for, what do you aspire to,
and in what way do you intend to conduct yourself in this
world?"

Clara didn't know how to answer these questions.

"Come now, answer," said Salomé with a tone which
indicated great desire to hear an absurdity.

"Say something, sister," the devout one exclaimed through
her nose.

"I...," answered Clara, after a long pause in which she tried to control her disturbance, "I...shall tell you...I am...a woman."

Paz nodded her head, a sign of assent, and looked at her cousins in a way which indicated the profound truth of Clara's reply.

"Come on, child, what do you intend to do in this world? How do you expect to live in the future? How? Let us see," repeated Salomé, vehemently hoping that Clara would not easily find the right answer...

"I...," answered Clara, "what I desire is, well, to live...."

Paz again inclined her majestic head in a sign of approval.

"And, nothing else?"

"To be good and..."

"And what?" insisted Salomé, provoked by the judgment and discretion which the defendant had shown in the previous matters. "And what else? And hasn't something for the future occurred to you? Haven't you hoped to see yourself in another position, in another condition than the one you now are in?"

Clara continued to not understand.

"Well, what we mean," added Paz, "is whether you hadn't thought about being happy in some other way, to imagine that it could be useful at the same time...well...because the young girls today possess certain thoughts about life and society which we need to analyze in you."

"How," Salomé asked, "do you believe that a woman ought to live in the world? How do you expect to live in society in order to serve it and to be useful to it?"

"Oh, yes," said Clara brusquely, as if a sudden ray of light had enlightened her understanding, suggesting an idea that would please the ladies.

"Let's see, how?"

"Let's hear about it."

Clara had a very great natural feeling. She evoked everything and thought what to her seemed to be the destiny of women. She understood that if there were not marriage the world would end. She recalled having thought on various occasions that by marrying, a woman would become what a woman ought to be. With this dose of logic she ventured to give an answer to her judges, certain that the three would be very satisfied and pleased.

"Let's see, child. Tell us now."

"What must a woman do in society in order to serve it and be useful in it?"

"Get married," said Clara, with the utmost simplicity. And at the very moment she uttered these words, she became terrified about what she had said, and blushed.

The reader will have observed, if he has attended some bombastic sermon, that at times the preacher, not knowing what means to use to move the female audience, will raise his arms, roll his eyes, and with a tremendous voice, name the devil, declaring that he is going to carry them off to hell in his knapsack. You probably also have observed how panic spreads among the devotees: one cries, another shouts, this one faints, that one starts to cross herself, and the whole church echoes with alarmed voices, the stamping feet of the hysterics, a murmur of sighs, and a tingling of rosary beads. Well, the effect produced in the three ladies by Clara's reply was entirely like that of the apostrophes of a bedeviled preacher in the sheltered, matronly audience of a novena.

"How awful!" exclaimed Paz, clasping her hands together.

"Heavens! Heavens!" said Salomé, covering her ears.

"*Et ne nos inducas*," professed the devout one, raising her eyes to Heaven.

There was a moment of confusion. The three stared at one another in astonishment. *Doña* Paulita fell back. *Doña* Paz shuddered in her seat, and it is still rumored that Salomé's yellowish face turned light purple. For that to occur, it was surely necessary for all the blood in her body to be divided between her two cheeks. It is said that even Batilo, the most taciturn of all the dogs, participated in the general opinion. He raised himself on his paws, extended his snout, and barked.

After the first moments of confusion, Paz caught her breath and said in a broken and angry voice, "Child, those ideas do not surprise me. We knew about you from hearsay. Now I understand your behavior....It is quite clear now....Oh! You require a strict upbringing."

"But ladies..., I...What have I said...? I," stammered Clara very upset. "A woman—if she marries—but do you mean that to marry is to offend God?"

"No, madam, no," answered the matron. "Marriage is a very important thing; without marriage there wouldn't be a world. But what surprises us is to see a girl of seventeen thinking only about getting married."

"But, if I haven't thought..."

"Don't interrupt me, child....Thinking of marriage! What other craziness from someone who at your age thinks only about getting married. So it is clear that you are very fond of men...that you are looking for them."

"Madam, I have not looked for any man," said the girl in anguish.

"We know everything, but you are mistaken if you think that we are going to tolerate your scheming here."

Clara's heart was filled with bitterness upon hearing those words. She was unable to control her emotions, and burst into tears.

The three displayed extreme cruelty in tormenting her. We cannot explain this. Was it, perhaps, the effect of seclusion and the dryness of spirit produced by the lack of love and enjoyments of life? Without doubt, the three mummies were unable to bear the thought that anyone might aspire to happiness.

Doña Paulita, who had it on the tip of her tongue to reprimand Clara, was moved on seeing her cry and consoled her by saying, "Mary Magdalene sinned and was forgiven. What you need now is sincere repentance."

"But what am I to repent of?" said Clara sobbing.

"Heavens! What a reply, so common today...and so...liberal!" exclaimed Salomé, who thought she had made a witty remark.

"There is no excuse for the false pride which you have demonstrated in this matter," said Paz with contempt.

"When older persons tell you that you are wrong," added the other, "they know why they say it, and you should behave and be quiet."

"But oh...! I don't know how I have offended anyone."

"When they tell you have, there must be reasons for it."

"But I have a peaceful conscience."

"It would be more peaceful if you did not answer back when your superiors say something...."

"Authority, child," exclaimed Paz, "authority is necessary....You have already sufficiently demonstrated the terrible influence which the ideas of today have produced. Satanic pride, at rebelling against your superiors, contradiction...This is unbearable. In this way society will head toward its ruin. But we will bring you to the righteous path."

"For the present," said Salomé, "be careful how you look out the windows. It remains definitively prohibited for you to go near a balcony or window, or for you to open the door to the stairway."

"And you must speak only when you are asked to."

"You have to get up at four in the morning. Laziness is the mother of all vices."

"I get up at that same hour, sister," said the devout one. "I shall provide you with the opportunity, at that hour, to keep your mind on holy things."

"And see if from now on you can be careful not to say those terrible absurdities which you have just uttered."

"She will not return to her old ways," *Doña* Paulita said in a sudden fit of compassion. "I know that she'll not return to her old ways. I am confident that she will be good and obedient to others; others worse than she have become saints."

"Be careful how you speak to anyone who comes to this house. You will do the work that you are ordered to do," continued Paz adding an article to that unalterable code of behavior.

"But not in excess," *Doña* Paulita pointed out officiously, "work is good to drive away occasions for sinning, but in excess, it is bad."

"It will not be in excess. Moreover, you'll have to try to erase from your mind everything you have thought of up to now. Be careful about the ideas of the day which have brought you to this haven of good principles! Forget the past; and since you are now entrusted to our guardianship for the rest of your life, you ought to think only of behaving yourself. As you have had the misfortune of losing your parents, we, being the authority that you need so much, shall guide and reform you."

The orphan lowered her eyes and sank into a profound depression. For life! At that moment she wanted to die. She did not look at the three harpies, nor did she answer them. Her fright was so great that her tears dried up, and she remained in that state of painful perplexity which follows the great crises of the soul.

Let us leave her in her confinement in order to assist Lázaro, who is grieving in another type of prison.

Chapter XVII

THE LIBERAL'S DREAM

When Lázaro saw the door of his prison close and heard the footsteps of his jailer fade away, he looked around and found himself in profound darkness. Light entered through a grating at the top of the wall, but, having come in from the street, he was dazed and could see nothing but shadows. For a moment it was hard for him to comprehend his situation. It seemed a dream. Had his trip to Madrid been real or was it a vision perceived in the prison?

The confused thoughts that crowded the youth's mind in great disorder cannot be described. The first feeling was of great self-pity, which emanated from the ridiculous aspect which the preceding events assumed in his own eyes. He had believed that each step taken in Madrid would be a step toward his future advancement and immortality. The most famous patriotic club in Spain had opened its doors to him, offering him a platform. Fate seemed to have smoothed all his paths, and then...But he could not blame bad luck. Fate had given him the occasion, the place, the audience; it had placed a popular uprising at his disposal. It had arranged for him alone an immense group of aroused listeners disposed to make an apotheosis of the first stranger. Destiny had organized for him a popular demonstration, quick to improvise a hero in every street. Destiny could not be blamed. He was at fault; he who had been born, perhaps, for an obscure life, that of a good artisan, a good laborer, and nothing more. And that presumptuous learnedness, those attempts at childish eloquence, and that premature vanity of the great man were, perhaps, just phenomena born of a series of the fantasies which always accompany youth at the portal of virility.

After these thoughts, he concentrated on his inner monologue. He was imprisoned. They would accuse him of disturbing the peace. What would become of him? Moreover, he had committed a great mistake in not visiting his uncle immediately. What would Clara think?

Submerged in a kind of sepulcher, his imagination began to wander. He was weak and very tired. Out of forty-eight hours he had scarcely slept five; besides, the lack of nourishment had weakened him. Yielding to fatigue he began to doze off, but he did not rest with that slumber which gives repose to the body and spirit, because tension prevented a deep sleep. He slept with a painful and indecisive sluggishness which reflected, in an incoherent and unnatural way, all the images of the previous night's vigil.

In his dream he thought he heard laments echoing off the vaulted arches of the prison. The old Villa prison was an ugly loft, divided into cells where the imprisoned had no comfort, nor were they secure. The jail possessed none of that majestic horror with which poets have painted all prisons. Lázaro imagines it to be a somber building, a gigantic grave of living beings with very high walls, thick and inaccessible towers with large pits of muddy, green water and long rows of dungeon cells, of which the most gloomy and subterranean was his. He thought himself to be many feet below ground. He believed that the grating communicated with some mysterious canal and that behind the walls there would be a water dam. In his dream he believed he heard the sound of a torrent of water: the water was slowly entering, and enormous rats were running between the prisoners' feet, looking for refuge against the shipwreck. Everything looked like the sinister tales he had read about the prisons of the Inquisition.

Later on, the walls seemed to him to be separating and he was in a large room whose walls were painted black. In the background there was a table with a crucifix and two yellow candles, and seated around this table were five men of frightening mien, five inquisitors dressed in the sinister livery of the Inquisition. The men were asking him questions he was unable to answer. Then four fierce-looking fellows approached him, undressed him, and tied him to the wheel of a horrible machine. They turned the wheel; the axles creaked; and his bones cracked. He screamed with pain, that is to say, he tried to use his vocal organs, but not a sound was heard.

Then the scene and the figures changed. They appeared to him as two rows of men covered with black hoods and with slits in their faces for eyes. From the rear came the same men who had interrogated him. One of them was holding aloft the same crucified Christ who presided over the torture. In a lugubrious voice they sang a monotonous song which seemed to come from the depths of the earth, and they all advanced, he among them, in a slow procession. The immense throng stared impassively and coldly at him; a friar, also impassive, stood at his side, speaking into his ear holy words he could not understand. He spoke to him about the other life and the soul.

Then, it seemed to him that the retinue was stopping. Face to face he saw a strange light changed into flame that shot forth from a pile of firewood. The flame increased. It grew until it reached an enormous height. The wood crackled, sparks flew, and a column of black smoke rose to the sky. Then some ferocious men, also dressed in diabolical attire, tied him firmly by his hands and feet. They drew him near the fire heap and threw him onto it. In a moment of sudden and indescribable horror, he felt his hair burning, consumed in a second, his clothes in another second. The soft hairs of his skin creaked tenuously. His flesh boiled with the intense and dissonant sizzle of any humid body which falls into fire. He breathed fire. He drank fire. He changed into living and feeling fire with the pain of his own combustion. He tried to scream. The flame did not carry the sound. He tried to flee; he had no movement; he had no body; he was merely a wick. He tried to pray; he possessed no thought; he was now only an ember, a mass of ashes. The wind crumbled him. He felt himself being scattered in burning space. It burnt up what was already burnt. He was only smoke. He felt himself rising in a blackened spiral and forever burning, forever burning and being consumed; scattered now, annihilated, evaporated, finished..., until he, at last, awoke completely covered with the perspiration of agony.

He awakened because a clamor of voices was heard at his side. The door of the prison had been opened. It was late afternoon. A jailer who brought a lantern lighted the way and guided the other man, who was coming to visit the prisoner. The visitor was *Coletilla*.

Chapter XVIII

DIALOGUE BETWEEN YESTERDAY AND TODAY

Elías stood before his nephew. Lázaro babbled a few words, greeted him incoherently, and finally, after several false starts, managed to say that he had been sure that his good uncle would come. But on seeing that his uncle did not reply or stop frowning, he fell silent, crestfallen and ashamed.

At last, the royalist spoke: "I shouldn't have come to see you, nor even remembered you. You deserve what is happening to you. I have no pity for you, and I am here only to meet you."

"Sir, I..."

Lázaro could find no words of explanation. *Coletilla* had learned from the abbot, *Don* Gil, what had happened to his nephew.

"I know why you are here. A friend who followed you this morning has told me everything. You raised your voice in the middle of a crowd of charlatans, and they took you prisoner. Justice has put you where all charlatans should be."

With each moment Lázaro felt more confused. Those words, spoken when he needed consolation more than censure, completely discouraged him. They showed him that the character of his uncle was the hardest and most inflexible that existed on earth.

"They told me about what you did," continued the old man in his customary hollow intonation, "and when I learned that the delinquent was my sister's son, indignation and shame took violent possession of me. I couldn't believe that you would disturb the public order. If I had known such a thing, you would have remained in the village. I found out more later. I know that you arrived, and instead of going to my house, you went with the nincompoops to The Golden Fountain café, where they made you speak, and you spoke...and you certainly did so badly. Everyone laughed at you. Afterwards, you created a racket all night along with those who stoned Morillo's house.

"Oh, no, sir, not me!"

"However it may be, your behavior was unforgivable. But tell me: Since when did you start to become an orator? I didn't know there was so much eloquence in Ateca. The harvesters probably applauded you in the fields, and, as a result, you thought you were Demosthenes."

The fanatic laughed with such wicked sarcasm that it seemed to Lázaro that some grotesque demon stood before him. Each word opened a new wound in the poor prisoner's heart, and humbled and shamed him even more.

"But I am not surprised at your wild ideas," continued Elías, "disorder spreads everywhere. No wonder that many of these young village pedants have such pretensions, when the wise men of the city offend common sense with their ridiculous debates. No doubt some den in Zaragoza was the cradle of your conceit."

Lázaro's mind rapidly measured the abyss which separated him from his uncle in ideas and sentiment, but he felt dominated by him and unable to contradict him.

"Here," continued the fanatic with his frightening scorn, "here you can speak all you want. No one will bother you. What might happen is that they will believe you to be crazy and take you off to an insane asylum. Half of Spain ought to be there. But no, what am I saying, half of Spain? Only a small part, because almost all of us Spaniards maintain good sense. Only a small segment of wretched men, wretched in judgement, character, in everything, demonstrate with their conduct all the immorality of which nature is capable. But that will end. I promise you that it will end. If not, we must believe that there is no God in heaven, lose faith, and detest all creation. Look, Lázaro," he continued in a vehement tone, squeezing his arm so hard that it made him step backwards, disturbed and perplexed, "Lázaro, if you are one of them, forget that my blood runs through your veins; forget that I am the brother of the woman who gave you life. An abyss separates us. Reconciliation is impossible. If this is so, we must hate each other to death. Flee from me; for me you are not a relative. There are things which are above family ties. Life does not reconcile itself with death, nor light with darkness. Good-by."

He was going to leave, but Lázaro, quivering in astonishment, stopped him and said to him, very disturbed, "But, sir, don't leave me, speak to me! I want us to think alike."

In spite of everything, the old man inspired respect and veneration, and upon hearing his ideas reproached, he felt an impulse of subordination that is natural in a youth of impressionable temperament.

"If you are one of those," continued Elías, "return to your town and don't speak of me; don't say that you have seen me; count me out of your life; because it's true, for you, I no longer exist."

"But let me explain..."

"What are you going to say?"

"I think...you will understand my ideas....I have read, and I have convictions, yes, sir. I am deeply convinced..."

"You poor kid, what can you know...? What convictions can you have? You only know the falsehoods written in four books which ought to be burned in flames fed by the bones of their authors."

Each word depressed Lázaro more.

"Can it be possible," he asked in grief, "that you can take away the beliefs which I have nourished with so much affection and which give me life? No, you cannot; but if, through the strength of your talent you were able to do so, I beg of you not to; instead, just leave me here. Let that abyss, as you call it, keep separating us, and if I am in error...But I am not wrong, I know that I am not...."

"Dreamer, fanatic, idler...! because all this is nothing but vanity, the vanity of Satan," said Elías with severity. Then he added more strongly, "But I'll free you from this misery."

These words were expressed with such a deep accent of conviction that the nephew could not reply to them and felt even worse.

"What do you intend to do? What are you waiting for? Do you think things are going to continue this way for a long time? You are mistaken, because Spain is on the verge of recognizing its error. Look at how it begins to stir everywhere. Hatred for the Constitution beats in every honest heart. You will soon see the King recover his sacred privileges which only God can take away from him, by causing his death."

"Oh, sir! And what this nation has overcome with so much spilled blood! Will it be lost through the pride of a single man? If it were so, I would vigorously deny our lineage, and if Spain let itself to be insulted in this way, it would deserve a better fate."

"Deserve a better fate!" said Elías with the most frightening expression of which his abominable countenance was capable, "it would deserve to be annihilated and disappear from the earth if it did not accept the Absolute King."

"No, I can't believe it although you say it to me. When the day arrives that I don't believe in Liberty, I shall not believe in anything and will be the most despicable of all men. I believe in the Liberty which is in my nature so that I may show it through the personal actions of my life. I, a citizen of this nation, have the right to make the laws which are to govern me;

I have the right to meet with my brothers for the purpose of electing a legislator."

"In order to give you laws and force you to comply with them, there is a sacred man anointed by God."

"No, my brothers and I anoint him. He is King because we want him to be. He is sacred for me if he fulfills the solemn pact which he has made with each and every one. If not, no. But he will fulfill it; he has sworn to it."

"There are oaths," answered *Coletilla* somberly, "whose fulfillment is a crime!"

Lázaro felt a chill in his heart. The confidence with which those words were spoken crushed and depressed him even more.

"And all those heroes," the prisoner dared to say after meditation, "all those heroes, sanctified by History, who live in the memory of good men will always be the pride of mankind, all those who have lived for Liberty and have died for it, martyrs dishonored on their last day by the hand of the hangman but later exalted by Humanity....Do you not want me to love them? I revere them; my own limitations do not allow me to emulate them, but I confess that I would give my life to have the opportunity to be like them. Oh, if Liberty were not the best thing, it would become the most beautiful thing just with the memory of so many heroes."

"And those are your heroes? That is what you admire?" asked Elías.

"Well, whom should I admire? Whom should I admire? Tyrants? Nero killing Seneca; Philip II assassinating Egmont and Lanuza; Louis XV dismembering Damiens?"

"The French must be taught that there should not be another Ravaillac."

"Well, the lesson was not effective, because it has been thirty years since a King died on the gallows."

"Those are your demigods, those men?" exclaimed Elías furiously.

"No, my demigods are not extermination, terror, or assassination. I lament any extremism, but I am not surprised that, on fleeing to escape the atrocities of one extreme, one reaches the atrocities of the other and by so doing pays for the crimes of entire centuries with the crime of one day."

"Don't speak any further," said *Coletilla*, his voice solemn and lugubrious. "I now know that you are one of those men. One of those I cannot describe for lack of harsh words. Your God is a blind spirit of anarchy. The rule of your behavior is scandal. Tell me, brainless one. What is your objective?

What do you see in that future? Suppose you were an outstanding man among those of your kin, the blindest of the blind, the craziest of the crazy, what would you do? What would be your aspiration?"

"I have no illegitimate aspirations. I do not want to thrive in the shade of a tyrant who rewards adulation with money. I do not aspire to anything but the gratitude of mankind, to glory."

"Glory by that path? Glory is not achieved except by following the path of loyalty, by serving God and the King. Moreover, glory on earth consists of being a submissive and an obedient subject, not in vociferating in the streets and squares. The glory that you dream of cannot produce heroes, only charlatans and bandits. Glory comes from fulfilling one's duties."

"Well, I fulfill my duty by trying to emancipate my brothers from an odious tyranny, telling them and convincing them that they are free, equals before God and before the law."

"The first of all duties is to obey what the King commands."

"Blindly?"

"Blindly!"

"I obey the law which is the law, made by those who should make it, those elected by me, my brothers and all the people."

"It does not behoove you to examine the law, but to obey it."

"And what if the law orders me to commit an infamous act?"

"It will not order such an act."

"And if I am commanded to do it?"

"I tell you that you will not be ordered to do such a thing. And if God should permit your King to order something contrary to justice, then do it. For God will punish him and reward you in the next life. You will be a martyr. What greater glory is there? The martyrdom of duty is great and sublime."

Lázaro felt more and more depressed.

"Observe," continued Elías, "the spectacle of this nation. A few soulless people make laws in the name of some absurd principle contrary to nature. God has given sovereignty only to the King. The King was obliged by a mob of rebellious soldiers to swear to obey an abominable code! He swore to it, but deep in his heart he detested it. It could not be otherwise. He is a prisoner, a prisoner of vassals, who toy with him. The

King was obliged to carry out the most horrible farce. Never has royal dignity been so degraded. But he will free himself from this horrible tutelage because Europe, if necessary, will join forces to save Spain. Spain has already saved Europe."

"No, no I cannot believe such perversity," replied Lázaro. That invasion would be more hateful than the invasion of 1808 and more severely punished."

"Have no doubt: the King will be restored to his throne. Moreover, Spain will not rebel, and if it does, it will be in favor of intervention. Do you not see how it shows its will? Can you not see the factions appearing everywhere? The provinces are arming themselves in order to proclaim the Absolute Sovereign, even though the principal factions have not as yet come forward. Spain will rise up against that absurd system, and Fernando will once again be our beloved King."

"Is it possible?" asked Lázaro, discouraged and even more disturbed.

"So very possible that you will soon see it. All of the charlatans who have filled your head with nonsense will flee, ashamed, running to hide their disgrace on foreign soil. Then the righteous hearts will cover themselves with glory; the loyal and patriotic will fight against a licentious common people; they will fight for right, God, and the King. They will live eternally in the memory of all, and their names will become symbols of justice and honesty. These men are the real heroes, Lázaro."

Lázaro was completely overwhelmed. His uncle's words so astonished him that he could only ask hesitantly, "Only those men?"

"Only they."

"No others. Glory is divine. It can only crown justice and duty. Do not expect anything else from this. The whirlwind of that blind mob draws you to it. Go with it. I have nothing more to say to you. Take the road to dishonor and death. Good-bye. Someday you will remember my words."

"No," exclaimed Lázaro, stopping him. "I want you to advise me and guide me....I...even though I have the strength of my convictions..."

"Strength of your convictions?" asked the fanatic, stopping to stare at his nephew with contempt.

"Yes," answered his nephew, "and I cannot lose them. I do not want to lose them."

"Well, stay on that path. Keep away from me and expect only dishonor and obscurity. I leave you to your destiny. Understand that I no longer recognize you. Perhaps they will

have you released. You will go along with them, be defeated
and then...then...you will either flee in disgrace, or will be
given over to the revenge of your unforgiving enemies, who
will punish you."

"But are you leaving me here?"

"Yes, now I know you. I came here only to get to know
you. Now I know who you are. I hope to see you again, at my
house, but only if you have changed."

"Oh, that is impossible! I shall not go there."

"Well, good-by," said Elías firmly.

"Good-by," repeated Lázaro, in distress.

Coletilla left. The young man dared not stop him. He did
not believe he would really leave, until he saw him outside and
heard the jailkeeper closing the door. Then, he had the impulse
to call him back; he shouted, but was not heard; he shed tears
of desperation; he beat violently on the door and the lock with
his hands; and finally, yielding to fatigue and mental upset, he
again fell into that wandering and painful lethargy from which
he had been roused moments before by his uncle's arrival.

Chapter XIX

THE ABBOT

The following day, the house of the three ruins held six persons in its narrow confines: the three Porreños, Clara, and two visitors.

Clara and the devout one were seated in the inner room dedicated to ascetic rituals. The saint, her silent prayers concluded, sat on a stool. Placing a large book on her knees, she was reading with head tilted to one side, brows arched, eyelashes lowered and hands crossed humbly. Clara sat beside her, and since, in her natural weakness, she could not hope to attain that degree of perfection, she was sewing like a sinner, like an unfortunate woman uncleansed by the flames of divine love. The devout one permitted herself only the recreation of telling her companion about the ecstasies and visions that she had had during the night. Then, she began a test about doctrine and asked her several moral and theological questions which Clara answered with simplicity, guiding herself by the little that she knew for certain, and by what her good sense suggested. But to *Doña* Paulita the disciple's answers always seemed poor. She reprimanded her, giving her unusual scholastic gyrations and phrases in explanation, and then called her ignorant and a heretic, greatly frightening and disturbing her.

Suddenly, interrupting her lecture with a reprimand, she exclaimed, "Oh! I forgot a part of my prayer. Now see, you distracted me with your errors, child. You must change your thinking and put aside your ideas...but I tell you that I forgot to pray...for..."

"What have you forgotten to pray for?" Clara asked her.

"I forgot to pray two 'Our Fathers' for the nephew of our good friend *Don* Elías."

"Heavens! What happened to him? What has become of him?" asked Clara intensely, unable to control herself.

"Do not be frightened sister; he has not died," answered the devout one coldly.

"Then, what happened to him?" continued Clara, pale and trembling.

"He's a prisoner in jail, and deserves to be."

"What has he done?"

"He created a disturbance in the streets and spoke in the clubs on matters so perfidious and infernal that to remember them would be horrifying. Last night, *Don* Elías told us everything that soulless youth had done, and I spent some uncomfortable moments listening to it."

For a while, Clara was unable to speak. The sudden news upset her so much that she did not dare to ask more.

"Sister," continued the devout one, "these modern boys! What horrible corruption! That young man must be a monster. Ay! but we should be compassionate, even with the delinquents who err. I do not believe like Orígenes that even the devil should be saved. But we should pity and love sinners, although they be very hardened and rebellious."

"But what has he done?" repeated Clara, making a great effort to conceal her emotions.

"I do not know every detail, but such horrible things...He has done what so many other shameless individuals who live around here have done. This society is doomed. Now let us see, you can quickly learn what I have told you about effectual grace."

"But is he imprisoned?" asked Clara with increased fear.

"Imprisoned, yes, and they will not free him soon. But you are upset....You now have compassion for him, as is natural. Compassion for your fellow man is one of the virtues Tertullian recommends most highly. You are pale, sister. But it is only the effect of compassion. I am going to pray."

Leaving her book, she picked up the rosary and prayed.

Clara lowered her head and continued to sew. Her grief was such that she could not make a correct stitch. She pricked her fingers several times, and the seam turned out so badly that she had to rip it out and sew it again.

Let us leave these two and turn to the visitors. In the living room sat María de la Paz, and Salomé, and before them, standing respectfully, were Elías Orejón and the ex-abbot, *Don Gil Carrascosa*.

Until now, we have not spoken about this unusual person's friendship with the venerable of ladies. Carrascosa, in his capacity of inquisitive abbot, often visited the Porreño house. We even heard from reliable sources that the meddling and audacious little man had played a principal role in the mysterious relations between Salomé and a certain young soldier who was sent to Peru after the young lady broke off with the beardless Duke of X—.

Carrascosa was a cunning and scheming man, subtle as the air, and capable of plotting the most clever entanglements within the very bosom of families. He used to come and go quietly under the pretext of preparing fiestas and arranging religious processions. In brief, he was a third-generation scoundrel. We call him that rather than use a somewhat cruder name, which someone appropriately applied to him and which was rightly remembered by many others.

His friendship with the three old ladies was cut short by the decline of the family, and he visited them only from time to time, reminding them of past times with an eloquence and warmth that displeased *Doña* Paz. Lately, his visits had become more frequent, and his displays of friendship were much more cordial. The day we refer to, he had gone there with *Don* Elías. He had surely gone there for some special reason, because his suit was well selected, and his face more scrubbed than usual. The sharp-pointed coattail of the best of his three dress coats swung behind him in time with his steps; his toupee had received a double quantity of pomade; and his cravat, increased by new folds, formed a white foliage, a frilled collar under his chin. When the abbot put on this attire, he had already pronounced the *ultima ratio* of his peculiar elegance.

Coletilla left after greeting the ladies. He had come only to ratify an agreement he had recently made with Paz. We already know that the ladies had the second floor of the house filled with family furnishings they had not wanted to part with. That apartment was very small and garret-like, connecting to the main floor by an inner stairway.

The ladies had proposed to Elías that he live there as a guest, eating with them. This arrangement suited the old man to perfection because it saved him money, and at the same time put him in close contact with his old employers, whom he greatly esteemed. Economy, comfort, security: he saw these three advantages in the proposal and accepted it. On that day he came to give them a definite reply; about the price, there were no disputes.

When *Coletilla* left, the abbot prepared to take the floor. He proffered a thousand pleasantries, displaying his complete repertory of smiles. We shall not be indiscreet if we mention, in anticipation of *Don* Gil's own declaration, that he was going to invite the three ladies to a religious celebration. With all imaginable reserve we dare to point out that this was only a pretext concealing other purposes.

As he began to speak, the first thing he did was to ask about *Doña* Paulita and Clara, using some discreet half-truths. Then he said, "Well, I came to ask you to honor with your presence a function that the Brotherhood of Passion and Death will celebrate tomorrow in the church of Las Maravillas. I am the secretary of the brotherhood, and thanks to me, the celebration has been arranged. I assure you that it will be the most spectacular that has ever been seen in Madrid."

"It will never be like the one we put on in 1798 in the Niñas de Loreto, when the *Virgen de los Dolores* was moved from the oratory of Olivar," said Salomé.

"It wasn't in '98, but in 1803; I remember it as though it were yesterday," said Paz.

"I know it was in '98," insisted the other.

"I am sure that it was in 1803," said Paz, "when our cousin returned from the war against France."

"It was '98, Paz," affirmed Salomé, " '98. It was thirty-five years ago."

"Heavens, woman! I assure you that it was 1803; I remember it well. I was then...fifteen years old."

"Ladies, the date is not important," said Carrascosa, cutting off the delicate debate. And then he continued, "Thanks to the collections which I direct, two thousand and some odd *reales* have been collected. We'll have a Mass with a chapel orchestra. Father Lorenzo de Soto, who is an orator worth all the gold in Peru, will preach to us."

"Oh! Don't mention him to me," said Salomé, turning her face away and screening it with her hand. "He is a perverted clergyman contaminated by modern ideas. After the liberals made him Vicar General of Astorga, he came under the power of the devil. I almost fainted at the fiesta of the *Virgen de la Leche y Buen Parto* when I heard him say, in San Luis, that we must reconcile ourselves with those who had turned our country upside-down. How can a person as learned as Father Lorenzo de Soto have reached such an extreme of perversion?"

"Madam, in my opinion he is a great preacher," said Carrascosa. "In 1812, he was, as you know, a delegate to the Assembly; in 1814, he signed the exposition of the *Persas*. A noble person! Later, because of his friendship with the King, he was elevated to very high posts. To prove his merit, let me mention that it was he who discovered the conspiracy of Porlier. After 1820, he became an enemy of the Constitution, which is praiseworthy because otherwise, he would have lost his sinecure. But none of this matters, because he will preach tomorrow, and this afternoon, we will have a completory in which the sopranos of Avila and Father Melchor, a Franciscan from Segovia, will sing. The Reverend Bishop of Michoacán will officiate, and in the afternoon there will be a procession that the confraternities of *El Paso* and *El Santo Sudario* will attend. The children of the orphanage will also attend."

"Oh, *Don* Gil!" exclaimed María de la Paz, with a note of profound sorrow. "How do they dare take the saints out into the street with such things going on? They should stay in their homes rather than to go out to see the sins men commit."

"I can assure you," said the abbot with a diabolically ironic smile, "that no one has yet complained, nor will anyone complain about the procession. The best thing about the procession is the retinue we have organized. Fourteen virgins will be dressed in white, with rose crowns, veils, scapularies, and holding wax candles."

"Those retinues," said María de la Paz in a very bad mood, "do not suit me at all. It is such a worldly thing. The men only go there to see the girls, and the girls who depict the virgins only go to be seen. And the thing that they least think about is God and the Saints. Those are French customs, *Don* Gil. Years ago, such immorality was not found here, and the day will come when such scandalous customs will come to an end."

The nasal timbre of *Doña* Paulita's voice from the adjoining room resounded in the living room, bringing the opinion of the saint who, although in prayer, had managed to hear everything said in the living room.

"Oh!" she exclaimed, raising her voice to be heard by *Don* Gil. "Do not mention those processions of worldly virgins! I wonder what kind of virgins go out with crowns of roses and wax candles in their hands. I once saw that, and such horror overcame me that I had to immediately confess the anger it produced in me. Do not ever mention it! What a scandal, Lord! Where will all this lead us?"

"Well, ladies," spoke up *Don* Gil, breathing heavily,...as though with his breath he would acquire the strength he needed against so many enemies; "I, while respecting your opinion, find such processions very moving, very expressive and very religious. In any case, the procession is already planned, and will take place. We have been looking for young women, and have found some, but we need five more. The celebration is tomorrow, and if we do not find them today, the function will be spoiled. What a setback! You can't imagine how hard I've worked to locate them. The ones I already found are very pretty."

"*Señor Don* Gil, for the love of God," shrieked Salomé in the tone of an honest woman scolding the effrontery of a suitor.

"Ladies, what's so strange about that? If God has made them pretty, what are we going to do about it? But oh! I need five more. That's why I am here."

And he stopped, somewhat perplexed.

"You have come here!" exclaimed Paz, opening her eyes wide.

"You have come here!" murmured Salomé with a sudden change of color.

The two ruins looked at each other. That quick glance was dreadful. An intelligent hidden observer perhaps would have noticed, that as the mutual flash was launched by one and the other, they were examining each other, each rejecting the other, their gazes changing to an expression of rancor. Carrascosa, although a keen observer, was not able to perceive the brief radiance of the glance. Quick as a flash of lightning, the two chasms opened up and for an instant faced and stared at each other, showing their full horror. Do not believe on account of this that aunt and niece did not love each other a great deal; they did love each other, if one cares to put it that way. They loved each other as much as two persons who mutually annoy each other can. Let us continue.

A deep and distant sigh announced *Doña* Paulita's wonder.

"Yes, I have come here to see if you would agree...," continued the abbot.

The altar-piece that served as Paz's face turned beet red, and Salomé's eyes gazed at the sky, whether due to a natural movement or a calculated combination of gestures, we cannot say.

"There is nothing surprising about it, ladies, not in the least. On the contrary..."

"*Señor Don* Gil," said Salomé, with something like a blush.

"*Señor Don* Gil!" exclaimed Paz with all the majesty of her character combined in a single gesture.

He, who had been an abbot and civil clerk, realized that they had misunderstood him.

"I am going to correct something," he exclaimed.

"Let us rectify it, as they say in the Assembly," suggested Salomé in a spell of sudden and unexplainable amiability she could not control, unusual for her and surely a sign of great emotion.

The other ruin's good humor was an ill-omen.

"I mean," continued the abbot, after coughing two or three times, "that I have come to see if you would agree to let that young lady...that young lady in your guardianship..."

Salomé began to cough convulsively, whether due to a physical cause or in order to hide from *Don* Gil's view the triangular wrinkles and the red color which appeared on her face, we cannot say. María de la Paz rubbed one eye as if it irritated her. The voice of *Doña* Paulita was heard praying in incomprehensible Latin.

"That young lady," continued Carrascosa, "who is named...I don't recall her name. Well, the one who is so pretty and so modest. There will certainly not be anyone in the whole procession to equal her beauty."

"*Señor Don* Gil!" exclaimed María de la Paz Jesús, in sudden anger. "How could you imagine that I would agree to such a thing? I have already told you that I think those retinues are very indecent, and if that child were to desire to become the scandal of Madrid, she would not ever enter this house again. I do not doubt that she would be willing to because she is so fond of flirting around that if she could she would be in the street all day long, chasing after men. But, don't...don't even speak to me about that!"

"I suspected from the first what you really wanted from us, *Señor* Carrascosa, but I wanted to wait until you had explained yourself," said Salomé with marked contempt.

"Ladies, I see that you are inflexible. I am well acquainted with the noble integrity of your character and the firmness of your principles."

At that moment *Doña* Paulita, who, without leaving the inner room had not missed a syllable spoken there, entered the conversation, changing her seat in order to hear better.

"Oh, Lord!" she said, "I shall not consent to such a thing. Even the most perfect persons may sin at times! The devil can use even good men with the best behavior for his perverse purposes. Who would think that you, *Señor Don* Gil Carrascosa, would be an instrument of ruination for this poor girl!"

"I? My dear woman!"

"No, I already know that it is unintentional; at times God may permit one good person, without knowing it, to cause the ruination of another. I don't blame you. But this poor child has someone to look after her. She will not fall from grace again; she has already left the abyss, poor thing, and has saved herself. The most important part is over, so that now, with an exemplary life, consecrated entirely to prayer, her soul will completely purify itself. Do not fear," she added, turning to the side where Clara sat, "do not fear that you will sin again. When you left the trouble of the world, it was in order to continue pure and stainless. Don't be distrustful of her..." she went on, looking about the room and directing her words to the two sphinxes..."don't lack confidence in her, because she is very good."

Salomé moved her head in a gesture of doubt.

"She is a very good person, a very good companion to me," continued the devout one. "Although the world tried to corrupt her, she has a very good nature, and her soul is saintly. I knew it all the time. She will lose the crust of vile passions which the world has taught her. I am so concerned about her salvation that I want to keep her always by my side and save her along with myself. I assure you it will be so! Love her ladies, for God commands love for sinners, above all when they are repentant. Isn't it true that you have repented, sister?"

No answer was heard. Clara no doubt answered yes with a nod of her head. The devout one's sermon left an echo in the room.

"Ladies, in conclusion, I shall permit myself one observation," said *Don* Gil. "I don't see anything scandalous in letting *Señora Doña* Clarita go out in the procession of the virgins. On the contrary, it is good for her to show off her beauty, which is a work of God; the woman who hides herself and doesn't go out prevents the admiration of a work of God, which is her beauty....That young woman is a marvelous example of God's handiwork, and to let her be seen is like publishing the praises of the Author of a thousand wonders."

"*Señor Don* Gil," objected María de la Paz, making an effort to appear calm. "I had no idea that you were such a libertine. Come now, we had another concept of you; we thought that..."

"I am a man, madam, like any other. I admire the beauties of nature, and a beautiful woman is..."

"For God's sake, *Señor* Carrascosa. The ideas that occur to you...," said Salomé, passing her hand through the strand of her hair which appeared between her dry, yellow forehead and her coif.

"Heavens! Control yourself, for heaven's sake," said the devout one from the other room. "Your words horrify me."

The important dialogue lasted a while longer, but when *Don* Gil saw that he was getting nowhere with the three, he tried to change the topic. He had little success, because his friends showed marked coolness toward him during the rest of the visit. Finally, deciding to leave, he stood up and paid a thousand courtesies; he reiterated his respect and admiration for them, promised to return soon and left.

Out in the street, he looked around as if searching for someone; and soon afterward, the young officer whom we have known from the beginning of this story stepped out from the doorway of an adjacent house.

"What's up?" he asked Carrascosa with great interest.

"Nothing, they refuse. Those old ladies are demons," answered the abbot, laughing wholeheartedly. "I think we'll get nowhere by this method."

"Damned old ladies!"

"We'll never get her out of that house unless we hand the three ugly shrews from the three balconies and *Coletilla* from the roof."

"I have already decided on what I told you about yesterday. If I can't get her out, I'll barge inside."

"Man, are you insistent!...Let's get away from here. If *Coletilla* sees us he'll surely fall of his donkey. Let's get away and discuss the matter."

"You are the most useless...You'll see if I don't get her out of there."

"I should like to see it," answered Gil, and they left, heading toward Santa Bárbara.

"You have already forgotten your old tricks, you devilish abbot; you've lost your touch. Let's see how I can get into that place; think of a means, any artifice. What good is your being a rascal? Let's see."

"There is one magnificent way," answered Carrascosa.

"Well, speak up!"

"I am going to describe it."

Chapter XX

BOZMEDIANO

Before reporting the entire conversation between these individuals, it is appropriate to provide information about one of them who is already well-known to the reader. The soldier, whom we observed in the second chapter of this story lending assistance to *Coletilla* and, later furtively gaining access to his house, was *Don* Claudio Bozmediano y Coello. He was thirty-two years old and served in the army with the rank of *Comandante*. His father was one of the venerable legislators of Cádiz. A man of talent and well-known integrity, of noble birth and pleasant appearance, he had always been well-regarded by his compatriots. With the return of the King, he was persecuted like all others, and had to emigrate. But once the Constitutional system was restored, the elder Bozmediano returned to Spain and held one of the highest posts in politics.

(In this story we will use the name Bozmediano to designate the son of that illustrious gentleman, whose real name we cannot use in this account due to the fact that he is a contemporary personage of very recent memory.)

Bozmediano, the father, was a liberal at heart. He had dealings with the King, and it is certain that he did everything humanly possible to guide the twisted will of that deceitful and perverse sovereign down the righteous path. He was rich, and his interest in political affairs never altered. Love for his son and patriotism were two deep sentiments which, joined and fused together, filled his entire heart.

Bozmediano, the son, who we will know better, was a man of excellent qualities, but he had a flaw which can be excused by his youth. He was so fond of the fair sex that he dedicated a major part of his life to gallantries, perhaps depriving the nation of important services. He was no libertine. He loved the ladies with all the good faith that the incipient nineteenth century permitted, and although he was, as he said, waiting for his ideal woman, he meanwhile amused himself with the others. But at last, he had found her, or at least he had found one who would without a doubt entertain him more than all others.

After he met Clara he had lost his calm. That young girl interested him, not only because of her personal qualities and charms, but also because in her life he uncovered a mystery which was for him, extremely intriguing. It provided him with what he always sought with great eagerness: an adventure.

Adventure presented itself in a singularly dramatic way, stimulating Claudio's love and curiosity at the same time. The loneliness of an orphan living in the company of an old eccentric, the sadness, and need for consolation, which he had observed in her, were sufficient to stimulate a spirit even less impressionable and gallant than his. His intention, his great aspiration, was to unravel the mystery of that house and to save the delightful and unfortunate girl from the hateful custody of her guardian.

"There are several ways of entering the house," said Carrascosa, taking the soldier's arm, "but there is one way which is excellent. Those old ladies have a tenant who is due to come now to pay them their rent, the little income that they have. I know about it through Elías. We will be on the alert; we'll buy him off by making him write a letter stating that he is ill and that he is sending his son with the money. You will disguise yourself as a peasant, enter the house, and once inside, boom! A fainting spell has seized you, a terrible accident. They can't help but leave you in the house...they'll put you up in the loft, and during the night, when they are sleeping, you will seize the girl and...escape into the street."

"Oh, hush up, you imbecile! That can't work. I don't remember which comedy I saw that in, and it's all very fine in the theatre...but in real life...Forget it! I want to enter the house in my own clothes, with my own name..., but I need some pretext, because I imagine that those old women will be suspicion personified?"

"They'll create a scandal, and the uproar will be heard in Getafe. We'll have to move with care."

"But, man," said Bozmediano, who had no idea that such types existed in the world, "What kind of people are they?...What is their character, their life, their habits? What do they do, and why is that poor girl there?"

"Lucky you, to not know those Porreño she-devils! They are the strangest birds that ever lived on earth. When I'm in a bad mood, I go over there to have a laugh, listening to them talk nonsense. They were rich, but have since come down, declined. I believe the day will come when they will suddenly eat each other up."

"And what do they do all day?"

"Nothing, or rather, they pray. One of them is a saint, and I assure you that when she starts talking about her own holiness, one could die of laughter. And how insolent they are! When I proposed that business of the procession, with the object of getting Clarita out of there, they acted like griffins. I had expected that they wouldn't consent, and in all truth, friend, the plan which just failed was a little daring."

"And how did Clarita get there?"

"I don't know—a decision by Elías."

"Man, tell me about that fellow Elías. The day I met him for the first time he seemed to me the strangest thing on earth. I had already heard talk about *Coletilla*."

"Elías is completely out of his mind. He is a royalist, but with a fanaticism which will lead him to martyrdom."

"And does he love the young girl?"

"I don't know. I doubt it. *Coletilla* doesn't love anybody but the King, excuse me, I mean the royal prince."

"Well then, let's see how you can get me into that den."

"You'll have to enter *ocultis*," said the abbot with a sly smile.

"And what good will that do?" replied Bozmediano in complete confusion. "Say I enter, for example, in the evening. If one of them sees me she will think I am a thief. She'll yell and then...a fine mess! Besides, Clara has no idea of this and has nothing to do with me. I want to get inside the house without suspicions and strike up a friendship with her."

"I have an idea," exclaimed Gil, pounding his forehead.

"Let's hear it."

"You are going to enter at a time when Clarita is alone."

"Alone? But if those demons go out occasionally, will they leave here there?"

"Yes."

"And when do they usually go out?"

"I'll undertake to find out and arrange everything."

"Explain what you mean."

"The first thing that you ought to do, *Don* Claudio, is to write a letter to the girl. I'll also take care of that."

"Well, they do go out. They'll probably leave her locked in. How can I enter? Am I going to pick door locks?"

"No, sir, you will enter comfortably and quietly."

"How do you figure it, you devil of an abbot?"

"Do you remember that abbot's robe I had back in 1810?"

"How could I remember that?" said Claudio, inquisitive and curious.

"Calm down, my friend," answered *Don* Gil, placing his hand on his chest. "Do you remember my cap and stockings, a marvel of needlework and fit?"

"And what does that have to do with the...?"

"Come on! That outfit, that cap, those stockings were made for me by *Doña* Nicolasa and *Doña* Bibiana Remolinos, outstanding in the art of sewing, whom I shall have the pleasure of introducing to you this very day."

"But what kind of double talk is this? What in the devil does that have to do with what I am asking you?"

"You don't get the point," answered the cunning abbot, "because you don't know that those two ladies live in the same attic where the blacksmith's daughter, Josefita Pandero, with whom the Count of Valdés de la Plata was so much in love, lived ten years ago, that is to say, at number six, Belén Street. I was involved in the matter."

"Now I recall hearing you say something about that. But what do I have to do with Josefita Pandero or the Remolinos ladies...?"

"You don't know what I mean because you don't remember that the Count of Valdés de la Plata, who could not get the girl away from the blacksmith who kept her shut up, as if she weren't already a woman, rented the adjacent house and did not stop until he established a means of communication which permitted him to profane the household of the stubborn Vulcan."

"Yes..."

"Well...my friends the seamstresses live in number six, where the smith's daughter lived, and my friends the Porreños live in number four, where the Count of Valdés de la Plata lived. In brief, if a door cleverly permitted a gentleman to pass from number four to number six, then it would permit passage from number six to number four if one were to grease the dear seamstresses' palms. One must say in passing, to honor the truth, that they possess hands which are glorious for backstitching."

"Now I understand. And that door, does it still exist?"

"How can it not still exist! I've seen it, and I'll answer for everything. I'll take charge of finding out when those shrews go out, delivering the letter, and facilitating the way...."

"It isn't a bad idea," said the soldier, "but, good or bad, I'll give it a try. And what shall we do so that owl *Coletilla* doesn't bother us?"

"*Coletilla* will not hinder us. The girl is what matters least to him. Her future does not concern him one iota. He doesn't worry about anything but..."

"Plotting, eh?"

"Well then, friend Claudio, Elías is an influential man with friends in high places. He is powerful, and as a result, despite his humility and melancholy, he is the man who controls the puppets. Believe me, he is going to bring about..."

"So, they are plotting? If the royalists conspire, it is certain that you will be one of them. Is it not so?"

"Well, I...," answered Gil mischievously, "I am only a man who loves order. If I go along with *Don* Elías and have dealings with his followers it is only to find out about their scheming, anyhow..."

"Always the same sly rogue. No one has learned better than you how to navigate in any winds."

"You already know, *Señor Don* Claudio," replied Carrascosa, "that they called me a royalist, and took away my job. What was I going to do? Was I to die of hunger? Ideas do not feed you, friend. You, who are rich, can afford to be a liberal. I am too poor to permit myself that luxury."

"You outright rascal, you!"

"What I do is to keep abreast of everything. Do you want me to stop being frank? You are a good friend and a fine gentleman. I am going to continue to be frank. Well, I want you to know that this is going to get you into a mess. All this is going to collapse, and fairly soon. You say that I am a terrible rascal. All right, then I say that you are a hopeless fool. You are one of those men who believes that this situation is going to continue, and that we'll have Liberty and a Constitution and all those follies. What a disappointment they are going to have. Mark my words."

"The factions are already forming, eh? Well, it is certain that they will cause a great deal of trouble for you because the liberals won't be happy just sucking their thumbs, dear Carrascosa."

"Oh!" replied the other, laughing like a demon, "Are you saying that they will not suck their thumbs? You will soon see what is going to come out of all this. You, Bozmediano, find a strong tree to shelter yourself under....Look, I know what I'm talking about....But let's get back to the matter at hand. Insofar as Clarita is concerned, I am going to give you some very important news."

"Let's see."

"This Elías fellow has a nephew in Ateca. Clara was there some months ago. The nephew is young, rather loquacious, and somewhat flirtatious. Need I say more?"

"Ah, it has finally come out," said Bozmediano, with a great deal of interest. "I'll bet that he is her suitor."

"Well, you win the bet. I was in Ateca back then and heard that they were in love. It seems to me that they still love each other."

"Come on now! Is that what we have here?" said Bozmediano, somewhat provoked. "And why didn't you tell me all this before?"

"Because until today I didn't know that the fellow had arrived and is in Madrid."

"In Madrid?"

"Yes, but it worked out in such a way that arriving in Madrid and being thrown into prison were one and the same thing."

"Well, what did he do?"

"He is very interested in politics. Back in Zaragoza he used to speak often in the clubs. The kid's conceited. When he arrived in Madrid his pals took him to The Golden Fountain; he spoke, and on the following day, he got mixed up in the tumult of the procession with Riego's portrait. He was one of the people shouting in the street, exhorting the people. The police came, took him into custody, and carried him off to jail, where he is right now."

"And doesn't his uncle try to get him out?"

"You don't know that beast. His uncle, when he learned that the boy was radical and was considered an orator, became really poisonous. He went to the jail, gave him a tongue lashing, and has broken off relations with him, telling him that as long as he has such ideas that he'd better not show up at his house."

"That man is the most eccentric..."

"Yes, sir. But the poor girl is surely suffering; she probably is heartsick at what is happening to her poor friend."

Bozmediano remained pensive a few moments. Then he said, very calmly, "Now I know what I have to do."

"What are you going to do?"

"Everything possible to set that young man free. We'll see how she takes it. I'm sure that I can get him out."

"Mister, you are really strange! I can't understand you," said *Don* Gil, smiling in surprise. "So you are going to court the girl and set her boyfriend free? You are a fool, *Don* Claudio."

"No, I am sure about this. I'll set him free. We'll see how she takes it. We'll let her know that I myself have set him free."

"A fine mess you're going to organize. Those chivalrous men are hard to figure out. That boy will be another hindrance to our plan to enter the house."

"It doesn't matter, we'll see later on. About all the rest, what was said stands. The letter, the departure of the three harpies, and the attic door..."

"Everything is set and in order. There is nothing more to say. May God help you."

After these words they parted. The ex-abbot left, laughing at the young soldier whom he wanted to serve for ulterior motives, hoping for very advantageous support in that political situation. The other headed home, thinking at the same time about *Don* Gil's repugnant cunning and the dangers of his coming adventure.

The amorous ruse Bozmediano planned to use was a very common thing at the beginning of the present century, which still preserved the rigidity of domestic principles that in past times had made each house a fortress.

In the seventeenth century, when our vigorous, original and profoundly characteristic national traits had not yet received foreign influence, Spaniards were a different kind of people. They achieved their objectives through more violent, more aggressive, and more romantic mean, placing passion before fear, that is to say, more by the resolute attitude of courage than by the ingenious intent of intrigue. That was the century of abduction from convents, of scaling garden walls, of elopements, and of attacks of the most sublime daring. Back then—so it is said—there was a gallant, the Count of Villamediana, who burned down his house for the pleasure of carrying a lady out in his arms.

The invasion of French customs which took place with the coming of the new dynasty at the beginning of the eighteenth century changed all this, along with other things. That society, which imposed itself on ours, was less great, less brave, less passionate, but more cultured, more refined, and more hypocritical. With its influence came the abbots, and cold classical literature, ceremonious, false, and also hypocritical.

Pastoral poetry, the highest degree of literary hypocrisy, had a sorrowful renaissance in the past century. To the beat of the madrigals, the abbots secretly made love in the salons. The lovers, who composed chaste and insipid pastoral verses, could not enter the houses as did others in the garb of the church dignitary, but entered disguised, or employing the most extravagant and involved means.

With the new society came new fashions. This brought white wigs, the most exaggerated and complicated hairdos; and with the craft of these coiffures came the ladies' hairdresser, a witty man who entered every boudoir and was the third person in every love intrigue.

No other century has seen, as did the eighteenth, guile serving love. Lovers absurdly faced very peculiar situations in order to talk to their ladies. The home was invaded, but not as our knights of the past century had invaded it, with sword in hand, beating down a swarm of servants and two dozen bailiffs, but by cunning and stealth, taking advantage of the family's confidence, or by hiding themselves behind ingenious and, at times, crude disguises.

In 1821 these procedures were still in vogue, and Bozmediano was a most accomplished master in such affairs. He knew the modus operandi of the barbers, third parties, abbots, and was very skilled in the use of disguises, deceits, and witty frauds, as such things were then called. If he was unable to use them in the adventure that we see him undertaking, it was due to the singular customs of the three ladies. It was not his fault; it was only because of the obstacles and difficulties of the terrain. Because of that, he said, he would resort to somewhat more violent means.

Chapter XXI

FREE!

Bozmediano, prompted by an easily understood impulse, was firmly resolved to do everything in his power to set Lázaro free. To him, doing a service for the man whom he could consider a rival seemed an act which would assure him of Clara's goodwill, and that sentiment, well and astutely guided, could turn into love. Nor did he proceed in the manner of ordinary lovers, in whom passion is nothing more than a slightly spiritualized egotism. In Bozmediano sensitive and generous gestures were spontaneous and fervent.

It was not difficult for him to achieve what he wanted. The secretary of the civil administrator, informed by the police, told him that the prisoner was an agitator paid by reactionaries, but Claudio made excuses for him as best he could, saying that he was a youth without experience or judgement, and finally, after much insistence and many explanations, the order was given to set him free.

Bozmediano set out for the Villa prison. Lázaro had fallen into gloomy depression after his uncle's visit. The feverish distress that filled his imagination with the torment of terrible hallucinations had degenerated into a lethargy that dulled his senses. His intelligence, so lively and brilliant on other occasions, was numbed, and, as he sat leaning against the wall in one corner with his gaze fixed on the opposite corner, his eyes sought the darkness as their only relief. Indifference, abandonment, lack of emotion, and dull stupor were reflected in his attitude.

When they told him that he was free, it took some time for him to grasp the meaning. Recovering somewhat, he assumed he owed that favor to his uncle, with which Elías momentarily regained his affection. But as he left, he ran into Bozmediano, who greeted him very courteously, repeating that he was free and could return home.

He was moved by that person's disinterested generosity, but soon doubts and confusion arose. Who was the fellow? Had he favored him out of generosity or for some concealed purpose? He did not know him. How had he learned his name and that he was imprisoned?

Lázaro did not think much about this. They talked as they left the jail, and he thought that Bozmediano seemed to be a good person, honest, and disposed toward friendship and good deeds. As they walked together along Atocha Street, the

Aragonese listened to the words of his unknown Good Samaritan with the serene attention of inferiority. He admired his manners, his understanding, his physiognomy, and his way of expressing himself. And at that moment, Bozmediano seemed to him to be the most complete gentleman he had ever seen. He also took him to be a distinguished young fellow, rich and influential, and his admiration held a great deal of respect.

"To what do I owe this great favor you have done for me?" asked Lázaro. "I want to know how I can repay you for..."

Claudio, who wanted to avoid naming his real motive for that act, rambled on, giving Lázaro a number of details which increased his confusion. He spoke to him of *Don* Elías, his town, the club in Zaragoza, and The Golden Fountain café.

"Well," he said, determined to get out of that awkward conversation, "I don't want to take any credit for an act you ought not to thank me for. Everything in its place. I have set you free, but I have only been an intermediary."

Lázaro began to feel uncertainty. They stopped walking and looked at each other. The smile sketched on Claudio's lips at that moment seemed a very bad omen to Lázaro, and he began to lower his benefactor from the high pedestal on which he had placed him.

"Indeed," continued the soldier, "you do not owe this favor to me, but to a person who apparently loves you a great deal."

Lázaro was going to pronounce Clara's name, but he checked himself because a flood of ideas, which came to mind all at once, made him stop, his gaze fixed on the soldier. That rush of ideas produced a dizzying series of swiftly changing conclusions. She knew him! She had seen him! Bozmediano was a pleasant person; he set him free; she had begged it of him! She felt pity for him. He wanted to please her! At what price? With what objective? Since when...?

Finally, the Aragonese dared to ask to whom he owed his freedom.

"Come, now," said Bozmediano with a somewhat impertinent voice. "You know very well what I mean. I do not have to name her, but it's only natural for you to play the innocent. It's very flattering to be loved by such a fine person. Don't be ungrateful, young man, she doesn't deserve that."

"I don't know what you mean," protested Lázaro in the tone of an unprepared student who asks to have a question repeated in order to delay admitting that he doesn't know the answer.

Bozmediano spoke further, but it came to the same thing. To Lázaro it seemed an inferred offense to Clara, to publish her affection and repeat such an honest and delicate confidence to an intruder. Yes, Bozmediano was an intruder who had stepped in to give him his freedom without anyone asking him to do so.

"You know very well who I mean," said Claudio, giving him a pat on the shoulder with simplicity and confidence, "but because you are so proud to be her beau, you use that tone."

"Oh, no," repeated *Coletilla's* nephew, in embarrassment. "The truth is that I don't know to whom you are referring."

Bozmediano extended his hand to the young Aragonese with good wishes and promises of friendship. Lázaro was so upset that he responded curtly and with minimal courtesy.

"I know where you live," said Claudio, as he departed. "We'll see each other there. And if not, at The Golden Fountain, where I frequently go."

Then he left. When he was some distance away, Lázaro felt the impulse to run after him to thank him more courteously, but his jealousy and pride were in conflict. He let him leave without saying anything.

Bozmediano walked away remarking to himself with much satisfaction: "He's an ordinary fellow, very ordinary...."

Chapter XXII

LAZARO'S WAY OF THE CROSS

Lázaro continued walking aimlessly. His sudden and mysterious exit from the jail, his acquaintance with Bozmediano, and the agitation produced by Bozmediano's words prevented him from clearly realizing for some time his difficult and exceedingly peculiar situation. But after walking alone for quite a while, he began to realize that he had no place to go, no one to go to, and no one with whom to live. Elías's statements had left him no doubt about his uncle's character. The old man was a fanatic royalist, a blind partisan of tyranny. With his eyes bright with anger and his speech venomous and emphatic, he had told Lázaro that he could not enter his house unless he changed his ideas. What to do? It was impossible to live with that bitter and cruel man, melancholy and violent as a Moslem fanatic. How opposed their two sets of ideas were! What could he do? Pretend, and be a hypocrite? Feign love for a tyranny which seemed criminal to him? "No, impossible," thought Lázaro. Moreover, in the present agitation of the parties, to pretend such ideas was worse than to profess them. The old man could not admit him into his home. Then, what should he decide? Where would he go? Should he return to Ateca? And what about Clara?

Remembering his unfortunate companion, the young man's thoughts took another slant. The sorrows of that unhappy girl, condemned to live with such a cruel person, began to torment him. He had to go there and see what was happening in that household. But how, if he could not visit his uncle?

Should he go or not? His need was pressing. He was alone, oppressed by exhaustion and hunger, and with no extra clothing. Twelve *cuartos* was his total fortune, because along the way he had lost a doubloon and the expense of the trip had consumed the rest. Meanwhile, night was approaching, and he had nowhere to sleep. If he went to his friends' house, he might not find them as benevolent as the night before. Besides, they were poor people like himself and could not offer him hospitality.

He had to go somewhere. It had occurred to him to take the road to his town and return there. He had met a muleteer at the inn who would have taken him there on credit. But what about Clara?

These were his thoughts when he happened to pass The Golden Fountain. He heard loud voices, stopped automatically and started to enter.

"No," he said, checking himself. "I won't go in."

At the same time, he took a step toward the door. An unavoidable attraction drew him toward that place, the tomb of his first and most beautiful illusions.

The din heard from within resounded in his brain like the infernal echoes of a strange fascination.

He retreated; then took a few steps forward. He hesitated, debating with himself, and finally, as curiosity joined his instinctive desire to enter, he made up his mind and went in.

They were having a very heated discussion. Voices everywhere were raised in the public area as well as in the club. The speaker managed to control the noise and was able to make himself heard, but shouts soon drowned his voice out again. He was expounding on the shameful defeat which the extremists had suffered under Morillo's authority; some had taken this matter personally. Zealous for the decorum of the society and their party's good name, some orators denounced "the infamous who, disguising themselves with the label of liberal, would corrupt that assembly, make shameful dealings in the name of the King, buy extremist eloquence, and promote disturbances which had no other objective than to discredit liberalism and give arms to the opposition."

"Wolves," said the speaker, "disguised as lambs who come here feigning a love for Liberty which they do not feel. They offer gold to the speakers to pay for speeches that will excite the spirits of the ignorant masses!"

"Yes, those scoundrels," said another. "They are the ones who organize the mobs and stone ministers' houses. The object of this association is to maintain a permanent center of good ideas and to guide the voters, but never to support licentiousness, scandal, or anarchy.

"No," shouted another speaker on whom all eyes were fixed, and who stood angrily to protest the preceding words. "No, there are no traitors here. Anyone who does such things does not belong to the human race! I don't believe it. If there are traitors, let them identify themselves. Let us find out who they are, let us know each other."

"Let them state their names!" repeated a hundred voices.

"We must purify this noble assembly," said the first speaker. Thanks to the scoundrels who have corrupted our club, insulting comments about it and about us are spread throughout Madrid. Get those scoundrels out of here!"

"Let them identify themselves," responded the multitude with a roar.

"No," said another, "that kind of person does not exist."

"Yes, he does exist," exclaimed the first, in exasperation. "People frequent this place who use the King's gold to buy the frenzied oratory which drives people wild."

"Who? Who?"

"Who among us," continued the speaker, "does not know the so-called *Coletilla*? He is a fanatic royalist, a wicked agent of the royal house. Do you know him? The man is a snake who slips in among us to corrupt young speakers. I know that many have accepted money in exchange for very heated speeches. The ridiculous mobs which we see every day—to what do we owe them? Have no doubt! Open your eyes, you blind men! They are due to Fernando de Bourdon's gold distributed by that insidious character, *Coletilla*."

"Who are the mercenaries? Let us know!"

"Do not trust the authors of disorder."

"That man is some kind of friend of the government," shouted someone in the public area, pointing to the speaker.

"Friend of the government?" said the speaker, indignant. "Why? Because I love liberty without license, petition without scandal? I am directing my remarks to those Aragonese who in this gathering distinguish themselves by their provocative language and their love of disturbances."

"What do you dare say?" exclaimed Núñez, rising like a fury to rebuff the first speaker. "What insult do you imply to my friends—and to me?"

"Yes, gentlemen," shouted the other, "don't trust the Aragonese. It was a man from Aragón who provoked the crowds on the day of the procession with the portrait."

Some looked at Lázaro, who, mute and cold observed the scene.

"And have no doubt," continued the speaker. "The man who spoke on that occasion was a vile instrument of the agents of the King."

"That's the one! Here he is!" exclaimed someone, pointing Lázaro out to the attention of the entire assembly.

"Yes, *Coletilla's* nephew."

"*Coletilla's* nephew! *Coletilla's* nephew!" repeated many voices.

A frightening uproar resounded throughout the whole club. They all stood up and looked at Lázaro.

"Yes, the one who spoke the other night to incite the rebellion!"

"The agitator at Plaza Mayor."

"*Coletilla's* nephew!"

These last words were the greatest mark of dishonor. Núñez stood up to defend his friend, but could not; his voice was not heard. Many who had feared being accused themselves, on seeing the landslide fall on Lázaro, unloaded all their anger on him.

"How much did they give you for shouting on the day of the procession, darling?" called august Calleja from the corner.

"Throw him out!"

"Out, traitor, out!"

"Throw him out, out into the street!"

Lázaro tried at that moment of supreme desperation to gather his aplomb and speak, to defend himself, to shout, to tell everyone that he was innocent, that he was an unfortunate victim, a poor devil, the most insignificant of all beings. They did not listen to him. He could not speak, to defend himself, or to rebuff them. He gave in under the unbearable weight of so many glares and so much anger. On seeing the amazement and humiliation of their victim, the multitude redoubled its fury, and after words came action; they ordered him to leave; they pushed him toward the door; they threw him out. The circle around him narrowed more and more. The unfortunate youth saw a hundred hands on his body. He felt himself caught as if a snake were twisting around him, tying strong knots, and squeezing him in its robust coils. The uproar, heat, anguish, and shame stunned him to the point of making him lose consciousness. He was dragged without seeing who was dragging him; monstrous forces were pulling him by the wrist. They were hitting him on the back. They were forcing him outside. He heard the door open with a crash, and his body received a strong jolt. He was thrown out and was free of those terrible arms; he fell to the ground. The clamor continued around him, consisting mainly of infernal coarse laughter. Finally, the noise faded little by little; the poor fellow began to experience pain from the fall and felt the cold ground. He was out in the street....

He remained on the ground for some minutes without being clearly aware of the event, and the sweat covering his face produced a glacial expression. He later became acutely aware of his situation and realized that he was on the ground with his back against a wall, his forehead bowed and his hair fallen and messy. His hat had been knocked to his side; his clothes were torn; and he felt an extremely sharp pain in his left elbow, badly damaged in the fall. The clamor in The Golden

Fountain resounded like a distant beehive; applause accompanied shouts, and an agitated and sometimes a sonorous voice raised itself above a storm of enthusiasm.

Lázaro noticed near him three little thieves who were staring at him mockingly; one of them was looking for a chance to make off with his hat. The passers-by began to form a circle, and some approached to lean over to see whether the fallen one was deceased or had simply fainted. He got up because their impertinent inquisitiveness bothered him as much as the noise coming from The Golden Fountain, and he moved away from the area and headed toward Puerta del Sol. Those ruffians, accompanied by some others, followed him. The night watchmen shone the light of their lanterns directly on him, and the passers-by stopped, watching him go away, thinking the he was neither dead nor unconscious, but simply drunk.

He went up Montera Street and asked the way to Válgame Dios Street, because he had decided to go to his uncle's house. He no longer felt doubt; his decision was made; and in that distressed trance, the fanatic's house at whose entrance he had to abandon his beliefs, his true sentiments, seemed a peaceful refuge to him.

After all, the few days spent in Madrid had been continuous suffering, and the idea of an apostasy he would be obliged to accept in the royalist's house did not really bother him. His imagination was destroyed, which meant he was weakening on his most powerful side. He was no longer the ardent youth who believed himself destined for great objectives; he was now a disinherited unfortunate without strength of spirit, without hope, and without ideas. He did not know what was happening. He was unable to gauge the immensity of the change that his uncle demanded of him. He only wanted to throw himself into the arms of the first person who could console him.

After many inquiries he finally arrived at Válgame Dios Street. He saw the number of the house and looked up at the windows on the second floor and the lights on in the rooms. Surely Clara was there, tired of waiting for him, never expecting to see him again. He entered the hallway and nervously went up the stairs so quickly that upon reaching the door he had to stop because he could not breathe. A few seconds later he extended his hands, grasped the doorbell cord, and pulled very softly, because it seemed to him that it would disturb his uncle and frighten Clara if he rang more strongly than necessary. He pulled so gently with his trembling hand that the bell did not ring. He pulled it more energetically, and because he was nervous it rang so loudly that the noise deafened the whole building. Lázaro became frightened, expecting Elías to come out in a rage, shouting at him for making such a racket. A long while passed before anyone opened the door, but at last he saw some light through the small window; he heard footsteps; a hand was running along the door; a space opened and two eyes appeared.

They were not Clara's eyes.

"Who is it?" asked Pascuala from within.

Lázaro asked for his uncle.

"Yes; but he isn't in."

"Will he return soon? I'm his nephew."

Pascuala opened the door and Lázaro took a step inside, surprised not to hear Clara's voice.

"He will come neither sooner nor later because he has moved," said Pascuala.

"How is that?"

"He moved this very day. I am still here because a few odds and ends and the armoire remain; so here I am getting ready, but tomorrow I'm going."

"And where has he moved to?"

"Near here on Belén Street, to the home of the Porreño ladies."

"And Clara?"

"Since eight days ago she has been living there with the ladies. The master sent her there because he was angry with her."

"Wait a minute! What are you saying?"

"Ah! But are you the master's nephew?"

"Yes."

"You are Aragonese. Tell me, by chance do you know Ventura Palomino of Cariñena, the brother of Jusepe Palomino, who married Colasa Sanahuja?"

"No," answered Lázaro impatiently. "I'm not from Cariñena."

"And do you know if Antón Telares's wife had a baby? He's the brother of my boyfriend, Pascual, I am going to marry next week, Lord willing."

"I don't know, dear; I don't know those people. But tell me, why has Clara gone to live with those ladies?"

"Oh!" said Pascuala, laughing heartily. "I keep forgetting that you were her boyfriend. The master sent her there because he said that he could not put up with her...,well I'll tell you...the master is that way....He said that she was a modern

girl, that she was brazen....But she's a very good person, and I
don't know why the poor thing hasn't rotted with sadness in this
house."

"Did she leave here willingly?"

"The truth is, sir...the master has such a temper...my
word. The two of us were always terribly frightened when we
would see him come home. He never spoke to us, and in the
evening after going to bed, we used to hear him stomping his
feet...."

"And why did he send her to that house?"

"See here. I'm going to tell you the truth because you are
one of the family. There was a young soldier who one day
came to the house bringing home the master, who had been
injured in the street. Then he started to come by here every day
and whenever he ran into me, would stop and ask about Clarita.
Oh! One day my boyfriend Pascual saw me talking to him and
almost....My Pascual has a devil's temper, and when he gets
angry...you don't know how he walloped the butcher across the
street....Because I'm so...so attractive..."

"Keep on with what you were saying; later on, we can hear
about what *Señor* Pascual does," said Lázaro, impatient with
the maid's digressions.

"Well, he said that the young soldier offered me money in
order to slip in here."

"And did he?"

"Hold on, and I'll explain. He didn't come closer than the
corner, but the master managed to see him several times.
Although the master appears not to see anything, he notices
everything."

"And she, what did she say?"

"Hold on...He told me that he wanted to come in."

"And what did he say about her?"

"That she was too pretty to be shut up here without seeing
the world; that it was a pity that a woman should live in the
company of such an ugly old man, and so...he said, 'I'll get her
out of here.' "

"And did she know that he said that?"

"Yes, he said it directly to her."

"He was here, then," exclaimed Lázaro with much anxiety.

"Hold on!"

"And she, what did she say about him?"

"That he was an amiable person and had very good
manners, that he was a good person and very courteous. One
day he dropped in on us here. Heavens, what a scare!"

"And she, what did she do?"

"She told him to go away."

"And did he go away?"

"Hell no, he stood here saying a thousand things."

"And she, what did she say to him?"

"That he should leave, because he was going to get her into trouble; that if he really was interested in her, he should leave right away, and not let anyone see him there."

"And he, what did he say?" inquired Lázaro, who could not contain his anxiety.

"A thousand things, a thousand trifles. It so happened that the master came home and saw him. He became very angry with us and scolded us an awful lot."

"And what did she say to him?"

"Nothing. He scolded us all day long. Then he said to Clarita that she was crazy, that he was finally fed up with her flirtations....The peculiar ideas of an old man, because she, poor girl....Finally he told her that he was going to send her to the three old ladies' house so they would reform her and teach her righteous living."

"But why did my uncle call her crazy? What did she do?"

"Nothing, but the master says that modern ideas..."

"And what else did he say to her?" asked Lázaro, who could not hear enough about the awful answers to that terrible interrogation.

"That she ought to dedicate herself to prayer and holy life."

"And that soldier, have you seen him lately?"

"These past few days I've seen him wandering around Belén Street, and I..., I imagine."

"Come on, what do you imagine?"

"I imagine....The soldier is quite a rascal....I'll bet he has made his way into that house."

"And do you know those three ladies?" asked Lázaro, trying to conceal the bad effect the previous reply had had on him.

"No, but the master said that they are good people; one of them is a saint."

"Where do they live?"

"On Belén Street, number four. Your uncle lives in the same house. You'll soon meet them."

"Say," asked Lázaro, after a pause in which he deliberated whether to leave or to prolong their painful talk. "Say, is that soldier a young fellow, tall, with a black mustache?"

"Yes, a bit taller than you. He has a very clear voice and walks gracefully. And he laughs with a great deal of charm."

"Do you know his name?"

"No, sir, I was going to find out, but since my Pascual is so jealous, I was afraid....Oh, what a man my Pascual is! When he gets angry..."

Lázaro was silent for a moment, contemplating the coarse effigy of that woman, the oracle of his misfortune. Then he repeated the address of the new house several times and left.

Now the decision was made to go there, and he would rather have died than change his mind. Curiosity, jealousy, and the need to find an answer to that sudden series of doubts drove him toward the new house.

And what about the perjury required of him? He had almost forgotten about that. Undoubtedly, Pascuala was talking about the same individual who had set him free. A new and painful mystery! He would have given up many days of his life to know everything clearly, and at the same time, he was horrified at the thought of knowing. The idea of Clara's infidelity, of her dishonor, was too horrible for him to accept, and he could not consider it. What confused him most was the strange rapidity and fatal impatience with which so many setbacks had been hurled at him, so many sorrows which gave him no chance to search for courage and hope.

He entered and slowly climbed the stairway of the eighteenth century house. I cannot omit the sensation of respect he felt toward those three ladies, still unknown to him, who seemed to be three perfect models of virtue. He rang; one of them opened the door for him. The surroundings disturbed him a bit; the historical portraits in the anteroom looked at him with their moth-eaten eyes. Lázaro was frightened. Following Paz, he passed through those shadows, made more mysterious by the weak light of the hallway, and then entered the parlor.

Chapter XXIII

THE INQUISITION

When *Coletilla*, after moving into the second floor, informed the ladies that his nephew would probably come to live with him, Salomé remained a little thoughtful, but María de la Paz said that there was no inconvenience, provided that the youth, under the vigilance and supervision of his uncle, maintained the moderation and dignity that that house imposed upon its inhabitants.

Preceded by María de la Paz, Lázaro entered the living room. The first thing that his eyes saw was Clara, who was seated next to the devout one and was sewing, with her head lowered, not daring to look at anyone. He noticed her embarrassment and her eagerness to conceal it. Then, he looked around the room and saw his uncle respectfully seated next to Salomé, who had planted herself to the extreme east of María de la Paz. Lázaro observed them, as motionless as wooden figures; they were all looking at him, with the exception of Clara, who persisted in sewing with her eyes so close to her work that it was difficult to understand how she kept from poking them out with the needle.

Elías stared at him in astonishment; Paz in astonishment; Salomé in astonishment; they all were looking at him with such astonishment that he himself began to belive that he was an invoked phantom, the fearful ghost of *Coletilla's* nephew. Finally, Salomé pointed to a chair with one skinny, bejeweled finger, and Paz said to him, in her most scornful and autocratic tone of voice, "Sit down, young man!"

When the young man responded, "Thank you, ma'am," his voice echoed weakly and painfully indicating so much suffering and prostration that Clara could not help but raise her eyes and look at him with sudden interest. She found him pale and depressed; she understood what the poor fellow had experienced during those days, and she needed all the strength of which her valiant soul was capable to keep from breaking into tears like a fool in the presence of those three rigid ladies and angry *Coletilla*.

"These ladies already know what you have done on your arrival in Madrid," said Elías to his nephew, with much severity.

Paz and Salomé furrowed their brows to make clear their indignation. Lázaro did not reply because he was terribly ashamed, and because at that moment the two ladies seemed to him the two most perfect personifications of human justice.

"Do you remember what I told you when I went to see you in the jail?"

"Yes, sir; I've not forgotten."

"I am now living here in the house of these ladies who have offered a home to Clara and myself."

"Only because of you, *Señor Don* Elías," said Salomé.

"I already know that," answered the old man. "But I," he continued, directing himself to Lázaro, "if I called on you while living in the other house, in this one I do not dare offer you any hospitality because..."

"*Don* Elías," said Paz, "as far as the upstairs is concerned, you can dispose of it as you desire. You already know what we agreed to. We are doing this just for you."

"I can't permit that," continued Elías, bowing his head. "I cannot ask this young man to stay in this house. His behavior has been so scandalous that I dare not..."

"There is no mistake, however great it may be, that cannot be corrected," said Salomé, looking with sublime protection at the unfortunate Lázaro, to whom those words seemed the epitome of generosity.

"Indeed," said Paz, in a tone of emphatic indulgence. "There are failures so great that their very enormity requires indulgence. My opinion is that this young fellow ought to stay with you, *Señor* Elías. If not, what will become of him?"

Elías indicated that he understood.

"What will become of him if he continues to live alone and without guidance?" continued the lady. "From what has already happened we can conclude what will happen. Without the protection of a person as virtuous and magnanimous as you, what will become of this fellow in whom the seeds of all the bad ideas of the day have budded forth?"

"I believe that there is still time, because although the contaminating influence has just taken root in a corruptly fertile land, a good system of education can uproot that bad weed and even expurgate and purify the bad earth," said Salomé, who since the days when the poets used to dedicate madrigals to her had preserved a great talent for allegories.

"What do you think, Paula?" asked Paz, who sometimes believed that in that house not a single word could be expressed, not advice of any value given, without its being endorsed by the devout one's orthodox sanction.

"She, who is a saint, will tell us what should be done," exclaimed Elías.

While all awaited her opinion, the devout one stared at the student's countenance as if she were trying to read his crime on it. An expression of affectionate pity and even frank admiration shone in *Doña* Paulita's eyes, which in that moment seemed to look out at the world naturally. But as soon as she realized that they were asking for her advice, she remembered her mission, arched her brows, and in her metallic voice, cast to the winds the following:

"Oh! What is there to discuss in the matter? Who could ask if an offender should be pardoned? Who is so un-Christian as to ask such a question? Forgive! Is the sin grave? Better: it requires more forgiveness and forgetting. And if he were even more delinquent, I would forgive him sooner."

Paz and Salomé looked at *Don* Elías simultaneously to enjoy seeing in his eyes the admiration which so much wisdom was bound to cause.

"Why do you even ask me that?" continued Paulita. "Tell me where there are sinners so that I may forgive them all. Are you going to deprive yourselves of the happiness of forgiving? Not only do I tell all of you to forgive him but also that you should love him as if he had never sinned. Remember the prodigal son? Today is a day of jubilation in this house because the sinner has returned. He who was believed lost has returned. I am going to give thanks to God for having provided me with the ineffable favor of receiving in my house a delinquent laden with blame, and to be able to say to him: Rise and sin no more."

It was easy to recognize by the saint's gaze that at that moment she spoke with deep truth and great conviction. The sinner felt moved with gratitude. Clara would not have spoken with so much eloquence, but surely she was thinking and saying similar things to herself.

Upon concluding her homily, the devout one smiled, an extremely rare event which would have surprised everyone had not the preoccupation of those moments kept them from noticing it. The youth saw that smile on the mouth of the woman he judged to be holy—and who was; and it seemed to him to be the most natural thing in the world. He felt relieved of a great weight, breathed tranquilly before that profession of goodness and indulgence, and thought himself present at the Last Judgment.

"Due to the admirable opinion of this saint," said Elías, "because she is a saint, Lázaro, mark me well, you will stay with me, but with the expectancy of certain restrictions."

"I do not allow censure, only a complete pardon," said the devout one.

"All right. Pardoned, but subject to vigilance."

In spite of the severe attitude of the two ladies and his uncle, Lázaro experienced a certain moral easiness in that house. He observed Clara, silent and distant. She did not raise her eyes or utter a word."

Whenever Lázaro looked over at Clara, he always found the devout one's black eyes fixed on him with tenacious attention.

The scene was arranged in this way: Paz and Salomé were seated in their customary ceremonious posture. Elías sat on the right, and Lázaro faced them in the position of a prisoner. Behind the two old women, Clara and the devout one formed another group next to a small table supporting the lamp whose weak light illuminated the scene; the reflection shone squarely on the young man's face. In the shadow sat Clara and the devout one, and the eyes of the latter, profoundly black, shone in the deep shadow of the living room with feline vivacity. The two old ladies, their backs turned to the second group, saw nothing, but Lázaro, who sat facing them, noted the intently curious and fascinated expression in Paulita's eyes and asked himself what there could be in his person to excite that lady's curiosity.

Elías, meanwhile, would not have felt the ecumenical council was complete without his pompously praising the virtues of the three venerable remains of the illustrious Porreños family.

"Truthfully, ladies," he said, "I don't know how to express my gratitude for so much kindness. I don't know what I, a person of such humble origin, owe to you, that you treat me with such benevolence and shower me with favors. What have I done to deserve this? Who am I? Oh! You are goodness and nobility personified. How apparent are the nobility of your origin and the excellence of your lineage. Oh! You have undertaken to be redeemers of all those around me who oppress me with hardships, making my life bitter! And what would become of that poor girl without your protection when modern ideas have planted such pernicious roots in her heart?"

The devout one stopped looking at the new arrival and said, "Don't scold her any more! She has suffered enough."

Lázaro noticed that Clara was trembling, blushing red as a poppy.

"Don't scold her any more. She has been scolded enough," added the pious one sorrowfully. "I will answer for her. I know that she is basically a good person, although the defects of the pestilent ideas of the century appear externally. I know she has a good heart. What do even the most serious mistakes matter if they are followed by repentance?"

Lázaro saw Clara make a gesture as if she were attempting to contradict those words, but in his blindness he did not realize, could not understand that at that moment the spirit of his friend was passing through the hardest trance of pain and patience that human nature is capable of.

"I know that she will reform herself," continued the pious one. "She is certainly going to mend her ways! Great sinners have become saints. Courage, my friend! With your vision concentrated on God, what is there to fear? I know how spiritual ills are cured, and my friend Clara is already responding under the beneficial influence of a good reaction. Let us also forgive her; I shall answer for her correcting herself."

These words filled Lázaro with confusion. What had Clara done? He felt like standing up, approaching her, and saying to her in a loud voice, "Clara, what have you done?" He looked at her and saw tears in her eyes. He looked at everyone, searching those parchment faces for the solution to such a great mystery, but none revealed to him the girl's sin, not even the face of the devout one, who, after her sermon, began to stare at him again from the somber depths of the room. The intensity of her scrutinizing and anxious gaze would have disturbed even a less timid person.

Chapter XXIV

MYSTIC ROSE

"I haven't prayed at all today," said the devout one to Clara the day after Lázaro's entrance into the Porreño home.

The two women were seated in their customary place. *Doña* Paulita held a volume of San Juan Crisóstomo in her hand. Clara was embroidering at a small frame. Her face expressed the most calm and profound melancholy. On the other hand, *Doña* Paulita, contrary to custom, was very restless.

An observer would have noticed her lips moving, spelling out in silence the mystic reading; while at the same time, she would suddenly direct her gaze toward the door, then look around the room, gaze toward Clara blankly, and finally, remain with her gaze fixed in space, as though carried away by something distant and unseen. At times she seemed to be paying attention to something happening outside the room; she started to leave, then stopped at the door, listening attentively, and returned to her seat. She picked up the holy book, read a bit, skipped over entire pages, looked at Clara, murmured a prayer, closed a folio, opened it once more, and so on, successively. Undoubtedly, her spirit wandered over the text of San Juan Crisóstomo without penetrating the meaning of the theology; this is not uncommon.

"Clara," she said after meditating for a moment, "Clara, do you know, I think the room they gave to *Don* Elías's nephew is a little cramped?"

"Cramped?" asked Clara, pretending indifference. "Not for only one man...."

"Oh!" exclaimed the devout one. "How the youth of today corrupts itself: A young man like that seems to have good instincts...."

"Yes," replied the other, without lifting her head.

"Did you know him before?"

Clara, who wanted to maintain the most absolute secretiveness, decided to tell a lie. She was ashamed of a denial, but in those circumstances, and in that house, the truth was not only embarrassing, but fearful as well. So she replied, "I? No...."

"It's a shame that youths like him are becoming so corrupted. Oh! But there will be no scarcity of good souls who will pray for them and help them emerge from their misery. Isn't that so?"

"That's true," answered Clara.

"And when one is basically good, like that young man, it's an easy matter. Oh! but you told me that you stayed in the town that young fellow is from. Wasn't he there then?"

Clara, who was unaccustomed to lying, was very embarrassed by the question, but by evoking what little evil her character held, she controlled herself and lied once more, saying:

"No, no, he wasn't."

"and what did they say about him there?" inquired the devout one, opening up her volume of San Juan Crisóstomo.

"What did they say?" answered the orphan, studying her needlework as closely as possible, "They said that he was a very loyal young man, very generous, very good, and very talented."

"Yes. It is clear that he's a young man with good qualities," said the Porreño woman, opening San Juan Crisóstomo. "And are his parents alive?"

"His mother is," answered Clara, bending over to pick up an object that had not been dropped. "His mother is an affectionate woman, very religious and very good."

"Surely. It is quite clear that she must be so," affirmed Paula, leafing through the saint's writings, "I imagine that she must be an excellent woman."

"So she is."

"That young man really deserves to be protected. When the soul is good…Who does not ever sin?"

As she said this, she arched her brows, stared at the book and made all imaginable efforts to read a half a line. After spending five minutes in such an important endeavor, she spoke again, saying, "Doesn't he have any sisters?"

"No, ma'am."

"Oh!" exclaimed Paulita, setting aside San Juan Crisóstomo. "I forgot about my prayer. Sister, you have distracted me with your conversation. Let us pray."

But instead of opening the prayer book, she picked up a volume of Saint Teresa and automatically opened it. Clara held the rosary while the devout one began the psalmody with her eyes fixed on the book, making mistakes the whole way through. Instead of saying the "Lord's Prayer" she said a "Hail Mary"; she got so mixed up in the prayer that after a while she was lost in a labyrinth, without knowing where they were in the Rosary.

"Oh! What a head I have!" said the saint, as she paused, "But, oh! you've distracted me with your conversation. Let's continue."

But instead of pronouncing the fundamental "Lord's Prayer," which would have let her start again, she fixed her eyes on the book and read mechanically, "I now want to deal with two forms of love: one is spiritual, because it seems to not touch on either the sensuality or the tenderness of our nature; the other is spiritual and links up with our sensuality and weakness…. What distraction!" she commented afterwards.

She laid the book aside scornfully, looked at the ceiling, and remained silent for a good while, without giving signs of being in this world; she remained motionless such a long time and with such deep ecstasy that Clara became alarmed and finally decided to pull on her sleeve, to make the devout one come back down from Heaven.

"Oh, sister!" she said energetically. "You don't know how to say the Rosary. Give it to me."

And she seized the Rosary from Clara's hands. She took it and began to count the beads one by one so very carefully that she spent at least ten minutes in that difficult operation. Then she prayed a "Hail Mary", to which Clara answered with a "Lord's Prayer." The two looked at each other. Clara trembled because she thought that the devout one was going to scold her harshly as usual for her mistakes. Much to her astonishment the saint's lips unfolded smoothly, as she smiled with an ineffable expansiveness which no one, absolutely no one, had ever observed in that house. And then she laughed openly and with relief, a phenomenal thing never before observed in such an exemplary woman.

But Clara, although quite surprised, did not give much importance to the event. *Doña* Paulita blushed slightly, and again picking up the book of Saint Teresa, said, "I am going to see if I can locate a passage recommending penitence."

She leafed through the book and read, " 'Sustain me with flowers, comfort me with apples for I am sick of love.' Oh! This is such divine language for my purpose! 'How, holy wife, thou kill with sweetness. For, as I have tasted it on occasion, it is so excessive that it undoes the soul and makes it seem as if there were no longer a soul designed for living…' No, this isn't the one. Let's see this other one," she said, skimming some more. "Well, this prayer is a little spark with which the Lord begins to light up the soul of his true love and hopes that the soul will gradually understand what a gift love is. No, it isn't this passage, either. I am not going to locate it today. Let's continue our prayer, sister."

She seriously began the rosary. Paula said "Hail Mary" the required number of times, but on reaching the place for the "Lord's Prayer", she continued saying "Hail Mary" up to thirty times, so quickly that she did not wait for the other to finish her "Holy Mary". Clara also answered rapidly, so as not to fall behind, and finally, with each of them it became a contest in rapid pronunciation. They reached the end breathless and extremely tired. Paulita needed to breathe fresh air. She opened the balcony and looked out into the street, an unusual occurrence whose importance Clara did not appreciate, either.

"Oh, I've opened the balcony!" she exclaimed, realizing the atrocity that she had committed. "I have opened the balcony!"

And she quickly closed it, like a nun who had found the iron gate of the locutory open.

"Sister," she said afterward, "I have decided not to fast tomorrow."

"You will do well not to fast. You are indeed a saint, but you ought not to fast so much, ma'am. That isn't good."

"You are right, Clarita, and I believe that my condition is caused by excessive zeal. Father Silvestre advised me correctly that piety in excess is injurious because it ruins the body, without which the soul has no strength."

"But what's wrong?" asked Clara, rather alarmed.

"I'm not well," said the mystic woman, rubbing both her eyes as if she had irritated them by a long vigil or by excessive use. "I feel feverish here inside...and a palpitation...But it's from fasting, sister. It's from fasting."

"Well, you should slow down. Rest a few days!"

"Yes, I'll do that, and this week, I shall not say double prayers as I have up to now. I'll eliminate my prayer hours in the evening."

"I should hope so! Doesn't it suffice to pray one time? You are a perfect saint."

"Does one time seem sufficient to you?" inquired Paula, with much anxiety.

"Yes, and you must do your best to get well."

"What's that you say, Clarita? Get well? I see that you know how to give very good advice."

"Get well, yes....Amuse yourself a little....Go out...."

"Go out!" exclaimed the mystic, so alarmed that Clara regretted the advice. "Go out! And go where?"

"Well...I mean...that you should try...well, when one is shut up in the house for a long time one's health breaks down....So it is that...it's always good...to go out a little...."

"Clara," said *Doña* Paulita with the expression of stupor and gravity which occurs when one makes a great discovery, "Do you know that your advice is very wise? I didn't believe...It's true. That's it. Why must it be bad? I now feel the need to go out, walk, breathe....Yes, it's necessary."

She was speechless. In her spirit and body a very important crisis seemed to be taking place. Her whole body relaxed as if that day she had suddenly lost the power of concentration, the internal bonds which had restrained her from birth. We still cannot explain to ourselves what happened to her.

"You should take care of yourself; you ought to live," said Clara.

"Yes, I should take care of myself. I have to live," repeated Paula in the tone of stupefaction of someone who hears for the first time the concise solution of a problem he has been working on fruitlessly all his life. "I ought to live!"

At that moment her eyes looked around, wandered vaguely, surprised, frightened, with melancholy and incomprehension, as would someone who has never before seen a horizon and views it for the first time.

But suddenly she stood up nervously. She went to her priedieu, knelt, and opened her prayer book. She bent her face forward, concealing it between her hands, and there she remained, submerged in profound and concentrated meditation. She was clearly resting in the bosom of God, who had reserved for his saint the ineffable pleasure of wandering and heavenly ecstasies.

During the ecstasy, who knows what occurred in her thoughts. God only knows.

Chapter XXV

VIRGO PRUDENTISIMA

Let us visit the two guests on the evening following their installation. Due to a prodigious effort of María de la Paz Jesús's domestic genius, the upstairs room managed to accommodate two beds.

Lázaro had just gone to bed, trying to recover his lost strength; his uncle, awake, and seated in the leather arm chair next to his bed, busied himself leafing through some papers, reading, and from time to time writing a little.

Suddenly the old man turned from his work, he looked at his nephew, who could not overcome a certain fear he felt whenever he saw those owl eyes gazing at him. He seemed to want to speak to the youth about something important, but to be afraid to because he lacked confidence in his discretion. After Lázaro's arrival at the house, uncle and nephew had not discussed politics. The fanatic believed that his charge did not possess the integrity and perseverance to sustain his beliefs. At the same time, the fervent liberal had had so many other things to think about that he had relegated politics to a secondary place and remembered little about the renunciation his uncle had demanded of him.

Lázaro yielded to his fatigue; he was slowly falling asleep when the old man asked loudly, "Lázaro, are you sleeping?"

"What?" replied the boy, startled awake.

"I am going to ask you something. Did you know a liberal in Zaragoza whose name was Bernabé del Arco?"

"Yes, sir," answered Lázaro, who knew and esteemed that person who was an orator and notable writer.

"He was one of those extremists, eh?" suggested the fanatic with sarcastic irony.

"Yes, sir, he's a man who supports the most advanced ideas," answered the nephew, fearful of saying even a word which might offend his uncle.

"He is..., no, he was, I should say, because he has passed on to a better life."

"How's that! Has he died?"

"They have killed him," said Elías with glacial indifference. "Look at the destiny which awaits the crazy, the depraved, the misguided, and the perverse. Do you see? Thus do the people punish those who deceive them! Oh! Thus should perish all the loud-mouths!"

The nephew was silent; the uncle returned to his reading, and not even a quarter of an hour had passed before Elías again spoke to the youth who, overcome by fatigue, was now sound asleep, yelling: "Wake up, Lázaro!"

And he awoke with a leap, terrified and trembling just as we will awake on the Last Day when the trumpets of judgment sound. The old man just had to take away Lázaro's few moments of rest after so much misfortune.

"Do you know a young fellow here whose name is Alfonso Núñez and another whose name is Roberto, commonly known as El Doctrino?"

"Yes, sir," replied Lázaro frightened and expecting him to announce that his two friends had also died.

"Good fellows, eh?" commented Elías, smiling like a witch at a Sabbath.

The nephew gave no answer, satisfying himself by mentally commending his good friend Alfonso Núñez to God.

"I have a plan...!" added the fanatic with a certain self satisfaction, "a superb plan. If you only knew, Lázaro. But you are very foolish, so you'll be unable to understand this. They are good fellows, those I mentioned to you. Isn't that so? So...very inspired, very fond of deceiving the people and giving speeches...well, just like you."

Lázaro became more frightened and understood even less.

"Those boys are very valuable. If you only knew how useful they are! Lovers of freedom, charlatans, impetuous ones, and enthusiasts. Oh! I don't fear them....They'll do all right. A magnificent plan!"

Afterwards, as though he regretted having said too much, he looked away from his nephew, mumbled something and began to skim through his papers again, making notes and constantly growling, at the same time gesticulating as though speaking to someone.

Lázaro stared for a long while at the livid face of the old royalist who, in the glow of the lamp, presented a fantastic and evil appearance. His ears became transparent, his eyes seemed like two burning coals, and his bald head shone like a convex mirror. The peculiar objects which surrounded him and those which covered the walls of the room increased the student's terror. That leather armchair, mute witness of the passing of a hundred generations, those old paintings and the carved furniture adorned with grotesque figures gave the room the aspect of a sinister laboratory where an alchemist wasted away, devoured by science and cobwebs.

After closing his eyes, finally overcome by sleep, Lázaro kept seeing his uncle and the objects which surrounded him. In addition the sinister figures of the Porreño ladies appeared before him, and in his frightful dream it seemed to him that those three figures were growing to the point of touching the clouds and occupying all space; Salomé, like a column, was supporting Heaven; Paz, like a gigantic cloud, joined the East and the West. Later everyone seemed to shrink and become very tiny: Paz like a peanut, Salomé like a pine nut, Paula like a lentil. He heard the friar-like voice of the devout one; he saw strange and complex lights flaring out from the old man's lamp. He observed the reddish translucency of his ears like two slices of incandescent meat; he saw the enormity of his baldness lit up like a planet. At last, all these confused and misshapen objects vanished, leaving in the dark background of the visions the image of Clara, who appeared to him, not distorted, but as an exact portrayal, raising her eyes from some task to look at him. Meanwhile, he seemed to hear constantly a subterranean voice which cried out, "Lázaro, are you asleep? Wake up, Lázaro!"

At dawn his sleep was deeper. He awoke at eight o'clock, and in the first moments he had to gather his thoughts and meditate a little in order to remember where he was and what had happened to him. His uncle had left. He got up and dressed. He did not know what time it was, but hunger led him to believe that it was lunch time. He opened the door, looking down the length of the hallway and as far as possible on the staircase. The first object that his eyes encountered was the figure of *Doña* Paulita, moving slowly.

"Have you rested?" she asked him with a voice less nasal and remote than usual.

"Yes, ma'am; many thanks."

"Do you need anything?"

"Nothing, ma'am."

"But you'll probably want to eat something. Here we are accustomed to breakfast at seven. It is the best thing. But it is eight; my aunt is very strict and has said that since you weren't at the table at seven you can't eat. This is a necessary discipline. As you well know, without discipline there can be no order. Now you can't eat anything until two in the afternoon."

"Ma'am, it doesn't matter. I...," said Lázaro who was courteous, although dying of hunger at that moment.

"But do not fear," continued the devout one, lowering her voice and looking around her. "I know that you are faint and you must be fed. Don't leave your room!"

She then went downstairs very quickly, trying not to be seen. The youth felt even greater gratitude toward the lady, who had already spoken in his defense the night before.

After awhile the devout one returned, bringing a breakfast which, although scanty, was enough to appease his hunger.

"My sister will not take it too badly," she said "but don't say anything to her. I am doing this for you because I understand that in a weak body the spirit has no strength."

"Ma'am, I don't know how to repay you for so many favors," answered the lad without looking at her.

At seven that morning, while Lázaro slept the sleep of exhaustion, a controversy was stirring in the kitchen on whether or not it would be convenient and disciplinary to call him to breakfast. María de la Paz said no. Salomé was in doubt, but the saint said yea. María de la Paz's reason was that since he preferred sleeping to eating he should be allowed his preference, then gradually accustom himself to discipline. In vain Paulita tried to oppose her with a great citation of theological and moral reasons founded on the principle of *mens sana in corpore sano*. That was all useless. Her words, heard with respect, produced no effect. Elías decided the matter by saying that his nephew, besides being a liberal, was a lazy bum and that he had given up on making anything good of him. They all ate in silence. Clara was not admitted to the family table.

Let us return upstairs. Lázaro ate his serving with great appetite. The lady asked him a thousand questions, and he answered her trying to be as courteous as his hunger permitted. The dialogue was along these lines:

"Did you think that you wouldn't eat today?"

"Ah, ma'am! No."

"I didn't forget that you were hungry."

"I thank you."

"But you didn't expect it," said Paulita, anxious to exploit that matter until the end.

"No, ma'am, in no way...; I...if...but...now."

"Your uncle was opposed to your eating."

"Ah! my uncle," said Lázaro leaving his meal "is a...no; he's an excellent man."

"Oh, yes!" said the devout one, looking to Heaven. "He is an exemplary man..., a saint."

"Yes indeed, a saint."

Lázaro, new in that house, had had no opportunity to determine the character of the person who sat before him at the moment of his breakfast. That is why nothing attracted his attention; he was not aware that her beautiful eyes had never had such a lively gleam, nor that the voice of any nun had never sung psalmodies with such melodious timbre as the voice of Paula as she asked, "Did you think that you would eat today?" In her, nevertheless, there was great naturalness, and we can affirm that at no time had her fine white hands ever crossed themselves with less affectation, unlike those contracted fingers she used to accompany and adorn her perorations.

"Here we will not permit any harm to you," she said in the tone of one who makes an important revelation. "Have no fear if you have committed some wrong."

"A wrong?" asked the youth sadly.

"Well, didn't they say that you were a great sinner?"

"I, a great sinner, ma'am?"

"It probably isn't as much as they say," continued *Doña* Paulita with a smile so worldly that it did not seem appropriate on a saint's lips.

"No," replied the youth effusively, "no, it isn't so much as they say, that's a fact. And if I were to tell the whole story..."

"Tell all," said the other with great interest.

"I do not know what wrong I have committed," added Lázaro sadly, "Yes, I have committed wrongs, I can't deny that...."

"Tell me, tell me, what wrongs?" inquired God's Favorite, anxiously.

"I shall tell you," he replied, preparing to confess.

"I understand, some misconduct of youth. Youth is full of dangers. And if youth is left alone..."

"That's true."

"I want you to reform. Perhaps the wrong is much less serious than you yourself think. Perhaps it is no more than a trivial indiscretion," said Paula, with even greater anxiety and interest. "Speak up and I shall give you advice. Tell me about it."

Lázaro thought for a moment and was about to open his mouth to formulate an answer or an excuse when Elías presented himself at the door. The devout one was a little upset, but recovered in a moment. The royalist was very surprised to see the lady there and, also the remnants of a meal, and his nephew became embarrassed at having eaten it.

"Come in, *Don* Elías," she exclaimed with her usual aplomb, "come in; I am pleading with your nephew that for the love of God he not give you any more unpleasantness. Oh! But he is beginning to repent for the errors of his youth. How strange it is that youth, involved in itself, sins only through thorny paths. I am recommending moderation, courtesy, and prudence to him. I see that you are surprised to see that I have brought him something to eat. Oh! I confess my wrong. I just couldn't resist the impulses of compassion. I have been weak-willed. I was not made to be strict, and I confess that I don't have the character, as I should, to maintain strong discipline. If I have committed a wrong, forgive me."

For a few seconds Elías did not know how to answer her, but he held too high an idea of that woman's Christianity to hesitate in approving what she did. That act seemed to him a sublime proof of charity.

"Madam, how kind you are!" he said.

"It isn't kindness, it's weakness. I know that I did wrong."

"Madam, you are a saint! Although he doesn't deserve what you have done for him, this brings out your virtue even more."

"Oh!" exclaimed the Chosen One of the Lord, "I confess that my duty was to follow your verdict, but I couldn't resist a powerful impulse of indulgence. Oh! If one could always conquer oneself..."

"Look and learn," said Elías, turning toward Lázaro, "look at that saint; learn what is nobility, generosity, virtue."

"No," she said, lowering her eyes. "Don't take this sinner for a model."

"Learn, Lázaro," exclaimed the fanatic emotionally. "Here you have virtue itself."

The saint bowed deeply and walked out, leaving the uncle and the nephew alone together.

Chapter XXVI

DISSENTERS FROM THE GOLDEN FOUNTAIN

That morning passed with no other incident than that which we have described. Lázaro went upstairs and downstairs furtively several times, with the caution of a thief, trying to see Clara, but it was impossible. He hoped to see her at lunch, but as on the day before, his wishes were frustrated.

At two o'clock the table was set, and everyone seated at his place. The table was large enough for twelve; María de la Paz occupied one end, with Salomé on her right and Elías to her left, while the pious one was seated to the right of her cousin. The youth was placed on the opposite end, at such a distance from the main group that in order to reach his serving he had to extend his arms. He was first served a soup which, in its thinness and lightness, looked like a seminary serving; then followed a pallid stew in which Lázaro was privileged to receive three dozen chickpeas, a leaf of cabbage, and half a potato; afterward, they divided up some six ounces of meat which, if the truth is told, was not as bad as it was scanty. And finally some grapes, so wrinkled and yellow that it was easy to believe there was some close tie between those noble fruits and the skin on Salomé's face. The small feast ended, during which the silence of a refectory reigned in the dining room, except when Elías commented that such lavish generosity seemed excessive to him and when he praised sobriety as the foundation of all virtues.

Then they prayed for a while, and the ladies left the room. María de la Paz had, during the period of their decline, acquired the habit of taking a nap, and now during the last *agnus dei* of the prayer she was making reverences with her eyes closed. Lázaro climbed the stairs disconsolate, because once again he had not been able to achieve the object of his constant preoccupation. He ventured downstairs undetected by his uncle; he traversed the hallway, full of worry and anxiety, but saw nothing. Everything was closed and silent. Undoubtedly the inhabitants of the house were submerged in the pleasant stupor of a siesta or the spiritual lethargy of religious contemplation. Only Batilo, the melancholy dog who had lost the habits of his race and could not even remember how to bark, was walking in boredom through the kitchen, from time to time scratching the closet door where the scanty leftovers of the meat served that afternoon were probably resting.

Lázaro went upstairs in desperation, but on seeing his uncle half asleep in an armchair, he could no longer resist the lethal influence that boring region exerted on all its inhabitants; he also prepared to sleep and stretched out on his bed. Not ten minutes had passed before he heard the vigorous ringing of the bell on the floor below and the voice of Salomé along with others, among which he thought he recognized one. He got up and peered down the stairs.

There were four persons who were looking for him, and the lady irritatedly directed them to the upper floor. Lázaro saw his friend Alfonso, *El Doctrino*, and two others he had never seen before; they proceeded upstairs. *Coletilla* had heard them in his owl-like sleep, and awakening suddenly he headed to the door.

"Hi, there!" he exclaimed suddenly, but changing tone very quickly he said with feigned coldness or indifference, "What can I do for you?"

As Lázaro was standing behind his uncle, he did not see Elías put his finger to his mouth and make an imperceptible sign to *El Doctrino*. Then making an effort to appear pleasant, he added, "Now I see! You were looking for my nephew."

The young student trembled at thinking how it would irritate his benefactor to see him in the company of those extremists.

"For me?" he asked, shaking his friend's hand.

"Yes," replied *El Doctrino*, who understood what he was to do.

"Yes, we came for you," said Alfonso. "We have a meeting this afternoon and we want you to come to it. It is the meeting of the dissenters from The Golden Fountain."

Lázaro expected his uncle to be furious on hearing them speak about a meeting of the Fountanists. But to his surprise, *Coletilla* was as calm as though he had heard them speak about an ecumenical council. The youth did not have enough discernment or memory to realize that there could be some relationship between the questions the fanatic had asked him the night before and the visit of those friends.

"Yes, you may go. Go," said Elías.

Lázaro's confusion increased, but before he had time to think, Alfonso took him by the arm and lead him down the stairs and into the street.

The other two youths were until now unknown to us, although we may have seen them in the noisy area of The Golden Fountain precisely on the unlucky day when Lázaro was thrown out of the club. One of them, born in Algodonales, was one of the most assiduous members of the barber Calleja's gatherings, and it is fairly certain that he intervened in the quasi-tragic scene we referred to in the first chapter. His name was Francisco Aldama, and, being an Andalusian and considerably fond of his dealing with bullfighters, he was called Curro Aldama, or El Curro. *Doña* Teresa Burguillos, the barber's happy companion, was a bit clumsy in the pronunciation of proper names and usually called her husband's friend and companion in arms Aldaba. He was Curro Aldama or Aldaba, a fervent Fountanist, grossly ignorant and as daring as any other fool. He boasted of being a great patriot, and no bell sounded in Madrid without his taking part in the dance.

The other youth was of a very different circumstance and figure. His literary zeal had made him a friend of the classical poet who he spent time with in the Olympus of *Doña* Leoncia, the semigoddess of De la Gorguera Street. There he met Alfonso Núñez, with whom he struck up a friendship, and very soon, although the muses were propitious for him, he opened successfully at La Cruz with his pastoral *sainete* entitled *Anfriso and Zenobia*. He left the muses for politics, wrote in *El Universal* and in *El Labriego*, spoke in clubs, and decided to support the extremist party.

He possessed much talent, and was gifted as an orator and newspaperman, but had very little education and was hopelessly fickle. He often went to Calleja's store and to The Maltese Cross club, but lately it had been said with certainty that he belonged to the shady society of Los Comuneros, although he denied it. We know for certain that they were suspicious of him in The Golden Fountain; we do not know whether there were grounds for this mistrust. It was rumored that he was one of the agitators paid by the opposition. Finally one evening, on seeing that they were looking at him with distrust and making stinging references to him, he left the club, never to return. This was Cabanillas, a well-mannered and talented youth. One could not avoid a certain repugnance at seeing his association with soulless men like *Tres Pesetas*, *Chaleco*, and El Matutero, whom we had the pleasure of meeting at the beginning of this timely narration.

"Lad," said Núñez, "did you know that we have had a falling out with those people from The Golden Fountain? The events of the other night obliged us to break off with that rabble. We took off and are now on the outside. We are going to organize another club."

"They slandered me," exclaimed Lázaro. "I don't know what demon tempted me to speak that evening."

"But they're only simpletons. They imagine that there are no other liberals but themselves," affirmed Núñez, "and we who defend true and total freedom are referred to as extremists, agitators, and they say that we are being bribed."

"We'll soon straighten our accounts with them," said *El Doctrino*.

"Well, listen," continued Alfonso. "We'll found another club, a true revolutionary club. Those fools of The Golden Fountain have now taken to preaching order. Order, what hogwash! We'll preach violence, because without violence there can be no revolution; without uprooting the obstacles and destroying them completely, one cannot change this nation. We are going to preach democracy; we are going to proclaim the supreme absolute sovereignty of the people; we'll fight the throne, and single out those who, during the great purification being planned, should be pulled out by the roots, exterminated, and finished off. Will you come to our club?"

"We'll see," answered Lázaro, very distracted.

"Our idea," continued Alfonso, "is to combat those lukewarm republicans who go to the Parliament and the clubs to preach order and moderation. We'll exterminate that mob, those hypocrites."

"Yes," said Curro, "because whoever lets himself be dominated by those lukewarm men, will stay behind; these are not times for lagging behind. Be alert, he who doesn't take advantage now..."

They arrived at Gorguera Street, and *Doña* Leoncia's house; they went up to the poet's room, which was the place designated for the organizational meeting of the incipient club. We shall refer to the poet's room as La Fontanilla—the official denomination the youths gave it.

They made themselves as comfortable as they could on three chairs and the poet's bed while the poet was elsewhere in the house at *Doña* Leoncia's side, paying little attention to politics. El Curro sat down next to the table and from the beginning displayed great interest in a bottle which had undoubtedly been placed there by the provident hand of the classical poet.

"Let us see," said Alfonso from the presidency, which was the bed, "let us see what we do to those liberals who slander us and say that we are drunkards and hidden agents of the reactionaries."

"Fight them with reason!" observed Lázaro, "prove to them that we are not agents of the reaction. But how do their ideas differ from ours? Aren't they liberals? Don't they love the Constitution?"

"But they love it halfway," said *El Doctrino*, "because they don't love the true sacrament of the revolution—which is destruction."

"Enough has been destroyed," indicated Lázaro, "let us do all that is possible to each provide at least a small stone for the great edifice which is to be built."

"None of that; without destruction it is useless to think about building. We ought to point out who are the enemies of the people, their perennial enemies," said *El Doctrino*.

"Well, that is what I was saying," affirmed Aldama, deciding after much hesitation to test the contents of the bottle.

"I feel the same way," echoed Cabanillas. "Today, we are worse off than before; the only difference is that there are a few more words in our mouths. The Ministers speak of liberty, the deputies speak of liberty, the club members speak of liberty, but there is no liberty, it doesn't exist; it's a farce. I declare, gentlemen, that rather than this farce I prefer the priests and the absolute King of the past."

"Exactly what doubts do you have?" said Núñez. "We have only tried a few formulas. And as for that, who is to blame but the liberals, who speak to us of order and the return of order?"

"That's exactly what I was saying!" exclaimed El Curro, again tasting the bottle which apparently had pleased him.

"To teach the people to ask for justice, and if it is not given to them, to make justice for themselves; that is what is needed," said *El Doctrino*.

"How often those hypocrites have spoken about the priest from Tamajón who took justice into his own hands! What could the people do when they saw that the government permitted constant conspiring by the Royal Palace and was jailing good liberals because they were singing the *Trágala*?"

"It's very clear. What they want to do is to deceive the nation, infuse fear with their talk about order, always with their order...."

"While certain men still live," said *El Doctrino* gloomily, "we'll never move forward. It's not appropriate yet to point out which men must perish. They'll be named at the right time."

El Doctrino was rather lugubrious; he spoke little and always with a melancholy deliberateness which hinted at concealed thoughts and a cold and sinister calculation he did not let show.

"I feel the same way," repeated Aldama who was resolved not to snub the bottle while it still had something inside.

"Well, the first thing, gentlemen," said Alfonso, "is to establish ourselves in any way possible. We shall see if we can locate a good place where we can accommodate the largest number possible."

"We will meet in the open air if it is necessary. What matters is for us to recruit people, and I'll take care of that. The day after tomorrow we will meet here, and I'll bring two or three friends. You will see what kind of lads they are!"

"Well, then, until the day after tomorrow; you come, Lázaro," said Alfonso. "I'll pick you up. I don't want you to be discouraged or bored. The future is in our hands, young man. We'll have to look for a new way out because this situation is sunk. Ideas are gradually going to decline, and it's only natural and right for young people to be the initiators and developers of great principles."

"I'll be there," said Lázaro, with little enthusiasm.

Alfonso and Cabanillas stood to leave. Lázaro did the same, and the three departed. *El Doctrino* and El Curro remained alone. It seems certain that the bottle Aldama had shown so much fondness for was soon completely empty.

When they were alone, and had heard the others go down the stairs, the one with the bottle asked, "How much did uncle *Coletilla* give you yesterday?"

"Look," said the other pulling out four *onzas* and some doubloons from his greasy pocket.

"Ah, you shrewd one!" exclaimed Aldama, observing the gold with shining and avid eyes. "Give me at least one! I owe four months' rent and have borrowed more than six *duros*."

"Little by little. One must not squander the King's treasury," said *El Doctrino*, majestically putting the revolutionary state treasury into his pocket.

"Come on, Doctrinillo, give it to me! You already know that I have come to terms with Perico Tinieblas from Plaza de Gilimón, who is perfect for these matters, and, of course, in Cebada Plaza there isn't a single horse-dealer who is not capable of devouring the government under one of my orders."

"Things are proceeding as planned. I can't pay out except at the proper time; those are my orders. But don't worry, when the assembly begins to yield fruits..."

"Tell me—does Alfonso Núñez know...?"

"No, he doesn't suspect anything. He's innocent and a dreamer. He's one of those who'll give his life for his convictions. These are the kind of men we need—talented men of good faith who can speak to the people and awaken their restlessness."

"And that other nitwit we picked up today?"

"That fellow is also bright, but innocent as an angel. We have many of these, who will do most of the work at no expense. Cabanillas is valuable, but he's expensive; the poor fellow is bad off and we must favor him. Yesterday, I found him crying at his home; I felt a great deal of pity for him. He works for us with repugnance, but he has no other choice because he hasn't a red cent."

"Well, look, I'm also..."

"You'll see how well this is going to turn out," said *El Doctrino* lowering his voice. "And by that time we will be able to count on funds. Times are bad, Currillo, and if one doesn't seek shelter in the shade of a good tree..."

"That's exactly what I say. But will you give me a little cash or not?"

"Wait until the day after tomorrow. I have orders not to distribute it as yet."

Curro and *El Doctrino* went downstairs after shouting good-bye to the classical poet from the doorway.

The Golden Fountain helped the King and the opposition more than the friars and partisans did, for within it grew a cancer, which a few prudent men tried in vain to cut out, by expelling an innocent man. The cancer of venality continued to corrupt assembly, for whom La Fontanilla was not a competitor, but rather a branch office.

Chapter XXVII

SHE STAYS HOME ALONE

When Lázaro returned home, he trembled in *Coletilla's* presence. But his fear very quickly turned to surprise on seeing that, far from showing indignation, the old man even managed to show a certain benevolence, which was a very rare thing in him.

On that evening and the following morning Lázaro again attempted the difficult task of seeing Clara. It was impossible because the system of confinement employed by the three jailers, like a female Cerberus with three heads and three bodies, was inexorable. Clara lived worse than a cenobite nun, worse than those prisoners whom the ancient history books say were buried alive—living bodies destined for pain and the horrors of loneliness. God pity that unfortunate girl!

But although Lázaro was not able to see her, the abbot Carrascosa did, with the consent of the devout one, entering that day to ask about Lady Clarita's health. Finding himself alone with her, he pulled a paper out of his pocket, signaled her to remain silent, and clandestinely handed it to her. Without saying a word to her, he departed.

Clara blushed. Her first thought was to tear the letter up, but it occurred to her that it could be from Lázaro. Perhaps the poor boy had decided to write to her, and being unable to see her, he had availed himself of the abbot who was undoubtedly his friend. She kept the letter in her bosom and waited.

The devout one soon arrived and sat down next to her.

"Did you know," she said, "that this afternoon we are going to watch the Divine Pastor procession?"

"Is that so?" answered Clara automatically.

"Yes, but you are not going. We have decided that you should remain here, because young ladies who are doing penance must never leave the house. Don't you agree?"

"Yes, I do," said Clara, trembling for fear that they might see from the expression on her face that she possessed a hidden letter.

"We are going to the balcony of a friend of ours from where everything can be seen perfectly. It will be very spectacular. From San Antón church will come three Statues, and they say it is also very probable that the *Cristo de las Llagas* Statue will be brought from the Chapel of Santa María del Arco. They will all pass by Calle de San Mateo, where we are going."

She said no more. She was already dressed to go out. Her dress was the one she always wore on formal occasions. But something unusual! Her wimple headdress was pleated at the forehead with a certain hint of a novitiate nun, a suggestion which did not lack charm. Her shawl, whose impenetrable veil on other occasions always covered her face, now was thrown back with an openness which a strict Dominican of that ancient house of the Porreños would have classified as extremely uninhibited.

If Clara had been less preoccupied at that moment and had possessed a more observant character she would certainly have been surprised to see Paulita so distracted. She would also have noticed that she was smiling frequently, bustling around incessantly, and that she suddenly would become sad, remaining still and rather absorbed in her own thoughts. The the quietness turned into an attack of despair; it made her nerves twitch, and she closed her eyes, extended her neck, and seemed to listen to distant noises, no one else could hear. There is even more. If Clara had not had her face bent over her sewing, as usual, she would have noticed that the devout one had stood up and approached a little rock crystal mirror—an admirable work of the seventeenth century, acquired in Venice by the eleventh Porreño—and was looking at herself with unusual singular attention for a span of three minutes. There is unimpeachable evidence that that historic mirror had never at any time reflected that lady's face. We also know that it was not the first time that she had looked at herself; the evening and day before she had also looked at herself, observing herself, above all in the evening, calmly and with pleasure. There is no doubt that she half-closed her eyes in order to see herself (we do not know in how much light) and that she later tightened her lips, displaying to the insatiable curiosity of the flattering mirror her two rows of beautiful pearly teeth. This phenomenon has obliged us to labor considerably in order to decipher certain mysteries which are essential for the continuation of this story.

In the other room, María de la Paz and Salomé had exhumed from their worldly drawers some very old dresses of Valencian silk which in better days had been elegant garments. On their heads, over very large combs, they draped black mantillas of thick lace, and Paz opened a small cardboard box shaped like a casket, which still held the aroma of the glove shops of 1790. From this same drawer she pulled a fan with two hundred spokes which when unfolded like a peacock tail, made more noise than bird shot. Salomé carried on the wrist of her left hand a small handbag, in which she placed, along with her glasses, a little vial of essence and other trifles.

"And will we leave that young man here?" said Paz looking at her sister in amazement.

"How is that? That isn't possible," replied the owner of the bag with fright. "If Clara remains at home..."

"How horrible! We must take that young man with us. But what will they say...?"

At that moment the devout one entered the room. Elías was just outside.

"What will they say if we take that young man with us!" continued Paz.

"That young man?" repeated Paulita.

"Yes, what will they say? Heavens!" exclaimed Salomé.

"What would they say?" expressed the devout one, looking elsewhere. "He is an escort, a gentleman who is accompanying us. And above all, evil lies in the intention, not in appearances. What can they say? It is true, we do not need gentlemen but it isn't improper for that young man to accompany us. Oh! Let us not pay so much attention to the opinions of others."

"They know him as a libertine," said Paz, "and if they see him with us..."

In the face of this argument Paulita hesitated for a moment, and almost did not know what to reply. But she was not a person who would let herself be easily defeated in a dispute, and gathering strength she continued, "Oh, the fragility of worldly things! Let us not fear what they will say! Above all, I do not believe that Lázaro is a libertine." Meanwhile Elías had entered and listened attentively to the devout one. "He has a good heart, and if he has committed some wrong it is due to a lack of experience and guidance. But I understand him very well, and I know that he will mend his ways, if he hasn't already. He is secretly shedding tears for his past mistakes. Let him come along."

Elías did not let her finish. Carried away by enthusiasm he raised his arms and shouted, "Lázaro, Lázaro!"

Before Lázaro arrived, the royalist leaped outside the room and brought him, or more exactly, he dragged him in.

"Kneel there," he said to him energetically, presenting Lázaro before the devout one. "Kneel in front of that saint. She has said that you have a good heart."

Lázaro was perplexed; the two old ladies were amazed, the devout one satisfied, and Elías enthusiastic. The youth had to kneel down, whether he cared to or not.

"Kneel down, man, kneel down!" said the uncle. "Now, kiss her hand!"

Lázaro, without thinking about it, obeyed his uncle's violent orders; he respectfully kissed the saint's hand and held it extended a moment between his own hands.

"Bow down before virtue!" said Elías. "You, a sinner, unworthy of being forgiven. She has said that you have a good heart. No, ladies, he does not."

Doña Paulita made a heroic effort to maintain a certain archiepiscopal dignity as Lázaro, on bended knees in front of her, was kissing her hand, but her saintly decorum was overwhelmed by her increasingly womanly nature. When she felt the young man's lips touch the skin of her hand, she trembled all over, first turning pale, and then in an instant blushed red. A current of ardent fever and a burst of cold nervousness circulated alternately throughout her holy body, which was not accustomed to the contact of human lips.

After a pause, she recovered her aplomb and said:

"How ridiculous! I, a saint? Stand up, young gentleman!" she did not dare use the words "young man." "I only said that I believe in your good sense and that you will reform."

"Well, didn't she say that she has forgiven you for the wrongs you have committed? What virtue! What Christian heroism!" exclaimed Elías. "Aren't you overwhelmed? But man, get up! What are you doing there on your knees?"

The youth stood up as Paz put an end to this intense and stirring scene by saying coldly and with contempt, "Let's go!"

"Prepare yourself to accompany these ladies!" said *Coletilla*.

This command greatly annoyed the student. He had heard at the table that morning that Clara would not be going to the procession and had made his plans to get to her that day. The duty of accompanying the three women seemed to be the greatest misfortune that could have happened to him that day. But, how could he possibly resist that tyrant's orders?

Full of exasperation, he picked up his hat and went downstairs with the three illustrious ruins, who took along one of the keys to the house, leaving Clara instructions to not leave her room. Elías, who also stayed home, had another key.

Not five minutes had passed since the Porreños began to make their way to San Mateo Street, when the abbot Carrascosa very hurriedly arrived and knocked at the door.

Elías went downstairs to open it for him.

"Come, friend, come right away," he said to him excitedly.

"But where, man, where? This house is all alone. I can't leave."

"What do you mean you can't leave?" said the abbot, in surprise. "Well, a fine mess you'll cause if you don't leave right away; come with me."

"Well, what's going on, Carrascosa?"

"Come on and we'll talk on the way."

"But, the house..."

"To hell with the house! Close the door and let's go!"

"That girl will be left here alone."

"We'll leave her locked up. Come; this isn't a matter for ifs ands or buts."

"But what's up? Let's hear it."

"Ah! If you don't come with me right away to La Fontanilla...it's the club those boys started...if you don't come with me, there's going to be a fight."

"But what's wrong, man?"

The abbot had not prepared beforehand the lie he needed to use to persuade Elías to leave the house; so that he was flustered for a moment, but his friar-like astuteness did not fail him.

"Well it seems that those fellows are getting excited and say that you have deceived them, that you don't have authorization from...from that person, that you..."

"That I don't have authorization?" said Elías. "Careful with those youngsters. What can you expect? Liberals to the end!"

"And it seems that they want to start an uprising this evening," said Carrascosa, now certain of the lie he needed to use on Elías.

"This evening!" exclaimed Elías, raising his hands to his head. "Those kids are crazy! They are going to spoil everything....But who told them tonight...? Damned kids! I'll go there right away."

"Come now, because if you delay..."

"I'm going, I'm going right now. I'll lock the door and I'll take the key with me. It really doesn't matter, the ladies have another key."

"Let's go."

The abbot had achieved his objective, which was to keep *Coletilla* away from the house that afternoon so that Clara would be alone. Meanwhile, the sphinxes were approaching the end of their trip and Lázaro followed them, turning over in his mind the plan he had conceived in a moment of choleric inspiration. His plan was to leave the three ruins in the middle of the street when they were most distracted by the procession, and return to the house.

But this plan had some drawbacks. How was he going to enter the house? Break down the door? And what about his uncle, who was inside? It was a terrible situation. To live in the same house with her and not be able to see her! To hear them continuously accuse that unhappy girl of mistakes and outrageous crimes, and be unable to approach her and ask her, "What have you done?"

The three Porreños walked along in cadence, pompously, without speaking a word. In this way they arrived at the house where they were to view the procession. It was the house of a clergyman, *Don* Silvestre Entrambasaguas, and his sister *Doña* Petronila Entrambasaguas.

Chapter XXVIII

THE HANDBAG

Don Silvestre was a round-faced clergyman, well-nourished, greasy, stingy, jovial, somewhat silly, and a bad theologian and preacher; he was as pompous as he was simple-minded. His sister was a housekeeper in her fifties, stout and very short, with a nose the size of an almond and the color of a tomato, a prominent bosom, and waistline and hips so voluminous that they gave the impression of a barrel. The three aristocratic ruins would never have condescended in their good times to have dealings with that pair of such low extraction—they were offspring of a pork dealer from Almendralejo, and *Don* Silvestre had been a swineherd in the pastures of Badajoz before he entered the seminary—; but in times of decline they could visit each other and deal with each other, although always maintaining a certain decorum and tacitly establishing the differences of the ancient hierarchies. They had met each other in the locutory of the Góngoras church, in whose convent there was a nun who belonged to the Entrambasaguas family. The friendship between the Porreños and *Don* Silvestre and his sister had been carried on now during four years of mutual courtesies, mutual urbane formulas and respectful familiarity.

The three sat down and informed their friends about the young man who was respectfully escorting them. María de la Paz, in her eagerness to tell all, revealed with her customary lucidity that the young gentleman had been on the road to ruination on account of bad acquaintances; but added that they were protecting him and hoped to be successful in leading him to the righteous path.

"Where are you from, boy?" said the priest, who was very brusque and frank and used the intimate *tú* with everyone.

"From Ateca, in Aragón."

"Ateca? Good land! Good bacon! Good fruit!...And are you not studying, son, don't you study?"

"Yes, sir. I am studying to be a lawyer."

"That's a fine thing!" said the cleric with brutal laughter. "Lawyer! What is that good for? Why don't you study theology and canon law?"

"I studied a little of that in Zaragoza."

"Zaragoza! Good land! Good mutton, good loin, but not like that in my own country, Estremadura...because I am an Estremaduran. Tell me, why didn't you study to become a priest?"

"Because I don't have a vocation for that career."

Doña Paz made a gesture of surprise and disapproval, as though the youth had said a great irreverence. Then, gathering on her face every sign of contempt and acrimony in her great repertory, she said, "Ah, *Señor Don* Silvestre! This youth's absurd behavior may rightly surprise you, but you must take into account that until recently he has lived in the most lamentable misconduct. He will soon mend his ways. Someone has taken charge of his education, and we believe that she'll achieve her intention."

"That he didn't have a vocation!" exclaimed Entrambasaguas in a thunderous voice, "That's irreverent."

The student, stunned and indignant, lowered his eyes. Then he looked to *Doña* Paulita for consolation, to see if, as on other occasions, she would come to his defense, but the devout one, who was watching with contemplative attention, was thinking something other than defending him.

"My *Señora Doña* Paulita," said the clergyman, addressing the mystic rose, "Do you know that I have read the book *De Albigensium Erroribus* and I agree with Father Paravicino, that *pietas in pietate contra ecclesia nulla contemnere pios*? How does this opinion seem to you? Because to *demonio numquam salus inveniatur*. Come on, speak up, you who are a great theologian."

Paulita did not reply; anyone less thick-headed than Padre Silvestre would have understood that at that moment an extemporaneous theological consultation was a great nuisance. Feminine instinct had just revolted against all the saint's usual ritualistic unction. She had no answer, and, how unusual! She who always had blushed in the presence of priests when they spoke of mundane things now blushed because one spoke to her of theology.

"I don't know....I don't understand....I haven't read that book," she finally answered noticing that the crackpot Entrambasaguas repeated his question adorned with two or three more festoons of Latin.

"But didn't you recommend it to me that day that we spoke together, in the nuns locutory, along with the Bishop of Calahorra, when you said something about Saint Dionisio Aeropagita which began...Let's see how it begins....Don't you recall?"

"No, I don't," said the devout one, very flushed, and uncomfortable at not finding a pretext for changing the conversation.

"But didn't you recommend that book about *Albigesium Erroribus*? You told me that it was the best that had been written...," insisted the stupid clergyman.

A buzzing of voices and the harsh twang of bassoons freed our friend from her predicament by announcing the procession. They immediately moved out to occupy the two balconies. On one sat the clergyman with María de la Paz and Salomé and on the other were the stout *Doña* Petronila, *Doña* Paulita and Lázaro. An enormous flower pot, in which an oleander grew with extraordinary vigor, complicated the seating arrangements of these three. The clergyman's fat sister sat in the middle, and it was impossible for the other two to sit down in comfort due to both *Doña* Petronila's size and the oleander's. At last, after a thousand formalities, the devout one seated herself in the center, with Lázaro on her right and *Doña* Petronila to the left.

The procession began to file by. The clergyman did enough explaining for six people. He spoke so loudly that the passers-by kept looking up at the balconies. Some of the curious people noted a great strain on *Doña* Paulita's face, and the author of this book, who was one of those passing by, noted with surprise—because he knew about her character from hearsay—that there was nothing more than a few leaves and an oleander flower separating the lady's forehead from the youth's hair. Lázaro paid no attention to the crowd, the saints, or anything. His despair at finding himself there against his will preoccupied him completely.

On the other balcony *Don* Silvestre was giving a detailed account of the confraternities, banners, standards, images, and associations which were filing by. Salomé showed off a handbag attached to her wrist, which hung over the guardrail, offering to the large crowd's surprise the bright colors of its tiny blue beads and golden sequins. Salomé's handbag was an elegant piece of beadwork, in whose elaboration its owner's delicate hands had taken part—a work of the past century, and the year '94 in which the lady had shown it off on the promenades of La Florida on winter days, to the approval of the youth of that time. Salomé professed a great deal of affection for that handbag, because she felt when she wore it around her wrist that she was carrying an amulet of perpetual youth.

"It's going to fall off," her aunt admonished her, watching the way she balanced it on the guardrail.

"I won't drop it," replied Salomé, who was fond of showing off that inherited piece of adornment on solemn occasions, and believed that from the street below it looked magnificent.

The orderly crowd of altar boys, clergymen, brotherhoods, privileged brotherhood members, and penitents continued to file by. Each time a standard (a cross) passed by, the fat woman and her brother praised it to the skies. Lázaro's elbow was touching the devout one's elbow, and she sat with her hands crossed and head inclined to one side, no doubt because the smooth contact with the oleanders pleased her. Later, she passed her hand across her eyes as if pushing aside an imaginary veil.

When the procession was at its peak, so to speak, a shout resounded from the adjacent balcony. Oh, what grief! Salomé's handbag had fallen into the street.

"And the key to the house is in it!" said Paz, terrified.

That was all Lázaro needed to hear. He made a decision in an instant. He left the balcony and said impetuously, "I'm going to look for it."

The handbag fell on the heads of the passers-by; it was passed from hand to hand and dragged by the multitude in such a way that moments after falling it was at a great distance. Lázaro, seeing this, ran downstairs rapidly; he reached the street and crossed through the crowd with great difficulty. "What a happy coincidence!" he said to himself. "There is the key. I'll take it, run home, and open the door; the old man should be upstairs napping; I'll enter, see her, speak to her, and tell her...who knows what I'll say to her...and I'll return on the run. If the old women are suspicious, I'll make up some kind of lie. It's the only way."

At last, panting with exertion, he caught up with the wandering handbag. The woman who had it was examining it, and seeing that it contained nothing of value, did not seem to show much interest in keeping it. Lázaro took it. The surging movement of the crowd had carried him a great distance from Entrambasaguas's house. He could not be seen from the balcony. He stopped hesitating and began to run home through one of the transverse streets.

The situation's nervous tension and the sudden departure had excited him so much that he had to stop to catch his breath. At last he would see her! He reached the house, entered, and went upstairs, but before deciding to enter, he stopped for a moment and had to lean against the wall because the excitement made him weak. He thought that she would be frightened at seeing him enter so impudently and at hearing the door open. Finally, with the greatest care, he put the key in the keyhole, gave it a turn, and very quietly opened the door. He entered; he turned to close the door and took a few steps. It was already late, the house was dark; he could not see anything. He felt his way around for awhile. Finally he could vaguely distinguish some objects and continued through the corridor.

Sepulchral silence reigned in the house.

"Elías must be sleeping upstairs," he thought, and continued walking until he reached the door of the room where Clara should be. "So as not to frighten her," thought Lázaro, shaking with emotion like someone about to commit a crime, "the best thing will be to draw near the door and call her quietly. In that way, she will not be frightened."

He advanced, reached the door, and taking a breath in order to pronounce the two syllables of that name he loved so much, he stopped, and in a low and emotional voice he called:

"Clara." But at the same moment he pronounced her name, he shuddered in surprise and terror. An intense cold circulated through his whole body; his blood all rushed to his heart, which beat with uncontrollable violence, and he stood next to the door, immobile as a statue. As he spoke Clara's name he heard from inside the room a man's voice, a woman's voice, and some hurried footsteps.

We shall soon learn what he did.

Chapter XXIX

THE FATEFUL HOURS

At four that afternoon, when, after the three ladies had left, Clara found herself alone, she tried to satisfy her curiosity by reading the letter the abbot had given to her; but she saw Elías walk through the corridor. She felt afraid and put it away again. A half-hour later, after *Coletilla* left with Carrascosa, she was alone, entirely alone and shut in. Then she opened the letter. She felt certain it was from Lázaro, and she knew almost point by point what it would say. But she was astonished to look at the signature and see the name *Claudio*.

"Claudio! Who is Claudio?" she exclaimed in great confusion.

The letter read:

"My friend,

I have already returned to you the young prisoner you love so much. I got him out of jail, where the unfortunate fellow was ready to die of hunger and cold; I had him released only because he's your friend. You know now that you and I are true friends. That young man seems to love you sincerely, but not so much as I, who adore you. I am so miserable apart from you that today I'm going to try to see and speak to you, entering by way of a neighboring house. Don't be surprised; my mind is made up. Because of me those three ladies have gone out today; on my account Elías has left; on my account Lázaro has left. You are alone and shut in, shut in against everyone but me; I'll see you this afternoon. Don't be afraid. I assure you that I only want to see you and speak to you. He who adores you.

Claudio."

"Claudio!" repeated Clara as she folded the letter. "Who is this man? And he wants to enter here! Lord, how frightening! What should I do? Lock the doors?"

Clara began to tremble with fear; she could not decide what to do. At last, pulling together all her courage, she went to the corridor door and locked it. Then she ran to the door which led to the next room, planning to lock it as well, but it was too late. Bozmediano had already very calmly entered the room.

"Heavens!" exclaimed Clara, retreating in fright. "Go away, for heavens sake! What audacity!"

But unable to continue, she burst into tears.

"Go away sir,...If they return...For heaven's sake, kind sir," she had forgotten his name. "Go away....You are very kind and will leave me alone. If they come home now, what will they say?"

"They will not come. Calm down," said Bozmediano, somewhat annoyed by that emotional reception. "We are already truly friends. Today I come to speak to you and to see you. You already know that I have declared myself your protector."

In Bozmediano's amatory system, it was his custom to use the more intimate *tú* form of address after his third meeting with a girl.

"I don't want you to protect me. I am fine here," affirmed Clara with anguish.

"Fine, here?" asked the soldier, clenching his fists. "Fine, here? I'm ready to hang those three harpies who are torturing you. When I think that an old fanatic and three ridiculous women are alive in the world today only for the purpose of mortifying you and slowly destroying the most noble and lovable creature who has ever been born..."

"But they don't torment me," said Clara, whose great distress manifested itself in intermittent weeping, giving the adventurous ladies' man a moment's pause. "Go away, for God's sake, I beg you. I ask you in God's name and for all the saints' sake."

"Leave without you? It's not possible."

"I'll never agree to leave with you," exclaimed the young girl resolutely.

"Go away, kind sir," for once again she could not recall his name, "you are a good person, I'm sure. But if you wait a moment more before leaving, I'll despise you for the rest of my life. Go away, for mercy's sake."

"And if I go, what's going to become of poor you?" asked Bozmediano sadly. "If I abandon you, what is going to become of you in the hands of those four demons? How can I go along with this frightful crime of confinement, this loneliness, this stagnation, this slow torture that these infamous people apply to you? Clara, you know me well enough, from the few times that you have dealt with me, to know that I couldn't consent to such a thing. If I abandon you, you will spend day after day here with no one doing anything to save you. The young lad whom I had released from the jail has a wild imagination and neither the determination nor the spirit to free you from these hardships. This is the truth; don't expect anything from him. He cannot or does not know how to do anything for you. Believe me; I am your only hope. And as for me, I'm certain that you will not oppose my decision, which has no other objective than your happiness."

"But I don't want you to worry about my happiness," said Clara with growing unease.

"Well then, who's going to worry about you? An orphan all alone in the world, surrounded by enemies and evildoers, with no one to take an interest in you."

"Oh!" exclaimed the orphan vehemently, believing to have found a good argument. "Yes, yes, there is someone concerned about me."

"No. Don't believe it, no. That young man will not do anything; I know him, I know his character. The proof is that he has been living here for some days, he knows about your suffering, and has done nothing to relieve it. Has he attempted anything? No, not that I know of. He doesn't dare to."

"He doesn't dare to? That's so, yes...but go away, for God's sake. If they return...don't stay another moment more; I beg you. You are going to get me into trouble."

"Clara, Lázaro will not do anything for you. His imagination is absorbed in politics. Don't expect anything from him."

"Yes, yes, I do expect he will save me. I am sure of it," the young girl said painfully.

"How do you know this?"

"He himself has told me."

"He did? That's impossible. According to what they have told me, I doubt that he has been able to see you."

"But he will see me, he will save me. I don't need you."

"Yes, you need me. I have that to boast of, the only compensation for the great love that I have for you," said Bozmediano with the clear expression of truth.

"But I don't love you nor can I love you. I have only seen you twice and at that without my permission."

"That little time has been enough for me to come to love you."

"I am grateful to you for that, but when are you leaving?" asked the orphan. "What a strange way you have of befriending me, frightening me like this and putting me in a compromising situation. Ah! go away, for God's sake. They are going to come back and will find you here. Lord, what a man!"

"They will not come back. The procession is long."

"But if he comes?"

"Who is he?"

"The old man."

"He would rather die than come."

"But if the neighbors see you? And even if they don't see you...I don't want you to stay here any longer; I do not want to see you."

Clara was so dismayed, and her attitude so determined that Bozmediano began to doubt his adventure's successful outcome, and lost his resolve for a moment.

"Clara," he continued, sitting down with familiarity, "you don't know me. You have no idea what I am capable of. I am even capable of suppressing my feelings for you, sacrificing my own happiness for yours. You don't know me, nor are you correct in your judgment of me, nor do you see anything in this undertaking of mine except harmful and vile intention. If I could see anyone near you who was capable of taking you out of this miserable situation, I wouldn't be opposed, as you have told me that you didn't want to see me. I would leave, then, to another the pride of loving you and making you happy. But this isn't possible. Your situation is so desperate that I want to save you in spite of yourself, facing even your ingratitude, which is what I fear most. I am here only because there is no one in this house who can help you."

"Well, I am grateful to you, kind sir, but please leave. Oh! If Lázaro finds out that you've been here..."

"If he finds out, it will not matter to him. He thinks of nothing but politics, nor does he have the discretion and cleverness that you need to be able to leave here. In that heart there is only room for the unbridled and vulgar passions of the masses, perhaps capable of a noteworthy deed but useless to console a weak and delicate being."

"Yes, he will save me, I know it," repeated Clara, somewhat less frightened and sadder.

"No, don't wait for him!"

"Yes, I'll wait for him. Why shouldn't I expect him? Why do you tell me that? How can you know what he can do for me?"

"But can it be true that you love him so much?" said Bozmediano, who had not expected to encounter such firmness.

230

"Yes, I love him. But you, why do you ask me such questions?"

"I ask you in order to be informed," said the soldier, very calmly. "Now I repeat that you have no idea what actions I am capable of. Can you believe me, that if you prove to me that you really love him so much, I will understand and will look out for the two of you, the same as I now look out for you? But one condition is lacking. I seriously doubt that he loves you as much as you deserve, and if my suspicions are confirmed, I will consider him unworthy and will keep him away from you as much as I can. I got him out of jail in order to prove to you that I am acting in these matters, as always, with good faith and gentlemanliness. When I saw you for the first time and understood what your life was like, how little hope there was for your future, and the goodness of your heart, I felt so much pity that...I don't know...I loved you almost from that moment. My love is so bereft of selfishness that no other thoughts have occupied my imagination, day and night. Later, I learned that there was a young man who loved you very much; I learned that this young man was imprisoned so I set him free for you. I never planned to keep the two of you apart; on the contrary, my desire was to unite you if he was worthy. Well, I am convinced that he does not deserve such a thing and is unworthy of you."

Clara did not know how to answer these words. The truth is that it was hard to know whether such an eloquent expression of goodness and affection was sincere or simply a gallant ruse used by seducers.

"Yes, but meanwhile," said the girl, "you are getting me in trouble; you'll ruin me forever. If someone from the household comes in and sees you or finds out that you have entered..."

"No one will find out....But is it true, Clara, that you love that boy so much?" asked Bozmediano, wanting to give his words a certain jovial tone, which was very distinct from his feelings at that moment.

The young gallant had misfired his shot; the adventurer of love thought he had dazzled Clara with his conversation during his first two visits. In truth, he held too high an opinion of his own personal endowments to doubt that a simple girl, reared by a fanatic and unaware of any aspirations other then the common inclinations of a village girl, could resist. He also believed that his act of setting free a man who could be considered his rival would be a formidable influence on the orphan's attitude. He had employed similar procedures on other occasions, with great success. Moreover, Lázaro had seemed to him rather crude, unfriendly, boring, and unworthy of being loved.

"Yes," replied Clara, "I love him. I swear it to you, who say you are my friend."

"And do you love him very much?"

"Very much. Go, now you can leave!"

The soldier remained very thoughtful. He felt somewhat ridiculous in that situation; but the goodness of his heart always triumphed over his self-love. At that moment he was thinking of completely renouncing everything and instead trying by any means to contribute to the two youngsters' happiness.

"But, aren't you leaving?" said Clara, fidgeting again.

"Yes, I'm leaving now. But...no," he added with determination, "I can't allow you to remain in this tomb. I feel that if I leave you here, I'll never see you again. But that man, that radical. What can he be thinking about? What is he doing? How does he have the heart to see you under those harpies' control and not set fire to this cursed house?"

"He loves me," said Clara, determined to say anything that would make him leave.

"No, he'll let you die of boredom in this prison. I know it. I know that crazy man well."

"Oh! He is concerned about me. I am sure of that."

"Just that? Just concerned?"

"He suffers a great deal, seeing me this way," exclaimed Clara, painfully.

"Oh! The three schemers who live here will have to answer to me for this. But is it true that they are cruel to you?"

"Oh! Enough of this!" exclaimed Clara, unable to contain herself.

"Damned women! But that man, what is he doing for you?"

"He'll do a lot, he will do all he can. He is poor..."

"Poor!" said he, very pensive. "And, what can you expect from a man who will only be able to make you more unhappy. Oh, I promise you that if that young man isn't worthy of you, he'll have to answer to me!"

Bozmediano rose to go. At that moment Clara suddenly turned very pale thinking that she had heard someone open the stairway door, but Claudio reassured her, saying that she was mistaken.

"Don't be afraid," he said, listening attentively. "No one can come in."

"But why are you still here?" she asked, recovering a little, "Haven't I told you what you wanted to know?"

"Yes, and I'm going. Right now. I'm going, but I'll be back."

"Again!"

"Yes. I still believe that I am your only hope. My leaving now does not mean that I am abandoning you, not at all. I am going to concern myself with you two, and I will find out what this youngster is worth. If he is not worthy of you..."

At that moment a muffled voice, tremulous and emotional, called clearly from the corridor: "Clara."

The girl stood petrified with fright, and the look she gave Bozmediano made him realize how greatly he had jeopardized her. He thought that the best thing would be for him to leave very quietly. Certain that whoever had spoken would not have heard him, he signaled Clara to be quiet, and walked rapidly and very cautiously to the door through which he had entered. Clara stood motionless. One could see her great distress by the look on her face.

Bozmediano left. The voice repeated, more loudly, "Clara, Clara, open the door." It was Lázaro's voice. From outside he had heard a man's voice in the room, and had heard the footsteps of his hasty departure. Then he heard, deep in the interior of the house, a sound as if someone knocked over a piece of furniture. He ran toward the sound, frantic with anger and alarm. Hurrying through the dining room and a small passage that faced the patio, he ran up the stairway that led to the second floor and the attic, but when he reached it, Bozmediano had disappeared, and he could only see a vanishing form, slamming a door behind it. In the fleeting moment before the door closed, he thought he had seen the diabolic figure of the abbot.

"Thieves!" he shouted in a terrifying voice.

Never had he felt so strong an emotion. He tried to force open that mysterious door, but on the other side strong hands prevented it. He ran downstairs like a madman, and, returning to the dining room and from there through *Doña* Paulita's bedroom, where Bozmediano had entered, he arrived, breathless and furious at Clara's room. He found her trembling, her eyes full of tears.

When she saw him enter, the unhappy girl was almost unable to speak:

"Ah! Lázaro, Lázaro, listen...I'll tell you, wait."

But her voice caught in her throat and she could only cry like a child.

"What are you going to tell me? Hush!" exclaimed Lázaro angrily. "Quiet! And don't speak anymore to strangers. Who was here?...That soldier!...But is it true what they are saying?...I wouldn't have wanted to believe it although everyone else did. Clara, Clara, what has become of you, what have you done? I didn't want to believe it! If all the saints in heaven had sworn it to me a month ago, I would have told them that they were lying. But now I've seen him, now I've seen him."

The orphan cried as if she were guilty....Finally, she was able to say:

"For God's sake, listen to me. I'll explain."

"What are you going to tell me?" he said more angrily. "I'm going to kill that man....Oh! Clara," he added, his anger changing to intense pain. "How could you?... No doubt I am out of my mind. What I've seen is madness."

"No..., I'll explain it to you," she said to him, recovering her courage. "That man, I don't know him....One day he came to the house..., he told me..."

"Don't speak to me, don't look at me....I knew it all. Why did my uncle put you in this house? What did you do there? Why do these ladies keep you locked up and without seeing anyone? What have you done? You can't excuse yourself, no. I am a fool if I listen to the excuses that you are going to give me. I have had sufficient proof. I was so blind that I refused to believe anything....I won't speak to you anymore....Why did I ever meet you? It's all my fault; I have no right to accuse you. You are a free person. Good-by."

He left very hurriedly without waiting for a reply. He left like a madman and whirled about the house without knowing where he was going. If his uncle had appeared at that very moment, reprimanding him with his customary harshness, Lázaro would have trampled him, maltreated him, perhaps even wounded him. He finally reached the door, tried to recover his serenity, opened it and went downstairs. Once he was in the street, he felt so oppressed that he could not stop his tears.

But he did not lose his composure to the point of forgetting that the old ladies were waiting for him, and that his absence would add to the seriousness of that adventure. He headed for San Mateo Street, trying along the way to master his agitation and dissemble as best he could. After crossing several streets without finding the one he was looking for, he arrived at the home of Entrambasaguas. He entered the house, went upstairs and found Salomé extremely impatient, while María de la Paz was in a state of terrible irascibility.

"You have been away more than an hour. Where have you been?" she exclaimed, looking distrustfully at the youth.

234

"Ma'am...ma'am..." said Lázaro, stuttering. "I could not...The people thronged together in the street...and I found myself among the crowd, unable to return. Then a woman seized the handbag and started to run through those streets. As you can imagine, I had to pursue her and I almost did not overtake her."

"Come now, young man...the street has been clear for some time."

Salomé took possession of the handbag which she had believed lost and examined it to see if anything was missing.

"Undoubtedly, you went to some club to speak," she said, when she noticed that nothing was missing and that is was impossible to scold Lázaro for any other reason.

"Come now, young man!" said Entrambasaguas. "Do you also speak in those clubs? That is an iniquity; be careful not to condemn yourself."

The devout one said nothing. Her admirable instincts, which recently had acquired extraordinary strength, could understand that something had happened to Lázaro during his absence. She did not suspect what it was or where he had gone, but she thought a lot about it, while the last figures of the procession filed by in the street.

"Ay! Let's go, it's late," exclaimed María de la Paz.

"Are you going so soon?" asked the clergyman, who could hardly wait for them to leave, because the odors of the mutton stew being prepared were reaching his nostrils from the kitchen.

"My dear *Don* Silvestre," said Paz, "we cannot detain ourselves, because now we are no longer free. We have taken upon ourselves a very burdensome responsibility: the protection and upbringing of a young girl who will give us many sorrows."

"What is that?"

"She is an abandoned child," continued Paz, "who lived in the home of our friend, a solemn bachelor who was not able to put up with her antics. It seems that she is somewhat out of her mind, and since he couldn't control her, he turned her over to us so that we could correct her....Everything for the love of God."

"And has she given you worries?" asked *Don* Silvestre Entrambasaguas's sister officiously.

"As yet," answered Paz, "to tell you the truth, she hasn't behaved badly, but I am never mistaken, when I have a person fixed here in my mind..." as she pointed to her forehead, "and she seems to me to be a fine jewel."

Lázaro heard this apology about his unfortunate friend with all his attention. But he did not become any more disturbed than he already was, since that would have been impossible.

"What's the matter, Paula?" Paz asked the devout one, who was very pale and obviously not feeling well.

Indeed, as they all looked at her they noted signs of a growing indisposition. Her eyes were bright and her breathing was labored.

"Nothing," replied *Doña* Paulita, trying to cheer up.

"No doubt you've caught a cold on the balcony."

"Yes, a slight breeze was passing by this afternoon, of course, of course..." indicated the clergyman. "But go home and if you bundle yourself up well..."

"It is probably nothing," said *Doña* Petronila Entrambasaguas, very impatient because certain aromas from the kitchen warned her that the mutton was getting burnt at full speed.

The ladies headed to the door. The cleric struck himself on the forehead like someone recalling an important matter and remarked to *Doña* Paulita, "Ah! My dear lady, if you would be so kind as to do me a favor..."

"What, *Don* Silvestre?"

"Would you be so kind as to look over a sermon I have written. I am going to preach in San Antonio Church on January seventeenth. You who are a great theologian and have given me your opinion on other great sermons of mine, I'd like you now to look this one over."

"I don't know anything about such things," the saint replied with repugnance.

"Of course she understands," said Paz with satisfaction.

"Such modesty!" exclaimed Entrambasaguas. "Holiness combined with talent. But I know, although you may want to conceal it, that you are a great theologian. At times, I have listened to you with my mouth open as if I were listening to all the fathers of the Church...."

"Stop that!" muttered the devout one, with visible annoyance. "I don't understand those things."

"It is on the theme of the fifth temptation of San Antón. You know when the demon presented itself to him in the form of...a girl, well..."

He ran hurriedly to his drawer, pulled out a bundle of papers and handed them to *Doña* Paulita, who took them in the worst possible mood. They fell from her hand; the preacher rapidly picked them up and gave them to her once more, saying to her:

"But are you truly ill? I see you can hardly stand up. As I have told you, fasting is good up to a certain point and no more...and you always are so persevering..."

"This girl, with her fasting and penitence..." said María de la Paz.

"Would you like a cup of broth?" the clergyman began to ask, but then stopped before finished his sentence, because his sister, with more speed than dissimulation, had tugged at his coat tail, pointing out the indiscretion of the offer he had just made.

"Thanks, it isn't necessary. This is nothing."

"Go home early," said the stout woman. "It isn't a good idea for you to eat broth or anything else."

Placing her hand on her forehead, she continued, "You have a high fever. Go home quickly!"

The retinue left. The cleric took the oil lamp in his robust hands and lighted the stairway for them. When they were already downstairs, Entrambasaguas called out from above:

"Pay attention, *Señora Doña* Paula, to that passage which says, 'When in a deluge of suns a corpulent body of an effigy came into the world...' Whether it means *corpus corporum in corpore uno*...Pay special attention to this passage, I have some doubts as to whether..."

Doña Paulita did not answer nor did she even look at the vulgar bombast. They went out into the street, and Lázaro was so involved in his thoughts that he began to walk ahead, leaving the two ladies behind.

"Eh, young sir!" said Salomé, who was in a bad mood that afternoon, "What manner of behavior is this? Are you leaving us alone in the middle of the street?"

"Oh, what a courteous gentleman we have brought along," said Paz, whose blood-thirsty temperament that afternoon, possessed a marked irritability, for no known cause.

Lázaro fell back and slowed his pace.

"You could well behave better," added the lady, "in front of strangers. You didn't even greet those...folk...." Paz used this general denomination to designate all persons who by their lineage were on a lower echelon than she in the social hierarchy. "What will they say about us? Ah! Paulita, you cannot walk. Come, *Don* Lázaro, give my niece your arm. Lean on *Don* Lázaro, Paula, you are very ill. Ah! It's a sad thing to bring along as escort a young gentleman like this one."

The Aragonese stammered some excuses and offered his arm to *Doña* Paulita. Walking along, he felt that the devout one weighed down his arm as though she were lead. She was bundled up in her shawl and walked with difficulty.

"You are going very fast," she said, weighing more heavily on the youth's arm.

Lázaro moderated the pace.

"Walk a little faster," she said after lightening her weight. Lázaro felt himself being dragged along.

Lázaro quickened the pace.

"Such a clear evening," she exclaimed, stopping and looking up at the sky. The other two were ahead of them at some distance.

"I have never seen an evening like this. I have never seen the stars shine that way without moving...and with that vibration that makes them seem to be talking."

"Talking!" said Lázaro, very surprised by the saint's simile.

"That surprises you?" she replied, looking at him with such firmness and intensity that the young lad thought that two of the stars had descended to take refuge in Paulita's eyes. "Yes, don't you think so?"

Silvestre Entrambasaguas's manuscript suddenly fell to the ground, released by the lady's hand.

"Ma'am," said the youth, leaning over to pick it up, "look, you've dropped the sermon."

"Leave it," she exclaimed vehemently. Pulling him by the arm to keep him from picking up the manuscript, she quickened her steps.

"There is no doubt," said Lázaro to himself, "that this woman has a high fever; she is now becoming delirious."

The mystic woman began walking so quickly that they soon caught up to the two oldest ruins. But soon she had to moderate her haste and walked so slowly that it took her a long time to advance only twenty steps. With each step she weighed more heavily on the student's arm. On arriving home, *Doña* Paulita was no longer able to take a step. Lázaro put his arm around her waist to keep her from falling. It was impossible for her to climb the stairs because the lady could not stop herself from weaving from side to side. At the same time, the young man saw that her face was changing color, her eyes were closed, and her arms hung weakly at her sides. He made an heroic effort, seized her in his arms, and carried her up. *Doña* Paulita's head rested against his shoulder, and Lázaro felt her forehead was burning his neck.

"She has a high fever," he said, putting her down in the corridor, since Paz would not allow him to enter her bedroom.

The other two, quite alarmed at her sudden illness, got her into her room. They soon came back out, much calmer, and went to the dining room to eat the meal they had prepared before they had left.

A profound silence reigned in the house. Lázaro went up the interior stairway to his room. On the way he could not help but stop, for he heard a voice that pierced his heart. It was Clara's voice, asking or answering who knows what of the devout one. Lázaro quickened his pace, fleeing from that voice which he never wanted to hear again.

Chapter XXX

VIRGO FIDELIS

Lázaro did not find his uncle upstairs. The unhappy lad was greatly disturbed by the afternoon's incident and could hardly contain his anger, bitterness, and shock. It was impossible for him to calm down, especially when he remembered the figure of Clara, kneeling, with her eyes full of tears and arms crossed. He felt first compassion, then anger, the two sentiments alternating so violently that he felt sick and dizzy. After the fits of rancor came the depression of disillusionment. He could not decide whether he still loved Clara or despised her.

The hours passed; the evening progressed; and he continued in a state of unrest. He did not plan to go to bed, nor did he feel sleepy or in need of rest. On the contrary, his natural impulses were toward anxiety, restlessness, and movement. Dismal silence, uninterrupted by any sound, reigned in the house. Everyone seemed to be asleep. Surely only he was awake. In the corridor, the fresh air of the evening gave him some relief, and he promenaded there for some time. Nine, ten, eleven o'clock struck. Finally, he stopped, stunned by his own backward and forward motion. He leaned against the railing and hid his head between his hands. He remained this way for a long time, devouring his agony. Suddenly he thought he heard a strange noise; he raised his head, and at the far end of the corridor he thought he saw a human figure moving forward. His heart beat so rapidly that he believed his chest would burst. The form, obviously that of a woman, moved forward, standing out in the darkness. She was approaching, clothed entirely in white, which made her even more fantastic, and the reflection of the moon seemed to project a mysterious light. When she was near, Lázaro recognized her. It was the devout one, whose countenance revealed the symptoms of insomnia and fever.

"Lázaro!" she said in a very weak and emotional voice.

"Ma'am," he answered with much surprise. "You here, at this hour...? With that fever...Aren't you ill?"

"I...?" she murmured in a kind of frenzy. "I? No..., I am well. I'm better."

"I thought you were sleeping. You need rest."

"I," she answered with a peculiar intonation which alarmed Lázaro. "I...I do not sleep, I can't sleep. It has been many nights since I could close my eyes."

"Well. What is the matter?" asked Lázaro, looking at her very attentively. "You are not well. You are a saint, but excessive holiness is harmful, ma'am."

"I am not a saint," said the lady. "I am a sinner."

"Don't say that, for God's sake. You are a saint. What happiness to have one's conscience at ease! To direct all one's love to Him who does not deceive, nor is false or disloyal: to God....This is the greatest of joys."

"Speak more quietly," said the devout one.

"And then," he continued, "to be free of hatred, rancor, and disillusionment...."

"Not so loud!" indicated the lady, and her voice resembled a sigh.

"To be free of rancor," continued Lázaro in a very low voice. "To love without distrust, without fear; to despise worldly things, betrayals, ambushes; to find happiness in suffering, and to derive consolation even from misfortunes!...Oh, how happy you are!..."

After a pause, the voice of the mystic woman resounded like a distant echo as she answered: "No, my friend, I am not happy, I am very unhappy."

Only someone standing very close to her at that moment, as Lázaro did, could have heard those words.

"I am very unhappy!" she repeated in a weak murmur, muffled and faded like those whispers of a prayer which disturb the profound silence of the cathedrals during quiet hours.

"What greater consolation," continued Lázaro, "than to live with the spirit in regions of peace, where there are no indignities or treachery; to elevate oneself in exaltation and love; to enjoy with purity the pleasantness of communication with God, and to live in prayer, confident in the payment of so much love and in the infallible gratitude of the object loved. Oh, what happiness!"

The young Aragonese's spirit was so absorbed in his own sorrows that he did not pay the kind of attention he should have to the strange signs of physical and emotional disturbance which anyone less distracted might have noticed in *Doña* Paulita's saintly face.

"To live in prayer!" he continued. "To live praying with the eyes of the soul fixed on the eternal and faithful love! To repeat incessantly His Name and His praises! That is truly happiness!"

"No," relied the perfect woman in the same way. "I do not pray; I cannot pray."

"Ay!" he exclaimed. "You say that in modesty, because you still don't feel you are perfect enough. If you knew the misery of others, you would understand to what immense heights you have risen."

The devout one lowered her eyes, and with deep melancholy and in a gentle voice said, "And what misery is there greater than mine?"

"You are too good. Everyone is well aware that you are a saint, a real saint."

"Do you want me to make a confession to you?" asked Paula, looking at him as one looks at a confessor. "Well, I also believed it; I also thought that I was a saint, but I no longer believe it."

"Oh!" exclaimed Lázaro. "I don't need anyone to tell me who you are. I know. When a creature as perfect as you are has descended to defend me and forgive my errors, it is clear that you are not like others. I was harassed everywhere. Here everyone else treated me with acrimony or contempt. You alone raised your voice, and you raised it several times later in my favor, stating that I wasn't as bad as they believed I was. Do you think I have forgotten, or that I could forget that? No, ma'am. I am probably all that they say, but I am not ungrateful. I shall always have engraved in my memory the words that you pronounced in my defense. You are a saint; I shall tell everyone."

"Oh!" said the devout one, in the same mournful voice. "I never believed that you were as bad as they said you were. I can read such things in people's faces. I am never mistaken, and I am almost sure that they have perjured you, that they want to oppress and confuse you with unfounded accusations."

"You actually thought that of me?"

"Yes. I am sure," she answered, "that your heart is good and righteous; that if you have committed some wrong, it was due to fickleness and lack of foresight. I also believe that they do not love you as you deserve to be loved."

"Ma'am, what did you just say?" asked the student impulsively. "That touches me, because it is a truth I was just thinking about."

"Yes, they don't love you as you deserve," repeated Paulita. "Your uncle is too severe."

An impartial observer would have noticed that the saint moved several inches closer to Lázaro, who, impressed by the truth he heard from that oracle's mouth, was about to embrace her, and would have done so had it not been for the respect which hierarchy and the evangelical decorum of the theologian had instilled in him.

"Your uncle, *Don* Elías," continued the mystic, "I notice he treats his nephew too severely."

"And others do, too," said Lázaro, turning away his face.

"And how do they expect you to be a good person when you aren't loved?" said the lady with admirable mysticism. "When one receives ingratitude and scorn, his sentiments become bitter and the fountain of good love that exists in every human breast becomes sterile. When a creature isn't loved, he has to be bad out of necessity."

"What discernment, what discernment, ma'am!" the youth exclaimed enthusiastically. "I considered you a saint before, but now I see that your wisdom equals your virtue, and standing at your side, I feel so small that I am embarrassed."

"Yes, a person who is treated so harshly can't be good," said Paula. "Love makes prodigies; it makes uncultivated and bad men become tame and good; the sad and unbelieving turn into happy beings, believers and affectionate."

"What wisdom you posses! That wisdom belongs only to holiness. Fortunate is he who can see the miseries of the earth from such a great height and can calmly judge everything! You certainly know the world."

"No, Lázaro, I don't know what the world is."

"Oh! then you should be even happier."

"I," said the perfect woman, after a pause during which she gazed fixedly at the ceiling, as if reading something, "I spent my childhood in the austere house of my uncles, receiving the most exemplary education from devout persons. As soon as I had use of reason, I learned to pray. My first words were a prayer. The first years of my life were spent in a convent where I was surrounded by holy and affectionate Mothers who showed me the path to perfection. My youth was passed this way, in religious occupations. I have been praying without ceasing for fifteen years, and unaware of it. I have lived in God since the cradle. I don't know what I am. I don't even know if I have existed."

"My God, what an angel you are!" said Lázaro. "What perfection! I admire and revere you, ma'am."

"I am not worthy of such veneration, but on the contrary, deserve pity," she answered him bitterly.

She gave out a deep sigh, which seemed to draw out the mysteries enclosed in the sanctum sanctorum of her breast.

"Worthy of pity!" exclaimed the Aragonese in surprise. "Well, what can you crave? What are you worried about?

Some scruple of conscience, the desire for greater perfection? I, to be sure, am a wretch. I, ma'am, ought not to exist in the world."

"But what's the matter?" inquired Paula, with much interest. "Tell me everything! Didn't you say that I have consoled you on other occasions? I shall console you now if you tell me of a new misfortune. Tell me about it!"

"My misfortunes are too numerous to mention. Moreover, you are too good a person to hear of them. You will be horrified, and your spirit's serene peace will be disturbed."

"Oh, no, tell me! Perhaps it is a very serious misdemeanor. It doesn't matter, tell it to me. I shall forgive you even before I know about it."

"It isn't my misdeed."

"Someone else's? Tell me," said the mystic with anxious curiosity.

"Leave all those griefs to me, ma'am. That's for me alone! It's a sad inheritance which only my heart can bear."

"What is it, Lázaro?…Oh! I know what it is. Your uncle is very cruel. He doesn't love you. But you should not grieve over that, my friend. Not everyone will treat you with the same severity. Someone will love you."

"No, that doesn't matter to me," manifested Lázaro, whose sorrows recurred anew at that moment, "it doesn't matter to me that they treat me with contempt, that they all abhor me, that they detest me. It is what I was born for."

"You are very upset. And, standing here before me, you despair in that way?" said the devout one in a gentle reproof.

"Forgive me, ma'am. I don't know what I'm saying. You are too good, and you don't understand these things. You don't know what the world is like. You do not know how much iniquity, how much perfidy, how much deceit, how much cynicism there is in it. You do not know anything but good. You only know about God."

"That desperation you express, Lázaro, is not at all good. That will lead you to misfortune and death."

"You, with your immense goodness, want to give me the consolations of religion; that isn't for me. I don't deserve it."

"You deserve everything, consolation, friendship, love. I know what you deserve and therefore, you'll have it. Sentiments like yours must not be forgotten for so long."

"May God bless you a thousand times! But you are mistaken: that isn't meant for me."

"You deserve love, and all that the heart can give. You call yourself unhappy, and your disquiet, Lázaro, has no basis.

There are worse evils, evils which are born suddenly in one's heart and grow so rapidly that there seems no hope of cure. Everything within and outside oneself becomes threatening. Life is an insupportable burden; anxiety is ever present: it gives one disgust for the past and terror for the future."

The devout one was speaking with lowered voice, and with a serious, sad inflection. The night had darkened, and Paulita's eyes, which had always, in given moments, had an extraordinary brilliance, shone that night like two glowing embers, whose light made the darkness of her eyelids look more penetrating and sinister, further blackened by insomnia, illness and the emotional excitement which possessed her.

"Woe to those who do not know themselves, who have deceived themselves and have permitted their natures to be distorted and their characters misrepresented without their recognizing it. They, when what is silent speaks, when what is hidden emerges, when what is disguised is revealed, will be victims of the most frightful sufferings. They will feel themselves reborn but advanced in years; they will see that they have lived many years without feeling; they will observe that the new being, product of a delayed transformation, grows intolerant, proud, demanding all that pertains to him, whatever is his, which a fictitious and disappointing life has not been able to give him; requiring feelings that the old being, inert, indifferent and cold, has never known. What terrible conflicts arise from that late awakening! Oh, this is frightful!"

We have reason to believe that *Doña* Paulita did not say all this in the same words written in our account. But if the reader finds these words unlikely, if they seem uncharacteristic, coming from this person's mouth, consider them said by the author; it makes no difference. But she did say something similar to this; the thought was the same, although the phrases were different.

Without doubt, as the reader surely understands, the confessions of the devout one are sufficiently obscure and do not yet shed any light on the crisis which was clearly disturbing that very pure and perfect spirit. In fact, a great transformation was taking place in her character. Lázaro, to tell the truth, didn't understand very well the solemn and somewhat oracular words which he heard from the trembling lips of the saint. He attributed the obscurity of such an explanation to the influence of her mystic readings and to the habits formed by a person absorbed in contemplation. So he limited himself to saying, "Yes, ma'am, it is frightful."

"How terrible love is in its demands!" said the saint, "especially when it feels offended, when it asks for the payment of a great debt it has contracted. When love waits it doesn't yield; on the contrary, it manifests itself by demanding everything all at once."

"Yes, how terrible this is," answered Lázaro. "You are lucky to not know about it except through hearsay."

"By hearsay?" she repeated. "Yes," she added, after a brief pause, "I have heard what lovers say; but most of them find among the world's accidents a thousand ways to maintain life in the terrible struggle. Only some, it is said, due to special circumstances of character and position, have the sad privilege of dying irremissibly without victory and without defense...."

"Oh, how she reads my mind!" thought the student, very moved, but without understanding the psychological depth of those words or their application and meaning at the moment.

"You do not understand those things, Lázaro."

"I don't understand?" said the latter. "I don't? Unfortunately, I do understand them....For you, yes, these painful miseries are veiled. You, who are a perfect creature, a chosen one of God. Fortunate is the blindness of those whose eyes God closed as they came into the world!"

"It is true....I do not understand it...," said Paula, with an irony so pronounced that it required the full wandering of Lázaro's mind to allow him to not notice it. "I do not understand it, I do not understand anything about it. I am a devout fool."

These last words, spoken with a certain despair, were enough to attract her listener's attention. He didn't answer nor question her further about the matter they spoke of. He stepped nearer to the lady, who had backed up, moving away from him, and saw that she was crying. Oh confusion of confusions!

"But what's the matter, ma'am?" he asked.

"Nothing, nothing, nothing," she answered in a gradually diminishing tone of voice. The last *nothing* was only heard by the lips which pronounced it.

"You are ill, and you have left your room at this hour! That's not good, ma'am. You are going to get worse."

"It is true, I am ill," she said, drawing nearer, "ill forever!"

"Ill forever! You are suffering, no doubt because of your excessive devotion. You aspire to reach Heaven; what else could a soul as beautiful as yours aspire to attain?"

"Yes," said Paula, in a very sad voice. "I only want to rest in peace."

"How beautiful is death!" said Lázaro pathetically. "Only it can console us. As for me, ma'am, I tell you frankly that I would like to die right now."

"To die!" exclaimed the devout one with a sudden fit of interest, moving closer, much closer to the youth. "To die, no! You ought to live. Who knows what future God has reserved for you?"

"For me?"

"Yes, perhaps days of happiness in the company of persons who love you. Oh, how many beings there must be who are themselves happy just to know that you are happy! I know there must be some."

"How good you are, ma'am," repeated Lázaro. "So far as I am concerned, there can be no such thing. Either I don't deserve anything better, or I am damned by God."

"Don't say such things!" she exclaimed, clasping her hands.

"Pardon me, ma'am. I don't know what I am saying. In spite of everything, you comfort me, and I find an indescribable pleasant relief in your presence. I shall never be able to forget that only you dared to defend me when all others accused me."

As he said this Lázaro could not help noticing that the saint dropped her arms heavily and looked up toward Heaven. Her face, a pale olive complexion without any shade of pink on her cheeks, was at that moment wan and shadowed by the projection of her hair, whose thickness, beauty, and blackness could only be compared to the dark intensity of her black eyes, which, after the metamorphosis, had acquired a strange expression. We do not know whether it was accidental or intentional, but instead of her normal custom her head was covered by a simple kerchief. During the conversation, her magnificent hair, a treasure concealed by mysticism, came undone and fell loosely onto her shoulders. Never had Lázaro seen such hair! In the evening darkness it seemed to be a veil descending to her waist. As she spoke she kept brushing from the sides of her forehead the two principal locks of her enchanting hair, an enchantment born that evening of the warmth of an intimacy scarcely intended. Lázaro, who observed the lady for a long while, saw that she was crying and that slowly moving away from him, she leaned on the wall with signs of great prostration and exhaustion.

"But you are crying," he said, repentant of having spoken so much and detaining her, "you are very exhausted. Why haven't you rested?"

"I can't rest, I can't sleep," murmured the devout one in a voice more hoarse and serious than usual.

"Why did you come out in this condition at this hour?"

"I was suffocating, and I had to come out to breathe the air."

"But you are crying. My God, what's the matter?"

Doña Paulita did not answer.

"Are you very ill, very ill?" continued Lázaro.

"Yes, " she whispered.

"Has it been a long time?"

"Since a short time ago."

"Ma'am, return to your room, I beg it of you. Your hands are on fire, and your forehead is burning."

Lázaro took her hands and noted an excessive warmth. He dared to lay his hand against her forehead and thought he had touched a fire. At the same time, she was trembling as if her body were on ice.

"You are cold, you are chilled," he said; "go back to bed."

She remained in the same position. She shut her eyes as if profoundly sleepy and inclined her head, seeking support. Lázaro was afraid. He was about to call for help. He seized her arm, determined to making her go back to bed. He said to her, "Let us go, ma'am, it's very late. You do not feel well. Let's go. Do you want me to call a doctor?"

"No," she said, opening her eyes and looking at him with a certain irony. "No, why call a doctor?"

"Your health is very precious," said Lázaro, as a suspicion quickly passed through his mind. "Take care of yourself; it will always be my greatest happiness to know that you are well and enjoying the health necessary to do good. I will not leave here without the assurance that you are completely well."

"Going away? You?" she exclaimed with a sudden animation.

"Yes, I'll leave."

"Go," she continued with another movement that was almost a jump, and putting a sinister brilliance into her eyes.

"Yes, of course."

On hearing this, the devout one, with sudden strength, seized his arm with her convulsive hand. Grasping him violently, she said, "No, you will not go!"

At the very moment she was saying this, the door to the street was heard to open. It was Elías who entered. They heard him climb the stairs. He came, illuminated by a lantern, and as usual, talking to himself.

"Leave," said the mystic vehemently.

"Are you going to stay here?"

"Go to your room! Don't let him see you awake! Get into bed. Pretend that you are sleeping."

"But, you...?"

"Get going. Enter your room! He will arrive soon....Quickly."

Lázaro left hastily, suddenly pushed by Paulita. He ran into his room before *Coletilla* arrived; throwing himself into the bed, he pretended to be asleep. The fanatic entered a moment later and went to bed, mumbling. When he put out the light, Lázaro very cautiously sat up in the bed, and leaning out through a window which faced the corridor, he looked outside. The lady was still there, with her face turned toward the window. Lázaro laid down again, and during a quarter of an hour thought all that a human head could possibly think. He leaned out again and saw the same white figure, immobile, in the same place, and two terrible black eyes fixed on the window. That confused him completely. For a long time he continued to look out every five minutes or so, and always saw the same figure until, at last, he no longer looked because it frightened him.

Chapter XXXI

THE MYSTERIOUS MEETING

Lázaro left the house at dusk the following day. He had spent the morning finding out where Bozmediano lived, and in the few hours he spent in the house of the three most noble ladies, he learned that *Doña* Paulita was ill and Clara was not well. Salomé, more insolent than usual, approached him several times to remind him that the previous afternoon he hadn't greeted Entrambasaguas; and María de la Paz Jesús did her best to find pretexts for reprimanding him. Her admirable inquisitor's character allowed her to do so more than once.

Lázaro left, and as night fell he entered the solitary neighborhood of Flor Alta, where the Bozmedianos lived. He entered the doorway and asked for *Don* Claudio. The doorman, who behaved badly with people of humble origin, replied in a very disagreeable manner that he was not at home.

Lázaro stood still for a good while, looking at the doorman as if the declaration of that sibyl in a chevroned overcoat were untrue. The doorman thought he hadn't spoken clearly enough, and repeated:

"He isn't home!"

But the youth, intent on seeing Bozmediano that evening, was not satisfied and inquired:

"When will he be in?"

The other man felt that the question, posed by a youth who did not seem to be of high nobility, had not arrived in a coach, who was not a soldier, and did not wear *farolé* style boots, was presumptuous and lacked good judgment. So he smiled with an air of superiority, putting his hands in his pockets, and answered, "How do you expect me to know when he'll come? He'll come...when he comes."

"I have to see him this evening. What time does he usually arrive?"

"He doesn't have a set time," said the servant, turning away toward the doorman's lodge. He then turned back and added, "If you want to leave him a message..."

"No," repeated Lázaro, "I have to see him in person."

"Well, early tomorrow," said the servant in a tone which was easy to understand as "Go away."

Lázaro realized that it was impossible to find anything out from that ogre, and left; but he felt compelled to see Bozmediano that very evening. It seemed to him that each hour which passed since that fatal moment when he saw Bozmediano

250

disappear through the attic added new intensity to his burden. To him, Bozmediano seemed at that moment the most odious and repugnant being ever born. He fancied him to be motivated only by the lowest and crudest sentiment, and he saw him as a cowardly seducer incapable of any good or generous behavior. He felt himself superior, highly superior, to that insidious man, and believed that just by seeing the criminal would he comprehend his true vileness. At times he felt sudden fits of anger, so strong and violent that if he had had the soldier before him, he would have attacked him, willing to take his life by any means. Feeling this way, the student decided not to go away from the house, but to wait around to seize Bozmediano as he entered or left the premises. He crossed to the other sidewalk and began to pace back and forth, determined not to abandon his post all evening, waiting with the unyielding patience that the desire for vengeance produces.

It was probably ten o'clock when Lázaro observed three persons leaving the house. He approached cautiously and saw that one of them was Claudio. Supported on his arm and walking slowly, was an elderly man who seemed to be Claudio's father. The other person was a soldier; the three were conversing heatedly. Lázaro followed them at some distance, realizing that this was not the best moment to speak to Bozmediano; but he decided to follow them, to see where they stopped. They walked several blocks and finally reached Afligidos Square. They stopped in front of one of those enormous doors which in that very ancient part of Madrid lead to the oldest houses of the seventeenth century, and the younger Bozmediano knocked. The door opened without delay, and they entered. Lázaro, who was observing them from a distance, noticed that they seemed to be concealing themselves, trying not to be seen. The soldier, after looking all around the Plaza, entered last. Soon a light was seen through one of the house's windows, but a hand closed the blinds, and no light was seen thereafter.

For some unknown reason, the student's imagination attributed a certain mystery to the entrance of those persons into such a house. He approached and looked at the house number, but as he was leaving, ready to return home, he noticed that another two persons, muffled up to their eyes, were approaching. Lázaro walked past them, pretending to continue on his way, and taking refuge behind the corner of Las Negras Street, he saw that they knocked at the door, that it opened quickly and that they entered the house. "Perhaps it is just a coincidence," thought the youth, "but there is something strange about the gathering of those people in that place."

Not ten minutes had passed before Lázaro observed three other persons, equally muffled, coming from the narrow street of San Bernardino. He saw that they stopped to see whether they were being watched, and, then, after knocking, entered. "Now there are eight," he said to himself, and waited to see if another shipment would arrive.

A little later on, one person, walking very quickly, arrived by way of Osuna Street. Behind him appeared two others who did not have to knock, and later, one after another, five more entered successively and separately.

"There is clearly something going on here," said Lázaro. "Sixteen have already entered. It must be a secret club, a conspiracy, perhaps a Masonic lodge."

At eleven he left, since an hour had passed without further arrivals; but he decided to return the following evening to see whether the same thing occurred. It was evident to him that a meeting of serious persons was taking place there, undoubtedly with some political objective. He hated Bozmediano, and this emotion led him to believe that whatever went on there could not be anything good.

He returned to Válgame Dios Street, very regretful at not having been able to have the terrible interview he had imagined with his enemy.

It is impossible to describe the anger which had taken possession of María de la Paz due to the youth's tardy return. In order to give an idea of the fury of the lady whom the poets of the time of Cadalso had compared with Juno, let it suffice to say that she arose, dressed not in underclothing, but definitely less pompously dressed, covered and adorned than usual, to tell the young man that if he imagined that the house was his own—that if he had planned to spend the evening in the clubs and joints of Madrid—She added that she was convinced that his behavior would never change, and that they ought to stop trying to make a ray of light enter such a thick and disorganized head. She also stated that it was to an excess of her charitable goodness that he owed the great favor of being admitted into that holy house. She announced, however, that he would not remain there for long, due to his wicked and abominable escapades...which dishonored that holy house. And she kept repeating the phrase "holy house." In this way she spoke to him, using a loud voice. The youth replied very quietly, "Ma'am, I had things to do..."

But she did not let him finish, and exclaimed, loudly: "Don't raise your voice, young man. Why are you shouting in that manner? My niece is very ill, and now you are going to upset her. If you have come here only to disturb us...."

"Is *Doña* Paula very ill?" inquired the lad in an almost imperceptible voice.

"Yes, sir, and you, with that loud voice of yours, do not let her rest."

"But I haven't even raised my voice..."

"Be quiet, Lázaro, keep quiet and don't contradict me."

They were involved in this dispute when Salomé appeared, saying, "For God's sake, Paula has a high fever, and with all this noise she is going to get worse!"

"This young man shouts so loudly," said Paz, raising her voice. "You see? He returned at twelve. What do you think of that, Salomé? He must have been at some club with those degenerates. We've accepted a fine jewel into our home! And you, young man, you say that you had something to do?"

"Yes, ma'am, I had some business," replied Lázaro a bit provoked by the two elderly ladies' impertinent comments.

"A fine business it must be," remarked Salomé. "But how about lowering your voice; my cousin can't stand that shouting. You had just entered....*Doña* Paulita heard you enter. She recognized your footsteps and awakened with much shock. And when she heard your voice, she sat up in bed, very upset, which shows that your voice bothered her very much. So keep quiet and try not to walk so heavily....All right, you may go now."

"Good night, ladies."

He had not yet taken a step when Clara appeared, very upset, and called, "*Señoras*, come! She wants to get out of bed....I can't keep her down. As soon as she heard your conversation she got up quickly saying that she was coming here."

"Oh! Let us see," said Paz, entering her room.

"She is becoming delirious," said Salomé, as she also entered with Clara.

Lázaro went upstairs thinking about this new mystery of the holy woman.

Chapter XXXII

THE LITTLE FOUNTAIN

Lázaro did not find his uncle, who had not shown up at the house that day. If we wish to see him we'll have to head for the newborn club, The Little Fountain where the good royalist was conversing heatedly with *El Doctrino* and the other youth named Aldama, whom we have already met.

Let us point out the change which had taken place in that house. The poet had flown. Carrascosa finally achieved his objective; the Basque landlady decided to throw the poet out, along with all his impedimenta of the Gracchus Tragedy, muses and classical nymphs.

Neighborhood opinion had been an important factor for the hefty and middle-aged landlady, as it became increasingly explicit regarding the bard. Conjectures could be drawn about the youth's disappearance, and there are reasons to believe that the landlady spoke very secretly with her boarder a few hours before his departure.

With the poet absent and little Mount Parnassus empty, *Don* Gil brought over from Las Urosas Street the trunk containing his three dress coats, a wig from the days of Esquilache, four shirts with lace pendants, a cape, and a rusty sword, and installed himself in the apartment inhabited by the author of *The Gracchus*. He hung on the wall a family painting depicting the last stages of man in extravagant and diabolic allegories and there he remained, his beloved's guest. We feel it opportune to point out that the cause of *Don* Gil's fondness for the Basque woman was the fact that he had found out, through some papers he saw while still a civil servant, about certain holdings in Oñate which *Doña* Leoncia had unknowingly inherited. The abbot planned to make a good deal by somehow becoming her attorney and pleading her case in court in exchange for a big cut of the estate. His greed was as great as his ingenuity, which probably meant he would succeed in his undertaking. We will leave him there, dedicated to the arduous task of winning over the semigoddess, and attend the session at The Little Fountain.

El Doctrino was saying to *Coletilla*, "I strongly feel that it will not work out well; I depend on aggressive people, but, the blow is too terrible, friend Elías, and I fear that public opinion will be aroused."

"But public opinion has already turned against them; it points them out with repugnance," observed Elías vehemently.

"It seems that you don't know the people. Don't you see what they're like in The Golden Fountain, Lorencini, The Maltese Cross, and Los Comuneros? Don't you see how the hot-headed liberals rail against those whom they call lukewarm, that is, against those who support the government and form the 'sensible' majority in Parliament? Well, the people are furiously angry at such lukewarm politicians. You already know that anger was sparked. The people are pleading for their destruction because they believe that it is the best way to obtain Liberty. Let us carry out the will of the people."

The sarcasm and diabolic malice with which *Coletilla* pronounced these words are beyond description. The reader will soon understand the course that the old absolutist demon's plans were taking. He proceeded confidently toward his goal. Patience, constancy, mature reflection, and astute discretion guided him. He was a skillful man and had an extraordinary faculty for devising and carrying out projects like the one we see him developing right now.

"Well," answered *El Doctrino*, "I agree that we must do what you say and find the means by which the common people can satisfy their bloody desire. They don't know what they want, or why they want it. They has acquired those ideas by various means, and their desires must be satisfied. But it seems to me that this is still not the right time, *Don* Elías. The men who are designated to be victims still have a great deal of prestige. The people do not like them it's true, because they have misled and deceived the people; but they do have support from the middle class and a segment of the aristocracy. I do not think the moment has yet come for the surprise attack you have been preparing."

"What a child you are!" answered the royalist. "What does it matter if those people are prestigious? And what about the support of that highly placed person..., who can do anything?..."

"You mean the King's support. Say it once and for all!"

"You already know what the King is thinking. In the eyes of the public, in the eyes of Europe, those men are his friends. Some are his ministers, others are his state advisors, and others, deputies who support his decrees in Parliament. On the surface the King seems to love them, but in fact, he hates them, detests them. It is their fault that the constitutional system has been enthroned. They strengthen liberalism. You see now that to get rid of liberalism one must get rid of them."

He said this with such cynical determination and shameless veracity that even *El Doctrino*, who was a scoundrel, felt a certain repugnance.

"Well, then," continued *Coletilla*, "all condemnation for the attack will fall on the hot-headed liberals, who will be the ones to perpetrate it. This uprising will wound liberalism directly. We will see liberalism destroy itself as its most extreme partisans devour the more moderate ones. What should the Nation do, terrified by this horror? Deny liberalism, and expedite the holy intention of the King to restore the former system. The assault is very well-prepared; one group of liberals burns with the desire to wipe out another faction. The suicide of liberalism is imminent. Let us encourage it and help it along. Tomorrow, perhaps, will be too late; perhaps if we delay, a reconciliation may take place, and then..."

"Reconciliation, no, that's impossible," said *El Doctrino*, in a worried tone. "The extremists of The Golden Fountain and of the other clubs have already reached such a state of intransigence that...a lot of doctrine on intolerance and extermination has been preached to the people. It can't be helped; those who oppose the excesses of Liberty in the Parliament and clubs are going to trampled by Liberty. Reconciliation is impossible. For that very reason, I believe that one ought to, and can, wait a bit to see if those men lose completely what little popularity they still have."

"These things have to be done aggressively; if not, they'll never be done," said Elías. "I see that you were not meant for the strokes of circumstances. I believe that my plan should unfold this week, and it will, whether or not you want to help me."

"Collaborate with you, yes, definitely. We have an agreement. You are in charge. Even though we differ on one point, that doesn't mean we will have a falling out. I'll follow your orders, but the responsibility for success falls on me. In the event of failure, you must not abandon me; this has been our pact."

"Don't worry. With respect to what I've said to you, there is no need for you to insist further. You will have what you desire, and even more."

"Then, I only await your orders."

"It is clear," said Elías after a pause, "that they have decided to act in agreement and eliminate the small differences that used to exist between them. Martínez de la Rosa and Toreno are joining forces with the Ministers, Felíu and Argüelles."

256

"So what?"

"That is what our plan requires."

"With the exception of Argüelles, they all are despised by the people; and I don't believe that there is any man around who is more despised by the liberal extremists than Minister Felíu."

"Well, then," said *Coletilla*, "I am sure, extremely sure, that those whom I have named, along with Valdés, Alava, García Herreros, Quintana the poet, Bozmediano, the State Advisor, and others are meeting together. I don't know if they meet with all the ministers and a few generals during the daytime or at night. It's clear they have some project in mind; some plot; who knows if it is against the King."

"Do you know where they meet?"

"I don't know, but I am dying to find out. Imagine what an occasion! They are precisely the men who...I'll tell you how I learned that those birds meet some evenings, maybe every evening, I don't know. Some days ago, Felíu was in the King's room. There was no counsel meeting. Count T--- was telling jokes. The King laughed a lot, and the Minister, too, so that they couldn't accuse him of irreverence. Later on, His Majesty mentioned that he wanted to see the welfare decree Felíu had prepared, because the Bishop of León was present and the King wanted to show it to him. Felíu pulled the manuscript out of his pocket, and at the same time, a very small paper fell out, and His Majesty, who is more crafty than Merlin, put his foot down on it immediately. The Minister saw that the paper fell, but pretended not to notice. He kept on reading the decree. The prelate said he did not like the decree, but the King was extremely satisfied with it. He was very curious to know whether the paper contained something interesting and hastened the departure of the Minister. When he was alone he called me. Together we read the paper which said, 'At ten Argüelles and Calatrava are finally going. Don't be absent.' "

"This increased our curiosity. At ten we sent someone to keep an eye on the exit of the Minister's house, to observe where he was going. But Felíu didn't leave; Argüelles and Calatrava did not leave their houses, either. It so happened that the wicked one, who saw that His Majesty had put his foot down on the paper, tried to mislead him by not going to the rendezvous, and he informed Argüelles and Calatrava in time so that they would not go either."

"And did you try to find out later on?"

"Yes. On the following evening, a person went to Felíu's house looking for him, and they told him that he wasn't there. He remained in the area, but didn't see Felíu enter or leave the whole evening. I suspected that Toreno, Martínez de la Rosa, Valdés, Alava, and Bozmediano had entered that meeting; and after ten, I sent men to their houses to inquire about them under some pretext. None were at home. I learned that Quintana, who often goes to El Príncipe, left before ten. I also learned that Bozmediano and his son, who attended the gathering at the Marquis de las Amarillas's place, left at about ten, the three of them together. This happened on several evenings."

"And aren't they followed in order to determine their destination?"

"Yes. It was observed that each one enters his own house. They do this to mislead anyone who may follow them. Some evenings they were seen heading to different places, but they were never observed going to one single place. But we shall find out, don't worry."

"Well, if that gathering is a fact," said *El Doctrino*, "it is undoubtedly a plot. What an opportunity!"

"And you wanted to let this chance go by! Those people must appear before the eyes of the people to be conspirators in a coup d'etat attempt against the Constitution. It is easy to deceive the public."

"The people will believe it, and that's all that matters."

"Well now, what did you do this morning?" asked *Coletilla*. "Have you spoken to the people from Lorencini?"

"We are in agreement."

"And the Comuneros, have they decided to go along with you."

"You already heard what the leader of the extremists there said. We also reached an agreement."

"Good," said Elías.

"Great masses of people will blindly obey our mandate. That is the good thing about extreme ideas. It is very easy to lead the people to the field of action by provoking them with such extreme ideas. The people let themselves be led, and they like to be led."

"Blessed be the nation!" said Elías, with a look on his face like Satan's when he tempted Christ. "Blessed be the nation which has so impressionable and docile a public, because while they may go astray, their gullible nature can also serve to return them to the righteous path; and then, with a system of repression in place, the people will not be impressed by anyone else."

Coletilla had scarcely pronounced these terrible aphorisms when a noise was heard on the stairway; some young members of the newly-organized club had arrived.

"Hide over there," said *El Doctrino* to *Coletilla*. "These fellows must not see you."

The royalist hid himself in an adjacent bedroom as Alfonso Núñez and Cabanillas entered with a third youth, whom we meet today. He was Juan Pinilla, a great orator of Los Comuneros, an apostle of the most divisive and extravagant ideas. He worked along with *El Doctrino*, both serving *Coletilla* for respectable sums of money and the promise, solemnly assured, of a government post either in Cuba or the Philippines. Many other young men took part in the infamous plot, among them many who were guided only by a badly understood patriotism, ignorance or ambition. They were the most unfortunate ones.

"What's new?" asked Núñez. "Are you still convinced that this can be put off? Tomorrow will be too late. I have seen that the atmosphere is perfectly prepared for our objective. The ministers and the deputies of the extreme faction are detested; the storm roars over their heads. We must make it explode. We'll save Liberty. Yes or no?"

"We'll save it," said *El Doctrino*. "When we count our ranks and see that most of Spain is with us, should we not be confident?"

"That's exactly what I say," said Aldama, who in *Coletilla's* presence never spoke, but who knew how to make use of his pet phrase in his absence.

"Hasn't Lázaro arrived?" asked *El Doctrino* of Alfonso.

"He wasn't at home. Perhaps he'll be here later on."

"Tonight Jorge Bessières, the great French Republican, will come," said Juan Pinilla, who was also a Republican.

Pinilla was a tall man, almost as corpulent as Calleja the barber, but endowed with more clarity of mind. He was a lawyer without cases, due more to the violence and informality of his character than to a lack of talent. He was a great terrorist, and his greatest desire was to undertake the role of accuser whenever the Junta of Public Health decreed the extermination of a large number of citizens, starting with the King. Fernando was already sentenced in Pinilla's papers, along with others less worthy of the guillotine than he. A little after this frenzied demagogue arrived, another person came on the scene.

"Who could it be?" asked *El Doctrino*, hearing footsteps. "I'll wager that it's Lobo himself."

A tall man, thin, and dressed in black, entered the room. It was *Don* Julián Lobo, a famous Republican who later became a partisan and one of the most bloodthirsty jackals of absolutism. It is not clear whether during this period, he was a real demagogue or simply an absolutist in disguise, like so many others. What is certain is that he professed the most exaggerated opinions, and his speeches, delivered in Lorencini, were eloquent and fanatic. He often plotted with the liberal extremists against the government of Martínez de la Rosa. There are those who insist that he was among the first members of the Misas and El Trapense factions; and it is true that at the end of the three constitutional years, he became shamelessly associated with a faction in Moncayo, where he caused nothing but devastation. Once absolutism was enthroned again he was named to a major order—he was already a member of a lesser order before 1821—; he then obtained the archdeaconry of Ciudad Rodrigo, with a seat in the choir of Salamanca, and he enjoyed it for many years.

"*Señores*," he said with great solemnity, "good news: The Golden Fountain is ours."

"What's up? Tell us," they encouraged him.

"They have left the field wide open. The last lukewarm ones who remained have now left, realizing that public opinion is with us. Last night they were given a terrible hissing. They all agreed to leave together. The owner of the Grippini Café came here to ask me if we wanted to continue to hold the sessions..."

"Well, are we not going to continue? This very evening," said Alfonso enthusiastically.

"Good for The Golden Fountain. The Golden Fountain is ours!" shouted *El Doctrino*.

"The same thing has happened in Lorencini. Those gentlemen left, taking along their order and common sense."

"The field is ours. Get the people together for this evening."

"Everybody to The Golden Fountain!"

"To The Golden Fountain at ten."

In the preparatory session of The Little Fountain nothing significant occurred. The principal leaders of the conspiracy set a time for a secret conference to take place that evening in the back room of The Golden Fountain at nine, and so they departed, leaving Aldama and *El Doctrino* behind. Once they were alone, they called Elías, who appeared with a jubilant smile—which on his face was the most diabolic and repulsive state imaginable.

"What do you think?" asked *El Doctrino*.

"Good! Good!"

"Let's have a drink," added the youth, taking from Aldama a bottle which he had taken out from somewhere after the group departed.

"I don't drink," said Elías, taking the bottle and pouring wine in the glasses of the other two, "I don't drink."

"This evening at The Golden Fountain. Are you going?"

"Yes, I'll go...why not?" responded *Coletilla* ironically. "I'm a liberal, too."

Chapter XXXIII

THE HARPIES BECOME SAD

Lázaro was amazed by what happened in the house on Belén Street, the afternoon following his excursion to Afligidos Plaza, on the same day as the session in The Little Fountain. It was about three in the afternoon when his uncle came in; the two harpies pounced on him at once, and with the gall characteristic of their venomous natures, began their tale, fighting over who would speak first, "Ah, *Señor Don* Elías! You don't know how upset this lad has us! Do you have any idea what time he returned home? Can you believe it? At twelve!...What a scandal! In a house like this, in a house of peace, of decorum, of virtues! This young man entered at twelve. He probably spent the evening in one of those clubs, as they call them, probably rioting and learning all the heresies that circulate there. What do you think about that? But aren't you angry, *Don* Elías? The worst thing of all is that he came in making so much noise with those footsteps of his...shouting...Since Paulita is so ill, the noise disturbed her so much that she wanted to get up out of bed. Oh, what a man! You can believe us that your little nephew has just about worn us out, *Señor* Elías, and you must make a decision in this matter because this house...you see...this house..."

Paz said most of this, although some words were Salomé's. But when the two realized that their sermon didn't effect *Coletilla*—and this is what surprised Lázaro—Salomé then took the floor to say, "And aren't you aware that this...youngster is the most ill-mannered person I have ever seen? Well, the other day we were at the home of *Don* Silvestre Entrambasaguas, and he behaved so rudely that it embarrassed us to be in his company. Later, he raced through the streets. In short, if you don't decide to keep him out of those clubs..."

Lázaro felt a powerful desire to grab first one monster and then the other by the hair, demonstrating the harsh condemnation which the historic aristocracy could suffer via the illustrious Porreños. But his indignation vanished when his uncle, far from listening with anger to those accusations, smiled and passed a hand over his shoulder almost affectionately (if one is permitted to use this word) and said:

"Don't be angered by such a small thing. If he arrived late, it was surely because he had something to do. There isn't anything unusual about that. Lázaro is behaving himself. I can assure you of that."

"Jesús! *Señor Don* Elías!" exclaimed Salomé, as if she had heard an obscenity. "Jesús, *Señor Don* Elías. I expected you to have some consideration for us."

"But, madam, I said that if my nephew arrived late, it was because he had something to do."

"I never expected to hear such words from you," remarked Paz, setting her eyes, mouth, and nose in the same aggrieved grimace as if she were about to cry.

"I don't know where we could have failed," observed Salomé, turning green and making a great effort to leave the impression that if she was not crying it was only due to her social propriety. "I don't know what we could have done to make you say such a thing to us."

"Since we are down and out..." mumbled Paz, bowing her head, as if accepting some terrible humiliation.

"But, ladies," said *Coletilla*, seriously. "I haven't insulted you, I have only pardoned my nephew."

"Ever since our misfortunes..." added the lady, resuming her interrupted complaint. "Certain considerations are no longer shown to us, and when we say something, it is contradicted."

"Do you think I do that, my dear ladies!" stammered Elías.

"During another period," said Salomé, breathing heavily and concentrating her feelings of contempt into a stare..., "at another time such things did not happen. Each person knew his place, and he who was obliged to obey us, never approached us except with respect and courtesy. Today, everything has changed."

"Today everything has changed! As it must!" exclaimed Paz, who after incalculable efforts had achieved her objective, which was to force a tear to roll down her tomato-like cheeks.

"Adiós, *Señor Don* Elías," said Salomé, turned poisonous because the royalist did not kneel at her feet, as she had expected.

"Adiós, *Señor Don* Elías," repeated Paz, seeing that her little teardrops did not soften the old majordomo's hard heart.

"But come now, ladies."

The two turned rapidly.

"I am confused; I don't know why you take this tone with me. I don't see how I have offended you. What have I said?"

"You have said something I don't care to remember," said Paz, wiping away the above-mentioned tear.

"You said that your nephew was going to change his ways. Oh! I can't believe that you...," exclaimed Salomé.

"Adiós, *Señor Don* Elías."

"Adiós, *Señor Don* Elías."

They left. The fanatic quickly recovered from his surprise, and then, conceding little importance to the matter, turned to his nephew and said, "Let's go, Lázaro. This evening your friends are meeting at The Golden Fountain. It will be an important session. Don't miss it. I do not object to every man expressing his opinions. You have yours; I respect them. I know that you have talent, and I want them to get to know you. Go to The Golden Fountain; go this evening."

Lázaro was amazed. He could hardly believe what he was hearing from that intransigent man, who had so often incriminated him for his liberal ideas. But he did not worry much about it, accustomed as he was by now to strange and unlikely events.

Mealtime arrived and the holy ceremony of the daily bread was so quiet that the house seemed to be in mourning. Let it suffice to say that Salomé forgot to pass the chick peas to Lázaro, and he, so as not to give rise to a new conflict, did not ask for them, or serve himself. And *Doña* Paz was not very generous in serving the royalist's portions. She forgot to serve him any meat, hence that great man who lived only for the spirit continued to do so. The other old lady did everything humanly possible to indicate that she had no appetite; but among all the means available to show such a thing, she failed to use the best method which is to not eat at all. Her efforts did not reach that extreme. Paz produced some sighs between mouthfuls of food. The only important event which upset the calm of that melancholy and silent meal was a minor dispute stirred up between the harpies, because Salomé had said that it was Paz's fault that the stew was overcooked, and Paz asserted that the opposite was true. On concluding the meal, Elías looked up from his meditations to ask:

"But isn't *Doña* Paulita better? Bah! I suspect it's nothing serious."

Salomé quickly placed a grape which she held in her delicate fingers, into her mouth in order to be able to say:

"Nothing serious? You can be assured that it is quite serious."

On saying this, the movements of her thin skin and the angular bones of her gullet indicated that the grape had been swallowed.

"But is it truly serious?" asked Elías.

"Does it really interest you so much?" asked María de la Paz, haughtily. She felt the vitality of her ancient and skillful parlor eloquence arise within her as she spoke.

"Well, why should it not interest me?" asked Elías, feeling his majordomo's self-pride offended. "But I am going to see her, if you permit me."

"You can't right now, because she's sleeping."

"You'll disturb her."

The two smiled, satisfied with the humiliation they thought they cast over Elías, by momentarily distancing him from their confidence.

"Well, if I can't see her, I'll retire."

"Good-night."

"If I can be of any service to you, ladies...," said the royalist.

And the royalist left the room, frustrating their expectations.

"Oh!" exclaimed Salomé. "Is it possible?"

"What?" asked Paz, in alarm.

"Could it be that the modern ideas have also...?"

"Is it possible...?"

"And he, too!"

The ambiance of the dining room resounded with the vibration of two sighs as expressive as two poems. But no harm came, from their bad temper, unless you consider the unprovoked kick which Batilo, the pup, received after the meal.

Chapter XXXIV

THE CONSPIRACY—LAZARO'S TRIUMPH

That day Lázaro was once more unable to find Bozmediano. His desire to speak to him, to ask for an explanation of his infamy, to demonstrate the nobility of his own conduct, and to punish him mercilessly increased by the minute. He was anxious to see him; for certain offenses inspire a patience and tenacity which even the greatest undertakings rarely provoke.

At the house he was told repeatedly that Bozmediano was not at home; he walked from one end of the street to the other without seeing him. Evening arrived, and about ten he noticed that the same three persons from the evening before were leaving. There they were. The Bozmedianos, father and son, and the other soldier left by a door which opened onto a dark, narrow alley, and they set out for Afligidos Square taking the long route.

The youth stationed himself once more behind the corner of Las Negras Street, and saw them enter the same house. After a short while, another person entered, later three more, then two, in short, the same people as on the previous evening. Then Lázaro, realizing that his great objective, which was to talk to and confound Bozmediano, could not be achieved by watching unknown persons entering an unknown house, left the area, heading for The Golden Fountain to attend the important session his uncle had told him about.

From dusk onward, *El Doctrino*, Pinilla, Aldama, and another two individuals who had further dealings with the revolutionary Elías Orejón's purse, sat in the café on San Jerónimo Avenue.

"There is no better way than the one *Coletilla* has proposed to us," said *El Doctrino*. "That fox is certainly talented."

"But it's important that effective measures be taken first," indicated Pinilla, "because if those blows aren't successful, the results will be terrible....We should choose good people and let them all follow us and work toward the same objective without saying anything until we are on top of it. Let only thirty or forty proven men know our true objective."

"It has to be that way; I'll guarantee it."

"They also apparently see the struggle coming and are preparing their defense. Today Toreno said it in Parliament," observed Pinilla. "But it's going to be difficult for them to escape. The people are fed up with them. The people want liberty and will trample anyone who stands in their way."

"The greatest difficulty is not being able to catch them together in a single location. The best thing would be to invade the Assembly, but the man in the big house does not want that. One must go hunting for them, lair by lair, and this makes things more difficult and complicated....But let's get to the point. In summary, what should we do?"

"The matter is very simple," said *El Doctrino*, pushing back his hat and lowering his voice. "Everything is reduced to the following: There is a party, a few men who call themselves sensible liberals, who preach order and respect for the law. That is fine. But the masses have come to feel a great hatred for those people, who are, as the King believes, supporters of the Constitution. The public has come, after many recommendations, to strongly desire the...elimination of these men. Well, let us lead the public to the fulfillment of its desire. The people want it, so let the national desire be fulfilled."

After these ridiculous and diabolical words, *El Doctrino* paused to read the effect of his exposition on the faces of his listeners.

"Well," he continued, "there are twenty or thirty men already designated by popular opinion as the proposed victims."

"As victims?" interrupted Pinilla.

"Yes, there must be some trampling. How far this destruction will go, I cannot say. We already know what these people are like."

"But this trampling, will it end up in killing?" asked one of the two unknown conspirators.

"That is what I don't know. There has to be some destruction. The names of the persons who will suffer are listed in my document case. They aren't exclusively ministers."

"And what will happen afterwards?" asked the other. "Assuming that the event has taken place, and supposing that the ultimate extreme becomes a reality, what will we have? We'll take the control of the extremist party; we'll have a period of dictatorship, of terror and frightening reprisals. Where will we all end up? In the most horrible anarchy."

"It doesn't matter," said *El Doctrino*. "The King is counting on that and wants it to happen. From that anarchy, absolutism will emerge triumphant. That is his objective, and he will achieve it; there's no doubt about it."

"And against whom is the mutiny directed?"

"Against many; you already know who they are—the so-called politicians of stature, those who guide the progress of

Parliament, the influential ones. And we will not forget either presumptuous Argüelles or the famous, more-than-famous Calatrava."

"Man, would I be sorry if that wonderful adviser, Bozmediano, managed to escape; he was brazen enough to tell the Government in Parliament that if it did not keep the extremists under control, Liberty and the Nation would be endangered."

"How would that fish ever get away? He is one of the first to go....He is the very man who encourages the Government. Who clamors every day for the clubs to be closed? He's the one. Who is the author of those printed decrees? He is. Who induced the Government to dismiss Riego? He did."

"Not to mention his son, *Señor Don* Claudio Bozmediano, who used to be a member of The Golden Fountain," said one of the unknown conspirators.

"Oh!" *Señor* Pinilla exclaimed strongly, as if his heart were wounded. "Is that dog going to escape? I hate him, despise him, I wouldn't feel compassion for him if I saw him roasting on a grill. I would join the conspiracy just for the pleasure of putting an end to that damned man."

"But what has he done to you?" they asked him.

"What happened to me?" said Pinilla, livid with anger. "Sometime ago that man used to go to Lorencini. One evening I spoke out against absolutism and the friars; the public all applauded me, and he did too. Then I said something against the military; he was silent, but when I concluded my speech, he came over and expressed his displeasure in a few words. I did not wait any longer; he had been getting on my nerves for some time. I had a grudge against him, without knowing why; I told him that I did not care about his opinion. He answered me, and I answered back more strongly. Finally one word led to another, and I said something about his mother who, everyone knows, was off her rocker. Suddenly he, without hesitation...I can't even talk about it, the blood rushes to my face. He punched me in the face, so strongly that I still feel it here...,here...,burning like a red hot iron. We had it out; he's much stronger than I, and he beat me up. Afterwards, we challenged each other and he injured me, I had another run-in with him, and again he...In brief, I hate him with a passion. One of us has to destroy the other; there is no other way."

"Well, he won't escape, and neither will his father."

"I agree," exclaimed Aldama, who was very regretful because the proprietor would not give him a bottle of Málaga on credit.

"Hush, someone is coming. Who is it? Ah, Lázaro."

Lázaro entered and greeted his friend.

"Good evening, you sly fox," *El Doctrino* said to him. "We are here again in The Golden Fountain; now we are in charge of the club, our club; that horde of fools has already left. This evening you will speak out and be applauded. They'll learn to appreciate what you are worth."

"I'll do no more public speaking," replied Lázaro, with a certain bitterness, for he'd become convinced that he was not born to grace a dais.

"Look," said Pinilla to *El Doctrino*, continuing their interrupted conversation. "That young Bozmediano, along with being an immoral man, known for detestable behavior, is also a libertine, as was his father, the scandal of the Court of Carlos III."

Lázaro was suddenly attentive.

"He spends his time seducing young girls. How many families are unhappy today because of his deeds! Oh! That kind of criminal should be done away with!"

"You're talking about a person who interests me a lot just now," said Lázaro. "Do you know him? Do you know about the bastard's habits?"

"Of course I do," assured Pinilla.

"I looked for him yesterday," said Lázaro. "I looked for him today but was unable to locate him. I have certain matters to straighten out with him. I'll find him if I have to walk the whole earth to do it...."

"Be careful, young man, that bastard knows how to handle a weapon. His aim is good."

"It doesn't matter to me. We'll soon straighten things out."

"And you've been looking for him?"

"Yes, but I haven't been able to find him; that is to say I located him, saw him, but not where I could talk to him. He was accompanied by two others, apparently heading to a secret place where other men who showed up successively were gathering and entering a house."

"Where?" asked *El Doctrino* with intense interest.

"At a plaza. They tell me its called Afligidos Square."

"At Afligidos Square?" the other exclaimed in astonishment. "At Alava's house...How many were there? What time?"

Lázaro gave all the details of what he had seen in the Square at the same time on two successive evenings.

"Say no more," *El Doctrino* warned Pinilla.

This conversation took place in a small room in the interior of The Golden Fountain where the proprietor had stored a few hundred empty bottles and two or three barrels, also empty, to Curro Aldama's deep regret. As Lázaro concluded his account, the sound of applause and enthusiastic voices were heard from within the café. Alfonso Núñez spoke very eloquently. More than two hundred fervent youths, full of expansive zeal, applauded him enthusiastically.   The young orator communicated his indiscreet faith to that mass of innocent and idealistic youths, while only two paces away from them sat the four infamous characters who were preparing a bloody disaster. Such iniquities, planned by a few and carried out by many with the innocence so characteristic of deceived masses, are common during revolutions. The masses sometimes act while obeying only one member's voice, whichever that may be; all move as one in a fateful solidarity, driven by only one member.

The Golden Fountain was eloquent that evening, blind and impressive in its state of delirium. The group was about to perpetrate a crime without realizing it. Its eloquence was the premature justification of a bloody deed; and to someone who knew what was to come about shortly, that juvenile oratory's pomp would seem frightening and somber.

Lázaro entered the café: he was still not bold enough to move to the center of the floor, although he felt confident he would be well-received. He stayed back in a corner, prepared to remain a mere spectator, but some people asked him to speak. Alfonso pushed him toward the speakers' dais, the owner himself pleaded insistently with him, and the majority of the youths who made up the crowd applauded him in advance for his words. He could not refuse to speak; and having made up his mind he approached the dais and began. This time, fortunately, there was no repetition of the unhappy events of the night of his arrival. He stayed calm while confronted by his audience's thousand attentive faces and despite feeling himself the focus of so many eyes. He easily decided on the theme of his speech. From his first sentences, he saw before his imagination the developing ideas which were to constitute his dissertation. As he spoke each word, he felt the next word come to him. He spoke without stumbling, with the flowing spiritual calm of true inspiration. The mute eloquence of his hours of silence and loneliness finally reached his lips for the first time, to his own surprise, and was heard with as much delight by the speaker as by his listeners. Those spoken pages, those words never uttered by a human voice, came to his lips so easily that they seemed to have been learned by heart. This time, without realizing it, he avoided becoming rhetorical. His speaker's instincts carried him away from that danger, and although at times he expressed himself with extreme simplicity, he did not indulge in careless or vulgar speech. The spontaneous brilliance of his oratory, the profound intonations of truth and sentiment in his affirmations and the skill with which he was able to exploit the listeners' passion and fantasy helped him in that undertaking, for which his genius appeared to be of the highest order—great, spontaneous, and vigorous in ideas and form—as it really was.

"How do you expect to have liberty," he asked, "If a few men pose as its exclusive priesthood, when in fact that great priesthood belongs to each of us and isn't the patrimony of any one class? The monopolization of wealth, knowledge, superiority, and influence have already occurred. Should we now consent to the monopoly of ideas? (*Great applause.*) If we continue along these lines, we are going to end up with something like the caste system of the Orient. (*Laughter.*) Among the millions of citizens who belong to the sacred community of liberalism, we see a privileged caste coming forward which believes itself to be the sole protector of order, the only executor of laws, the only one able to direct public opinion. Must we agree to this? Must we always be slaves? Yesterday the slaves of one man's despotism, and today the slaves of a hundred men's false pride? We are a thousand times worse off with this absolutism than with the one we got rid of. I prefer to see the tyrant unmasked and frank, displaying his devilish, bloody and fierce face. I prefer the bare insolence of an abominable barbarian, conjured up by the devil, to the hypocritical cruelty, the hidden and disguised despotism of those men who command and direct us. Shielded by the label of 'liberal.' They make laws at their whim, then try to force us to respect the law. They seduce us in the name of liberty, then gun us down in the name of order. They call themselves our representatives, then insult us in Parliament, calling us bandits. (*Applause.*) This empire of injustice cannot endure. Happily, they have not yet gagged all our mouths nor not tied all our hands. We can still lift an arm to point them out. We still have enough breath left in our lungs to cry out: 'That one!' They are among us; we know them. This great revolution has not reached its august apogee; it has not reached the supreme point of justice. Until now it has only been one step, the first step. Shall we now draw back timidly, fearful, from our appointed task? No! We are in a terrible period, for the half-way point on this thorny road is the most dangerous of all. To hesitate now is to fail; it is worse than retreat; it is worse than never to have begun. We must choose between two extremes: either to continue forward, or to curse the hour in which we were born. (*Great and deafening applause.*)

As Lázaro spoke he noticed among the thousand figures in the audience, a face in the darkness of a corner, whose eyes shone with enthusiasm and eagerness. His thin and bony hands applauded, echoing like two concave stones. The individual watched him continuously during his speech, and if Lázaro had not been very sure of his theme and so confident of his position with respect to the audience, he would have been irremediably confused and his speech ruined. For the person who looked at him so fixedly and applauded him was his uncle. Such a reaction incomprehensible, and the youth would have puzzled over it if the public's affection and enthusiasm had not distracted him so completely.

Another person spoke after him, and finally, after many speeches, the public began to file out. Alfonso and Cabanillas went out to the street, carried along as the crowd broke up into large groups. All Madrid was restless that evening, and the authorities, ordinarily fairly weak and off-guard, had taken some precautions. *El Doctrino*, Pinilla, Lobo, Lázaro, and some others remained inside The Golden Fountain until the early morning.

"You have done well!" *El Doctrino* told Lázaro. "I expected as much of you. This evening our party will acquire tremendous influence, thanks to your words. *Don* Elías, you can be proud of your nephew."

"I certainly am," said *Coletilla*, smiling with the same diabolical facial contraction as Nature has given to jackals and foxes, "Yes, I certainly am. I hadn't thought that the lad was so clever. If I had known earlier, I would have done everything possible to..."

Lázaro began to see something odd about his uncle's intrusion into the radical liberals' meetings. A frightening suspicion passed through his mind. As he left for home, he remembered the accusation that the members of that very place had directed at him on the evening of his expulsion. He remembered the conversation he had with his uncle in the prison. He recalled all his uncle's words and his expression of the blindest fanaticism; and the more Lázaro meditated and recollected, the less he could explain how his uncle would ever let himself be called a great liberal. Although some vague suspicions disturbed him, he did not perceive the deep abyss in all its horror. He could not foresee the movement he had impelled with his words, not did he understand the dark scheme, the bloody collision that would take advantage of the bewildered heads at The Golden Fountain and the fervent will of some young men.

But as he arrived home, a surprise awaited Lázaro which made him forget his speech, his uncle, and The Golden Fountain. On entering, near daybreak, he found *Doña* Paz agitated, Salomé walking around the house with a lantern, and the two so angry and upset that he had to laugh despite his own emotional state.

"Thank God you have come! We are alone here," the eldest said to him, as she shook with emotion.

"What has happened, ladies?"

"We fear that someone may enter the house through the roof."

"What do you mean?"

"How is that? Who would dare do that?"

"You don't know what has happened, young man," said Paz. "That Clarita...What a horror, what perversion!"

"When will the execution be?" exclaimed Salomé. "A man, some man made his way in here to get to that girl. A seducer. And we were so blind, and gave her shelter!"

"Oh, my Lord! What an outrage!"

"And when did that man enter?" he inquired, understanding that they had discovered Bozmediano's entrance.

"On Sunday, the afternoon we were in the procession."

"And the girl, where is she?" asked the youth, believing that the moment had come to clear up the matter.

"How horrible! And you ask where she is? We have thrown her out, we have thrown her out!" said Paz, with an expression of satisfied vengeance. "Should we accept such a monster here?"

"What degradation! And in this house!" exclaimed Salomé, placing both hands over her face. "Lord, what kind of atonement is this? What sin have we committed?"

"And where is she?"

"What do you mean, where is she? How should I know? We've thrown her out!"

"But where has she gone?"

"How do I know? Out in the street, where she should have been in the first place. Oh! She's probably very happy out there."

"Her kind of people were born for the street," said Salomé, with a gesture of repugnance. "How humiliating!"

"But did you throw her out just like that? Where will the poor thing go?" asked Lázaro, who despite the girl's crime could not stand by and watch someone harm and mistreat a helpless being.

"How do I know where she went? To hell!" laughed María de la Paz.

"Lord, is it possible that so much infamy exists here on earth? Oh! The modern ideas..." mumbled Salomé, raising her hand to the sky in a declamatory manner.

Before we relate what Lázaro did after such a startling event, let us recount what happened earlier that evening in the three ladies' home. *Coletilla* had left, saying that he would return in three days, after attending to a certain matter. The ladies were commenting on his unusual decision when something happened that brought about the orphan's definitive expulsion.

Chapter XXXV

THE NUNCIO'S BIRETTA

During the past century clerical tailoring was a very busy and flourishing industry. There were many clerics and a great crop of abbots, all of whom dressed with elegance and style. Those who were engaged in such tailoring earned fat returns. For this reason many artisans of either gender, originally educated in secular tailoring, later dedicated themselves to cultivating this specialty. During the present century, the industry in question has been in decline; we cannot say whether it is because there are fewer clerics or because there are more tailors. On the fifth floor of Tócame Roque's house, located on Belén Street, two sisters made their nest, two female tailors of sacred clothes who lived in reduced circumstances. In their youth they had sewn many cloaks and surplices for the canons of Toledo and Palace clerics, but during the time of our account, for social reasons they were reduced to devoting their miserable existence to mending some charity school monk's dark green vestment or some poor and tattered military chaplain's gown. Once in a blue moon, they would make a biretta cap for a palace chaplain or for a judge from La Rota. They were very poor, but they bore their misfortune patiently, never uttering a complaint. One of them used to sigh while turning over the meager black fabric of her holy industry, and remark: "There is no religion any more."

Their only friend was *Don* Gil Carrascosa, the abbot who, according to what we've heard, once had certain bickering dealings with one of them. He visited them, provided them with some work, and long chats, during which he told them of goings-on in Madrid. But if the Remolinos—as they were named—had only one friend, on the other hand they also had an implacable, blood-thirst and ferocious enemy. This enemy was another female tailor who lived in the room next-door, and due to the predictable differences of opinions between professionals in the same trade, she had declared war to the death on them. To torment them, in addition to insults and nicknames, she kept a cat who seemed to have been born expressly to enter the sisters' room and perform the indignities that an enemy's cat can produce. Moreover, *Doña* Rosalía had a suitor, a merchant who visited her every evening with his guitar; and this suitor was an individual designed expressly to sing and play until all hours in that house and not let the two female tailors go to sleep.

Doña Rosalía had more work than her neighbors, the Remolinos. And furthermore, she did all that a covetous woman could to take away her rivals' work. Once a page from the Nunciature's office, an old client of *Doña* Rosalía and an admirer of her healthy color, dared to aspire to certain frank intimacies with her. The lady was annoyed, the page even more so; and on the following day, when he brought the Nuncio's biretta cap for mending, he handed it over to the two sisters instead of giving it to *Doña* Rosalía.

When *Doña* Rosalía found out that the papal nuncio's biretta was in the hands of her rivals, she took great offense, broke off relations with the Roman Curia, insulted the page a thousand times, and summoned her cat for a certain errand to be accomplished near her two neighbors—a delivery the animal carried out at once. She went to the unfortunate ones' door and fired a thousand terrible insults at them, causing the older of the two to react with her usual lamentation: "There is no religion any more."

But Rosalía sought to bring about a terrible revenge. How? She was surprised to see the abbot enter with an unknown soldier. The house was built in such a way that as one approached the door he could hear everything being said in the adjacent apartments. We all know the reasons for Bozmediano's visit to the Remolinos' house. *Doña* Rosalía guessed the reason, too, when she saw Bozmediano pass through the old attic door to enter the adjoining house. She waited quietly. The crafty woman realized that an amorous adventure was taking place, and at this point discovered a happy means for her vengeance. She saw Bozmediano enter and exit, and expecting him to repeat his fraudulent entry, she waited for the repetition, so that she could immediately run to the house next door to denounce the act while the youth was still inside. The youth would be caught in the act, there would be a terrible scandal, inquiries, and she would be able to point out his point of entry. She imagined the Remolinos en route to jail for their complicity in the crimes of illegal entry and abuse of confidence.

She waited one day, two, three days, and seeing that the entry was not repeated, she decided to go ahead and denounce the happenings to the interested family, for fear that by delaying she would lose her chance to denounce altogether.

No sooner thought than done. She put on her shawl, went down to the Porreños entrance, and rang the bell. They opened the door, and she faced the majestic countenance of María de la Paz Jesús, who grumpily asked her: "What do you want?"

"I came to see the owner of the house, to tell her something," said Rosalía, stepping inside.

"What a lack of respect!" thought María de la Paz, seeing her enter brashly. "Salomé, the light, please."

It was getting dark, and in the darkness she could not see the visitor's face clearly. Salomé brought a kerosene lamp to the room where the two held their conversation.

"What can I do for you?" asked Paz, scrutinizing *Doña* Rosalía at a glance.

"Who is the owner of this house?"

"I am," answered Paz, somewhat alarmed by the mystery surrounding the unexpected visitor.

"Well, I've come to tell you...Do you know what is going on here?"

"What's happening?" inquired Salomé, thinking that the ceiling was caving in.

"Don't be frightened, *señora*, when all is said and done, if one knows about a problem, one can prevent it from happening again."

"For God's sake, explain yourself, *señora*!" scolded Paz, in a tone of impatience and superiority.

"Well, you should know," *Doña* Rosalía began mysteriously, "that this house...Well...Let me explain. I live on the fourth floor of the house next door; I am a lowly seamstress, and sew all the home attire worn by the Papal Nuncio and the Patriarch of the Indies; I sew for the whole Archbishopric of Toledo and at times I have sewn for the Palace chapel." This recitation of the high hierarchy which the needle of *Doña* Rosalía served gave her a certain importance in María de la Paz's eyes.

"I live upstairs there, and I have seen...But are you really not aware of it?"

"Of what?"

"Of that man who entered here."

"What man? What are you saying?" exclaimed the two ruins at once, with a noise like a volcano erupting.

"Well, I've come here to inform you about it so that you can keep it from happening again. You see, in the attic of the house where I live there is a small door which faces the attic of this house."

There is no way to describe the look that came over the Porreños' faces as they heard those words.

"Yes," continued the seamstress, "and a young soldier came in here one afternoon through the door I refer to; he made his way in here. When I saw him, I suspected that there was a young girl living here."

"But, *señora*," said Paz, rising to her feet, "are you sure of what you are saying? A man entered here..., here in this house!"

"Yes, ma'am, I watched him. He slipped in through the apartment of some neighbors...friends of mine. I saw it."

"When?" asked Salomé, gasping breathlessly.

"Sunday afternoon. At about five."

"While we were at the procession! What a scandal! That shameless child..., that wicked child...I was right to be suspicious!" exclaimed Paz with her hands to her head, and pacing around the room as if crazed.

"Ay! I'm no good at dealing with such things....I get all upset!" babbled Salomé, leaning against the sofa dizzily.

"But, *señora*, calm down," said *Doña* Rosalía, trying to reassure the two ladies. "Do you have a daughter?"

"No, *señora*, we do not have a daughter," replied María de la Paz, angrily. "There is a girl, a crazy girl we admitted here out of compassion, hoping that she would reform. But...I was already suspicious! What a prize! Do you see what I mean? My Lord, how could we have let such a wicked young woman live here?"

"*Señora*," replied Salomé, pressing her hands to her chest in an effort to revive herself. "Please explain this. It's too horrible. We are not used to hearing such things, and these goings-on confuse me. It's too much to bear, for me, especially."

"Well, don't doubt what I'm telling you. The youth slipped into this house on Sunday afternoon and was here about an hour. Check on it, and you will see that it is true."

"But it seems incredible," said Paz, sitting down again. "This is a decent home...and how did that door get there? How is it possible...?"

"It has been there from way back, but was condemned and sealed shut. If you want to see it go up to the attic, and if you look for it very carefully, you will locate it."

"But he, that monster, how did he enter?"

"That same door," continue *Doña* Rosalía, "joins the apartment of some seamstresses who live next door, friends of mine. The poor things sew badly, and only work for sacristans and village priests. They try to put on airs and tell people that they sew for the cathedral of Segovia, but it's a lie. Don't believe them."

"And that man, did he enter through that apartment?"

"Yes. He is a tall, good-looking soldier."

"Jesús! How awful! I can't listen to this!" exclaimed Salomé, stretching out as if suffering a second attack.

"He gave those women money," continued *Doña* Rosalía, "because they are very poor. They don't earn much, because they sew so badly...They only sew for people like the junior grade military chaplain of San Martín."

"We have to make a decision, Paz, a quick decision," said Salomé, recovering her composure. "Because if we don't, the good name of this house will be ruined. *Señora*," she added, turning to *Doña* Rosalía, "don't be surprised at our anguish. We are not used to shocks like this. Thanks to our birth, our upbringing and religious devotion, we have always been above such disgraces. Oh! We are to blame for excessive charity. Imagine, we fearlessly accepted a wiper into our household although we had had reports on her conduct. We took her in, believing that she would mend her ways. But you now see how perverse some souls are! What a society! What a century! How right I was to be suspicious, despite what my niece, who is a saint, was saying, insisting that, guided by her good heart, the girl would reform. How can such a monster change? How disgraceful, how contemptible! Oh! I cannot deal with such matters, I get upset, fall to pieces and don't know what to think."

"Yes, a decision must be made," affirmed María de la Paz, with noticeable rancor. "If not, what will become of this house's good reputation? We must immediately put that youngster out into the street, without even consulting *Don* Elías. He will surely approve. Or even if he doesn't agree with us. Well, didn't he even tell us just this morning that his nephew would straighten out? Yes, this is one horror after another! What a century! What customs! Even he...!"

"Do what you please, Paz," said Salomé, affecting meekness and a certain nervous humility which she believed was flattering to her body. "Do as you please, pay no mind to what that majordomo may think; he has no voice here. Get rid of that girl; let her join the rest of her kind. Oh! I can't even think about what this woman has told us!"

Even the dog did not bark; poor Batilo was terrified. He sat across from *Doña* Rosalía and with a worried dog's attention studied the face of the seamstress who had brought desolation to that household.

"*Señora*," said Paz, somewhat more civilly. "We are grateful to you for the information you have given us, displaying, as is natural, zeal and interest in the good name of our house. Once we get rid of that girl, we'll move away from here. Oh! And I had really gotten fond of this holy refuge! We were living here in peace and tranquility, not as comfortably as in our old house, but still, very tranquilly....And you, *señora*, have saved us from dishonor; what would have become of us, alone here and exposed to that soldier's intrigues? Oh, I prefer not to think about it."

"He is a young soldier, tall, handsome, and seems to be a distinguished person."

"Young, handsome, and of good carriage!" exclaimed Paz, once again highly indignant. "Is this believable? Such aggravating circumstances!"

"Don't continue, for God's sake," begged Salomé, who was already half-faint.

"Don't continue; my niece is very sensitive and cannot bear to hear such things. We are accustomed to..."

Doña Rosalía got up to leave, for she believed that she had satisfactorily fulfilled her mission. Then a peculiar thing happened. As the seamstress approached the door, Batilo, the misanthropic dog, who for a moment had forgotten the habits characteristic of his race, ran after her, became convulsively excited as if making a great effort, and barked like a Great Dane pursuing a thief. He chased the woman with sharp howls, and caught her dress and shawl between his inoffensive teeth. Paz was alarmed, and Salomé covered her ears as if she had heard the howls of a jackal. Between them, they defended *Doña* Rosalía from the dog's unexpected attack. The seamstress left, and the two harpies looked at each other face to face, mutually communicating their respective wrath.

In their eagerness to get to Clara quickly, they became bewildered, unable to open the door, and knocked into one another in great confusion.

"Woman, you are pushing me over," said one.

"Woman, what strange ideas come into your head," answered the other.

They entered the room where the devout one lay in bed. She was resting quietly, but was not sleeping; her eyes were fixed on the ceiling, indicating deep meditation. Seated next to the bed was Clara, who was serving as the saint's nurse and companion. When the two Porreños entered, Clara saw by their faces that a terrible scene was impending. She became frightened and drew nearer the bed, as if seeking protection next to the sacred person of *Doña* Paulita.

"Child!" said Paz, with her speech flustered and her countenance showing distress. "We have found out about all your infamous acts. You deserve to go to jail for jeopardizing the good name of a household like this. If I weren't afraid of lowering my dignity..."

"*Señoras*," murmured Clara, solemnly. "What have I done?"

"What have I done?" said Salomé, mimicking her with a grotesque gesture. "Look at the hypocrite! What a monster! Oh, my Lord! Paula, don't be frightened," she added, drawing near the bed. "Don't cause us any more unpleasantness. We now know what kind of person we have accepted into our house."

"Everything has been discovered, child," continued Paz. "You will no longer deceive us with your put-on, innocent face. But, how daring, what iniquity! You should die of shame."

"Ma'am, I don't know what you are talking about," replied Clara, completely losing her serenity.

"Insolent girl! And you still dare to try to conceal it after so much shamelessness. Do you think that you are dealing with people like yourself? Look, you fool! You're as foolish as you are perverse! You are going to leave this house right now!"

Clara's first reaction on hearing these words was sudden happiness. To leave that place! She had almost lost that hope. But it was not a happy situation. She soon realized it and awaited the final verdict with resignation.

"Tell her, tell her the reason," suggested Salomé, affecting great respect for proceedings.

"She is well aware of the reason," said Paz. "But I can control my anger. In truth, I tell you that if I weren't the kind of person I am...How horrible! The reason is...don't be frightened, Paula. The fact is that while we left the house, a man came in here through the roof. Yes, a soldier, a good-looking chap, tall, a person...How did she put it? Of a good stature...But don't be frightened, Paulita. We must accept it with resignation."

If Salomé had not been afraid of frightening her sick cousin, she would have gone into her fourth fainting spell. But she satisfied herself with looking at *Doña* Paulita with terrified eyes. The holy one just looked at Clara with a certain perplexity, and contrary to what her relatives had expected, she did not cite any Latin text, nor preach a sermon on the impropriety or irreligiousness of a good-looking, tall, military man's entering by way of a rooftop. Clara, despite her innocence, remained as terrified as though she were really guilty.

"Do you dare deny it?" asked Paz, taking a few steps toward Clara, with anger shining from her eyes.

"I...no," said Clara, retreating in fright. "Yes! Yes! I deny it." Then she added, as she tried to calm herself and to pacify her judge, "Listen to me, ma'am. I shall tell you the truth. I shall tell you what happened. I am innocent. I have not allowed..."

"Jesús, Jesús! I cannot bear such things," clamored Salomé, turning her face. "I can't. I can't listen to this. What haven't you allowed? You still have the audacity to deny it?"

"I..., I don't deny it," answered the orphan, in dismay. "But how is it my fault if that man...?"

"Do you also want to excuse him? This is all that we needed to hear. There can be no pardon for such treachery. What a way to repay us for the protection we have given you, without you deserving it, especially when I predicted that nothing good would come from you."

"*Señora*," said Clara, breaking down in tears, "I swear to you, for God's sake, by all the saints, that no man has entered this house on my account. I am not to blame for all that you are saying. I swear to you, by God and the Virgin."

"Insolent girl! And you still dare to excuse yourself!"

"This is more than my weak constitution can stand," said the other harpy. "Paulita, don't be upset. Try to remain indifferent. You'll just get sicker if you don't."

"My God! How can I explain it to you?" exclaimed Clara, with deep bitterness. "What can I do, or say, for you to believe me? To whom can I turn? I don't want to live this way. I have no parents, brothers, friends, or anyone to defend and protect me. *Señora*, I swear to you! Don't say such things to me again, because I don't deserve to hear them."

"Come on, get ready to leave immediately," said Paz with frightening cruelty.

"Leave? Yes, I'll leave. I don't wish to disturb you any more. But...Oh! Those things you said about me...I haven't dishonored this house; I haven't dishonored anyone; but I am very unhappy. I am an orphan, poor and alone. I don't have anyone to protect me; that's why no one has consideration for me and everyone treats me with contempt. I don't deserve that; I haven't done anything like what you are saying; I am innocent."

"I don't know how I can control myself," said Paz. "Not a moment more. You are going to leave here, and you can go wherever you desire. I know that it will make you very happy. You only want to roam those streets alone. You were born for the streets. Let's go, hurry up. And it doesn't matter to me whether *Don* Elías objects or not. He'll approve of this. He knows that it is useless to take an interest in a despicable creature like you. Leave right away."

"*Señora*," said Clara, kneeling next to the bed and reaching out her hand to the holy one. "*Señora*, you will defend me, you who are so good; you are a saint. Isn't it true that you know that I am innocent? Say it. They are perjuring me. What is going to become of me if you do not defend me?"

The pious woman had not uttered a word. She seemed absent-minded and aloof. When she felt the hands of the girl who had, although briefly, been her companion and friend, she turned her pale face toward Clara, and, looking at her vaguely, asked in a faint and somewhat indifferent voice, "I?"

Then she remained silent. With a disdainful gesture Salomé moved Clara away from her cousin's bed, saying, "Our patience is going to destroy us. Careful, Paz, we are too acquiescent. Why is this woman still here?"

"Out to the street, right away. Come, be quick about it," ordered Paz. "Gather your things right away. Pack up your clothes and go."

"*Señora*, for God's sake, don't make me leave this way," begged Clara, kneeling and clasping her hands. "At this hour and alone...I don't know anyone...What's going to become of me? Where will I go? By the Holy Virgin, wait until my guardian arrives. When I was an orphan, he gave me shelter...He will not abandon me this way, I am sure.

"No, not a minute. Do you still think you can fool him again? Get out of our house this minute."

"But ladies," continued Clara, "Where will I go? Alone, at night, I'm afraid...I'm very afraid...I don't know anyone..."

"You say that you don't know anyone? Do you really have the nerve to say that?" exclaimed Salomé, turning her face away and crossing herself with her pointed fingers. "Well, what about the young, tall, handsome gentleman?"

"Ma'am, wait for God's sake, until my guardian comes. I beg of you, for the sake of your mother's glory."

The idea that *Coletilla* would come and prevent the orphan's expulsion put Salomé in serious danger of having her fifth attack.

"What agony!" she said, sitting down. "Frankly, it's our own excessive generosity that has brought us to this extreme."

"Don't delay another moment," said Paz, with the satisfaction of vengeance. "Leave immediately!"

The unfortunate orphan turned as a last hope once again to *Doña* Paulita, who lay in her bed as immobile and listless as a prostrate statue in a tomb. Clara took one of her hands and kissed it effusively, sprinkling it with tears provoked by her executioners' cruelty.

"Ma'am, I am pleading with you once more," she exclaimed in an almost inaudible voice, "Please don't abandon me! You are a saint. Don't let them throw me out...at this hour...I am afraid. Don't abandon me!"

The mystic woman slowly withdrew her hand and hid it between the sheets. She turned, looking at the victim, and without altering her facial expression, asked in the same frigid voice, "I?"

"One cannot tolerate such insolence," affirmed Paz, seizing Clara by the arm and violently pulling her away from the bed. "If you don't leave right now, I shall call a policeman to teach you how to behave."

Salomé had already stepped to the bureau where Clara kept her few possessions, and gathered everything into a bundle.

"Don't worry, Paz," she said, "I am searching her clothes so she doesn't carry something off. She doesn't have anything of ours."

"Dear ladies!" Clara cried at the height of desperation. "Please don't throw me out this way; I haven't done anything wrong; I haven't done what you say. I am innocent. Let that woman tell you, she who is a saint and knows me. I am sure she will say it."

The devout one moved again and with a voice like a ghost's, repeated once more: "I?"

"Don't throw me out," continued Clara, not knowing to whom to appeal. "I don't deserve it! Where can I go alone at this hour? I don't know anyone. I'm afraid...I might get lost."

"Let's go! Here, take your clothes," said Salomé, handing her the bundle.

"No, I can't believe it. You can't be so inhuman. Can't you wait until he returns tomorrow?"

"He said that he will not return for three days. Do you think he has nothing better to do than to protect young girls like you?"

Having said this, Paz took Clara by the arm and led her toward the door with a great effort. The poor orphan undoubtedly had a strong character, for she didn't collapse, unconscious. No doubt because she was very angelic and delicate by nature, she didn't answer in like manner the insults made by the aristocratic Eumenides, a disgrace to the Porreño name. The unhappy girl still believed that her pleading could soften those two hearts hardened by boredom, unsociability, and the bitterness of a cloistered life. She continued to plead with them; she again kneeled before María de la Paz and took those hands, undoubtedly born to hold a dagger. The old woman pulled her hands away violently. She lifted her arm, and despite the dignity she strove to impart, even though her nobility of race should have been equaled by nobility of character, she struck the unhappy orphan, whom she had just slandered. The ridiculous old woman, presumptuous, devout, the human expression of great stupidity and great pride, slapped the abandoned and defenseless girl, whose youth and simplicity, offended the self-love of those two insolent demons.

"Ay, Ay, Ay! Paz, for God's sake, don't take a chance," said Salomé, screeching with horror as if poor Clara had a dagger in her hand. "Let her go; let her go."

"I could kill her," hissed Paz, clenching her fists and choking in anger.

Salomé put the same shawl across Clara's shoulders that she had worn when she first entered the house. Then she extended her bony arms and pushed her toward the door so violently that Clara nearly fell to the ground. At the same time she remarked: "I was not made to deal with such matters. I'm all broken up. Go away quickly, child. Don't make us use force."

Clara left. She was thrown out by old Paz's arms and old Salomé's weak and nervous arms. It is even probable that the latter, on giving her that last push, had clenched her sparrow hawk talons and digging her nails into her victim's arm. The door closed with a great crash, and the discordant voices of the demons reverberated inside for a long time. The orphan found herself in the street—alone in the world, without shelter, with the sky above, desolation all around, and not even a familiar face. Where was she to go? In the doorway, she heard a noise and turned around. It was the sad dog who followed her. The poor animal had left the house for the first time and seemed determined to not return; he was jumping and yelping with joy, mischief and an air of relaxation he had not known before.

Chapter XXXVI

CLARIFICATIONS

When Lázaro heard the news of his old friend's ejection, he wanted to seize the two noble ladies by the nape of the neck and punish them for their cruelty. In spite of her offense and without knowing why they had thrown her into the street, a great interest in the unhappy girl was awakened in his heart. Clearly, it was his responsibility to protect her at this critical moment, and to remove her from the sinfulness to which her solitude might expose her. He had to rescue her, in short, because she had been his friend, he had loved her, and in such cases it behooves a good and generous heart to forgive offenses and to repay them with noble deeds. Since they gave him no information about her whereabouts, he went out to the street and started out, determined to look for her. But where, where would he find her? Clara didn't know anyone in Madrid. No, wait, she knew Bozmediano. This idea suddenly chilled the youth's generosity. "Perhaps," he was thinking, "she left because Bozmediano persuaded her to do so; perhaps she was already with him." The thought revived the student's jealousy and rancor, and he decided not to rest until he had uncovered the mystery of her departure and called Claudio to account for his great betrayal.

With this idea in mind he headed toward Claudio's house, prepared to create a scandal there if they didn't permit him to see him. It seemed probable that Clara was there. Jealousy blinded him when he thought that the young girl who some months earlier had seemed to him to possess all the charm of simplicity and grace, of strictest virtue and domestic calms, had yielded to the propositions of an unscrupulous libertine. Such an infamous act could not go unpunished. "She still means a lot to me," he said to himself, "I love her so much that I pardon this offense, though it seems directed at me, personally..."

He arrived at Bozmediano's house and waited, pacing the street until dark. When he heard eight o'clock strike, he entered and asked the doorman whether Bozmediano was at home. The doorman, who now recognized him from seeing him there on previous days, was not as unpleasant to him as before, because he recalled a certain conversation he'd had with his master apropos of that visit. He had told Bozmediano that a young man came looking for him sixty times in a row. The master's curiosity was awakened, and he wanted to know more details. The doorman gave them to him accurately, and Bozmediano, suspecting it was Lázaro, instructed the domestic to let the young man in immediately if he returned while Bozmediano was at home. Claudio suspected why the youth was calling there, and far from shrinking from a visit, he was anxious for one.

But despite his clear orders, the doorman felt that it was disrespectful to receive a visit at that hour from a youth who wasn't a soldier, who neither came by coach nor wore *farolé*-style boots. He made him wait for quite a while and finally let him in, telling the servants to awaken the master. The latter took another quarter of an hour before leaving his room.

"You must already know why I have come," said Lázaro, without greeting him. "You know me; you freed me. I thought since then, out of gratitude, that there could be friendship between us, but you didn't want it that way; you have seduced and dishonored a poor girl whom I consider my sister. If you got me out of jail in order to make the offense which I received even greater, you have done that, for I am now free to demand an account for your action, which is the most infamous act that a man can commit."

"I do not commit infamous actions. I'll not permit you to say another word until you retract what you have said. Indeed, you will retract what you have said. I have not seduced or dishonored any young lady. You are blind with rage and misled by passion. You have been deceived, and it is only because I know that you have been deceived that I tolerate the words I've heard. But it will be very easy to set you straight."

"That's exactly what I want," said Lázaro. "If you convince me to the contrary...But you'll not be able to convince me. I have seen you, I saw you leave the house where Clara was sheltered, like a thief. You entered there to see her, perhaps you were summoned by her."

"Oh, no!" exclaimed Claudio, interrupting him. "Sit down; let us speak calmly. Don't jump to hasty conclusions. I am going to dispel your doubts."

"Tell me. There are no words; there is nothing that can dispel the judgment formed when one sees a man secretly enter a house where a young girl waits alone, and more so when the judgment is based on clear antecedents. I haven't come here to hear you explain anything. I don't have doubt, only certainty, about the infamy you committed. I've come solely to have the pleasure of telling you that you are no gentleman, but a corrupt man. I'll take the consequences of that accusation because I fear no adversary, however powerful, when I feel obligated to avenge an offense."

"Well, I have never tried to avoid the consequences of any such act," said Bozmediano emphatically. "I have never allowed anyone to reprimand me, nor have I permitted any man to say damaging things against me, not even a half-truth or an allusion. I want to clarify this matter in the hope that you'll be convinced and that you will take back all that you have said. I understand your reaction, it is only natural; for this very reason, I'll forget it. Let us see if after what I tell you you still insist on repeating the accusation.

"Speak up! I am anxious to hear what you have to say."

"I have seen Clara only three times," began Bozmediano. "She doesn't know my name nor who I am. She has seen little of me, and I am so unimportant to her that I can guarantee you that I am the same to her as an unknown person. One day I found that wretched old fanatic in the street. I took him to his house and saw Clara for the first time. She spoke to me, and with the simplicity characteristic of her personality and the openness born of the need for communication and sociability, she told me something about that household. I shall not deny to you that at that time I was extremely interested in her, that I thought that nothing would please me as much as getting her out of that prison, to give her some happiness and to free her from the supervision of that gloomy man, who could turn happiness itself into sadness...."

Bozmediano then told of the second conversation with Clara, even remembering some words of his dialog with her. The other youth listened attentively to that account, told with great truthfulness.

"So that you can judge me better, I shall be frank and not hide my sentiments, my first intentions," he continued. "At first I saw in Clara the object of an adventure, and even though I felt a great deal of pity for her and a true interest, I couldn't help but proceed in the formation of my plans with a certain indiscretion. I shall not deny it; I am not trying to disguise the facts; this confession is like that of a dying person to a priest. But either the circumstances or she herself altered my initial plan. She has an angelical character. Full of goodness and simplicity, she is capable of overcoming the intentions of any man, unless he were a villain or a libertine. I confess to you that the first affection and compassion which she had inspired in me acquired such force that I ended up by falling in love with her. I can't deny that in spite of this true love, I persisted in my intention of getting her out of that house by any means and carrying her off with me like a possession. I didn't consider this an offense and would have killed anyone who

stood between us or would try to take her away from me. I
learned, although she didn't tell me, that there was a person
whom she loved a great deal. This threw me off. I learned that
you were in jail, and I acted immediately. I understood that if
she loved you sincerely the best action was to get you free and
return you to her. What a complication! In this way, I
intended to win her esteem. Don't be so surprised! I have
always considered myself a practical person in these matters,
and due to Clara's character it was clear that the longer you
remained in jail, the more she would love you. But I didn't
count on the many other treasures of goodness that her
character possessed. You were living there and the vigilance,
the cruelty of three ridiculous women and a fanatic old man
prevented you from seeing her, helping her, or freeing her from
so much suffering. You were living there, but never spoke to
her, and seemed not to love her. That was my chance. I said,
'Lázaro seems ungrateful to her. I wonder if she despises him?
Her situation in that dismal house and the sadness she lives in
must be consuming her. Couldn't they be cause enough for her
to desire freedom, affection, and all the things she doesn't have
nor can have there, if that indifferent youth, occupied only by
political passion, doesn't know how to give them to her?' You
see that the situation was such that I could expect something
more than mere gratitude from her. I decided to get her out of
there and take her with me. I was so blind that I didn't foresee
her resistance, her fidelity, and her great affection for you, her
first love, an affection stronger than all her sufferings and
privations. I was determined to enter the house while she was
alone, and I did, through the door you know about. On seeing
me, she became so frightened that I was almost sorry to have
taken that step. She pleaded with me to leave; she begged me
on her knees to do so. I told her she had no other hope, and
that you wouldn't be able to, nor knew how to, save her from
the grasp of those cruel people. She didn't listen to a single
word I said. Her purpose was irrevocable. I recognized that
fidelity was the greatest of her virtues, and realizing that it was
impossible to uproot her first image, the image that nothing can
erase, I gave up my attempt. She didn't want to listen to me.
She was desperate at the thought of how much trouble I could
have gotten her into with my entry. Crying, she pleaded with
me to leave her to her sadness and loneliness. I confess that I
never have felt so small as at that moment, in the presence of a
delicate creature who was not only incorruptible in a young
man's promises of love, but also incorruptible before offers of
liberty, happiness and social standing. As I left, I heard

someone entering the house. I don't know who it was. I fled so as not to involve her. I fled terrified by the idea that despite my precautions, someone in the house might discover my entry."

"It was I," said Lázaro. "I saw you leave by way of the attic."

"What I have told you," Bozmediano solemnly affirmed, "is the full truth. I haven't omitted anything which could flatter me, or compromise me or make me look ridiculous. It is the full and absolute truth. I swear it to you by my mother's salvation, she whose portrait is hanging over there and who always seems to be looking at me."

Claudio pointed to a portrait hanging on the wall, and in this pledge his words held such a sincere tone that Lázaro could not utter the thoughts that had crossed his mind just a moment earlier.

"Nevertheless," said Lázaro, who was not yet satisfied by the other's declaration, "I want you to give me some positive proof. You can understand that in such matters, words do not suffice."

"What do you mean, words do not suffice? They do not suffice, no doubt, to satisfy obsessed spirits. There are certain things that cannot be proved in any other way. At times one person's affirmation is sufficient to transmit the deepest conviction to the soul of another. I cannot believe that, if you were to make the same accusation to Clara that you have made to me, and she, with the serenity of innocence, were to reply truthfully, that there is any way you wouldn't believe her. Speak to her; break the silence of that house. See her a moment, listen to her voice; and if upon hearing her statements you persist in believing her guilty, you are an unworthy being. I tell you a hundred times that you will not be worthy to look at her."

Lázaro couldn't defy the great strength of these words. A man's duplicity and guile could not possibly conceal the truth in that way, he thought. Bozmediano wasn't lying.

"Oh, be quiet!" said Lázaro, unable to control himself. "Either you are the best actor on earth or you are telling me the truth. I, who have never lied and don't know how to feign, feel a strong inclination to believe what you have told me. But the human heart has weaknesses and scruples from which reason and words cannot free it."

"Let's go see Clara," said Claudio decisively.

"Where?"

"At the home of those demons. If possible we'll subdue

those three old ladies."

"Clara is no longer there. They have put her out."

"But why? Where is she?"

"I don't know," said Lázaro sadly.

"But where has she gone?"

"That is my worry, my anguish. Where could she have gone? She doesn't know anybody. Finding herself alone in the streets, where could she have gone? I thought...frankly, I thought she might be here."

"Here?"

"I thought that you had induced her to leave, that she had come looking for you, whom she knew."

'Do you still believe she is here?" asked Bozmediano, smiling.

"Now...I am not claiming anything...I doubt..."

"And if I prove to you that she isn't here and that she never came here? What will you think then?"

"Even so, it will not be enough to tear out the last root of my distrust. I still don't have the evidence that I need; that is evidence which nobody has and nothing can give me."

"You will acquire it through your own feelings. There are beliefs that come to us through revelations which no thing, no person can destroy. There are things one cannot doubt, because their proof is imbedded in our very being and to doubt them would be something like death. Let's go look for her."

"Where?"

"Let's look for her! Just the fact that she doesn't know anyone will make it easier to locate her. I am sure that we will find her."

"We'll walk through every street; we'll talk to the police; we will ask everyone," said Lázaro.

"Yes, yes. We'll do all that."

"We'll go to hospitals, shelters; we'll enter every house if necessary."

"Yes."

"We'll go to the old apartment house; we'll ask the janitor, neighbors, the neighborhood storekeeper."

"That's it. Say, wasn't there a maid at the old house?"

"Yes, there was one, but I don't know her name."

"I wonder where she is. If we locate her, perhaps she can give us a lead. Perhaps Clara has gone to her. I remember that the maid told me that she was going to marry a tavern owner and that she would own a tavern. If that woman has set up house and Clara knew where, there's a good chance she went there."

"Exactly," said Lázaro. "Let's see if we can find that woman."

They left and headed toward Válgame Dios Street. They asked the janitor of the old house if he had yet rented the apartment on the second floor. The janitor said not. They asked him about the maid's name and whether he knew of her whereabouts.

"Her name is Pascuala," he replied. "She's married to a tavern owner named Pascual, but I don't know where she lives. The saloon keeper on Barquillo Street should know, because he is a friend of his."

The saloon keeper told them that the Pascual couple lived on Humilladero Street, and the two youths immediately headed there.

Chapter XXXVII

CLARA'S WAY OF THE CROSS

Although she had nowhere else to go, the Porreño house filled Clara with horror. So, her first impulse on leaving it was to flee, to run anywhere just to get out of sight of that odious place. She walked a short distance, turned the corner and stopped. Then she began to understand how bad her situation was. When she realized that she knew no one, that she had nowhere to go, she thought about waiting near the house until Elías or his nephew returned. But Elías had said that he would not return for three days, and Lázaro, who already suspected the worse about her, would be reassured in his belief if he knew the Porreños had thrown her out. However, she still needed to see Lázaro and tell him everything. And even if he believed her story, what could the two of them do, the one as helpless as the other? Nevertheless she decided to wait there for him, huddled against the corner of the house. But she was very frightened. She imagined that a great black hand was about to come out of the nearby grating and pull her inside. What horror!

Then she heard loud voices at the end of the street. Some very drunk men were approaching, scuffling, cursing and laughing uproariously like a pack of reveling demons. She was too terrified to stay there for another minute, and began to run away as fast as she could. The men ran after her, and she imagined their hands on her back; she heard their shouts in her ears. She ran through Barquillo Street, followed by the dog, and finally stopped, exhausted and breathless. The laughter faded into the distance....They were no longer following her....She stopped to gasp for breath when she couldn't take another step. Then she continued walking slowly. She dared not turn back, because the laughter had stopped and she heard terrible shouts and oaths. Some stones, strongly thrown, fell near her. Batilo turned, spitefully, and began to bark as he never had before, with true canine eloquence.

After this, Clara quickened her steps, and reached Alcalá Street. She looked both ways, uncertain which way to proceed. She walked toward Puerta del Sol, but had not yet reached San José when she saw a crowd of people. The street seemed endless, and she had no point of reference by which to judge distance, for to her the houses formed the horizon, and the approaching crowd seemed a mutely turbulent sea, advancing, advancing as to swallow her. Without thinking, she turned away and walked down toward the Prado. The crowd was also heading there; their muffled rumble echoed in the street. The people were carrying lights, and from time to time a voice shouted a loud hurrah, answered by a tremendous chorus of voices. The people were walking down the street behind Clara. This frightened her more than the drunks had; but when she came face to face with Cybele, the nature goddess, when she saw that great white figure in a chariot drawn by two white monsters, she was completely overwhelmed. She had seen a representation of Cybele on one earlier occasion, but now, the darkness of the night, her solitude, and her excitement and suffering made any object she saw seem fearsome, with strange and fantastic forms. The marble lions seemed to be running at top speed, galloping without moving from their place. The poor girl looked back and saw that the crowd was still coming toward her, making more noise. Wanting to avoid them she turned to the right and entered the Prado. This place seemed so huge to her that she thought she would never reach its end. She had never seen such an extension of level land, a dismal field of unlimited extension. The trees on the right and left seemed to her to be black phantoms with open arms, enormous arms, with horrifying hands and long, twisted fingers. She walked quite a distance until she finally saw before her a white object, some sort of human figure, very tall, and above all very white. It appeared to be drawing closer to her little by little, taking enormous steps. It was the Neptune from the fountain who, in the darkness of the trees' shadows seemed to be another phantom. The unfortunate girl was unable to think clearly due to emotional shock. She turned to the right to avoid that white figure and saw San Jerónimo Avenue before her. She started uphill, but was so tired that the steep incline of the street seemed impossible. She climbed along the avenue very slowly, scarcely able to walk. In the Italian sector she was confronted with what seemed a mountain, and looking up at its peak, she reflected that it would take her all night to climb it.

Clara could go no further, and sat down on a doorstep. She felt a complete exhaustion, along with an intense chill which grew by degrees, to become a painful coldness. She bundled up as well as she could and thought about returning home and waiting for Lázaro in the doorway. Then suddenly it occurred to her to try to find Pascuala's house. She remembered very clearly the name of the street where the tavern owner was living. She knew that the tavern was on Humilladero Street, but how could she get there? She decided to ask some passer-by, and if she located the house, she would spend the night there, putting everything else off until the next day. She knew that Pascuala would welcome her with open arms. But, where was that street? She instinctively prayed to the Virgin Mary, praying that Humilladero Street might be nearby; but the Virgin didn't hear her, because the street was quite far away. She stood up, resolved to ask any passer-by for directions. She saw a man coming, but she didn't dare stop him; another walked by, then others, but Clara didn't ask anyone. She was afraid to approach them. Finally she approached a woman, stopped her, and respectfully asked for directions.

"Humilladero Street?" replied the woman, a wrinkled old lady with a nasal voice.

"Yes, ma'am."

"Does it seem proper to you to stop decent persons in this manner?" answered the old lady, very annoyed. "I know exactly what these loafers want when they stop someone; they only want to pick your pocket while you answer them. Go to the devil, you louse, before I call a policeman."

Clara left before the old lady finished her diatribe, and became so anguished at the thought that everyone else would treat her in the same manner that she was ready to give in to desperation, allowing herself to die of hunger, cold, and pain. But misfortune infuses valor. She recovered some courage and was ready to keep on asking when she saw a ragged woman holding a child by the hand and another in her arms. That woman seemed to Clara generous and compassionate person who would answer her question. But before she could be asked, the woman spoke to Clara, saying, "Alms, *señora*, for the love of God. My husband is sick in bed, and these little children haven't eaten anything during the whole blessed day....Even a centavo."

Then, seeing that Clara did not look like a person who gives alms, but rather was a destitute and ill girl, she assumed that she must also be begging for money. Changing her tone, she remarked, "Listen, girl. Come with me, and we'll get a *duro* from that fat guy on the corner."

"What?" asked Clara, confused by the proposal.

"I'll bet that you haven't made a single centavo this evening. I've already got a *real*. See? Over in that store there's a blessed dry goods merchant who is very charitable. Yesterday, I told him that I had a sick daughter at home, and he gave me a *peseta*. If you like, we can get more out of him. Come with me this evening, child, and you'll see. We'll go in and you pretend to be near fainting, and put a handkerchief to

your face, and start to moan in a way that will break his heart.
Listen, like this: 'Ay! Ay Ay!' "

She let out some laments which were so pitiful that on
hearing them Clara was overwhelmed by anguish. Then she
continued, "Look, come on. We'll enter. I'll say that you are
my daughter and that you haven't eaten a mouthful, that the
doctor has given you a prescription which costs a *duro*. You
will say that you don't want to take it. If he pulls out a *duro* for
you to buy bread for the starving children, I'll say that the
money is for the medicine, and you'll say that it's for the
children, and then...you'll see how he'll soften up....And then
he'll give us both....We'll leave. I'll give you two *reales*...,
and...come on, put this kerchief on your face."

"Ma'am, I have to go, I can't," said Clara, who was too
polite to give her any other excuse. "Do you know where
Humilladero...?"

"What in the hell street is that?" asked the woman, and
seeing that two gentlemen were approaching them, she told the
child whose hand she was holding, "Start limping, boy!"

The boy limped toward the approaching gentlemen,
repeating his prepared statement. Clara departed at that
moment. She walked a good distance, and finally reached
Espíritu Santa Square.

She continued until she reached the corner of Prado Street,
and from there, she planned to go on, because she saw quite a
few persons who could probably give her information.

Batilo was walking ahead. A lively and small dog, an
impudent rat terrier, one of those that parade their vanity
through the streets of Madrid, approached the sad dog, a sitter,
and sniffed at him. Batilo was very shy, but he barked
anyway, feeling his self-esteem hurt. The rat terrier, who
needed very little provocation, also barked, and then took a nip
at the lap dog. Batilo defended himself the best he could, but
soon a massive dog began to pursue the terrier with terrifying
growls. Then came another dog, another and another. In two
seconds, twelve dogs had gathered there and set up a frightful
din. They fought with each other, falling and getting up in
scrambled confusion; biting each other, they jumped on and
trampled over Batilo and the rat terrier, who, caught in the
midst of the contenders, received the others' insults. Some
people stopped to watch. The owner of one of the dogs
intervened in the conflict and made some slighting remarks to
the owner of another dog. Since so many people were
gathering there and some young men were eyeing her with
impertinent attention, Clara quickened her steps. She headed

up the street fleeing from their stares. But the young men followed her, and when she tried to speed up they did the same. She decided to run and ran with all the speed that she could muster. Then a woman shouted from a doorway, "That one! That one! That one!"

A man grabbed her by her arm and stopped her. Many women encircled her and in a single moment formed a group of more than thirty persons. The orphan was so shaky and petrified that she didn't say a single word. She didn't attempt to flee, nor did she even cry. She imagined that she was surrounded by a circle of assassins.

"What has she done? What has happened?" said one.

"She has stolen that bundle that she's carrying under her arm."

"Girl, where did you get that bundle?" asked the one who had grabbed her.

Clara didn't reply.

"To jail with her," said one of the crowd.

"Where did you steal that bundle, girl?"

The young girl composed herself somewhat and with a tenuous voice, said, "It's mine."

"So, it's yours," said one of the women. "But I saw you run like a flash of lightning. I'll bet she stole it from that house, number fifteen."

"I'll bet it's Mrs. Nicolasa's house, the boarding house across the street," said another woman.

"You are lying, señora," said a tall man, who seemed to be a bullfighter, judging from his attire and a bullfighter's braid on the back of his neck. "This woman didn't come out of the boarding house, nor from number fifteen. She came from farther on down the street."

"Look at that clown," shouted the woman. "Are you trying to tell me that I'm lying?"

"You are lying, señora. That girl hasn't stolen anything. She was coming from way down the hill and ran because those young flirts were following her. I saw it, and if anyone tries to contradict me, I'll take on any man."

"So much fuss over nothing," said the man holding Clara, as he released her.

"Whether she stole something or not...When I say something...if my Blas were here, we'd see whether you were willing to face down another man," the woman who had provoked the disturbance muttered, turning away.

"Let's go, nothing was stolen here," insisted the dandy, aggressively. "You aren't needed here. Get on your way!"

The public—let's call them that—found the bullfighter's explanations very convincing, especially the suggestions he made with a lead pipe he carried in his hand; they began to drift away.

"Let's go, dear. Don't be afraid," the man with the bullfighter braid said to Clara. "Come with me. Don't be afraid! I am a man who'll face down any other. Well, can one ask where the little woman is heading? I'll go along with you because I am a man who..."

"I am going to Humilladero Street."

"Humillo...what?"

"Humilladero."

"I know now....But why are you going so far? If you start out now you'll arrive there the day after tomorrow in the evening. So, don't rush...."

"Yes, sir, I am in a hurry; and though it may be far, I have to go there immediately. Will you please tell me which way I should go?"

"Listen, take this street all the way up, all the way....But I am going to show you the way. Although it would be better if you came with me. Jesus Christ! What a pretty girl you are. I hadn't realized...Come on."

"I can't delay, *Señor* Caballero," she said, very fearfully. "Tell me where the street is, and I shall go there alone."

"Alone! Could I be such a brute as to let you walk alone through those streets on an evening when there is an uprising? I am just the person to...Come with me! I assure you that nothing bad will happen to you. I know a tavern near here where they serve some pork chops that..."

Having said this, the bullfighter took Clara by the arm and tried to steer her toward Lobo Street.

"Let me go, sir," said Clara, freeing herself. "I have to get going, for God's sake, let me go!"

"Well, you are like a porcupine! Bah! You're too pretty to be so touchy. I'm telling you...Well, all right, I'll go along with you to that street."

"No. Tell me which way I should go. I'll go alone."

"Alone? But there is an uprising going on. What if they shoot you down and leave you in the middle of the street?"

"I wan to go alone," she said, moving away from him.

The man's impertinent companionship and solicitude made her distrust him. She planned to flee from him and to ask another person for directions. But although she hurried along he stayed at her side, talking on and on. A fortunate incident—something pleasant had to occur that night—finally liberated

Clara from that sly fellow. They were passing through Santa Ana Square when they heard a woman's shouts from behind them. The dandy didn't turn around; but he carefully wrapped himself in his cloak so as not to be recognized."

"Scum, ingrate," called the woman, who was tall, stout, and mannish, with a terrifying whiskey voice. "Wait! Wait! I'm going to plant my five fingers in that parchment face of yours."

She then pulled at the dandy's cape, and with a hand more powerful than the piledriver of a fueling mill, she seized Clara by the arm and held her.

"If it wasn't for the fact that this woman is here," said the dandy, assuming a serious air to impress the stocky, middle-aged woman, "I would turn your nose inside out."

"Scum," said the snappy woman, standing up to him and moving her head. "Do I look shameless? Do you think that I am going to tolerate a broom face like yours...?"

"Shut up!" exclaimed the man. "Or I'll chop your legs off!"

"Look here, Juan Mortaja, I'll gouge this whore's eyes out if you don't come with me right away. Do you think that a woman like me would let you...? Juan Mortaja, I'm telling you that we are going to have to..."

"Don't pay any mind to her," said the bullfighter to Clara, who was breathless, crushed by the stout woman's hand like a dove in the claws of a sparrow hawk. "Don't pay any mind to her child; she'd even tell Saint Cuartillo off."

"Despicable!" the woman exclaimed in tragic fury, releasing Clara and quickly pulling from her waist a knife which she handled with a smuggler's gracefulness and speed.

"You bag of demons!" answered the man, brandishing a stick.

We cannot say how the dispute ended, because we are following Clara; the latter, on seeing herself freed from Juan Mortaja's lady's claw escaped quickly, and at a rapid pace, she reached Angel Square, with Batilo following behind her. The unlucky girl didn't know what to do next. She was horrified to think that among these thousands of swarming inhabitants, not one person would tell her how to reach the only refuge which would accept an abandoned orphan who was alone, wronged, and half-dead with fear and pain. She believed that God had abandoned her or that there was no God, that her destiny was forcing her to choose between the Porreños' frightening Inquisition or this abandonment, this roaming through a desert, either rejected by all or solicited only by depravation or vice.

She decided to try once more. She paused near a man with a lantern and a hook who was picking through a rubbish pile, and asked him for directions.

"Humilladero Street?" repeated the ragpicker, straightening up and making movements with his hook like an orchestra conductor swinging a baton. "That street it...I am going to tell you a way to find it right away. Well, just keep walking...keep looking carefully at all the street markers. Do you know how to read?"

"Yes sir," said Clara.

"Well, when you find a marker which says 'Humilladero Street' that is the very place where it is."

The ragpicker was very satisfied with his explanation. Turning away and bending over again, he reburied his search hook in the pile of garbage that lay on the ground in front of him. Clara walked off in great distress and, as she began to lose a clear understanding of her misfortune, found herself approaching the emotional shock that precedes extreme derangement. She again directed silent pleas to God and the Virgin Mary to rescue her from that situation. She was still praying when she noticed a person coming toward her who inspired her confidence. She took a few steps toward the person, a short and fat clergyman, somewhat past middle age. He was walking with a rosary in his hand and his eyes fixed on the ground. The orphan breathed a sigh of relief because the venerable person she saw before her was a holy man whose earthly mission was to console the afflicted and to aid the weak.

Chapter XXXVIII

CONTINUATION OF THE WAY OF THE CROSS

The priest, to judge by his well-worn, dark green attire, was a man of small means, but his round, protruding belly showed that he had not led a life of deprivation. He was middle-aged, with a round, livid face, lively little eyes and a nose which seemed to have served as Nature's model for the creation of potatoes. One cannot call his physiognomy unpleasant; he smiled benevolently, and above all, his eyes reflected a certain charm and amiable volubility. When he saw Clara and heard the question which she asked with the greatest respect, he put aside his rosary and tilted his hat, which was so big that it obstructed everything before him, and answered "Humilladero Street? Yes, my child, yes. I know where it is, yes. But it is very far from here. You will not be able to go alone. You'll get lost, my child. Come on, and I shall show you the way."

And he turned back. Batilo and Clara followed him. Clara thought that finally she had found a way out of the labyrinth.

"But, my child, how is it that you are alone? At this hour...All alone!" the priest asked in a bittersweet voice.

"I have to go to a friend's house," replied Clara, for the sake of an answer.

"But are you going alone? At this hour! Why is that?"

"I don't have anyone to accompany me. I am all alone."

"You mean to say that you are alone? Jesus, Mary and Joseph! What a calamity! But don't you have parents?"

"No sir."

"Are you alone, completely alone? Jesus, Mary and Joseph! This is not good at all, my child. But don't you have any relatives? Come on now. You can probably go to some relative's house."

"No, sir, no. I am going to the house of a woman I know. I don't know anyone else."

"Come now, you surely must know some other person," insisted the priest, stopping and turning with a roguish expression to look at Clara. "Where are you coming from?"

"From the house of some ladies, where I used to live."

"And didn't you know anyone else there besides those ladies?"

"No, sir," said Clara, frightened by the turn the cleric's questions were taking.

"Come now, I would have sworn that you'd met some young lad....There's nothing wrong with that, my child, that's what youth is for. That really doesn't matter....Bah! Don't be embarrassed. By Christ's wounds, I am not angry about that..., definitely not."

Having said this, the priest stopped and once more gazed at the orphan with his lively little eyes, accompanying this stare with a holy smile which would have done honor to any seminary student familiar with Sanchez's *De Matrimonio*.

"Because that's how things are, my child," continued the priest. "I, who know the weaknesses of both sexes, can speak on this subject. And then too, I have such insight that I understand everything immediately. Especially since you are such a pretty little thing..."

Clara was disturbed by is words; but the hope that they would soon reach much-pondered Humilladero Street calmed her, making the good man's amiabilities more tolerable.

"Yes, my child. I am a great admirer of works of nature, and when they are beautiful I admire them even more. I confess that I am not a prig. Courtesy does not take anything away from bravery. Although one may be a priest...it's not a sin to admire nature."

As their conversation continued, they had passed Atocha Street and arrived at the Main Plaza. They crossed it, heading toward San Miguel Square.

"Come, come!" he said, taking Clara's arm on seeing that she was a little reluctant to pass through the dark archway which faces Conde Miranda Square. "You will be safe with me....Well, I was saying that courtesy doesn't detract from bravery....But you didn't finish telling me about your young man."

"But I haven't said anything," replied Clara, subtly removing her arm from the priest's hand.

"Yes, there must be something, my child. I felt it from the start. But that really doesn't mean that it's anything unusual. Now...are you a bit shy? Come now, tell me about it. I'll absolve you right away. Pretty little girls are always forgiven for everything."

As he said this, he looked at Clara again, but he was no longer smiling. He was serious, and his voice carried an excited emotion she did not notice.

"Be careful not to fall," the priest said, putting his arm around the orphan's waist as if she had stumbled.

"Oh! she exclaimed, very confused and pushing herself away from the priest. "When will we get to the street?...Is it still very far?"

"Yes, my child. It is far, very far. But why are you in such a hurry?"

"Ah! Yes, I am in a great hurry. But don't bother yourself with me. Tell me which way I should go...and I shall continue on alone."

"Ah, you'll not find it if you look all night. It is very far. But why are you in such a hurry, my child? I see that you are very tired. Wouldn't it be better for you to rest awhile?"

"Oh no, sir. I can't rest," said Clara, terrified at the idea that she would be taken to a sacristy.

"Yes, my daughter. You are very fatigued, and I don't have the heart to see you walking these streets alone at this hour and in the cold."

"It doesn't matter, Your Reverence, I can't delay."

"Jesus, Mary and Joseph! I have never seen such an iceberg as you. I...don't like people to be this way because I like little girls to be affectionate and nice."

At this point, they entered Puñonrostro Street. The priest stopped and took Clara by the hand, but she stepped away from him.

"My daughter, by Jesus, Mary and Joseph! It breaks my heart to see you all alone in these streets in this cold weather....Look, I have a good brazier upstairs....I live here in back of Saint Justin, which is my church. Well, if you want to rest a bit..."

"No, Father. I want to go to Humilladero Street. Tell me where it is, inasmuch as you haven't taken me there."

"To heck with Humilladero! You are driving me crazy with that street! Well, you sure are impertinent," said the cleric, more excited and very impatient. "Come on, my daughter, tell me about the young man."

Clara's mind suddenly perceived his vile plan, with horror and repugnance.

"Sir," she repeated, "tell me how to get to where I'm going."

"Come upstairs, come up," said he, already inside the doorway of the house. "Come up, you'll not be sorry. If you knew how good I am..., because I am a priest does not mean that I'm not friendly. Tomorrow, you will go to Humilladero, or if you don't wish to go..."

"Sir, for God's sake, tell me in which direction I should go. I'm going out of my mind. Why have you brought me here? Where am I? I may even be farther now from the place where I want to go."

"Come upstairs, my child, come up," said the cleric, opening the door. "And we shall talk about it. I'll tell you where that street is, and tomorrow you'll be able to..."

"No, I don't want to spend any more time with you. Tell me which way I ought to go. Why have you deceived me?"

Clara broke out in tears like a child. The cleric's amiability had disappeared; his little eyes expressed terrible spite; his lower lip, a formless and hanging mass, trembled with angry annoyance and disappointment.

"Is that street far from here, sir? Is it far?"

The priest looked at Clara scornfully, made a contemptuous gesture and went inside, saying, "Yes, girl; it is far, very far,"

And he slammed the door.

Clara was somewhat relieved at being liberated from that wicked individual; but realizing that she hadn't gotten the information she needed, and finding herself in that narrow and darkened alley where no signs of human life existed and where somebody might be heading toward her from either side, she became so frightened that she was ready to swoon. It seemed to her as if the enormous walls of the priest's house and Saint Justin were pressing toward each other and would crush her in the middle. A supreme effort, a race in which the overwrought spirit rather than the body seemed to move her, took her to Sacramento Street. Finally, she saw a moving light. It was a night watchman. Seeing him restored some of her courage. She approached him and repeated her question, asked so many times and never answered. The night watchman, in a very bad humor but with good intentions, gave he exact directions.

"Go down that hill behind Sacramento Street; keep going downhill until you reach Segovia Street; go immediately to the right, then keep going straight ahead until you come to Moorishtown; go through it until you reach *Don* Pedro Street and then follow *Don* Pedro to Carros Square, and across from the chapel of San Isidro you'll find Humilladero Street."

He repeated the directions to her and said good night.

The orphan left him gratefully. At least she had found the way to that cursed street. She took the indicated route and went down the hill to *Los Consejos*. What a sick and frightening place! The ground seems to fall away from beneath a pedestrian's feet; it is that steep. Clara, who was totally weak and debilitated, felt as if she were falling with each step and the ground were inclining more and more steeply, refusing to support her weight. She began to think that the sharp descent would never end, until her feet finally touched level ground.

Finally she reached Segovia Street and imagined that she had fallen into an abyss. "Maybe," she thought, "the night watchman did not tell me the truth. Was this place inhabited by creatures from earth?" In the darkness, it seemed to her that the two groups of dwellings on either side of the street were leaning over, threatening to fall onto her.

Clara continued, nevertheless, along this route the night watchman had described to her. Ahead of her she made out the steep shape of Blindman's Peak and thought it unscalable. She attempted it anyway, stumbling over piles of rubbish and trash. The houses above her seemed to be suspended like vultures' nests at the top of the peak. She felt too weak to climb; she could find no path, nor any sign of movement by human beings. Once in a while a voice could be heard, and in the far off distance the women's shouts echoed. Their cries resounded as if a flock of birds with human voices were cackling in the sky. Suddenly, a child's voice rose from below. It was a girl who climbed alone, singing along Segovia Street and heading for Moorishtown. Clara was surprised to see that little girl singing as she made her way up the hill among so much debris. She stood up and tried to follow her. The girl did not see her and kept moving on ahead, apparently very happily. But suddenly she became aware of the sound of footsteps, of someone following her. The little one turned around, noticed a form walking behind her at midnight, and began screaming as she broke into a sudden run: "Mother, mother, witches, witches!"

The orphan then heard more clearly the women's shouting voices, and she, too, thought that there were witches in that place.

The women seemed to be coming downhill, and their confused and discordant voices were like the frenetic altercation of one of Eumenides' hordes. Clara retreated and started downhill, nearly slipping and falling several times. She stood again on Segovia Street, and the women's shouts reached her ears as if a horde of birds with human speech had taken flight to the high regions.

It began to rain; the heavy drops which fell to the ground seemed to the orphan's fevered imagination to be the sound of a music box. The rain increased; the raindrops fell extraordinarily fast, leaving a dark shape on the surface of the rocks, which when repeated again and again finally colored the ground with a shiny black color. Clara bundled herself up, leaned against a large stone base, her spirit defeated, and gazed up at the sky, looking for the moon, a star, anything that wasn't black and horrid, anything which she hadn't seen around her that night. She saw neither star nor moon. She only saw, far below, toward the bridge and along the horizon outlined on the other side of the banks of the Manzanares river, a reddish light; that striking clear bright color which on stormy nights looks like a fever in the sky. It was seen burning brightly and flickering in sudden precipitate flashes of lightning, while the rest of the sky's immense expanse remained dark and frozen. The light affected Clara in a strange way. Far from being frightened, she imagined it to be some internal light, more infinite than the wide sky, that seemed to open up there. She thought she saw waves of light emanating from an incandescent center, human forms, shadowless bodies that oscillated in whimsical revolutions. It seemed to her like an array of human stars, of heavens and worlds shaped like living beings, formed within the space of a never-ending flame. Each star engendered thousands, and each thousand, a million. They moved away and returned. They faded to become tenuously obscure and once again acquired the brilliance of the most intense light.

When her gaze left that brightness, she looked in the opposite direction. She looked at the street around her, and saw nothing. She waited a while, still looking, yet could not see anything. She thought she was blind and tried in vain, with eager attention, to make out some object. The rain had increased frighteningly. One torrent came down from Blindman's Peak, and another from *Los Consejos*. The street received the two floods and hurled a muddy gorge toward the bridge. She went on, unable to see anything; her feet were buried in mud; the roaring sound was horrible. Her courage left her. She felt that the only possibility that remained was to close her eyes and die, letting herself be dragged down into the river by the dizzying current.

An intense bolt of lightning lit up the abyss. Suddenly she could see, by its light, two dark masses of houses which stood on both sides of the street. Then she was submerged once more in deep blindness. Her knees folded up; the water had soaked her clothes. Batilo whimpered like a shipwrecked dog. In spite of the sound of the rain, the shouts of women could be heard once more, discordant, sharp like the shrieking of night birds echoing on high. Clara's sick fantasy recognized in the voices a horrid, harsh trio of Porreños, who were flying, wrapped in frightening clouds, tossing to the winds their insolent voices, their bitter spite and their envy. She even seemed to see Salomé, who soared on high, waving her long vestments like wings and revealing her bent, angular fingers tipped with owl-like talons.

The rain began to lessen. The clamor of bells and wheels told Clara that a wagon had just passed the causeway of the bridge and was entering the street. This encouraged her a bit because she heard the driver's voice as he used heavy blows to urge the mules to climb the hill. The young girl stood up, determined to make one last attempt by asking the driver for directions. She reached the wagon and walked into the middle of the road; but one of the mules, who was nervous, jumped, and almost overturned the wagon. The driver began to shout curses. The animal refused to take another step. The driver started to whip the balking mule, and the mule started kicking. The other mule, happy for a chance to rest his tired body, which had made the journey from Navalcarnero in six hours, threw himself on the ground sybaritically, waiting for the dispute with his master and his fellow mule to be resolved. The mule was almost completely buried in mud, and when the driver saw that, and that the coach was leaning to one side sinking the axle into the ground, he became a demon. He called for help from all the saints in Heaven and all the demons in Hell; he pulled out his hair and began to furiously use the whip.

Clara, who felt responsible for the damage, had enough strength to flee from the anger of the mule driver, who, if he had seen her, would have beaten her as well. She started to run uphill and didn't stop until she reached the corner of La Paja Square. There she met another night watchman and asked him the same question.

"You are very near it," he said. "Go up to that Square. Then go past that arch which is located there where the statue of the *Virgen del Farol* is, and you'll arrive at the Los Carros Square. On the opposite side of it is Humilladero Street."

Clara started to believe in God again, and followed the directions indicated. At last she was near; she was finally arriving. Hope gave her courage. But when she approached the arch, her fear revived. She assumed that the arch could only lead to a cavern, and, moreover, she thought she saw a corpulent figure beyond it, who was none other than María de la Paz Jesús, waiting there to seize her as she passed, to snatch her with a large and twitching hand, and to carry her off in the air.

But hope can do a great deal. She closed her eyes, and running speedily, she passed it. Los Carros Square now seemed more livable to her and less sad. Some people passed. Very few lights were seen. She looked at all the streets and their markers, and finally, full of happiness, she read the name she was looking for. She entered the street, and within a few steps, noticed a door on whose sides were painted a bunch of allegoric grapes and some bottles which indicated that it was a tavern. "Here it is," she said and drew near. The door was open, and inside there were two women and a man. She asked if a certain bartender named Pascual was living there with a certain Pascuala.

"There ain't no Pascuala here," said one of the women.

"Do you know if it is near here?" asked Clara. "Is there another tavern on this street?"

"No, not that I know of."

Clara once more began to doubt that God existed.

"What are you saying, troublemaker?" exclaimed the man. "You always stick your nose in where it's none of your business. Yes ma'am. There is another wine shop owned by a man named Pascual....Yes ma'am, over there in number fourteen."

The orphan thanked him and headed there, palpitating nervously but happily. Before arriving at number fourteen, she heard the sound of guitars and men's voices. As she approached the door, she saw many people singing and dancing with tipsy abandon. Although she didn't see Pascuala herself and those people frightened her, she went up the entrance step, and introducing herself, asked to speak to her old servant.

"Bravo! Bravo!" said two or three of the drunks, while one of them advanced toward the young girl and embraced Clara tightly, leading her over to the center of the tavern.

"Long live all that is good!"

Clara cried in terror on finding herself in that creature's arms, and screamed with all her strength: "Pascuala!"

"What? What is it?" called a woman's voice. "Let's see, what's going on?"

Pascuala came out, and finding a woman in her husband's arms, gave him a punch in the face which, if it had just been a little stronger, would have left him without a nose.

"It wasn't I," answered Pascual. "It was that demon *Chaleco*."

"Yes, it was he. He brought her and had her hidden," declared *Tres Pesetas*, with one of his frequent displays of maliciousness.

"*Doña* Clarita!" said Pascuala, embracing Clara more gently than her husband had, and leading her to an interior room.

In the Pascuals' bedroom *Coletilla's* niece, who had

exhausted all her body and spirit's strength that evening, collapsed on a chair and lost consciousness.

Chapter XXXIX

A MOMENT OF CALM

Bozmediano and Lázaro spoke very little on their way. It must have been ten in the morning when they arrived at Pascuala's house. They found her washing glasses and asked her if Clara had come to her house.

"Last night, yes, sir; she arrived after midnight. Ah, now I recognize the young gentleman, my master's nephew who came inquiring about his uncle."

"Thank God!" exclaimed Lázaro. "We're in luck!"

"The poor girl arrived this morning and fainted," said Pascuala. "She is very sick; she still hasn't spoken a word, except for talking nonsense. She was such a mess, all wet, trembling from the cold and with tears running down her face."

"Where is she?"

"There in my bedroom, in my bed. Pascual slept in the loft, and I slept on the floor at her bedside. She's very sick. She made some gestures, saying that some things were flying down...what did she say? 'The three, the three flying,' she said, and kept on until an hour ago when she stopped talking and fell asleep."

The two went inside, and Pascuala opened the window to let a little light fall on the graceful figure whose drawn, pale face showed signs of complete exhaustion. She was sleeping, but the contorted position of her head indicated that before she fell asleep she had been tormented by the delirium of a troubled mind. Pascuala took the girl's head between her hands and placed it in a more comfortable position. Then she pulled the sheet up over her arms, rearranged the pillows, and closed the window a little so that no more light than necessary would enter.

"Don't leave this room," Bozmediano said to Lázaro.

"No," replied the latter, worriedly watching the unconscious girl so closely that he heard her irregular and difficult breathing as though a small volcano lay between the sheets.

"I think that when she awakes, she will be disoriented. You must remain here until we see how this turns out," suggested Bozmediano. "I'll leave. I believe my presence would disturb her. I shall expect you at my house tomorrow, without fail, as we must talk."

Lázaro didn't reply. If his jealous suspicions hadn't been completely allayed, it was because he was unable to think about such a delicate matter at that moment. His powerful emotion did not allow him to occupy himself with cruel doubts and selfish rancors, which a lofty spirit always abandons when faced with really great misfortunes.

After Claudio left, Lázaro sat down next to the bed, and sat motionless there for a long time—one statue contemplating another statue. He was almost as pale as she, expecting with each breath that she would awaken, and observing with the hopeless attention of a lover the fluctuation of that life in crisis. Finally, Clara moved, muttering some badly articulated words. The youth was able to understand clearly, "*Señora*, for God's sake…!"

Then she shook one of her hands as if trying to push something away and finally opened her eyes. She pushed back the hair which, disarranged, had covered her face. She held her hand against her eyes awhile and then removed it. Her eyes fixed on the man beside her, and she stared at him for a long time, as if she could not believe what she was seeing. Then she extended her arm slowly toward him and spoke to him in a weak voice.

"Don't you know why I am here?" said Lázaro, touched with emotion. "It's as if we hadn't seen each other since the time we were in my town. I still cannot believe that you ever were in that cursed house."

"In what house?" asked Clara, as if deeply confused.

"There, in the house of those women," he answered, sadly recalling the pain suffered within that dwelling.

"No!" exclaimed Clara. "I don't want to return. I would rather die than return. I am in Pascuala's house, am I not?"

As she said this she looked around the room with anguished eyes.

"Yes, you are no longer…we are no longer there," said Lázaro, leaning closer to her.

"I won't go back. They won't take me. Isn't it so? You'll not return, either."

"What do you mean, return? That house has been worse than hell itself to me. I detest and despise those who live in it. I've suffered more there, in one single evening, than in my whole life. I'll never return, no."

Clara seemed to listen to this attentively. Then she looked at him fixedly, with a certain astonishment, for a long time.

"Why are you looking at me that way?" asked Lázaro.

The orphan paused before answering, but finally, with a slow and affectionate voice remarked: "It has been a long time since I've seen you."

"It hasn't been so long. You saw me one afternoon, on a Sunday."

"Yes....Now I recall. What a day! Do you know that they threw me out because they said a man had entered the house? Can you imagine? How wicked they are!"

"Didn't he enter?"

"Yes, he entered, yes....But, how was I to blame? They say he entered to look for me. How evil they are!"

"Did he enter for you?"

"For me?" answered Clara, her voice broken and very weak. "For me?"

Then she paused as though recalling something and said, "Yes, he did come for me. He told me that he was going to get me out of there, that he wanted to make me happy. He really frightened me."

All this she said with a vagueness which indicated how disoriented she was.

"He frightened me a great deal," she continued. "It seems that I can still see him. At the beginning, I thought he was going to kill me; but...he didn't kill me. He told me he wanted to take me with him, that he wanted to see me happy....He had written a letter to me."

"A letter?" Lázaro asked sharply.

"Yes, that ugly, ugly man handed it to me...."

"Where is the letter?"

"The letter?...the letter?...I don't know. I had it in my pocket."

"Where are your clothes?"

"I don't know....The letter..., ah! Now I remember...I tore it up into very little, little pieces."

"Why did you tear it up?" asked Lázaro, sorry not to have gotten hold of that document. "And do you remember seeing me that afternoon?"

"Yes, yes, yes, I remember," she replied, indicating that she hadn't forgotten that event. "You came in very angrily. I cried all evening. Then I had a dizzy spell. I thought I was going to die and that thought made me happy."

The sad serenity of these declarations moved Lázaro in such a way that he didn't dare ask anything else, for to offend that angel's delicacy would be an unsurpassed cruelty. Still, he tried to ask the last question in this way:

"And what did I say to you that afternoon?"

"What did you say to me? Well, that has slipped my mind....No, now I remember; you said..."

Here she paused. She seemed to lack either words or

understanding. Her eyes were full of tears, and she again pushed back her hair, which hung over part of her forehead. Lázaro felt humbled. He was almost ashamed of the cruel and brusque accusation he'd made that memorable afternoon. He hadn't yet dispensed with the social convention which demands positive proof for the explanation of certain acts. Although he still felt that unreasonable suspicion, he couldn't resist the persuasive strength of the orphan's reply. His heart could not tolerate any doubt once he heard her words; and if the voice of a tormenting demon echoed within him to remind him of the social obligation not to admit satisfaction, he was resolved to postpone the investigation of that matter to a later date, allowing himself to be guided for a time by the consoling warmth of an affection as strong as ever.

"Don't explain anymore," said Lázaro, seeing her tears. "I see that those demons are to blame for everything. Cursed be the man who took you there. Elías has slandered you; I am sure of it. They were always talking about wrongs committed, about sins..., and I don't know what else. They were saying the same about me. The two were certain that I was an evildoer and that I had committed some crime. This astonished me because I had never committed any serious wrong. I judged the same was true of you. You were the victim of their inflexibility, their distrust, their discipline, as they called it."

"I don't want to see them anymore," said Clara. "Last night I saw them all night long in my dreams. I imagined that *Doña* Salomé was fluttering above me, showing me her rancorous eyes and terrifying nails. And *Doña* Paz stood behind the bed and from time to time extended an arm to slap me. I was trembling and wrapped myself up in the sheets so as not to see them, but I kept seeing them anyway. How ugly they are!"

"Calm down," said Lázaro, hearing in her voice the symptoms of a renewed hysteria. "You will never return to the house of those beasts. You have thought yourself abandoned while I was there. I don't know whether I am to blame for this: but if it has been my fault, it is a carelessness which I will know how to correct. I have lived only for you! You have been the guide and inspiration for all of my actions! How right I was, when we met, to tell you that God had brought us together so that we would never be separated. Wherever I have gone I have held you in my heart, on my mind, believing in you and waiting for you. Since we met, we have always been together, traveling together along life's path, at least so far as I am concerned. When I came to Madrid, although we didn't see

each other immediately, I didn't take a step through the streets
without having you in my mind. They imprisoned me for a
foolish action of mine, which was certainly no crime, as those
women were saying. If I managed to endure that setback, if I
didn't commit suicide by beating my head against the prison
walls, it was only because in the darkness I imagined I could
see you standing there in a corner, with your face serene, as
always. Since I met you, I have not been able to think of the
future without also thinking of you, as a part of me. I could not
think about any acquisition, any happiness, without thinking
that you would enjoy it with me. I have not undergone any
misfortune or loss without imagining that you were at my side,
crying with me. If I have dreamed of some future happy
moment, I always had in mind that our two lives would be
united in that moment. I could not imagine one of us living
alone in the world: that has always seemed impossible to me.
You know, it seems like it was only yesterday that you left my
house to return here. And I would like to erase everything that
happened afterward from my memory. I abhor those days as
one abhors a nightmare. Didn't you tell me that you also
detested that house and those people? I believe it. I can't get
used to the idea that our thoughts could be different. If I could
really accept that you didn't love me, I wouldn't know how to
exist; and if I remained alive after that sad afternoon, it is
because doubt kept me alive, doubt I no longer want to think
about: it has been a sort of duty for me, one I imposed on
myself; but I refuse to accept this tyranny. When I saw you
time seemed to turn back to those earlier days. To doubt you
seems a crime to me; and if I have been guilty of it, I don't ask
you to forgive me, because I know that you have already
forgiven me for thinking so."

During this emotional declaration, Clara listened to him as
if in a trance. Finally she released such a flood of tears that it
seemed in a single moment she shed her life's pain, along with
those tears, starting with the bird incident in Madre Angustia's
house, and up to the scene of her expulsion from the Porreños'
house.

The youth refused to lessen the eloquence of those tears by
a single spoken word. The fever and rapid pulsebeat in Clara's
hand, which he held between his own, showed him that her
fever was increasing, perhaps due to the excitement of their
dialogue in which she had poured out all her sincerity and he all
his eloquence.

"You must take good care of yourself," said Lázaro.
"Yes," she replied. "I want to live!"

Chapter XL

THE GREAT ASSAULT

The doctor sent by Bozmediano arrived in the afternoon. He saw the patient and left after prescribing much bedrest, apparently unconcerned about a crisis that had originated in a profound emotional disturbance. Clara fell asleep, entering a new period of calm. Lázaro, who was eager to make a decisive determination in his life, decided to speak to his uncle that very evening, break off relations with him, and separate himself from the man who was the author of his misfortunes. He wanted to see the two Porreños, to reproach them for their cruelty and hypocrisy. If manly dignity had not prevented it, his first act surely would have been to seize *Doña* Paz by the hair she rolled into a bun at the back of the neck and lower her head to the ground.

The urgent and correct thing was to break off relations with that fanatic man, who seemed to him even more repugnant after shamelessly meeting with the impetuous youths and assigning himself the title of liberal. Lázaro did not care that he was alone, without support, poor, poorer than ever. He would work in a profession, in any trade. And if he could not manage in Madrid, he would return to his town, where at least he had bread for sure.

He left, then, in the late evening, leaving Pascuala to care for Clara. Remembering that his uncle had spoken of not returning to the Porreños house within three days, he decided to head to The Golden Fountain or the abbot's house. He went to The Golden Fountain and entered the back room, where the main figures of the club used to meet confidentially, but he did not find Elías. The only one there was Pinilla, who was pacing back and forth very nervously with his hands in his pockets and his hat pulled down over his forehead.

"Hi, pal," he said on seeing Lázaro. "What brings you here at this hour?"

"I am looking for my uncle."

"Ah! You won't find him. He's in a place...Now I know where he is. He's where only a few enter."

"Will he come by this evening?"

"This evening? Oh, no! How could he come here this evening?"

"Well, what's going on this evening?"

"The big move," said Pinilla mysteriously. "But, bah!

You know more about it than I do. If you're his nephew..."

"No, I don't know anything," said Lázaro, surprised.

"But haven't they given you a post? Haven't they told you what you have to do? Aren't you working like everyone in this great undertaking?"

"What undertaking?"

"This evening, this is it, this evening."

"Well, what's coming off? As a matter of fact, on my way here I noticed a certain restlessness in the Villa."

"Well, you'll see, at about ten...."

"And isn't there a session this evening?"

"A session? Brrr!" exclaimed Pinilla, making a strange noise with his mouth. "This isn't an evening for words, but for deeds. Too much has already been said."

"I didn't know anything about it. In truth, I haven't been here since the day before yesterday."

"Well, look for *El Doctrino*, who must be somewhere around Lavapiés, and he'll tell you what you have to do, because I imagine, my friend, that you will not want to remain behind. All fear aside! I know that this is rather frightening the first time, above all for someone who has never heard gunfire. But, in short, with courage..."

"But tell me what's going on," said Lázaro, faking a certain complacency so that the other wouldn't hesitate to tell him everything.

"What's happening," said Pinilla, "is that this evening is the big blow, the decisive blow, the last effort of shameless liberalism. We must trample the discreet ones, who keep us from acting. Yes, my friend, we'll have freedom at last."

"Come on," said Lázaro, pretending disbelief in order to learn more, "a small, unimportant uprising..."

"A small uprising? It's more than that," said the other, sitting down and reviving the scant fire in the brazier.

Robespierre jumped up onto his knees and settled there with admirable republican frankness.

"Well, I am also going there," said Lázaro, encouraging Pinilla to disclose more.

"Go look for *El Doctrino* who'll assign a position. I suspect that you would look bad if you don't take part in this after having made the speech we heard last night. What a speech, friend! You are a great speaker. If you only knew how much it was liked; the people are enthusiastic. I heard a shoemaker on Comadre Street repeating long passages by heart from what you said last night."

"But tell me: what will happen?"

"It's very simple. We must push aside the false liberals who are in power today. We have to trample them. Well it'll take place this evening."

"And how will that be accomplished?"

"These things are only done in one way, as you will soon see. The revolution requires quick and decisive measures. One tramples over them, exterminating them."

"Exterminating them!" repeated Lázaro, horrified.

"Well, that's the only way. It's the only way to uproot a bad seed. It is the only way. I agree that it's terrible, but it's efficient."

"So there will be a massacre?"

"The people are enraged, and rightfully so. We thought that we were going to have freedom, but we were deceived. Four small tyrants rule us constitutionally, and they persecute us constitutionally, just as before. This does not satisfy us. We want something more. Let's move forward, then."

"But the method is frightening. I don't want my country to experience the horrors of the French Revolution. After terrorism, only dictatorship can result. I don't want it to happen here as in France, where on account of the excesses of revolution, liberty had died forever."

"That is music, friend, music."

"That is the truth. Is it possible that my friends, those who have lectured in the club on the exercise of acquired rights as the only means of achieving liberty...? I can't believe it."

"Pal," said Pinilla, looking at him cunningly, "you said it yourself. Don't you recall that part of your speech where you said: 'We shall not stop our own effort because of timidity! No! We are in a horrible interim. Halfway up this path of thorns is the greatest of all dangers. To stop halfway is to fall, it is worse than not having begun at all?' "

"Yes," said Lázaro, in a state of confusion. "But I did not mean that it should reach the extreme of removing every obstacle at knifepoint. I want that goal to be achieved by legal means."

"Of course, that's what you meant to say. But the people understood it differently, and this evening you are going to see how they understand these things. Don't fool yourself, my friend, this is the only path. Legal means are foolish, believe me. You'll see this evening. This is the most appropriate moment....Just imagine!...they will all be in the same place. Yes a fatal meeting, and we won't have to mark each one's house with blood."

"Who will be gathering?" inquired Lázaro, restlessly.

"They will! The 'cautious' ones. They have some secret meetings now, undoubtedly in order to brew up some conspiracy to rid us of what little freedom that we possess. By accident, we have discovered that some of the most influential ministers and deputies of the majority meet in a certain house on Afligidos Square."

"But is that a fact?" asked Lázaro, trying to control his emotions.

"Yes, I don't know who discovered it. What I do know is that they told *El Doctrino*, and he went there and saw them leave. Afterward, he somehow ascertained who they are. Quintana, Martínez de la Rosa, Calatrava, Alava...even Alcalá Galiano has put in with those people."

Lázaro was mute with terror.

"What pleases me most," continued Pinilla, "is that the younger Bozmediano will also fall. He too has plunged into politics, guided by his father."

"Bozmediano!"

"Yes. So far as I am concerned, he's a hateful man; if I don't see him run down, it'll just kill me."

"And what has he done to you?"

"We had a dispute in Lorencini's. We argued. It was on account of one of my speeches. It's a long story. He won't escape nor will his father, either, who is pride personified. His father is the one who asked in Parliament for the secret societies to close. They are a fine pair! But they will not escape. That will never happen. I'll be there just for that. At midnight, no one will dare pull me away from the Square."

"And so you are going to assassinate those men, catching them all unprepared?"

"In simple language, that is it! The people of Madrid will do a good job. They despise those men, and there'll be a mob which, you'll see, you'll see...So then, you are going now, so that they can give you a role?"

"Yes, I'm going."

"I am waiting here for a message from the café owner."

"So long," said Lázaro, leaving hurriedly.

His resolution was irrevocable. He could not let that infamous conspiracy be carried out. It was his fault, and only his, that they had found out the meeting place where the previously cited victims were to be gathered, and it was up to him to pass by that mysterious house and warn them of the assault which was being prepared.

On the way, he observed many groups of suspicious people. Some were carrying blunderbusses, their heads covered by Aragonese kerchiefs, a comfortable headdress for revolution. Their attitude and their murmuring signaled the excitement which reigned among the people. A great crime was going to be committed. Did the people know what they were going to do and what principle they were obeying by doing it? Lázaro meditated about all these things along the way and thought, "No, this isn't what I preached." The idea that the speech he delivered the night before could have played a part in the complicity drove him to despair.

He noticed more and more suspicious groups, and he even heard some "down with them" remarks in the distance. When he arrived at Ancha Street, he saw a larger group. He passed nearby without planning to stop, when one of them headed toward him and hailed him. Who could it be but pompous Calleja, the famous barber of The Golden Fountain Café? Creating a great stir and raising his high-pitched voice, he set his heavy hands on the youth's shoulder and said, "Eh! fellows, here is a great guy, our man. I was right when I said that he would not let us down. Eh! fellows, here he is."

The whole group gathered around Lázaro in a minute.

"He is the one who spoke last night. Yes, he has a golden tongue," said one.

"Let him come with us. Let us name him Captain," said *Tres Pesetas*, who had promoted himself to Lieutenant and was wearing a yellow band on his sleeve.

"No, let him get up there, on top of that barrel, and speak to us," exclaimed another, who appeared to be Matutero, the one who pummeled *Coletilla* as we related at the beginning.

"Let him speak, let him speak!" shouted a tall, bony, lean and sinister woman, who seemed the very image of anarchy. "Let him speak, let him speak!"

"*Señores*," said Calleja, raising his index finger as if to puncture the sky. "It is no longer the time to speak, it is time to act. This man put it very well last night. 'Let's move forward; to retreat is death; to stop is infamy.' I would have said the same thing, only I haven't decided to speak as yet; but if I become angry..."

"Good, good!" screeched many voices.

Lázaro sweated with impatience and anguish. He did not know how to break away from the circle of intellectual giants surrounding him. He made some excuses, pushed to the outskirts of the group, and opened a breach on the other side, but even so, he couldn't manage to free himself completely, because the barber threw an arm around him, and spoke to him in the confidentially mysterious tone which two great men assume when communicating an idea which is to solve the world's problems. "I, *Señor Don* Lázaro, have this whole area under my command. Isn't it true that you have been given orders to take command here? I...frankly admire you a great deal as a speaker, because last night you said things that made our hair stand up, but..."

"What are you trying to say?"

"That I, *Señor Don* Lázaro, am a man who has saved the country many times and shed much blood in defense of Liberty, and for that very reason I...am in charge of this area, and it seems to me that the area is in good hands. Therefore, I want to know whether you have come here to take charge of this area; because the way you spoke last night and said...they may have designated a place of honor for you....And, frankly, although I don't speak well, I am a man who knows how to run things, and if you were to take charge of this area, I would protest..., you see how it is."

"No," said the youth, reassuring him. "I shall not take away the command of this section or any other from you. I do not command anyone."

"Just as I was saying," replied the barber with the greatest satisfaction. "I felt that you wouldn't take the command of this area away from me, but I thought that perhaps they had sent you here because they didn't have confidence in me. But you must know that anywhere Calleja is, liberty is a certainty."

"Oh, yes! I imagine so," said Lázaro, managing to get rid of the arm which was weighing on his shoulders in a most despotic manner. "Be at ease!"

"Are you going on some errand for *El Doctrino* or *El Lobo*?"

"No. I am on some other business."

"This is no night for business."

"Good night," said Lázaro, moving away.

The measures which the extremists, authors of the plot, would have taken had they known that Lázaro would cause their plan to fail, would have been frightening. But what did their revenge matter to him? The crime had to be avoided. It mattered little to him that the moment of mutiny would start with a simple political objective. What he couldn't bear was the assassination of a dozen defenseless and innocent men. What was the reason for this planned attempt? It was absolutism's horrible invention, taking advantage of the extreme liberal faction, and which had excited the passions of the people in order to make them the instrument of its loathsome objectives. All of this was clear to the youth's natural discernment and he could easily confirm his suspicions by recalling some of his uncle's words and mysterious and puzzling behavior.

He reached Afligidos Square near eleven o'clock. If there was a meeting that night they would all be inside by now. The Square was deserted. He checked the adjacent streets to see if there were people spying, but saw no one. Only on Las Negras Street were there some shadows visible in the distance, a group of people, about ten persons. Some figures were also moving toward the narrow gate of San Bernardino. He figured that there was no time to lose; he reached the door, seized the knocker and knocked forcefully.

Claudio Bozmediano, who is the person to whom we owe the news and information that make up this story, informed us that when the members of the meeting heard those very vigorous knocks, they were speechless and petrified with fear. They all knew that that evening there would be an uprising, but they thought that it would be one of so many and that with the precautions taken by the military authorities it would only be a demonstration with a few shots fired, two or three wounded, and a fair number of prisoners. They waited a moment to see whether the knocks would be repeated. In fact, they were repeated with even greater force.

"Someone has to go downstairs to see who it is."

"I'll go," said the younger Bozmediano. "But what will I do if it is…Who could it be?"

"That is the question," said another. "No doubt the evening's uprising has some high mission to carry out regarding us. No doubt about it, gentlemen, this uprising comes from the Palace, as they all do. Our meeting has been discovered."

"We must go downstairs," said Bozmediano, hearing the knocking repeated with greater force. "Three of us should go downstairs, we who seem less involved. Are there two others like me who are neither ministers nor deputies?"

Another youth and an elderly man stood up.

"We'll go downstairs. The others can leave through the orchard on Príncipe Pío, which is entered through the yard of this house. There is no time to lose. Gather those notes together and get to the orchard!"

"It's probably better to burn them," said another, throwing some papers into the brazier, which quickly consumed them.

The men went down the inner stairway, heading toward the orchard, except for Bozmediano and the other two who, going downstairs by the main stairway, arrived at the front door. Claudio shouted, "Who goes there?"

"Open up!" said Lázaro.

"Who is it? What are you looking for?"

"I am looking for *Don* Claudio Bozmediano."

The latter thought he recognized the voice of *Coletilla's* nephew and assumed that despite his fears, the social call would be a simple personal matter between the two. He opened the door and repeated, "Who is it?"

"Is *Don* Claudio Bozmediano in?" asked Lázaro, not recognizing him. "I have to speak to him about an extremely urgent matter, which cannot wait."

"Come in, friend."

The house servant brought a light. Lázaro entered, and with no further ado, knowing the gravity of the circumstances, exclaimed very nervously, "Get out of here, there is still time."

"What's the matter?"

"A terrible plot—the most frightening attack possible. I know it...I am certain. Leave immediately, right now."

"But, who? But, who?" asked the others angrily.

"Those..." answered the youth, "the radicals. There is an evil plan behind this evening's movement. I know it...I have come to warn you and to prevent this assault." The three moved inside, heading for the orchard where the others were waiting.

"Gentleman, what will we do?" asked Bozmediano. "This evening's uprising is directed against us. They have stirred the people up to attack us in the name of liberty. A horrendous crime! The uprising is being organized in the name of the extremist liberal faction, but you know who the true author of this movement is."

"The King, the King!" all who were gathered there cried out in terrifying voices.

"Well, we'll have to give those miserable creatures the welcome they deserve."

"The best thing is to flee; they will not find us here, and that will be the end of the matter," said the other.

"No! We must show the King how his vile pawns will be treated. We've had enough of contemplation. This was to be expected. Some of the most frenzied speakers are paid to foment the anger of the people against the constitutional authority. The climax of their diabolical undertaking has now arrived. Many imprudent people help them without knowing what they are doing. But today we cannot distinguish between them. Let's teach them a lesson."

"What will we do?"

"Over there, two steps away, is the barracks," said one of the men, who was a military leader of high rank. "I am going to bring two companies. I'll get them out by way of La Ronda, and with great secrecy I'll set them up here in the orchard. Not a man, not a sentinel, nor anything on the street. Then, when those mobs arrive, they will believe we are unprepared. Let them attempt to level the house; let them knock down the door."

"And will we leave?"

"I am of the opinion that we shouldn't. Everyone should remain here."

"Then everyone remains here!"

At midnight a tumultuous mob, animated by riotous voices, the howls of a bacchanal, invaded the streets of San Bernardino, Duque de Osuna, and Conde Duque. They reached Afligidos Square and occupied most of it, joining those entering through Portillo, who had arrived a little before. The door of the house to which we have referred resounded with tremendous axe blows. The wall along Príncipe Pío was occupied by people, and some groups of armed persons were on La Montaña, adjacent to the aforementioned house. The alleyway of Cara de Dios held more than three hundred persons. The uproar was so great that the shouts of the most radical ones, cries of Down with and Long live, could not be distinguished. It is impossible to describe the seesawing, the convulsions, the roaring with which that immense mob's collective passion filled that small area. The monstrous crowd pressed its great weight against the door of the house. The door gave way, and fifteen to twenty persons pushed themselves headlong into the entrance way, with terrifying shouts. When they reached the patio, there was a moment of hesitation, of horrible surprise. A double file of soldiers stood aiming at the mob, which despite the confidence it felt in its own strength, fell back, terrified. "Retreat," said the voice of their leader. "Advance, those traitors must die," exclaimed another in the entrance hall. At the same moment, a shot sounded, and a soldier fell. The troop opened fire without stopping, and a heavy discharge sent more than twenty bullets into the crowd. The confusion then was horrifying. The troops advanced, the mob retreated not without firing many shots and waving their knives, a surer weapon for them than the blunderbuss. The people in the street heard them retreating from the entranceway and fell back, opening the way for them. At the same time, a squad of cavalry came down the street from Conde Duque and a battalion of National Guard entering through el Portillo prevented the mutineers' exit. There were some small conflicts, but, nevertheless, the people completely dispersed. Those in the doorway who received a discharge of fire retreated toward the Square. The stampede that crossed San Bernardino Street and San Marcial Square dragged along in its haste the majority of persons gathered there either out of curiosity or to participate in the mutiny. Some of the so-called chiefs tried in vain to halt that disorganization with an improvised excoriation. The crowd continued to disperse, until only Perico Ganzúa, Pinilla and Lobo remained in the Square, along with the body of *El Doctrino*, who had been mortally wounded in the head on entering the doorway and had managed to retreat to the Square, where he collapsed. Fifteen or twenty people gathered around him, wondering whether to escape with the others or to defend themselves there. The troops had not left the house; the cavalry was advancing, and the Nationals had already reached Liria Palace.

"It is madness, let's run," shouted Pinilla.

"And what do we do with this one?" said another man, pointing to *El Doctrino's* body.

"What are we going to do with him? A fine relic to be carried off."

"Does he have any papers in his pocket? Let's see, remove them quickly."

Pinilla searched him carefully.

"He doesn't have any papers, but he does have a purse."

"Let's see, come on," said Lobo.

Pinilla put it under his belt. They all ran out of the Square leaving it for the troops.

Chapter XLI

FERNANDO VII

We have only examined one aspect of that restless society. The high regions of power have remained impenetrable for us. But it is now our turn to take a trip to higher places, to a place referred to as *The Big House*, in order to get to know, although not with the depth that the subject requires, the source of the abominable plot previously described.

Fernando VII was in a room of the hammer-shaped pavilion found on the eastern side of the palace, on the very evening of the uprising. He did not receive his ministers in that small office. That room was not the cabinet chamber; it was where he met with his private clique. Often favored there in previous periods were the Duke of Alagón, Lozano de Torres, Chamorro, Tattischief, and other memorable personages of the six years which followed the return from Valençay. At times the ministers were also privileged to be admitted to that alcove of perfidies and adulation, where Fernando's smiles toward his secretaries were always sinister. When he smiled at a liberal, it was a bad omen. That was a common palace axiom from 1820 to 1823.

That evening he was with *Coletilla*, his favorite lapdog. Seated at a table, opposite each other, they had before them some papers which were undoubtedly important, as indicated by the attention paid to them and by the satisfied attitude with which the King looked upon what was written there. Fernando permitted himself some witticisms from time to time, for he was a man who possessed to a high degree the tendency toward joking which has always been a trait of the Bourbon character. *Coletilla*, who wasn't used to laughing, laughed along with him, as he thought it irreverent not to imitate in complacent and slavish manner every change expressed on his master's royal countenance.

"Sire, this evening is the evening of redemption," Elías said. "May God in His very high justice grant that our undertaking reach a happy ending! That is what I hope for. I have a great deal of faith in the courage of those in charge of the matter. Your Lordship will recover the divine attributes, usurped by a mob of charlatans who have neither honor nor nobility. Spain is going to awaken. Woe to those who are caught in their error when the country shakes off its lethargy, opens its eyes and sees...."

Fernando didn't reply. He had inclined his head and

seemed very pensive. The light of a luxurious lamp completely lit up his face, that loathsome face which to our great misfortune was reproduced by an infinity of artists, from Goya to Madrazo. The very abundance of portraits of that repulsive face which his reign bequeathed to us is deplorable. Spain is plagued with effigies of Fernando VII, on stamps as well as on canvas. That face doesn't look like a tyrant's; for Fernando himself did not resemble a tyrant. His physiognomy is as unpleasant as his character, the vilest character possible in a human being. A stupendous nose, which without being deformed like Count Duke of Olivares' nose, nor long like Cicero's, nor broad like Quevedo's, nor coarse like Louis XI's, was uglier that any of them, and was the most important feature of his face, a face quite full and massive in the jaw and set upon a body of good proportions. Austrian vanity couldn't have placed a prominent mouth under his Bourbon nose (a symbol of double dealing) more appropriately and symmetrically than it had in the case of Fernando VII's face. Two small and very black sideburns adorned his cheeks, and his hair, standing up on both sides of his head, seemed placed there to give him the appearance of a tiger, in case his cowardly nature ever let him cease being a jackal. His eyes were large and very black, with very thick eyebrows which cast a shadow, giving them a very sinister and gloomy appearance.

With regard to his character—what shall we say? This man did so much harm to us; he struck us too often for us to be able to forget him. Fernando VII was the most cursed monster who ever miscarried divine right. As a man, he combined the worst elements possible in human nature; as King, he summarized all the weakness and infamy possible in royal power. The Revolution of 1812, the first convulsion of this fifty year conflict which is still going on and will perhaps last much longer, tried to overcome that demon's tyranny, but in two attempts did not achieve its goal. The revolution would have defeated Nero or Philip II, but it did not defeat Fernando VII. That is because he never fought his enemies face to face, nor gave them an opportunity to do so. Our tyrant wasn't frankly and openly abominable; he was a clown who would have been ridiculous, if not for his attempts to deceive the people. He deceived us since his childhood, when he forged a conspiracy against a detested favorite, very superior to himself in intelligence, and acquired a popularity which Spain promptly paid for with the blood of its best sons. Fernando was a bad son; he conspired against his father, Carlos IV, whose imbecility didn't diminish the value of his benevolence. He

326

conspired against the throne which he was to inherit later and even threatened his father's life. Subsequently, he groveled at Napoleon's feet like a beggar, while all Spain put up a struggle for his sake that astonished the world. Upon returning from exile, he repaid the efforts of those whom he called his vassals with the coldest ingratitude, with the most unwise arrogance, with the revocation of all the rights proclaimed by the constituents of Cádiz and the exile or death of the most illustrious Spaniards. He relit the bonfire of the Inquisition and was surrounded by vile, contemptible, and ignorant men who influenced public destiny just as Aranda seemed to influence the decisions of Carlos III. He persecuted virtue, knowledge, and courage and encouraged foolishness, double-dealings, and cowardice, the three facets of his character. Once the constitutional system was re-established, in spite of him, he applied the brake: he pretended as only he knew how to pretend, putting aside the venom of his rage, swallowing his own despair, hiding his intentions with words he had never spoken before except in jest or with scorn. Any behavior that such a human being, as hypocritical as he was cowardly, could contrive, Fernando was guilty of during those three years, from a thousand factions and conspiracies, devised by him, to the final plot of the Hundred Thousand Sons of St. Louis, which France sent to the Trocadero. Thus he regained what, in his royal jargon, he called his rights, inaugurating ten years of executions and persecution during which the figure of Tadeo Calomarde appeared at Fernando's side like Caiaphas at the side of Pilate. The bloody pact of these two monsters ended in 1823, when God reclaimed the soul of the King and gave his body over to the basements of El Escorial, where, we believe, it is still in a state of decay.

But our misfortunes did not end with this finale. Fernando VII left us a legacy worse than he, if that is possible. He left us his brother and his daughter, who instigated a frightful war. That King, who had deceived his father, his teachers, friends, ministers, supporters, enemies, four wives, brothers, his people, his allies and the whole world, thwarted Death itself, which had thought to make us happy, delivering us from such a devil. The vestiges of scandal and poverty remain among us.

But let us not recite history; let us continue with our story.

"And will you forget, Sire, what you promised me for my little nephew," asked Elías. "Ah! I should like Your Majesty to know him. He is the biggest braggart ever born. Yesterday, he spoke at The Golden Fountain and drove them wild. They applauded him with such enthusiasm...I also applauded him.

With three speakers like him, we would have saved a lot of money. The poor thing has done enough. Yes, sire. My nephew deserves it, he deserves it...."

"Let it suffice that he is your nephew and that you are anxious to give him that post....Yes. I'll name him Counselor to the Administration of the Philippines. He will make a career of it. I like youngsters...like that...hot-headed...."

"Sire," said Elías, bowing his head until his nose touched the table, "I, who never conceal the truth from Your Majesty, dare to tell you respectfully that my nephew doesn't deserve such a favor. He is crazy; his head is full of nonsense, and I believe that he will never be a responsible man. If I dared to ask Your Majesty for that favor, it was for the services that he had rendered to our holy cause, uniting, although indirectly, the instruments of justice who are going to save the nation tonight."

"Your nephew deserves the position, and that's all there is to it. Here, I have the decree," said the King, displaying one of the papers.

Then he added, smiling, "At last a day will arrive when I can proclaim a law at my own risk. If Felíu could only see these decrees, made and signed by me without consulting him..."

"It seems to me that he will not see them, nor many others for that matter. I will attest to that," said *Coletilla*, sinisterly. "God will permit that wise laws from a just King will come out in public and bring order, obedience, and respect to the spirits of all Spaniards. Tomorrow, sir, tomorrow. The first thing, sir," he continued, after gazing at the ceiling in thought, "is to appoint the Captains-General and Regents for all the Tribunals, trustworthy people who will immediately carry out the urgent laws of public security which you will give to them."

The King made a very common gesture with his hand to indicate the posture of punishment. His grimace gave the ultimate meaning to that exaggerated gesture.

"Sire," continued the advisor. "I shall permit myself to recommend to Your Majesty one thing, and that is that nothing would be more tragic than clemency. That would be criminal. Remember, Your Majesty, what occurred in 1814. If now, as then, Your Majesty contents himself with sending certain prisoners to the Fijo de Ceuta..."

Coletilla, although always observing absolute etiquette in the conversation, made a gesture with his hand, fixing his thumb under his chin and moving the other fingers, which the King understood perfectly.

"You will soon see what will be done," said Fernando,

signifying with a twist of his lip that he wouldn't be as easy-going as in 1814. "It is already twelve," he added, looking at a clock. "Do you realize we do not hear the noise from over there that one would expect to hear?"

"They'll not come this way, sire. They already know that the Royal Guard doesn't allow foolishness."

"The Guard has been instructed to stay near here and not to permit demonstrations in favor of anyone. Then..."

"I seem to hear the sound of voices..., over there...towards Los Caños," said *Coletilla*, approaching the balcony and turning his ear with the insidious caution of a thief.

"Yes, but it is towards San Marcial, down below. I believe something is going on in Afligidos Plaza," said the King.

"Yes. They must be there now. Isn't Your Majesty horrified to think what iniquitous plans those people could brew up over there? Perhaps an attempt against the throne or against the life of Your Majesty. Who knows? One can expect anything from those liberals."

"A parliamentary coalition, as they say. They probably would attempt to present some law and would arrive at an agreement with the majority to vote on it."

"That many people don't gather at night for a reason like that, Sire, with such precaution and the greatest secrecy..."

"The fact is that they are afraid of me," said the Bourbon. "They know very well that I can destroy their plans here with my clever tongue, without getting into constitutionalities. Oh, how well they know me! I also imagine that they have somehow received news of my dealings with the Holy Alliance or have learned of my correspondence with Louis XVIII. But as long as tonight's business turns out all right, the rest matters little."

In the Palace, alarm spread with news that arrived of tumult in the capital. The King, receiving his-gentlemen-in waiting and the Chief of the Guard, appeared very surprised and even pledged that he would give the mutineers quick and exemplary punishment. He then returned to the small room and to his court advisor, who was overjoyed on having heard a louder disturbance than the one before.

"Sire," he murmured, "there, there. From the noise, it sounds like they are returning."

"Returning?" asked the King anxiously. "From where?"

"From over there. Yes, they are! Perhaps bringing us a prize...."

The two listened very attentively and anxiously for a long

time. They spent half an hour in silence, only occasionally interrupted by a phrase from *Coletilla* or some monosyllables of the King. Finally, they heard the sound of a coach which stopped at the Palace gates.

"I wonder who it can be," remarked the King, and, with a great change of countenance, he passed to the royal chamber.

The Minister of the Government was announced. Fernando returned to the small room and looked at Elías with an expression in which the court advisor read contempt and discouragement.

"The Minister of the Government! Didn't you tell me that he was also going there?"

"Sire," said *Coletilla*, with the attitude of a beaten man, "surely something unusual has happened. Felíu was also going to be there."

"He's here!" said Fernando, stamping his foot. "Everything has failed. Felíu is coming; hide yourself over there. I'll receive him right here. I want you to hear what he says."

Coletilla hid himself. The King had the minister stop into his private chambers. Felíu came in very excited, but Fernando was serene, at least in appearance. He indicated that he had just received information at that moment about a popular demonstration which he deemed to be of little importance.

"Sire," said the minister, "more than one uprising was produced by the discontent of the people. This indicates a conspiracy originated by persons who are using that same public as an instrument of dissolution and anarchy."

"But who? Who?" asked Fernando, pretending anger; in reality he was angry, but for a different reason.

"Those extremists, constant enemies of the government of Your Majesty because it doesn't permit them to extend their rights to the point of licentiousness."

"But what are they asking for this evening?"

"They attempted to break into Alava's house. They intended to assassinate him, judging by the attitude of the mob which gathered there. Through a timely warning by a youth who was in on the conspiracy, some forces were stationed inside the house; thus a tragic crime was avoided."

"And where did this take place?"

"In the Afligidos Square."

"Wasn't Alava living on Amaniel Street?" asked the King, with an expression that nearly revealed his disgust.

"Yes, Sire. He used to live there, but some time ago he moved to this other house which is also his. Fortunately, the mobs weren't successful in their infamous design. On leaving my colleagues, the Minister of War had given the necessary commands, and order was completely re-established."

"But I cannot understand why the entire population would want to crush a single man. Could it be that there was a meeting in that house of many men the people despise? However it may be, prompt punishment is necessary. I hope that you don't allow yourselves to be deceived by that riffraff. Let the weight of the law fall on them, and let us see once and for all that these riots stop. Felíu can certify that since the Spaniards have had their liberty, we cannot sleep a single night in peace."

"Sire, the efforts of the Government are useless toward achieving that end. It despairs and bewilders us to see how difficult it is to pacify certain people. There are rebellions everywhere and factions instigated by a segment of the clergy. There are still many lowly spirits who refuse to believe that Your Majesty's interest and the nation's constitute the system which we all love and defend. There are people so blind that they still don't understand that Your Majesty is the man who most loves the Constitution and who most desires its fulfillment. All the liberal laws which Your Majesty sanctions and proclaims with great wisdom are not sufficient to convince them. What can we do with such people?"

Fernando was blinded with anger as he realized where the minister's obscure allusions were directed. He was still so base and cowardly that despite his anger he pronounced anathemas against anyone who still dreamed of the restoration of absolutism.

"This evening's attempt has been suppressed," said the minister. "May God grant that we can prevent what they intend to try tomorrow. We must find a remedy by seeking the origin of this illness. I believe that the extremist party isn't the only author of these disorders."

"Well, who else?" asked the King, who in spite of his cowardice felt his dignity hurt in that moment and became very incensed. "Who is, Felíu?"

"Sire, I'll take responsibility for finding out, and I shall suggest to Your Majesty some means for giving them appropriate punishment. It is known that among the most passionate youths, certain persons are meddling who never had the reputation of being at all liberal. It is said that those persons are working continuously to encourage the people to the extremes which we lament. Those people, Sire, are to my way of thinking Your Majesty's greatest enemies. We should keep the eye of vigilance and the hand of justice upon them."

"Yes," answered Fernando, with his usual hypocrisy. "Yes, there are foolish people who presume that there is glory and dignity for me outside of the Constitution. I am prepared to punish them more rigorously than the fanatic demagogues. What I need is power, power."

"Sire, I have no words strong enough to condemn the behavior of a man who is very well-known in Madrid; one who has had the audacity to use and profane Your Majesty's name in order to excuse his schemes. That man is more criminal than the greatest assassin and the most rabid anarchist. That man corrupts the people, he corrupts impressionable youth. He frequents the clubs. But none of this would be serious if he didn't dare speak the name which all Spaniards love as a symbol of peach and liberty. That man's name is Elías, and he is known as *Coletilla* in the clubs."

"Well, he and others like him should be exterminated," said the King, using his favorite word. "That cur is the one who does the most damage to my intentions by alienating the people's opinion."

"I reply, Sire, that this time I'll do everything possible so that man doesn't escape. He has already been picked up on other occasions, but somehow he manages to avoid justice and afterwards parades his cynicisms through the streets of Madrid, and in all the clubs. I believe that this time he'll not escape us. We will catch him soon, tonight to be exact. Bozmediano, who is stationed in Alava's house, has informed me that he heard of the plot a few hours before the assault from *Coletilla's* own nephew, whom the scoundrel tried to put at the service of his vile purposes."

"Well, we should reward that young man," said Fernando, trying harder to conceal the nervousness which overcame him.

"Yes, Sire, he is a worthwhile young man, according to what Bozmediano has told me, and a very good liberal. Before this episode, he had been suggested to me for a position on the Council of State, and I have already granted it."

"Good. I like that kind of service to be rewarded."

"Tomorrow I shall bring Your Majesty a detailed report of what occurred this evening. Moreover, I believe that the Minister of War will not delay in informing Your Majesty of the precautions which we have taken."

"This evening?" inquired the King, with distaste.

"I see that Your Majesty wants to rest. There is nothing to fear this evening. Your Majesty can rest peacefully."

"Good, then you may leave."

The minister left, probably satisfied at having said certain things to his sovereign which he dared speak only in those moments of irritation and excitement. Felíu was a timid man, and in face many of the unfortunate events which took place in that disturbed period were due to his indecision.

When Fernando was alone he folded back the screen, and Elías who was hidden there, stepped forward. The Palace advisor's face was frightening. He was livid; his lips were trembling and dried by the heat of a breath which drew his fiery rancor up from his chest. He wrung his hands, and even punched his own forehead with them, producing the unpleasant sound of two bones colliding in dry vibration.

"Do you see?" said the King, incensed with fury and banging the floor with a royal kick which shook the room. "Do you see what has happened? Did you hear? Tell me again how everything is taken care of. That I should have confidence in you, that you will take care of everything. Ah, how unfortunate I am!" he added, breathlessly. "I cannot find a man anywhere. A man is what I need! A real man!"

"Sire," mumbled Elías, standing away from the King, Like a dog who has received a blow from his master. "Sire, they sold us out....That nephew of mine, that scoundrel, has sold us out."

"No," said Fernando, in a sudden fit of anger. "You, with your imprudent conduct, you have gotten me involved. You see now, everyone knows that you are my agent. Didn't you notice how Felíu said it to me in such a nice way? Oh, I wanted to pull his tongue out. You have sold me out!"

"Sire," replied *Coletilla*, with a voice in which there was something of a sob. "Pierce my heart, but don't say that I betrayed you. I am not capable of betraying you. Slap me; spit on me, Sire, rather than say such a thing. Your cause has always been my only goal; I have dedicated myself to it with all the diligence I am capable of. The fact is, Sire, God permits certain things. God tests our mettle and our courage. Don't blame me, Sire, I have served you like a dog."

At that moment *Coletilla* would have been happy if Fernando had seized the august sword of his ancestors with his cowardly hand and run him through; but Fernando did no such thing. *Coletilla* felt his master's full contempt, and that moral blow hurt him more than a stabbing. The fanatic royalist would have viewed with terror, but without surprise, a royal order to have him hanged from a battlement or to rest his head on the executioner's block and receive the axe stroke. He approached the King, knelt before him, and pronounced with great fervor:

3

"Sire, I swear to you in the name of your forefathers that this apparent defeat that we have suffered is merely the prelude to the great victory which will conclude our undertaking. I promise you! Forget Felíu's allusions, forget it all. Continue on, let us continue together. You have loyal followers, only the first step is needed. If we blundered this evening, we'll not blunder again tomorrow. I assure you of that. I promise."

Rising slowly, he bowed deeply, as deeply as he could, and began to walk toward the door, turning his head several times to see whether the King was watching him. The King did not see him. Completely self-absorbed, he sat with his head in his hands, silent, from time to time kicking at the floor with one foot. *Coletilla*, from the door, waited for a glance from his royal patron; receiving none, he went out, feeling, along with Fernando's consuming rage, a pathetic sense of injury and hopelessness, which filled his heart with profound pain.

Chapter XLII

VIRGO POTENS

Lázaro remained inside Alava's house during the brief and anxious moments that the short-lived conflict took place between the people and the troops. They heard the uproar of the conflict from there, and for a while thought that their final hour on Earth had arrived. The objective of that illustrious group's meetings had been to find some means to impede the Palace's frequent conspiracies. A conspiracy by one party can be laughed at, or even two; but what strength can a Ministry have against the plots hatched by the sovereign, the symbol of legality? If there is anything more terrible than anarchy, it is the palace coterie. There is no efficient weapon against it, except the weapon of regicide. We cannot say whether those meetings proposed putting into effect an article of the Constitution, an idea which later on, to the great surprise of Europe, was achieved in Las Cortes of Seville (Parliament) in the year 1823. But we can guarantee that those men were concerned, distressed and discouraged, about the rumors of French intervention, about the secret relations between Fernando and Louis XVIII, and finally, about the reconnaissance army stationed on the border by the French Government, under the pretext of a sanitary cordon.

Let's return to our story. When the danger ended and the crowds dispersed, most of the ministers remained in the orchard; only the three who were to carry out the reconnaissance ordered by the authorities went up to the house. Everything was arranged so that in the Captain General's report, which was to be issued on the following day, no mention of a secret meeting or anything similar to it would appear.

At dawn everyone left, carefully guarded by the troops, and Lázaro, with no guard, went to Humilladero Street. Clara, who had heard of that evening's disturbance, waited in great suspense. She sat up, nervous and frightened, at the least sound in the street, and Pascuala told her a thousand amusing stories to distract her. During the night Pascuala had relied on her craftiness so that her Pascual wouldn't join the mob in the street. She locked him up in the house and hid his shotgun down in the basement. Pascual, who was by nature a peaceful man, on seeing that she had locked the door and prevented him from covering himself with glory in the streets, drank up the best part of his stock-in-trade, and, without creating a disturbance, because his drunkenness was also peaceful, he stretched out on the bench and began to snore.

Clara waited all night in mortal fear as hour after hour passed. She said all of the prayers she knew, including the ones *Doña* Paulita had taught her. Lázaro didn't return until morning. When she saw that he wasn't wounded, that he wasn't missing an arm, or half a head, nor bore a tremendous bloody hole in his chest, as she had dreamt in horror, she was relieved and extremely happy.

"If you had seen what I saw last night," said Lázaro, sitting down next to the bed, fatigued and breathless. "I saved the lives of more than twenty persons, the most illustrious figures in Spain. They were to be vilely assassinated."

"Jesús!" exclaimed Pascuala, holding her head in her hands. "How happy I am that my Pascual didn't go out. If I had let him go, they would have killed him."

"There was an infernal plot to kill them in a place where they were all gathered. All on account of that wicked man....If you had seen what chaos!"

"Oh! Don't leave, for God's sake," said Clara.

"I must go. I know that they are trying to take my uncle into custody, that they are trying to bring him to justice. He deserves it, that's for sure, but I, who did so much to prevent the realization of his iniquitous plans, will also try to save him. He is my mother's brother. If by telling him that they intend to imprison him he can escape, and I fail to inform him, my conduct would be criminal. He's a scoundrel; I must shamefully confess it, but if I don't prevent his persecution and his death, I'll probably have it on my conscience all my life."

The orphan could not help feeling pity and sorrow toward that eccentric man who, while still her tyrant, had been her protector and support in her childhood.

"Yes, yes," she said. "Poor man! What has he done? But don't go yourself. Couldn't you send him a message?"

"I must go myself. I'll return shortly. Have no fear! What can possibly happen to me?"

"Oh, dear God! I still seem to hear last night's shouting....And what if he becomes angry with you and quarrels with you?"

"Who?"

"Him! That man. He must be angrier than ever."

"I don't care. Today will be the last time that I'll see him."

"And if you go to the house and find the two women there, and *Doña* Salomé says something to offend you and tells you that I am incorrigible?"

"If she says something which offends me, it will not matter

to me, but if she speaks to me about you, I think it will be the last time that she'll ever dare to mention your name."

"And what if they discover that I am here and come to torment me, saying that I am very rude? Oh! If I ever saw them come in, I would die."

"They'll not come here," assured Lázaro with a smile. "And if they do come, I'll be here."

"Go, then," said Clara, with a sadness which detained the Aragonese for a moment and softened his irrevocable resolution.

"Good-bye…, I must…I'll return shortly."

He refused to wait any longer. He left and headed for the inquisition on Belén Street. It was probably eight o'clock when he entered the very noble ladies' house. Paz and Salomé had gone out to look for another house, and the devout one opened the door. When she saw Lázaro her surprise and turmoil were such that she stood a good while without saying a word to him, looking at him carefully as if she thought that his image was a vision.

"Oh!" she exclaimed, closing the door once Lázaro was inside. "I thought I would never see you again."

The youth felt relieved when he learned that the two harpies were out. *Doña* Paulita inspired his respect and gratitude, for he had never heard the slightest incrimination from her, nor had Clara told him of any complaints against her. The memory of the mysterious scene and dialogue which had occurred some evenings earlier made him very pensive. When he found himself alone in that gloomy house in the company of that pale woman with her wandering vision and her face worn by three days of delirium and fever, when he noticed her light tremors, irregular breathing, and intense gaze, he was shaken without knowing why.

"Is my uncle in?" he asked. "I have to see him."

"He isn't; he hasn't shown up here since yesterday. Perhaps he will come at suppertime."

"I don't want to wait; I have to see him sooner. Besides, I am not eating here. I will not return here, *señora*…I must say good-bye to you now; I am leaving for good."

Doña Paulita kept staring at the youth as if she heard the most unlikely and absurd thing possible from his lips.

"Never return?" she said, closing her eyes. "No, I can't believe it; it isn't true."

"Yes, ma'am; it is true. I can't stay in this house a single day more. Good-bye, *señora*."

"Lázaro," murmured the devout one, seizing the youth's

right arm the way a shipwrecked victim might seize a board in desperation. "You are going away...going away! And I'll be here forever. Oh! I would rather die a thousand deaths!"

The young man was stunned; the mystic's pained reaction terrified him. Her dry and trembling lips and the expression on her face revealed extreme desperation.

"I am dead; I no longer exist," she said. "I can't live this way. I already told you that I am not a saint, and it's true! I changed a long time ago...I can return to reality; I can save myself; I can save my soul, which is destined to succumb if I continue this way. I hope to live....When I saw that you were late, I began to lose hope; but you've come. May I not believe that God has sent you to me? There are things we women can't say, but I am saying them because I feel destroyed within. The moment has come for me to abandon an illusion which is killing me; I don't know how to pretend. I thought that God was reserving me for an exemplary life, one of continuous devotion and tranquility; but God has made fun of me; He has deceived me; He has made me see that the virtue I was so proud of was only a farce, and that my apparent perfection was delirium. I hadn't lived yet, nor had I known myself. I can't stay here any longer, because that would prolong the deceit that used to be my greatest pleasure and is now my greatest punishment."

"*Señora*," said Lázaro, who finally realized the depth of the devout one's new character, and clearly saw what had previously been a mystery to him. "Don't be upset over nothing. Be free and don't sacrifice your happiness to family demands. The two women who live with you are stubborn."

The youth wanted to avoid the impossible reply which the saint's words and attitude seemed to demand of him.

"I don't care about their temperaments," she said. "I love them; they are my relatives and lifelong companions. Once I have made an irrevocable decision, what they may say or do matters very little to me. I have made up my mind, Lázaro."

And her eyes searched in vain for any sign in the youth's face of the sentiments she so eagerly asked of him. He made an effort to remain immutable as he stood before the holy woman, who was overwhelmed by the violent emotions of a mystic trance; then, not knowing what to say, he took a step towards the door.

"No," cried *Doña* Paulita, clinging to him with great fervor. "Are you leaving? How can you? What's going to happen to me? Alone forever! The slow death which awaits me is worse than if you killed me right now....And you said you were grateful! You are ingratitude personified. I always thought so. There are people who do not deserve to receive the slightest display of affection. You are one of them. Nevertheless, by a strange and painful twist of fate, the greatest treasures of love are always directed to the people who least deserve them."

"No, for God's sake; don't call me ungrateful," responded Lázaro, realizing that it was impossible to evade the declarations the theologian so urgently demanded. "I am not ungrateful and especially not with you, who have been so kind to me."

"If you had forgotten that, you would be the most infamous of men. In spite of everything I always believed that you were not as bad as they said you were. You'll be a good man; happiness makes people good....I also hope to be good....Oh! Do you know what I have been thinking about? These past days I have had my head full of ideas....Never before had such things occurred to me....I can't repeat them....Do you understand? I think that I am destined for many days of peace and happiness, which someone else will enjoy with me."

"Tell me," said Lázaro, somewhat calmed by the hope that the new idea would divert the conversation from the disquieting theme with which it had begun.

"Well," continued the saint with forced amiability which made her seem more pathetic. "I thought there could be no greater perfection than domestic life, with all the duties, pleasures, and griefs that family life provides. Ah! meditating on this theme I have come to realize the sterility of my rosaries and prayers. What condition can be as dignified and noble as that of a wife, on whose care the happiness and lives of so many beings depend?"

"Actually, *señora*," said Lázaro very confused, "that is the truth. But people who, like you, can raise themselves through meditation and abstraction; who can free themselves from human weaknesses by means of strength, are much more perfect."

"Perfect? How absurd you are! And what did you say about human weaknesses? Do you use the term 'weaknesses' to describe nature, which God has created?"

The youth was completely bewildered.

"Aspiring to create the happiness of many beings through love and family ties," she continued, "is that what you call weaknesses?"

"No, *señora*, not that."

"Oh! You are going to be shocked by what I am about to say. You won't accept it; it's unbelievable."

Lázaro, who already thought that *Doña* Paulita couldn't say anything more inconceivable, trembled at the idea of new and stranger confidences.

"To achieve the happiness and peace which I have dreamed about, love alone is not enough; that is to say, one other thing is needed to avoid unpleasantness and a thousand irregularities. When difficulties occur in life, mutual love becomes embittered. One fears for the other; the two fear for their children; happiness is threatened at every moment; one fears the future. Both regret having united. I have learned this from meditation, and it seems to me that I have also read it in a book, whose title I can not recall."

"It's true, *señora*, I understand what you mean," observed Lázaro, astonished by so much wisdom.

"Well, I'm going to tell you something which will surprise you a great deal, Lázaro," said *Doña* Paulita, directing all the sadness and gentle interest of her eyes toward the young man. "I'm going to tell you something which will surprise you beyond measure: I am rich."

Lázaro stood fascinated.

"Yes," she continued, "I am rich. You're surprised. Knowing the life we lead....This is a secret which I confide only to the one I should confide it to....The use I intend to make of that treasure, you have already understood. I shouldn't have to make unnecessary proposals. We have understood each other; we have fused our purposes into a single one. Isn't that so?"

"Yes, *señora*," said Lázaro, for the sake of giving some answer to that profound and serious question.

"I am rich. A short time ago I would have given up my fortune without any effort at all. I have always scorned all that. But not today, no; today I think of that treasure as a way of life. I want nothing for myself; but ambitious men need all that. We need it. Isn't that true?"

After a moment of anguished hesitation, Lázaro repeated, "Yes, *señora*."

"I was very young," continued the woman. "My uncle had passed away. Great sadness reigned in the house. We were preparing to move from home; we were poor then. My aunt and uncle wept, but at the same time we were very involved with moving and gathering the few pieces of furniture which remained after the confiscation. On an old walnut couch I made an altar, where I used to pray a great deal. I used to close it up in the evening, and when I opened it in the morning and saw my saints and images, I felt that I had a small piece of heaven there. That day was a sad one for me because I had to remove my altar from its place, and as a result, many saints were broken, leaving marks where they had been glued. As I did this, I felt the plank in the rear give way under my hand, leaving a small opening uncovered. In this space there was a little box of beautifully carved wood. I attempted to open it and did so easily. It was full of money, almost all in very old coins. I closed the box, carefully adjusted the plank which covered the space, leaving it as it had been, and then remained silent. They brought the piece of furniture to this house, and it has been in my room until now. At first I looked upon it as a toy, a relic. At night, in the silence of this house, I would open it, contemplating with astonishment the beautiful coins which were inside. Several times I thought to tell someone else about it, but a superstitious distrust prevented me from doing so. At times I dreamt of one day founding a pious undertaking. I never touched that money; and in spite of the austerity in which we have lived, I never dared to spend a single cent. I felt compelled to save that money for some unknown purpose. Instinctively I kept it intact, although I never expected to change my situation. The treasure is in the very place where I found it. The time has come to use it for the necessities of our life together. It's mine. Who can doubt it? It belonged to some relatives, who put it there to keep it safe. Now it belongs to me; I found it. Nevertheless, I shall give half of it to my cousin and aunt, if they accuse me of having kept it from them. But first, I'll tell them that if I had not done so it would have been impossible for me today to bring about the happiness which I intend to give to my life and the lives of others."

Lázaro refused to make the situation worse and simply repeated, "Yes, *señora*."

The devout one went to her room and quickly returned with a small box which she showed to the youth, saying affectionately, "Here it is. It's mine. It's ours."

And upon saying this she drew near him with the box held in her two hands and supported by her bosom. The box touched Lázaro's chest, and he felt the thrust with so much force that to keep his balance he fell back a step and extended his arms to touch the saint's shoulders.

"You are doing the right thing," said the Aragonese. "What good does it do to hold on to money which can be useful to you and others?"

"Yes," Paulita replied effusively. "It is ours."

Lázaro no longer knew how to act. He decided to end a difficult situation once and for all.

"*Señora*, I am leaving. I have to go."

"Yes," she answered, "so do I. Let's go. We'll leave together."

"You, *señora*...You...!" Lázaro exclaimed, upset.

"Yes, the two of us. Let's go."

"*Señora*, you're out of your mind! That's impossible."

"Impossible, impossible! We cannot stay here."

"We have to part, *señora*. Anything else would be an impropriety...a disgrace, perhaps."

"What are you saying?" the saint babbled in disbelief.

Her appearance at that moment was frightful. It was like that of an epileptic when about to fall into a terrible convulsion. A contraction of the mouth, a caricature of a smile, a violent lifting of her eyelids as if expressing extreme bewilderment; mortal paleness, interrupted by sudden flushes; and a voice like a tired moan, were signs of her deepening anxiety.

"What are you saying?" she repeated, after a pause.

"You are ill, very ill, *señora*," answered Lázaro, who began to believe she was either delirious or out of her mind.

The mystic smiled ineffably, staring at the ceiling and clutching the treasure box to her breast as if it were Lázaro himself. Then, she took the youth by the arm and gently drew him toward her, saying, "Let's go; we'll never enter this tomb again."

"You shouldn't leave, you cannot. What will the other ladies say? Calm down, for God's sake, and think...."

"Let's go."

"Where would we go? The two of us! Don't you see that it's impossible? Why? Why would we leave together?"

On hearing this, the devout woman trembled from head to foot. As if all the accumulated and hidden passion of so many years had burst forth at once, she exclaimed with emotion, "Fool, don't you see that I adore you!"

Lázaro was petrified. The woman had expressed human truth; she had revealed herself once and for all, and in the most categoric manner. That violent confession left her exhausted and breathless, as though with those words she had breathed out half her soul. Lázaro said to her, vehemently:

"I don't deserve this, *señora*. I am not your equal. I am a wretch, undeserving of such passion...but I can't stay here any longer. Now more than ever I must declare that I would be the most evil of all men on Earth if I didn't get away from here right now. Terrible obstacles which I can't nor will ever be able to overcome prevent me from saying more. Let us part forever; anything else is impossible, impossible, impossible...."

He said this forcefully, and prepared to leave. The devout woman made an anguished gesture as if she wanted to speak. She seemed to have remained silent. Finally, she was able to utter these words:

"Come..., listen, let's go...."

"Never, *señora*, never!" exclaimed the youth, heading toward the door.

The devout one bowed her head and dropped her arms, releasing the box. After hesitating for a moment, she swayed moving back and forth, cried out, and fell to the floor. The impact shook the room. The coins scattered around her. She moved her head repeatedly, apparently affected by deep inner pain; she placed both hands on her bosom, her fingers twitched, and, finally, she lay still with no other symptom than the violent heaving of her breast, and her labored breathing. Lázaro quickly lifted her up and, at that moment, he heard the sound of a key. Salomé and María de la Paz entered very calmly.

Imagine the strangeness of that arrival and scene: Paulita stretched out with the symptoms of a serious accident; Lázaro pale and confused; a great quantity of gold coins, unknown in the house hold, scattered carelessly across the floor; and the two harpies in the doorway, looking at each other like ghosts.

The first object to attract Salomé's attention was the scattered gold; she threw herself on it and began to gather the pieces. Paz looked at Lázaro, and became pale with fear; she looked at the devout woman and was overwhelmed with anger. She took a few steps, and finally recovering the majesty of her character, asked, "What is all this?"

"Ma'am," said Lázaro, trying to deal with his situation, "a very sad event...*Doña* Paulita is very ill....She had an accident. We were talking...What a dilemma! Just now, she just now fell down."

"But what about that money...?" asked Paz.

"It is hers."

"Hers!" the harpy exclaimed greedily.

And turning to Salomé, who was gathering the gold she added, "Give it to me, give it to me; I'll take care of it."

"I'll put it away."

"But where did she get that money?" asked the other woman.

"She's had it for a long time," said Lázaro, trying, while the two Porreños busied themselves with the gold, to comfort the poor sick one.

Paz, on her knees, was picking up the coins. Salomé, also
kneeling, did the same, but the stout one's clumsy hands could
not keep up with the speed of her nervous niece, who was able
to grab two pieces for every one her aunt trapped. Salomé
seemed crazed. When Paz's left hand received an *onza* or
doubloon from the right hand, it would close, squeezing
together her robust fingers and clenching the gold with the
firmness and precision of a machine. The golden coins were
slowly disappearing from the floor. Four were left, three, two,
and then one. The hands of both Porreños both grabbed at the
last one with stunning speed, and they fell on each other, with
repeated blows. The two ruins glared at each other as if each
wanted to eat the other up. Which of these two characters
would overcome the other? Paz was swollen with anger and
pride; she was purple, apoplectic. Salomé looked yellow and
panted with rancor, avarice, and anxiety. Her half-opened lips
revealed her sharp white teeth, as if she intended to terrify her
rival with that weapon. They were on bended knees, leaning
on their hands. Sitting there like a couple of sphinxes, the two
harpies, displaying their new-found passion with poorly-timed
vigor, were like ferocious beasts. After a moment of silence
during which all the forces of human avarice seemed contained
in a single glance, along with the forces of pride, the panther
told the seal: "This is mine!"

"Yours! What are you saying, imbecile? This is mine; it
was my father's....I knew that he had hidden it some place, but
I didn't know where."

"Vain!" said Salomé, as she stretched and arm and a foot
forward. "You have submerged us in poverty; you hid this
money from us. What infamy!"

"Hypocrite!" exclaimed Paz, drawing back, "Get out of my
sight! Give me that money; never steal from us again."

"It was my father's. It is my inheritance."

Paz saw Salomé closing in. She raised her right arm, and
slapped her niece's face with all her strength, hitting her so hard
that she fell to the ground as if struck by a mallet. But she got
to her feet, dropped the coins in her hands into her purse,
stepped back a little like a carnivorous animal about to attack,
and rushed at her aunt. Before Paz could defend herself, her
adversary's fen sharp and steely fingers were on her face,
clinging as though each possessed a hook. She frenziedly dug
her nails into those fleshy cheeks and pulled, leaving eight
bleeding furrows across the vain one's face. The latter shouted
in pain. Lázaro had to intervene; and while Paz was getting up

344

from the floor, Salomé gathered up all the coins that her rival had let fall during their battle, hastily wrapped herself in a cloak, and hugging the purse, she raced from the room, took to the stairway, and fled.

Lázaro refused to witness that scene any longer. The old woman belched forth her anger at him, shouting the greatest insults, and calling him a coward, ordered him to pursue her niece. The youth could no longer stand the horror of that evil house. Lázaro looked at *Doña* Paulita, who still lay unconscious, and grieved by that unhappy woman's unrivaled misfortune, he left the house.

Chapter XLIII

CONCLUSION

Lázaro, eager to see his uncle that morning, headed to Abbot Carrascosa's house, and there found another scene of desolation. The ex-abbot was in his room, slumped in a chair with his feet on the cross-piece and his head in his hands. In that position he looked like a bird perched on a bench. His sad expression was so apparent and so unusual that Lázaro couldn't help but ask, "What's the matter, *Don* Gil?"

"Ay, *Don* Lázaro! What wickedness! She has left. Can you imagine such wickedness? And I loved her so much..."

Lázaro understood then that *Doña* Leoncia, the little Basque bird, had flown the coop.

"But how was that? For what reason...?"

"It's the most horrible conspiracy!...That schemer, that bum, that good-for-nothing poet who lived in this room has taken her from me. What an atrocity! I've always hated those versifiers."

"Cheer up, *Don* Gil. Let's turn to another subject. Do you know where my uncle is?"

"I tell you, I have never seen anything like it," mumbled the abbot, ignoring the question. "And she had an inheritance, a small legacy...Fickle woman!"

"That's life, *Don* Gil...One must accept it."

"She had an inheritance coming...I found out about it while I was employed in the Ministry."

"Please tell me, where can I find my uncle?"

"I...I should tell you the truth," continued the abbot, obsessed by his misfortune, "I'm not as much upset because of her, for in the final analysis...But she did have a small legacy..."

"Aren't you going to answer me?"

"She had a legacy."

"I just can't get an answer out of you."

"She had a legacy..."

Lázaro understood that any inquiry was useless. He left the house, leaving the abbot in the same attitude of a perched owl, and went to Humilladero Street, where he found Bozmediano anxiously waiting for him. On seeing Lázaro arrive, he said, "Friend, they are after you. We have to take precautions."

"Who's after me?"

"It's easy to understand that some people will be unhappy

about what you did last night. Those people are after you. I'm sure of it."

"I understand," replied Lázaro. "But what do I care?"

"We have to take precautions, because if they get revenge it will be in a terribly way. Be careful! Just now there were four persons in the tavern, assigned, I believe, to watch your comings and goings. The best thing, it seems to me, is for you two to leave Madrid tonight. Once you are out of town and far away..."

"What a setback! But I do want to leave Madrid. We'll go."

"Well, in the meantime, don't go out in the street. I'll arrange the trip so that no one knows about it. I know that they're looking for you, and they know their business."

"But how did they find out that I am here?"

"Forget about it for now. You must leave this evening or at least by tomorrow. You will not be safe here. Take care! I'll return and we'll find a safe way for you to depart. I believe we can find a way. So long."

Bozmediano left, and Lázaro went in to see Clara.

"Did you find them?" *Coletilla's* niece asked him with curiosity and some fear.

"Yes," he answered, smiling as he recalled the coin scene, which he told her about later, including *Doña* Paulita's strange behavior.

Clara listened to this last point with great interest, and then remarked sadly: "I already knew about that."

"How! Did she mention anything to you?"

"No, I just knew about it. It seemed that way to me. I had a suspicion...that woman is very strange. If only you knew how frightened I used to get whenever she began to pray, remaining silent and unfeeling for a spell, as though she were dead. She would kneel, looking at the ceiling, and remain motionless for two or three hours. She did not even seem to be breathing. I used to touch her and nothing happened. I would call her name and she would not answer me. Finally, after a long while, she would sigh and return to herself."

"And did that happen frequently?"

"Yes, many times."

"There's an illness," said Lázaro, "called catalepsy. It consists of a seizure during which the person loses movement and speech, becomes like a corpse. It is said that one of the causes of this illness is religious mysticism and the custom of religious ecstasies and visions."

"That must be what she has. Poor Paulita!"

That evening the two were found in the same room, sitting together by a scant fire. Clara had gotten up from her rest, completely recovered. Lázaro was turning over in his mind the strange incidents of the previous days. The two were very sad; they wordlessly shared their sadness, gazing into one another's eyes and remaining silent. Perhaps they were thinking about plans for the future; maybe she worried about the difficult situation in which they found themselves.

Then Pascuala entered and said, "How frightening! Since nightfall there have been some men loitering around the doorway....They were here this afternoon, too. What ugly faces! Sometimes they stop and peer into the tavern, and I'm afraid that if Pascual arrives and sees them he's going to kick up a storm...because he has such a temper!...he'll think they are looking for me..., because since I'm so...so attractive..."

"Lock the door!"

"I already did."

Clara was as pale as a ghost. She pictured a horde of villains, climbing in through the windows and breaking through the doors, armed with daggers, pistols, ropes, and other horrible instruments.

"Close it securely. Turn off that light. If they come in through that window..." he said, pointing out a skylight that the cat, whom Mr. Batilo respected so highly, used to enter with difficulty. That skylight faced the house's yard.

Batilo, who seemed to understand the danger the young couple faced and who wanted to prove that, although he was a misanthrope, he was a dog resolved to face any enemy, barked in a tone which meant, "There is nothing to fear as long as I'm here."

A little later Clara, who was fearfully watching the cursed skylight, shuddered and screamed. Her eyes reflected her terror.

Perhaps overwhelmed by fear, she had thought for an instant that she had seen the sharp eyes and pointed nose of Elías Orejón, her protector and tyrant.

"Are you crazy!" Lázaro asked her. "Don't you see that it's the effect of fear?"

He looked about and checked carefully. There was no one there. They went out into the patio yard, which was full of rubbish and firewood, and saw nothing there, either. It had to have been the effect of fear.

The following day went by quietly, and at dusk Bozmediano arrived. Lázaro knew from that moment he entered that he was worried.

"What's up?"

"A lot of danger. They are watching you. I have brought some men along, in case of a clash. But have no fear. I have brought enough people and we are safe. You are going to leave right away."

"And will we leave right now?" Clara asked happily, for she hoped to never again see that skylight and to leave Madrid forever.

"Yes, right away. I have already arranged for a coach to take you to Torrejón, where I have a house. You can rest there until the day after tomorrow, when a stagecoach will pass through to Alcalá. From Alcalá you can head to Aragón whenever you wish."

"And how soon will we arrive in Torrejón?"

"Before daybreak. You will go in one of my coaches and with people I trust. You have nothing to fear: good mules and good company. You'll be safe in Torrejón....Here...I don't think so. You must leave this house and Madrid immediately."

"Well, let's go," said Lázaro resolutely. "Let's not lose any time."

They quickly prepared to leave the city.

"Isn't there a door which faces onto another street?" Bozmediano asked Pascuala.

"Yes, sir, but one must pass through the collier's house, which opens onto another street."

"Well, we'll leave that way. The coach is waiting at the Gilimón Gate. The men I brought with me are out in the store. Let them enter, and we'll all leave by the other street."

A few moments later they all departed, including the Porreños' dog, which Clara refused to leave behind. The travelers said good-bye to Pascuala and accompanied by Bozmediano and his party, walked to Gilimón Gate. Very quickly then, so that no one would have time to notice them, they climbed into the coach. The coachmen and footman sat on the coach-box, and Bozmediano's servant, a strong man armed with a rifle, rode inside with Lázaro and Clara. Bozmediano warmly and somewhat emotionally, said good-bye to them. The coach left by way of La Ronda to take the road to Aragón.

So many precautions were not unreasonable; without them the fugitives would certainly have had a bad encounter, and perhaps an unfortunate experience, which might have knocked their happiness from the course it was following. Lázaro's uneasiness and Clara's fright continued until they were beyond Alcalá; and there was reason for concern, because *Coletilla's* pledge against his nephew—according to reports received by the author—was that he had sworn to take his life. But God willed a different course of events, and led the two main protagonists of this true story, sound and happy, to the Aragonese's villa. The two, once rested from the trip and recovered from their fright, thought only of marriage, a wonderful idea which would occur to anyone else under the same circumstances. None of the notes which the author has before him recalls the specific date they got married, but it is well-known that they didn't wait very long and had strong and healthy offspring. Proof of this were several strapping young fellows whom Bozmediano and the author met, years later, on a journey they made to Aragón for purposes not relevant to this story.

How Lázaro settled in this town, and how he made his living, is another long story. Let it suffice to say that, persuaded by his wife and his own wisdom, he completely renounced Madrid's tumultuous political successes and disputes. He possessed the rare ability to suppress his newborn ambition and to confine himself to his town, seeking within a quiet peaceful, hard-working, and honorable life, the satisfaction of man's legitimate desires. Neither he nor his irreproachable wife, ever rued this decision during the course of their long lives. So during a period of many years the name of our friend, who had seemed 'eligible' (let's put it that way) or about to become a celebrity, never appeared in any lists of functionaries, corporations, juntas, nor anywhere else outside the physical limits of tiny Ateca. With patience and work he increased his parents' small property, and he achieved a comfortable financial position. I was informed of this by Bozmediano, from whom I also received very interesting information about the other protagonists of this story. I was especially interested in hearing more about *Coletilla*, and one day fate provided me an opportune meeting with *Don* Claudio. We discussed the events already referred to. *Coletilla* came to my mind, and we spoke at length about him.

"The Devil made off with him," my friend told me. It seems that the eccentric old man received the most terrible punishment possible, given his character. After the success of 1824 the King rejected and ignored him. One day on his way home from a partisan meeting, he made a special trip to see the King. He had fought for absolutism as only such a man could struggle for such a cause. Fernando, whose ingratitude was among his outstanding flaws, sent out his lackey with the direct and specific order to thrash *Coletilla* wherever he might find him. The lackey went down and whipped the royalist. Such is the payment little tyrants receive. After this episode, the fanatic became ill. Some said that he had let himself starve to death; others, that he had gone crazy; and others, and this seems most possible, that he died of profound hypochondria.

"And the Porreño women—what became of them?" I asked Bozmediano.

"I haven't been able to find out anything about *Doña* Salomé," he replied. "I believe that she has disappeared from Madrid. *Doña* María de la Paz Jesús was living in Segovia, where she owned a boarding house. With respect to *Doña* Paulita, indeed I have received news."

"What a strange passion hers was!"

"Indeed, later on she began to suffer very frequent attacks of catalepsy. Insofar as her passion is concerned, one must recognize that the confinement of her life and her having created a fictitious character contributed to her sudden explosion. She had been raised in the pious life, and nature's worldly condition did not develop by her at the usual age because of her odd childhood. She was a child until thirty years of age. I believe that she could have become an excellent woman, endowed with the loyalty and gentleness which a good wife possesses, if that false perfection, produced by her odd upbringing, had not distorted her true character. Repeating her own words, although changing them to avoid blasphemy, we can be assured that Nature, not God, scoffed at her."

Shortly after the final scenes of this story she retired to a convent, and there was treated like a saint, which greatly contributed to her catalepsy. On several occasions they believed her dead; on one occasion they were about to bury her, but during the funeral service she recovered, pronouncing a name which all the nuns interpreted as a sign of holiness, since they assumed that she was repeating Jesus: "Lazarus, awaken!". She was undoubtedly a saint. Eight theologians proved it with 800 syllogisms. Her life was exemplary; her social life extremely sad; she used to pray a great deal until she fell asleep; she spent ecstatic periods in prayer nearly every day. One of those ecstasies was so long that the nuns did not expect her to ever come out of it. And in fact, they were right; on one occasion she didn't return to her senses. But the nuns, in order to avoid being disappointed again, waited as long as possible, and finally, certain that she was really and truly dead, decided to bury her.